THE TROUBLE WITH SERPENTS

Dear Clare
Book three - this copy with it's
own story!
With Love, Toni x

THE TROUBLE WITH SERPENTS

TONI GRANT

Published by Brolga Publishing Pty Ltd
ABN 46 063 962 443

PO Box 452
Torquay Victoria 3228
Australia

email: markzocchi@brolgapublishing.com.au

National Library of Australia
Cataloguing-in-Publication data

Toni Grant, author.
ISBN 9780645372311 (paperback)

A catalogue record for this book is available from the National Library of Australia

Printed in Australia
Cover design and typeset by WorkingType Studio

BE PUBLISHED

Publish through a successful publisher
National Distribution to Australia & New Zealand
International Distribution to the United Kingdom
Ebooks Worldwide
Sales Representation to South East Asia
Email: markzocchi@brolgapublishing.com.au

OTHER TITLES BY TONI GRANT

The centre of our world. Together we worked on every chapter, every project, every idea in the same modus operandi – you covered in the red dirt sand from the dam and paddocks, satisfied from your daily walk and swim; and me, having walked that bush track with you, had watched out for snakes and kangaroos, photographed all manner of interesting natural finds and enjoyed your antics and zest for life.

On our return to home, by the time I'd made coffee, you'd have finished breakfast and were ready to come inside. Then you'd settle beside me on the timber floors, halfway between the sun and shade. Smelly in that wet doggy hair kind of way. Together in the quiet, accompanied by the sound of distant tractors and finches playing in the garden outside, I'd work and you'd help.

After we lost you so unexpectedly, I admit I had a lot of trouble and it took a very long time but, my friend, I did eventually finish what we started together and the ghost of you was with me every step of the way.

And in spite of me, I eventually found your beautiful tranquillity, if for a moment or two, whilst I wrote and when I walked a new track, thinking about you and how much you loved life.

This book is for you Buster, and the endless joy and love you brought to our family, our friends and me. I miss you so.

1

Le Maschere, Season of Carnevale
Venice, Italy

A golden eve, rich with rose and yellow clouds, and if one dared to look, the view from San Giorgio Maggiore's bell tower witnessed the distant plains alight beneath the purple night encroaching.

In the immediate view, the protected lagoon of the Canale di S. Marco didn't disappoint. Washed in shades of aqua and pink, shrouded in that peculiar Venetian light, it shimmered in sunlight's last rays.

Across the watery divide, glowing yellow orbs emphasised the shoreline as elegant streetlights, two abreast, protected a wide promenade like silent bronze sentries. They created a grand sweeping arc, an illusion as islands joined together as one by light and bridge.

A hard edge, elegant in uniformity and repetitive design, defined by blocks of smooth stone held the silky water at bay.

Slap. Slap. Slap. The gentle, continuous motion of the sea rose and fell against the barricades and the wide, seaweed covered steps. On schedule, the waterbus came and quickly went. Elegant timber hulled craft glided past, cutting through restless watery motions with well-manicured bows.

This was no meditative experience, despite outward observations. And only the truly, most dire romantic revelled in tonight's magical natural display. Because, a spectacle of make-believe had captured this most elusive city, its visitors and residents alike.

Venice was alive with the season of Carnevale. And like a seasoned grand old dame, she would never disappoint.

Stacked to the brim, the city glittered in festival, anticipation and hype. On this particular night, most were dressed in costume, their faces hidden by mask and hat. Others arrived to observe the chaotic, noisy scenes through the lenses of cameras and phones clipped to telescopic sticks.

Whatever your pleasure, whatever your fantasy, everyone was here to celebrate the season. Utterly and completely mesmerised by the heady spectacle that was a Venetian party to end all parties.

In a plush bedroom suite overlooking the hectic lagoon the tension was different.

"Tighter. Pull it tighter." Giuliett Seta instructed.

"Are you sure Madame? If the corset is too tight it will be difficult to breathe." The older woman looked at her with an expression of motherly concern.

"Pull it tighter." She breathed out, expelling the last of her breath from deep inside her belly. She smiled at the seamstress. "The mask, Madame."

"Thank you." Giuliett said.

Stiffened black lace in a filigree design formed a desired

effect, placed to cleverly disguise her eyes. It curled delicately over her angled cheekbones towards crimson lips. Next, the black velvet Venetian hat, trimmed in exotic feathers, lace and pearls was pinned upon flaxen coloured hair that had been bundled into an elegant French knot.

A short swing coat wrapped her slim shoulders and brushed lean hips. Pleated lace and black crystals brought focus at the extended cuffs. Masculine high waisted pants and low heel brogues finished the costume, blurring the line between masculine and feminine.

Amidst the dark exotic decoration, the eye was drawn to the naked expanse between cheekbone and the corded black lace along the top of her corset. Here, the exquisitely tailored velvet coat and bustier were relegated to a supporting act. The soft fullness of her décolletage was now dramatically framed. It screamed out for attention. Giuliett smiled.

"Magnificent Madame!" The tailors gasped in unison. Giuliett breathed a shallow out and in. She turned from side to side. She smiled at them reflected in the mirror.

"The back Madame?" A manservant handed her a large oval shaped mirror and she turned. The heiress nodded.

"Yes, that will do very nicely." She said.

She returned her reflection.

"I need that." Giuliett said, her voice cracking slightly as she pointed to a velvet rectangular shaped box on her nightstand.

He strode quickly towards her, presenting the box to the heiress with a slight bow.

"Thank you." She said.

Giuliett held it reverently for a long moment before suddenly snapping open the lid. With a wistful smile, she acknowledged the glittering contents, opulent against the dark inlaid silk. Peeling the stunning decoration from the box, Giuliett held it gently in her palms as the stones dripped through her open fingers. She stared at it for a long time.

"You may help me Sir." She said to the manservant, and her voice faltered again in emotion. He nodded and stepped behind her. Her head tilted softly as he fixed the clasp.

Giuliett faced the mirror again. The elaborate collar set with sapphires, rubies and emeralds glittered around her neck. Brilliant cut diamonds sparkled in caught light. Large teardrop pearls dripped at intervals at her neckline.

Its beautiful audacity rivalled any Romanov piece. It was her favourite gift from the Russian, Anya Frida Volkov. Giuliett fingered the creamy white orbs at her clavicle. With the money piece wrapped around her throat, no one could challenge her authority and a calmness washed over her.

"Now, we are perfect." She said quietly to herself. "What would you say Anya? Am I now as beautiful as you?"

"Thank you." She turned towards the help. "Please wait one moment." She said. The heiress opened the drawer of a small writing desk. She took out three neatly written envelopes.

"For you. And you." She said, smiling at them. "And for Henri. Tell him I am very pleased and he has certainly outdone himself today. Tell him 'Prepare to be the talk of Venice!'" Giuliett concluded with a flourish and a smile.

"Thank you Madame, this is very unexpected." They glanced between them. The matron spoke. "We shall pass on your message. And from our House to yours, we hope you have a wonderful evening. Good night Madame."

"Good night." Giuliett turned back to the mirror, leaning in to closely inspect the heavy eye makeup hiding her identity. Was she really there under that mask?

She glanced at the clock on the sideboard. She paced and waited.

At the click of the connecting door between the suites, she turned elegantly towards her tall, wiry consigliere. The feathers moved around her in a gentle hush. She smiled mysteriously up at him.

"What do you say Enrico?" Giuliett asked, spreading her hands out for him to notice her. "It is the season for diamonds and pearls. Decadence before sacrifice."

He ignored her. In his long slim fingers, he held a small painted box and, on his face a churlish, dark expression.

Giuliett looked at the item glittering in his hands. She looked at his belligerent face. Her confidence faltered.

"No thank you, not tonight. I don't need it." She said quietly and half smiled. It felt good to reject that habit. "This evening is the most important night of my life. And I want to remember everything about it in every satisfying detail."

His eyes held hers with sullen coldness.

"Enrico, my mind is clear and I don't need it." She repeated, her voice gaining strength.

Setting it down on the small desk, he began the ritual. Unfurling the sides of an enamel origami butterfly, its wings opened dramatically to reveal the mirrored lid fitting snugly on a lantern shaped box. Inside the box, a gold-plated card separated two small compartments and its contents. He scooped some onto the mirror, and deftly cut a cocaine line.

"It's ready." His authoritative tone reminded her of her father. She looked at his stern expression as he poured a liqueur shot.

"And this." He held a small goblet for her. It was a combination of gold plate and glass, on a short stem, and decorated in enamel flowers and butterflies in the Venetian style. He pushed it towards her. In the late afternoon light it gleamed, filling the interior vessel of red Venetian glass with a warm glow.

Giuliett looked at him, tilting her head upwards towards his challenge.

"Did you not hear me Enrico. I said 'No. Not tonight.'"

"Do it." He demanded loudly without ceremony. "We don't have time for your stupid games. You will take it now. When and how much you require, I will determine."

"No." She said. "I'm *doing* tonight on my own." She stood her ground.

"*You* can't." He eyeballed her, intimidating her with his height and the set of his mouth twisted in anger at her refusal of him. "Giuliett, you will do as I say." He acknowledged the diamonds around her neck with a mocking sound.

"That," he said, fingering a large ruby at the hollow of her throat, "is why you will take it." He held the stone in the palm of his hand, like he would pull it roughly from her neck. Instead, he pushed the large gem roughly into her throat, pressing it painfully into her windpipe.

His eyes mocked her as she fought the instinctive urge to struggle as her airway blocked under his ongoing pressure. He released his hold and she gasped, filling her airway and lungs. The corset bindings snapped tight. Giuliett leaned against the back of a chair, panting light breaths until the fainting lightheadedness subsided.

She gathered herself as quickly as she could. Straightening her back, she stared at him for a long moment and obeyed.

Next, she snatched the glass from him. Spitefully she poured a second drink.

"To us." She toasted, sculling it. After the third, Enrico grabbed the glass and bottle from her, placing the items deftly on a marble topped credenza.

"Enough!" He shouted in a metaphoric slam of his fist on the table. "Now you're being juvenile!"

Giuliett shrugged her shoulders, dismissing his anger and went to the large picture windows overlooking the lagoon. The sun was setting and quietly she fought her internal urges. Reigning in her thoughts, as the drugs wired her mind and body, she fingered the diamonds around her neck. Her energy rose and she resisted the temptation of being swept along with it.

The brief altercation bounced around her agitated mind. An endless of words said and not. This heightened activity of brain and heartbeat threatened to unseat her shallow confidence.

This was her weakness. Conforming to his ways as she almost always did at critical times in her life. It was not a good start to the next phase she'd planned so carefully in her mind. Time to take hold of the situation and the man who openly challenged her. And she would do it in a manner she'd spent years perfecting. Her expression was as brutal as his. She stalked slowly towards him.

In an even tone she said, "Once upon a time you were my father's choice. Now he is dead, remember lover, it is your time to serve me. Let me be clear. Tonight, the Commission will recognise me as leader. It's the final act for our family and for all the families. I will not tolerate disrespect from you or anyone else."

Giuliett paused. The air grew tense and quiet. She stood

deliberately in his space, facing his dark expression staring spitefully back at her.

Pointing at the decorative butterfly she added. "*That* will never again spread herself open for me. My actions will no longer be dictated by my father's shadows and his weaknesses. This is your weakness Enrico. Your addiction shared with my father and the preferred method to control me. And tonight it stops."

"Or what?" Enrico tested.

Giuliett held her silence for a long moment.

"I am the Capo of Seta Clan. This is *my* destiny and I will lead with a clear head and a strong heart. Both you and Gatto will fall into step behind *me*. Obey me in every way as you obeyed my father. Or you'll face the fate of another dearest."

"You wouldn't have the guts to do that on your own." He spat.

"Try me." She responded dangerously calm.

She watched his wariness at her threat. Her eyes, glowing like dark sapphires and devoid of emotion, held his. Facts were facts. His bullying tactics to control her had overstepped the mark one time too often. She watched him tense liked a coiled spring.

"I see you understand." She said.

At the right moment Giuliett changed tact. This was not the night for separate agendas. There was only one way to flip the situation fully in her favour. History proved he would do anything for her once they were done. The slap then the hug. She pounced on it. Long ago Giuliett learnt how to play the game. Everyone has a price, and she used his guilt to get what she wanted.

"Let's not fight my love. Not tonight." She said, softening her tone. "As you always say, two are better than one."

She stepped into him, reaching up to gently rest her hands on his old shoulders, fingers spreading up his neck towards his ear lobes. He resisted as the hidden language of the familiar, wordless gesture, invoked a trigger for both forgiveness and foreplay in their complex relationship of lover, servant and commander. Family.

"Instead, let's celebrate this moment with shared passions." She watched his face change as he stood still as death and each sensual stroke of her touch melted away his anger. She played him, waiting as his agitation subsided to a more malleable tension.

"Your resentment at our past sins only fans my desire." She breathed softly into his neck, close to his ear. She bit gently.

She glanced around the hotel suite and smiled knowingly.

"I remember this very room, do you? It is why I chose it, you know. To remind you of us; of our shared risks and actions of the wrong." She spoke shyly in their intimate space as her body yielded to his need. Her face was close to his. She breathed his manly scent deeply and let her warm breath out lightly brushing against his throat.

"For many years we've nourished our guilty pleasures. Moments of lust enhanced by the threat of discovery. Zio, do you remember our power over everyone we met? Do you remember Enrico?"

"Yes." He whispered. He bit her lip, tasting blood.

"Come Enrico." Giuliett murmured. "Take this body. Drink from this forbidden cup."

Every deliberate word was followed by another deliberate action designed to bring his arousal to action. She unbuttoned his trousers. She knew he could bear it no longer, fully submitting to her and his needs.

He pushed her hands away and held them together behind her back. She was forced over the back of the chair and her legs kicked apart with his foot.

"That's right little one, you are mine in every way. Our secret." He gloated gruffly. "No other fuck buddy owns you like I do." He pulled at the clasp of her pants.

Giuliett stiffened at his last remark. Her hands unclasped from his and she straightened upright, stepping out of his hold.

"Fuck buddy. That's a new and interesting term for an old man like you." Now she was facing him, with words and expression laced in suspicion. She would never tell their secret. "You've been talking out of school. Who are you courting Enrico? And why?"

One look at his response and the overheard whispers were confirmed to her.He couldn't look her in the eye. When he did, his face was a carefully constructed blank expression and his eyes raged with the temper of one who had been found out.

"You little bitch!" He spat, cornered like a filthy rat. "I should soften you before we go for such an allegation." He taunted, his fists ready for the beating, but she sensed the bite was gone from his threat. They both knew he was walking the thin line of betrayal.

Giuliett stood her ground. "You will not."

Her eyes deliberately dropped to his exposed groin and the pants crumpled at his shoes.

"Get dressed." She said, coldly assessing him. She watched his aggressive actions as he hurled through the need she'd created in him. Giuliett licked her lips, lit a joint and poured herself another drink.

"I assume everything is in place." she said, knowing that

behind his tortured expression his mind was playing out tonight's fantasy. She took a long draw, watching as he buckled his belt.

"Of course." His response was haughty. "You need to ask?" She felt the restraint burning from his eyes. He refused to look at her when he spoke. Giuliett basked in it, knowing control had shifted to her as he chewed on his self-disgust and carelessness.

"Are you focused on the job at hand or do you need to relieve yourself in the bathroom?" she asked pointedly.

"And give you the satisfaction?" He retorted, finally glancing in her direction. "No. Thank. You."

She took one last draw and pressed the joint into a small metal cigarette box and shut the lid. Giuliett breathed out, as her eyes slowly ran up and down his sinewy aged frame, critically examining his attire for the first time.

He'd chosen a white Venetian hat trimmed in black braid. His long dark hair sat in fashionable 17th century rolls around his face. A fitted tapestry coat elongated his willowy structure.

It featured the same braid in military detail along the lapels and cuffs. At his neck, a flouncy white lace cravat billowed over a pale gold waistcoat. A Venetian coat of arms brooch secured the cravat. He looked like a dandy and she suddenly laughed out loud, saluting the present irony.

"What is so goddamn funny?" He spat angrily.

"You look like the aging, two-way poof that you are Enrico." She said, deliberately offensive in her choice of words.

He simmered at her insult.

"I won't be intimidated by you. Or play your sick games. Not anymore." She spoke quietly and didn't resist baiting him further. "Look at the pair of us. You desire to be a woman and tonight I am the man. And *I* am the new leader."

The clock on the mantel chimed. "It's time."

2

....

I t was standing room only along the Riva San Biagio and the length of Riva degli Schiavoni. Crowds of enthusiastic onlookers lined front to back, taking part in the party atmosphere and waiting for those all-important glimpses of the rich and the fabulous.

From the restaurants alongside, music enticed. People spontaneously danced in the street amidst happy laughter. Many stopped to gawk at the strange human statues dotting the area willing them to move. Or blink. Six robust young men dressed as ancient Roman soldiers moved as one through the crowd.

Some held elevated positions, pressed together like sardines on the Ponte della Ca' di Dio as the ancient bridge groaned under their combined weight, until a city official came and cleared the area save a lucky few.

On the water, jammed together in an equally tight flotilla, watercraft bobbed outside the cordoned security zone testing security measures and the patience of the local police.

The eclectic mix of human interest spread the length of the lagoon arc in both directions from the Arsenale stop that had been closed to members of the public for this prestigious event.

But it was those guests in the bell tower across the lagoon, equipped with binoculars and cocktails, who rallied the loudest

13

at each approach of the hotel's launch to the event. Their cheers whipped across the lagoon, as the excitement gathered momentum.

It was a hectic, messy scene enhanced by the chill night air and waning moon. And the focus was a long length of red carpet from the Arsenale stop to the entrance of the exquisitely refurbished former hospice, turned luxury hotel.

Tonight's official opening was invitation only. And anyone who was anyone was desperate to be there.

Tickets to the infamous Masquerade Ball was the talk of the season every year and invitations to this premier event were scarce. That it would be held in the opulence of Venice's latest luxury offering brought its own storm and urgency to be the first to see and experience the magnificent new palace.

This was more than hype. Rumours around the elusive guest list drove the frenzy, fuelled by social media reports. This ball was the hottest event in town. And the status of those excluded only added to the drama.

Movie stars, patrons, and royalty took turns on the red carpet laid from the pontoon to the luxuriously appointed foyer. Those who chose to be recognised faced an adoring public with a familiar gesture, wave and a smile, posing patiently for the obligatory photographs and taking media opportunities.

Their names began as a whisper and were soon shouted loudly to draw attention, and with hope, the perfect Hollywood dress up picture.

Others were more mysterious. Dressed in full mask and costume to hide their identity, they exited quickly from crowd's view into the secure hotel, inciting harried whispers and wild guessing games amongst the onlookers.

A grand ballroom filled with the masked, painted and

downright curious making it at times difficult to determine exactly who was enjoying the pageantry. From his vantage point on the second level within the interior's circular space, Nicholas Delarno watched for familiarity amongst the assembled guests; a stance or gesture that could not be hidden by mask or clothing.

The unmistakable gait of Bruno Poccolini, known to all as Pocco, weaved through the crowd. His hurried actions resembled a nodding puppet as his head tilted, heavy in headdress, angled sideways and forwards at those he pushed rudely past.

Nicholas watched him head towards a doorway in the middle of the long room and disappear through it. He knew the doorway led to a small chamber and a stairwell to a second-floor room which once housed the bedroom quarter of a ruling Doge's mistress. In this century, it constituted a meticulously decorated boardroom for a hungry conference market.

Nic stood his ground in the hideout, overlooking the ballroom. He watched another disappear through the door. That would be Mario Zanda, his longtime friend and confidant. Still, he waited. When Alessandro Delarno entered the room, the younger man inhaled sharply at his uncle's unexpected appearance.

The last to arrive was Giuliett Seta and her consigliere, Enrico Nero. Nic watched her stride confidently across the floor. She was high and chose a place within the crowd that allowed her access to the room and her consigliere, the opportunity to scrutinise. She settled into a conversation with another guest. Enrico watched over the fair-haired heiress, his eyes restlessly surveying the room, settling on everyone and no one in particular.

The room plunged into darkness. A million stars lit the ceiling in a digital night sky. Nervous energy built in the dark hush.

It began as noise. Venice in surround sound as distant voices, tolling bells and the constant lapping water were gathered together into the rhythm of a steady single heartbeat.

Then came the light. Projected images cast onto the ball room walls. The story of Venice began with the reeds, the flowers and the dragonflies. A nod to the early settlement of the island state. A gentle gliding movement through the space and the audience was the eye witness.

Simultaneously the noise softened as quiet, more sedate sounds filled the air. Oar and gentle splash, bird song and breeze combined with muffled conversations of the first Venetians. The ba-bump, ba-bump, ba-bump of the beating heart increasing in tempo was accompanied by the sound of breath and the distant rumbling of war.

An orchestral symphony steadily amplified to a roar filling the cavernous space. Instantly a timeline of a proud history was projected in larger-than-life sea battles. Symbols of power and actions of conquest filled the room.Hologram waves, violent sea storms and the city's famed pink light washed over the assembled group, coming at them from every angle in a light projection that immersed and fascinated everyone. The heartbeat was racing.

Hologram market vendors, past saints and pious Doge appeared, walking through the room in ghostly silence, engrossed in their own world. The sounds of market filled the air. Then came the rush of bells. And the low melody from the priests as mass was sung in surround sound, bouncing off the upper balconies and vaulted ceiling.

2

The crowd parted. Frankincense and myrrh incense filled the space as the swinging, golden thurible was ceremoniously carried through the centre of the room by performers on stilts in a blur of real and pretend.

The projections continued. Flocks of pigeons raced skywards and around the walls accompanying the sound of a thousand flapping wings. The birds seemed to land at guest's feet. Some faded into another projection of the cobblestoned forecourt of Saint Marks Square. Others spiralled upwards towards performers encased in gilded cages that lowered slowly from the ceiling.

In the middle of the room, a winged lion landed on a pedestal, roaring his presence. Faded and surreal the images captured the decay, the political and social nuances and the glory of the city.

Death, lust and religious fervour. Opulence, mystery and magic. Venice was on show tonight and when you couldn't absorb the wonder anymore, the room dipped again into complete darkness and the sound of a steady heartbeat.

Suddenly the whole room lit brightly with the radiant golden glow of a new day and falling glitter. It flushed out every hidden corner before collapsing the room into darkness again. Dance music pumped from a first floor balcony and the room moved as one to the beat in another light sequence as the real and the fantasy blurred together.Nic took his opportunity to leave as the orchestra joined into the contemporary mood. It was time for business.

Silently he entered the small chamber attached to the boardroom. He checked the stair well with a cursory glance and paused at the threshold. The door was slightly ajar. Not a soul and no sound. Pistol drawn he entered the lavish room.

Company entered the room behind him. Nic sensed the presence of another and stepped aside as the blade shaved his jacket. Silently he twisted into the associate, continuing the downward motion. His forearm pushed the henchman against the wall, driving the blade under his ribs and into his chest. The dead man was pushed into a dark corner and Nic moved further into the room.

There were no windows and one door. Gilded furnishings gleamed softly in the subtle electric candlelight directed upwards from regularly placed wall sconces. They adorned each long length of the room. His eyes adjusted.

Typically Venetian, every inch of the wall space was decorated. Carpaccio dominated almost every plaster surface.

The artist's patrons immortalised in religious and everyday scenes gazed from the ceiling and walls at the intruder. Nic caught his own shadowy reflection in one of the many ornate mirrors lining the walls between artworks.

"Fuck it." He swore under his breath. How could he get it so wrong? He'd watched them all enter this space tonight.

He made a quick assessment and the decision to leave. A brief look at the floor found a shadow at his feet extending forward into room. He turned to see a dull light appearing from a long crack, millimetres above the marble tiled floor. It marked a hidden doorway.

The Doge's hole. Nic crouched and felt the doorway give slightly. He waited, listening for a moment. He stepped boldly into the tunnel and face to face with the second associate.

"E questo il bagno?" he asked. Is this the bathroom?

The henchman lunged forward. Nic drew him from the small space and into the boardroom.

They traded fists. Outside the ballroom music and light show escalated into the last scene. A sudden noise and shaft of light reverberated around the chamber as the chamber door opened and shut.

He'd run out of time.

Nic slammed the henchman's head against the marble doorframe and quickly dragged the limp body into darkness. He waited in the shadows.

3

. . . .

Dominating the small windowless room was a long rectangular slab. Its subtle patina, brought about by the regular use of a nourishing olive oil blend, gave the wood a supple, glowing appearance. In its centre, the timber was inlaid with fragments of human bone, reputed to be those of Saint Theodore.

The slab was supported by four magnificent hand carved, gilded legs. The equally impressive decoration repeated around the table apron.

Ten tall backed, timber Venetian chairs, with padded seats of blush velvet, were set around it. An antique silk floor rug centred the arrangement within the private second storey room.

Opposite the only doorway, quietly crackling within the limits of an Istria stone hole, a small fire warmed the room. The pale surround, illuminated by the glow, contrasted with the deep green stone of the malachite floor. Absorbing most of the light, it gave the illusion that the beings silently moving to their designated seats were in fact floating on the thick suspicious air filling the room.

Eight sat as one. A sombre atmosphere belied the costumed group. The seated removed their masks, replacing them with serious expressions of mistrust and tension.

Don Mario Zanda spoke first.

"Nicholas Delarno is alive." He looked around the room, man-by-man, and paused at Alessandro. "You might like to tell us more Alessandro."

"Yes. It's true. I have seen him." Alessandro responded truthfully.

"Where?" Mario enquired. "What business did you have?"

"I went to Fiji to warn my brother Silvio of an eminent attack on him. I came across Nicholas there."

"Did you talk with him?" Mario asked.

"No. I had not the chance. The attack was already underway when I arrived."

"Have you seen Nicholas since that day?"

"No. I have not." Alessandro replied.

"So you are unaware of his movements?" Mario asked.

Alessandro nodded. "That is correct."

"I recently heard he has acquired a place in Venice. I'm surprised you've not come across him. It is a small community." Mario pushed.

"The boy's been hiding for many years. Who knows where he's been in that time. I did not know of him being in Venice because I was not looking for him." He paused. "None of you ever found him."

"We thought he was dead." Don Bruno Poccolini spoke plainly.

"As did I." Alessandro turned to face the Florentine crime boss. "We *all* thought he was dead, Pocco."

Every head turned towards Alessandro. He waited quietly, unflinching under their silent scrutiny. At the appropriate time, he turned to Don Zanda, who nodded and faced the men.

"Gentleman, tonight we elect the new Capo de tutti Capi." he said. "And I am proposing we return to our roots and restore the Council of Ten."

Pocco looked at the assembled men. He breathed out importantly and began his address. "We can no longer be sure that Nicholas is one of us."

"You have no way of knowing that Pocco." Zanda interrupted. "He dealt with Seta as his father would. A traitor plays with his life."

"That may be so, but his loyalty is to Francesca Salucci. A crime detective!" Pocco spat. He took a moment to gauge support. Encouraged he continued. "He murdered his own father for that woman."

Some of the men nodded in agreement.

"And we only hear about Seta's devious acts after he is dead." Pocco continued. "Again, a man murdered by Nicholas Delarno. How is it that none of us knew Carlo Seta had turned on Silvio in such a way?"

Pocco's focus drilled into the silent group, man by man. He silently challenged for a response. It came from Alessandro Delarno.

"Because you were too close to Seta." He stated. "The warning signs were clear. You must remember! Nicholas told you eight years ago to be wary of Seta. That he was undermining our cause. None of you would listen.

"Instead you believed *he* was the traitor within the group. And he suffered at your hands as was appropriate for such an allegation. Surely *you* remember Pocco. Zanda and I were the only two who supported Nicholas. We were witness to Seta's damaging actions in Genoa and we confided in you."

Alessandro lifted his chin towards the Florentine, challenging a rebuttal. Pocco remained silent. He knew that was true.

"You may be satisfied that Francesca Salucci is no longer a problem. The girl is out of the game. Now that he has proved his point with Seta, Nicholas' focus will return to our cause." Alessandro finished the plea with a reassuring conclusion.

The group remained silent.

"How can you be so sure? Have you spoken to him?" Pocco pressed. "How can we be sure we're safe from his rage and his pistol?"

Alessandro took the high road, ignoring the last inflammatory remark.

"As I said before, I've had no contact with Nicholas since the altercation in Fiji. But I know that boy better than most." Alessandro reminded the group emphatically.

"None of you have anything to fear with Nicholas. He has acted, as we would expect with Seta. His support to our cause is assured. As is his place within our group." His tone was even as to not offend any member of the group.

Alessandro's right hand was curled in a loose fist and his knuckles rested gently on the table. His left hand lay flat in front, fingers splayed facing the group. His chest rose and dropped as he breathed an even tempo. His bearded jaw that had tightly clenched moments before, relaxed into its natural place. He steadied his gaze on Pocco.

Silence fell upon the room.

"You're not proposing Nicholas to be Capo." The Florentine suddenly spluttered. "He's not even here! You are loco old man." His short fat arms flayed dramatically in front of him. Puffy small hands whirled around his head in circular cuckoo movements.

Alessandro's fist gently slammed the table.

Mario Zanda quickly intervened, easing the tension between the two long-time rivals.

"Nicholas has the birth right.' He said pointedly. "We all agreed he was suitable before Seta betrayed us. The boy's done nothing to undermine our group. His obsession with bringing Salucci on board with us is ended. I think we have the obligation to show him the respect such an honour deserves."

"I think our group needs new direction and a firm steady hand." Their attention turned to Don Sebastino Nero. "I have those qualities. As well as new alliances across government and the support of the people in the south." He said, joining the conversation for the first time. The young man straightened his big shoulders, leant forward slightly and stared at each member one by one. His dark eyes shone with determination. "I would be honoured to lead."

"You? You would be honoured to lead as our Capo?" Pocco repeated sarcastically, spluttering. "A pup! You insult us! Besides a Nero will never lead."

Pocco turned to the group. "Gentlemen, *if* we are casting votes, I should be chosen."

"Are we leaders or are we children?" Mario Zanda interjected, his warning focused on Pocco.

"How would you like to be my second, Mario?" Pocco taunted from across the table, pointing at the Genovese crime boss.

"I may be young but I know where my loyalties lie." Sebastino looked directly at Alessandro.

"What are you suggesting boy?" Alessandro replied coldly. "Be careful here. Your dead uncle can't save you now."

"I don't need my uncle to protect me." He said, unperturbed

by the threat. "I want to know a little more about your time with Nicholas. I'm not satisfied with your tidy summation of events. I get the feeling we're being stitched up." He glanced pointedly between Alessandro and Zanda.

"Do you require a full briefing Minister?" Alessandro taunted.

Pocco laughed and slapped his hand on the table loudly. Sebastino inclined his head slightly towards Pocco, his lips set in a firm line of displeasure.

"Tell me Alessandro, how it was that you came across Nicholas and arrived too late to save your brother. There was no way you could warn him of impending danger? A simple telephone call would have been sufficient." The young member of the Italian parliament held the floor as suspicion shifted back to Alessandro. "Perhaps you've wanted the leadership all along. You're not a Don. Nor do you have the birth-right."

Sebastino briefly paused before executing his challenge. "Did you take part in a plan to remove Silvio and Seta? Is there a deal with Nicholas Delarno?"

The room was sucked of air as the tension scaled up again.

"No, Sebastino. There is no deal with Nicholas." Alessandro paused. He looked directly into the hungry faces of the men around him.

"Of course," he continued, "it would be an honour to be chosen as Capo. But it is not a role I seek. I believe our best choice going forward is Don Mario Zanda."

Pocco stood and clapped loudly. "Such humanity! Such humility! Nice pitch. Great show. But I will not be deceived. This *is* a stitch up. Nothing more than another Delarno alliance designed to lead and influence. Nero. Delarno. Zanda. Gentleman, don't be fooled. There is another way..."

Their attention was interrupted by the sound of quick footsteps ushering along the tunnel. The consiglieres standing in place along the walls of the room, prepared. The steps breached the doorway. In one violent movement, the door was flung open and a rush of cool fresh air pushed through.

"Gentlemen." Giuliett Seta stormed into the dank crowded room. "You dare start without me? Drop your guns you imbeciles." She addressed the guard. Enrico was one step behind her. He menacingly circled the room.

"Now, I see everything is in place." She began. "Ten cups, the gilded knife, the holy card. A fire. The brand. Bravo!"

"Giuliett." Mario Zanda abruptly stood. "We're just beginning. We weren't expecting you tonight, so soon after your father's death." He bowed his head in respect to her recent loss. "Gatto has already apologised on behalf of Bice and yourself."

"Gatto! Apologised on behalf of my mother and I!" she repeated, astonished.

"I'm sorry Giuliett," Zanda said humbly. "There's been a misunderstanding."

"I have mourned my father's death." She said without feeling. "Now is the time for action."

She eyed the men assembled around the table.

"What you're really trying to say Mario is that you didn't think a woman would be capable of filling the role as Capo, so you all thought you'd meet without me. It is not a good start to our friendship; to betray me as my father was betrayed." She said stopping at the older gentleman who was taking the Chair.

"Let me assure you all, I am more than ready and capable. As my father was Head, upon his death, I am the new Leader." She eyeballed each of the men representing their family's consortium.

She arched an eyebrow. "Does anyone wish to challenge?"

The men turned to Don Sebastino Nero.

"A boy? You can't be serious." She scoffed. "And a Nero at that!"

She walked behind him, circling his chair like a vulture. Her deliberate steps lapped the table. She stopped beside Sebastino again and looked him up and down as he sat facing the group.

Suddenly Giuliett reached out with the blade. Sebastino caught her wrist close to his ear and held it tightly within his strong fingers. His chair scraped back abruptly and the mafia boss stepped behind her in one athletic movement.

Twisting her hand into a wristlock, he held it high behind her back. He roughly pushed her elbow further up her spine. His deft fingers caught the fabric of her cape and corset and he pushed her forward, face first towards the table.

Giuliett sprawled theatrically. Her left elbow propped heavily saving her head as it braced inches from the dark timber surface. She flattened her back. Shoulder blades pushed together coercing the pale creaminess of exposed skin and her flaxen hair into play. The light and smooth textures contrasting dramatically with the dark surrounds like a Rembrandt portrait.

She knew the power of her beauty and used it. Pocco licked his lips, his lecherous eyes wandering from the outline of her arse pressed against Sebastino's groin to her ample breasts pushing ever higher in the unforgiving lace corset binding.

Scraping noisily across the timber, the ornate decoration of pearls and stones hanging from her neck moved with her, competing with the crackle of the fire and the silent room.

Sebastino angled the wristlock harder. The knife released. He caught it, driving it forcefully into the table beside her hand.

Giuliett laughed at his show of strength and masculinity. A scoffing deep sound that came from her chest hit the back of her throat and vibrated out from the roof of her mouth and her nose.

"You may be a Seta, Giuliett." He menaced, pushing her downward again between the shoulders for emphasis. He grabbed a handful of hair, using it to pull her head back. Her long smooth neck was exposed. Pocco salivated.

"I am Nero." Sebastino said. "Our family has protected yours for decades. In spite of my youth I have earned the right to sit at this table. You have not. So, you'd do well to remember your place around me. Don't ever threaten or touch me again."

"Or what?" she goaded from the vulnerable position.

"Or you will find yourself in hell beside your dead father."

He released his grasp on her wrist abruptly, pushing her face towards the table one last time. He levered out the knife, folded it and put it in his pocket. The young man calmly took his place in his seat, his eyes challenging Enrico to act, before eyeballing the remainder of the group.

Giuliett scoffed.

"Well, Sebastino. You are still the tempestuous young buck I remember." She said in a condescending tone.

Alessandro seized control in the moment.

"Giuliett, please, take your seat at the table. Your father's place is next to Don Poccolini."

She turned towards the older gentleman, bowed her head slightly, then made her way to beside Pocco. Her steady gait echoed in the silent room.

"Thank you, Alessandro."

4
· · · · · · · · · · · · · · · · ·

"Now we have nine." Mario began, assuming authority in his tone and manner.

"Recent events have left our organisation at risk. The rise of the Guardians, internal power struggles and the changes in our operations to include outside groups has left us vulnerable.

"Information has been sold. Trust is broken. Tonight, as well as appointing a new Capo, it is my wish to re-form the Council of Ten. Tradition is the only way we can move forward with confidence and survive. We need to reinstate the old ways."

Mario looked pointedly at Giuliett. "Young lady you may think you are automatically Capo, but your father did not facilitate it with the Commission. You have the right to occupy a place within the organisation. That is your birth-right as you are the eldest child. However, you will have to undertake and pass the initiation and the tests, as we all have, to earn the title Don. You must be made in your own right, without relying on your father's contribution.

"After that time, you may take part in Commission decisions and be eligible for the Council of Ten. Currently you have no voting rights. You may only contribute to the discussion. Until you are Don, you have the same rights as our loyal servant Alessandro."

She glared at Mario Zanda from across the table.

"In fact, the only person who has the *right* to be Capo de tutti Capi is Nicholas Delarno." Mario continued.

"What?" She said incredulously, eyeing each of the men. "You're not serious. That murderous traitor!"

"Yes. It is true. He has the right." Pocco said nodding dramatically as if consoling a small child. He continued in the same tone as he gave her a summation of events as the Commission saw it.

"Silvio had ratified Nicholas with the Commission long before his death. We had approved this change upon Silvio's death or renunciation. After we believed Nicholas to be dead, your father stepped in without authority and undermined Silvio."

"My father had to step in," she spluttered, rudely interrupting the Florentine. "You stupid fool! Prancing around trying to facilitate another was costing us all."

"Giuliett," Pocco interjected, "we have a code. A structure based on honour and respect. It may be difficult for you to understand, but your father's actions undermined our positions and brought unwanted attention upon our activities. Time was our friend. It gave us an opportunity to deflect, withdraw and rebuild.

"Your father betrayed our group. It was only a matter of time before a Delarno settled the score. That is the way of the code. Your father knew the risks."

Giuliett shook her head. "You would rather stick to your traditions and protocol? How would you feel if the head of our organisation were a motor-bike rider? An outlaw from Australia."

She paused and looked around the table. "That's right. After Nicholas died, Silvio lost his mind. And whom do you think he was grooming as leader?

"Robbie L, a motorbike lord from Sydney! His initiation and stages are complete, under Silvio's guidance. In fact, he has already advanced to Capo of the Delarno Clan and is running the operations in Australia. All this has happened right under your very noses. Time? Phah! Your precious time gave Silvio Delarno another opportunity to rule.

"My father did what had to be done to save our business. And your arses."

She turned to Sebastino. "If you weren't so busy sleeping with prostitutes and running to Italy, you would know *that* Don Nero. You should've stayed in Melbourne. You could have achieved your desire. You could have won Silvio's heart and been leader." She taunted. "Instead we now have Robbie L making claims within our group."

Sebastino Nero glared at her. His rage reverberated from his bulging eyes to the tightly held fist, he'd clenched on the table-top. The room's heartbeat stopped.

"And if you hadn't been busy shoving powder and cock in your every hole," he said in quietly, "you would know that the south is on the rise and my political standing in our country has risen with it. *I* have won the support of the moderates and the fascists. Something no-one in our group has ever been able to achieve."

She returned insult for insult. "Ha! Il sud ha il dito nel culo! The south has its finger up its arse!" She spat.

Capitalising on the reverberating shockwave, Giuliett returned to their attention to the outlaw, Robbie L.

"Even in his death Delarno has you by the balls! My father had no choice but to take control before all was lost for us!"

She stared at them in the silence, barely able to keep her seat.

She looked for support from Enrico. At his raging expression, she closed her mouth.

"Giuliett," Pocco spoke first. "This is a lie. *Your* father betrayed *us*." He insisted steadily. "Seta knew the code. He should have come to the Commission with his concerns. I have to defend Nicholas in this case. He has acted as we expect from our leader.

"May I take this opportunity, on behalf of the Commission to express my condolences to you Councillor Castello for the treatment and ultimate death of your mother, Maria, at the hands of Carlo Seta."

"Thank you Don Poccolini." Castello replied. He looked at Giuliett and his lips pressed tightly together in displeasure. "Our family appreciates your loyal gestures and ongoing concern."

Giuliett glanced from Castello to Pocco to Mario Zanda and their hard expressions directed to her. She chose not to retaliate.

The room was at snapping point.

"Now then to the business at hand." As Mario Zanda spoke, his deliberate calm tone created the necessary, soothing rub to move the business forward.

"I propose that someone is appointed to seek out Nicholas and bring him back. In the meantime, I will oversee the operations and negotiate the mess with the Russians and the Australian bikers. Don Nero, perhaps you would like to assist?"

Sebastino bowed his head towards to the Genoese. "It would be a challenge I seek. Yes, I agree."

"Thank you. I also propose a commitment to the Council of Ten. Don Poccolini, Don Nero and myself as the three leaders. Of course, Nicholas will take his place at the leadership when we locate him. Alessandro Delarno is our advisor. Next I'd like to appoint Don di Tutti, Don Castello, Don Moretti and Don Bienvien to make the nine. That leaves one space for you Giuliett. When you have completed your initiation, you will be the tenth councillor."

He sat calmly with his hands folded in front of him resting lightly on the table. In the soft light of the room, his salt and pepper stubble enhanced his middle-aged looks, as did the springy dark charcoal hair. His dark expressive eyes settled on his worn fingers and he raised his head at the end of his thought process as if to punctuate the full stop.

"Do we have an agreement?" he asked. "Pocco, I find it hard that you remain silent. What do you say?"

"I think Alessandro should locate Nicholas. And you, Mario should be leader for the interim."

Mario raised an eyebrow. "Really."

"Alessandro has many connections in Venice. We've been told Nicholas is seeking shelter here too. It will not be too hard to get him I imagine." Pocco turned to Alessandro. "He's your nephew after all. You clean up the mess with that family."

"And the leadership? You were so vocal only moments ago."

"I have no interest in temporary roles. I will contest leadership when there is leadership to contest, you can be sure of that." He turned to face the room. "But we have history and protocol. It has stood us on steady ground for generations. I will not break the code for my personal satisfaction." Pocco concluded emphatically.

"A fair fight. That's very admirable of you Pocco." Sebastino interjected and it was hard to gauge if he was baiting or genuine.

"Well if there are no objections, it is decided. Let us begin the ceremony. Consigliere unmask."

Giuliett looked at the man standing directly across from her and recognised him at once.

"What the fuck are you doing here?" she screamed. "How dare you come into this room with us!" she rose from her seat and lunged across the table towards him.

Enrico, who'd been watching her from the shadows near the doorway, stepped towards her, pushing her behind him to protect her. The man, who by now had been securely contained by Mario Zanda's consigliere, continued to mock her. From his compromised position, the bulky stranger of islander descent laughed at her furious expression.

"Gentleman, may I introduce Robbie L." She frothed, struggling free from Enrico's grasp.

Enrico looked around at the faces in the room. Two were missing. He checked again.

"Where are Giuliett's men?" he asked.

"In the tunnel and boardroom, securing our meeting." Mario replied.

"They are not." The consigliere replied.

The room went quiet. "Secure Robbie L. Take my man." Mario yelled as Enrico made to exit the chamber and then he swore. "Fuck it! We've been compromised."

"No. We are secure." Nicholas Delarno stepped calmly into the room. "The traitors have been dealt with."

He looked directly at Giuliett Seta.

5

....

Enrico didn't conceal his disgust and shame at the evening's conclusion. He openly stewed on it as they raced across the lagoon towards the Jewish island, La Giudecca.

Despite the freezing conditions, he stood outside, away from her, fuelling his growing anger. He'd have to find a way to salvage whatever they could with the Commission. She'd embarrassed them all tonight. The whole Seta operation was now destabilised.

He could not protect her from the families who'd demand recompense for her disrespect. Her only hope was negotiating a way forward for the Seta operation under the guise of her grief.

He looked at the approaching wharf and tossed the options in his mind, wringing his hands and cracking the knuckles at regular intermission.

Each option was marked by one glaring fact. Notwithstanding the situation they now faced, she'd been right about the biker, Robbie L.

Enrico made his decision. He would bring about the change. In the way her father should've done. Her lack of discipline and respect for the organisation was coming to an end.

The consigliere unleashed as they entered her apartment.

"Fuck me, Giuliett! What the hell was that about? Learn your lesson." His open palm connected with her cheek in a resounding slap.

"You have a hide!" she screamed, pushing him back against the door. He pulled her towards him, roughly shook her and flung her across the room with another resounding slap.

She turned towards him quickly, beginning a steady advance. She took another swing at him, which he aptly dodged. She caught the epilate at his shoulder as he stepped past her and used it to pull him sideways.

Enrico pushed into her, with his shoulder, his momentum propelling her sideways. The whole room shook as she connected heavily with the wall. She screamed at him in equal frustration and pain, releasing her hold on impact as her fingers twisted and caught in the fabric. He stepped out of range as she fell to the floor.

Giuliett recovered quickly and lunged towards him again without success.

"Yeah? Come on wench. You want a fight? Take *me*! Not the whole flaming establishment." He yelled back, taking menacing steps towards her. He closed the space between them and grabbed her jacket front and gathered it together in his left hand. His right pushed her cheeks together and they ground against her teeth, slashing the inside of her mouth. He hit her again.

She reeled towards the marble topped credenza as the force connected. Glasses shattered across the surface and onto floor. Giuliett reached for it. Her fingers grabbed at the broken shards jutting upwards from the drinks tray. She found purchase with the bottle and threw it across the room at him.

He weaved from its path as it smashed into the papered wall behind him. The consigliere promptly left the room.

"That's right." She yelled. "Piss off out of my sight."

She spat the blood filling her mouth onto the floor in his direction.

Enrico returned with a towel from the bathroom. He threw it to her.

"Here!" He said. "Clean up your mess!"

Turning on her heel, she crossed the entire room to put some distance between them and remained there with her back him. The brutality was over for now and an uneasy understanding settled on them both.

"I want to scream. That bunch of arrogant, crusty old bastards won't know what hit them when I take over." She stormed. "And as for Nicholas. I want to scratch his eyes out. Have you ever seen such arrogance?"

"Yes!" Enrico responded in exasperation. "You! Tonight!"

He joined her by the window overlooking the lagoon. "*You would do well to learn from those crusty old bastards.*" He said accusingly. "They can make or break your entry into the Commission. Unless of course you want to sit on the side lines for your whole life like Alessandro."

"Ha! Like hell!"

"Release me." She demanded suddenly, turning her back to him so he could undo her corset. She gasped as the tight binding cords released, taking in a deep breath. She began to plot her next move and gain control of the organisation.

He undid the last of the fastenings. "You're done." He said coldly.

"What do you make of Sebastino Nero? Young. Powerful. I wonder what it would take to turn his alliance from Delarno to me."

"Unbelievable!" the consigliere said, shaking his head at her. "How about you focus on what's in front of you."

"I sense jealousy. Don't worry Enrico we have too much history. There'll always be a place for you in my bed."

She threw the bustier onto the floor at his feet, posing as her breasts spilled. She held them, pushing upwards before stretching upwards. The diamonds dripped against the smooth skin between her breasts.

"Give to me lover." She cooed seductively, as her arms fell gracefully to her side.

He threw her a robe. "Cover yourself Giuliett."

"It will be a night to remember." She said, stepping towards him, holding the robe in her hand.

"No Giuliett."

"I'll pretend to be Sebastino. He's definitely your type. We can finish what we started." She said, sidling up to him and wrapping her hands over his shoulders to caress his neck.

"Let me pleasure you." She whispered gently sucking his neck.

"Go to bed Giuliett. I'm not interested. You embarrassed yourself tonight. As well as your family." He paused. "For what it's worth ... do you want to know what would please me?"

"This?" She pulled the tie from the robe, wrapped it around one wrist and clasped her hands together as she knelt before him, bowing her head subserviently.

He unceremoniously pulled her up by the wrist so she stood in front of him. He wrapped the robe around her and pulled the cord tight around her waist.

"You growing up." He said. "Tonight, two men lost their lives protecting you. You'd do well to show some respect."

Enrico left her.

"You're not irreplaceable." She yelled as he slammed the door behind him. "I might secure Sebastino Nero *and* Robbie L."

6

. . . .

Giuliett would not settle. In the silent room, she paced like a caged lioness. Everything irritated her. Her clothes. Her hair. This room. She stripped down, leaving items where they fell and pulled every pin from her hair, shaking it out. Next she opened the windows and the cold damp air rushed in. She stood looking at the sultry lagoon. She'd give anything for a swim in its icy blackness.

She watched the boats come and go and turned her back to it, shutting the window. There'd been enough erratic behaviour tonight.

At last she flicked on the television as her father often did when he came home late at night. Scrolling through her mobile phone she selected a playlist. The devices competed for her attention.

But none could drown out the noise of her desperate thoughts. She'd been outgunned tonight. Outwitted and outplayed. And it scratched and burned, festering a seething internal battle.

Vulnerable feelings re-surfaced. Anger and torment crashed through her in waves of emotion. Everyone was against her. Giuliett was no stranger to that particular feeling. This time, her father wasn't there to soothe over the hurt.

The heiress wondered what to do next.

She had to figure this out. Her inability to sway the

Commission tonight was because of one man. Nicholas Delarno. Dealing with him would solve everything for her.

Giuliett quietly laughed. She'd been trying to deal with him for years. Every time she came close, Francesca Salucci would step in the way. The heiress leant forward in her chair subconsciously. Bare arms rested on her thighs.

Her focus closed in the former detective and then it was lost again, as though her brain could not rest long enough to string one thought to another.

Muddled by grief and temper, she faced the downer and loneliness with listless energy. In the end it was too much, and so Giuliett did as she had learnt. Beside the second coffee martini, she formed the powdery line. When she was done, she mixed another alcoholic blend and drained the glass in one gulping motion. She looked blankly into the blurred room until it came to focus.

Enrico lay in the adjoining room. At another time, she'd march right in and take his attention. Not tonight. She didn't dare. There was too much anger between them.

So, with no sex to be had, she located the knife.

She bled. Watching the drip slide along her inner thigh, she cut a second.

"Giuliett?" He was there within the next second, violently taking the knife from her grasp. She looked at him. Her eyes welled. She burst into tears.

Carlo Seta's consigliere was not the kind of man anyone would call soft. His face resembled an overripe passionfruit, round and wrinkled with age and battle scars. His physique was stocky but strong. His reflexes were sharper than most half his age. He was grumpy, antagonistic and disliked almost everyone he met.

"Poppa-Gatto." She sobbed, using her pet childhood name for her father's right hand man. "What are you doing here?"

"I heard about tonight. I came to check on you. Where's Enrico?" he asked, looking around the war zone that was her suite.

"He went to bed. I frustrate him." She added, "Besides, I don't need a nanny."

"You need someone by the looks of you. Let's get you cleaned up." He looked at the old linear scars scratched into the tops of her legs and scowled.

"Here, use this." He said gruffly, handing her a cotton towel still damp from her late-night shower. "Press down and hold pressure. That one's quite deep."

He collected the empty alcohol bottles and threw into the bin.

"Enrico get this for you?" He said referring to the remaining evidence of cocaine.

She nodded. He continued to tidy in silence, straightening the furniture, picking up her discarded clothes and hanging them on the dressmaker rack. He disappeared to the bathroom. Giuliett heard him fussing around before flushing the narcotic evidence down the toilet.

Next, he collected the broken glass shards off the floor with a blood-stained towel and threw them all in the lined bin. He tied the top.

The old man made two strong espressos. He took off his jacket and wrapped it around her naked shoulders. He pulled up a footstool opposite her.

They sat together in the small sitting room.

"I suppose you're surprised I chose this room." She said, referring to the hotel suite. The very room Nicholas Delarno had murdered her father, the mob boss, Carlo Seta on the day of her ill-fated wedding. She glanced at the vacant spot where her father's favourite chair once stood.

"A little." He said.

"I needed to be close to dad." She said.

Her father's consigliere simply nodded. "That was a very stupid thing you did tonight."

"Don't trouble yourself Gatto." She commented dryly. "Enrico will sort it out with the Commission and I'll get over myself. I usually do. There will be compensation paid to those I've allegedly offended."

"I'm talking about inviting Robbie L into the boardroom. The Commission is already angry with this family. Delarno and Zanda have been working the numbers against us. You shouldn't have pushed it."

"I didn't invite him!"

"Don't lie to me child." He warned.

"I'm not. I didn't invite Robbie L. I'm telling the truth. Why would I want him there?"

"You tell me." Gatto said bluntly.

"I have no clue. I was outplayed tonight. For all I know Nicci invited him. Did you know I lost two men tonight? Because Saint Nicholas Delarno called them traitors, the Commission distrusts me more."

Her mournful tone quickly turned to anger.

"What the fuck? The man goes AWOL for eight years, comes back and everyone treats him like he's a fucking hero. That's going to change. This is my organisation to run. Delarno's have had their day."

He stared at her for a long moment.

"You can't go around making wild accusations." He warned. "If you want them to take you seriously, you'll need to take yourself seriously."

He looked at her sternly.

"That's more or less what Enrico said to me tonight." She conceded.

"So, what's going on with all this then? The cutting? The drugs? The fighting? This room looks like a rubbish tip and smells like one too!"

"It's my coping mechanism." Her hands gestured, palms facing upwards.

"Well I'd suggest you find another way to cope. Look, I know a place. Your father used it sometimes. There's a little island in the south. It's very private. Very secure. Think about it. I can get you there and back. No one would ever know. It would give you a chance to get yourself together. Your mother and I can oversee things in your absence. Enrico will be busy enough appeasing the Commission."

"You want to incarcerate me? Is this an intervention?" Giuliett was incredulous. He had a hide.

"No!"

"I know what my father used to get up to. I've fucked his mistress. She told me everything. Every dirty little secret the old bastard hid from mum and me."

"Giuliett!" Gatto raised his voice in surprise.

"And I know why my father was not protected the day he was murdered." She looked pointedly at the consigliere.

"So, you can take your little island and shove it up your arse!"

she screamed at him at last, pushing her now empty chair in his direction.

Enrico burst into the room. "What the hell is going on *now*?"

"Gatto was just leaving." She said, striding towards the bedroom and slamming the door behind her.

7

·················

Nicholas Delarno left the secret meeting chamber and wound his way back towards the A-list crowd gathered on the first-floor of the exquisitely restored hotel. Not quite ready to reveal himself to all from the shadows of his former life, he took the stairs and exited through a service doorway.

It opened onto a narrow, lonely street. Suddenly, he turned left. Another sharp right-hand-turn and he'd reached the Fondamenta del Piovan. Even with his expert training, his footsteps seemed to echo too loudly around the claustrophobic pedestrian streets.

It was cloudy and crisp. To his left, the murky green water of the canal silently slid in time with his pace. Nic pulled his jacket around him. Behind him, the hurried footsteps of his uncle echoed in the stillness. Nicholas recognised them and ignored them. He belted headlong towards Ponte Storto.

"Nic!" Alessandro yelled. "Wait up."

Nicholas reluctantly slowed his gait, but he did not stop. Alessandro caught him in the open space around San Martino.

"You took a hell of a risk tonight." Alessandro began as they met. He spoke in a hushed angry whisper. "It was important to discuss your plans with me first. You could have destabilised the whole operation."

"Well I didn't." Nicholas replied tautly.

"I want to know why." Alessandro said. "Why expose yourself now?"

"I don't wish to talk about it." Nic said resolutely.

"Why not?"

"Because I don't. Look Zio, you have nothing to fear from me. Neither do the people within your organisation."

Alessandro grabbed Nic's shoulder. The action forced the younger man to spin round, turn and face him.

"I should bloody well hope not." He said angrily. "Talk to me Nicholas. What's going on?"

"There's nothing to talk about. The leadership was mine and I took it. End of story." He shook his shoulder to loosen his uncle's hold.

Alessandro searched his nephews closed facial features. "There's something. Something is eating you. You know you can talk to me. There is trust between us."

"Zio, you're looking for something that's not there." Nic said.

"You gave me an opportunity. I'm grateful for that. But this is my rightful place. I'm home. And frankly, I feel damn good about my choice." Nic said, squaring his shoulders.

"Bullshit. I don't believe you. I know you Nicholas." Alessandro replied. "This is an act of wilful arrogance. And it's not going to end well if you don't address what's eating you."

The older man stepped closer and lowered his voice.

"You put everything we've worked for in jeopardy. Talk to me!"

"There is nothing to say."

"You think you can lead and do what I do? You're a fool. You cannot lead the Commission and remain a Guardian. It's a foolish and reckless notion." Alessandro whispered angrily.

"I can do whatever I want." Nic said stubbornly. "And I will."

"Hear me Nicholas. The wolves are at our door more than ever. The leaders are asking questions about your absence. They're suspicious of your loyalty."

"Let them ask Alessandro. Is it not what we would expect from another in our group?" Nicholas faced his uncle. "I will address their concerns in time. Me. Not you. I'll never forget the care and love you showed me in my recovery. I've embraced the training and lessons I learned under your watchful eye. But this is my time. My fight. And I will take what's mine."

Alessandro eyeballed him.

"Goodnight Zio."

Alessandro watched him leave. He pulled a cell phone from his pocket.

"We have a problem." He said.

8

....

Alessandro Delarno was a mysterious man with simple but exquisite tastes that leant towards the antique nautical variety. His passions were an extension of his business interests as sole director of the world's largest maritime insurance agencies. The sea was his lifeblood. It nurtured his soul.

He was a well-groomed gentleman with a pleasantly weathered face and full beard of black and silver. His longish hair flicked out from a centre part, over his temples and ears, and was trimmed neatly at the collar. It matched the dark and silver patina of his beard. When he spoke, his voice was thick and deep and rumbled along in a unique blend of Genoese dialect and European gentry.

His home was in a little town on the outskirts of tumbling Genoa. There was no room for flight or fancy in that harbour city. It was a straight up kind of place, bullish and straightforward in its daily life and attitude. It was one reason he didn't enjoy the staged atmosphere of Venice, or the Venetians for that matter. And, it is why he preferred to stay at his country estate near Treviso when in the area.

However, when Nicholas took up residence in an old part of Venice, rather than the family home in Rapallo, Alessandro thought it necessary to source a small apartment close by.

Not that his nephew needed constant attention. In truth, it was Alessandro who needed the comfort knowing he was close by to protect the younger man as he learnt how to live a double life. A deadly game Alessandro knew only too well. He'd spent his own adult life undermining his brother and the organised crime outfit Silvio Delarno had overseen.

For many years, Alessandro had led the secret organisation known as The Paladini. They were the Guardians, formed by Francesca Salucci's grandfather to undermine and disrupt Mussolini's reign of terror.

After Mussolini's capture and death, the Guardians had turned their attention to the organised crime entities emerging under the guise of political parties. Parties bound by common religious beliefs and sympathetic clergy, were forming a strong power base across the Italian northern and Emilia-Romagna regions.

The Guardians watched as the power void left in Italy at the end of World War II enticed new entities from a population exhausted by war and poverty. Stronger and better organised, these developing organisations infiltrated the burgeoning political parties. In some cases, they even had the backing of the Catholic Church.

And so, rewarded with increased power, their activities propped up and stabilised an emerging Government desperate to regain control of her country. The Guardians held them in check where they could with less capital and a different skillset.

Alessandro had watched in horror as his brother's admiration for Mussolini's tactics would define and influence his entire life. Where Mussolini had failed, Silvio Delarno thrived, as he crafted and applied that which can only be learned through hindsight.

Nicholas's father nurtured a brutal, sadistic soul behind a congenial façade. His time in control of the organised crime group saw unprecedented growth that pleased the Commissions, who in turn tolerated his unorthodox, cruel ways.

Lost in his thoughts, Alessandro marched on towards his apartment in a reflective mood as he thought about Nicholas's actions that evening and how the manner in which they'd been carried out reminded him so much of Silvio.

The brisk breeze that had been swirling around the courtyard of San Martino wasted away as he strode deeper into the maze of winding narrow Venetian streets. He unwrapped the scarf that had been tightly bound around his neck, letting it fall each side of his jacket lapel.

The action diverted his attention from his brother and his nephew to another current conundrum. Alessandro pondered the new regime formed at tonight's Commission meeting; namely the rise of Sebastino Nero in the political space. Sebastino was as dangerous as he was charismatic.

Alessandro had watched in wonder and fear as the political tide in Italy returned to fascist rhetoric and beliefs. He'd closely followed Sebastino's pathway to political greatness. The young man held rock star status in Italy. Savvy across social media platforms, he'd engaged a whole new audience who were keen for meaningful change.

Not only did Sebastino speak their language, he'd tapped into their unrest and dissatisfaction. He was creating a new order that was tinged with the nostalgia of good times, and was placing it firmly into the present.

You can have your cake and eat it too.

Alessandro was less convinced. Italy's flawed political systems and the imperfect arrangements with the European Economic Union were gouging deep scars.

The financial damage inflicted on his country because of the failings of that system as well as the influx of human traffic not only magnified the breaking economy, it fuelled the illicit activities of his brother's organisation.

Shaking his head, Alessandro wondered again at how they could be brothers. He mentally shrugged to dismiss the thoughts. Alessandro had always resembled the Zanda traits of the Delarno connections, unlike his dead brother.

At last he was home. He sighed heavily, leaving the burden of his thoughts at the exterior. In the entry hall he paused, his eyes adjusting to the dimly lit interior. The small space led directly to the front sitting room, and here he draped his coat over the back of the lounge chair, unbuttoned his shirt and took out the cufflinks, placing them in a small Murano glass tray nearby.

The scent of a woman's perfume alerted him to her. "Bice!" he said in surprise.

"Alessandro." She came to him and kissed each cheek in greeting. "I hope you don't mind. Your housekeeper let me in." She added by way of explanation.

"Not at all." He was lying. "I'm sorry, I was unaware." He quickly checked his mobile phone for a missed message from her, and raised his head. "Have you been waiting long?"

"No, not long." She looked at his face lit by the reflected streetlights, and the slight frown indicating his uncomfortable surprise.

"This is a lovely room." She said walking to the centre, her arms spreading gracefully to encompass the space. "I've always been a little intrigued by you Alessandro. We've known each other for such a long time, yet I don't really know you at all. But I think this room must hint at your soul."

She turned to him, her dark brown eyes engaging.

At his curious expression, she stepped lightly towards the space of his writing table. "These water colours for instance. Not the usual palette and medium for nautically inspired paintings. But I think they show a certain kind of feeling. They're beautiful. Movement. Light. Detailed, though not pretentious. I would even say joyous – a reflection of the kind of feeling one must feel when one finds something that makes them truly happy."

She smiled at him.

"Thank you. The sea is an agile mistress. She possesses many faces and temperaments." He smiled congenially at her in return. "May I pour you a drink?"

"Only if you'll join me." She replied. "It's late, I know. I'm sorry my timing is never on point."

Alessandro shook his head. "Anytime you need, you know that." He said, choosing a whiskey. "I have a fine Scotch. Would that suit?"

Bice Seta nodded. "Sounds perfect."

The gentleman indicated she sit opposite him in the single armchair.

"So, what business brings you out this evening? I dare say it's not a sudden interest in my paintings or me. Is something on your mind?" He asked, adding quickly. "You know we met as a group tonight."

"How did it go? I saw Giuliett before she left. She was … hmmm … lively."

Alessandro nodded. "Your daughter has been under immense pressure since the death of Carlo. As has you. The Commission has been working hard and understands she is very fragile at the moment. We're able to take that into account for the moment. But she will need to make recompense."

Bice smiled. "My dear Alessandro, you're very sweet. However, you and I both know Giuliett has always been very ... difficult."

Alessandro grimaced.

"There were a few surprises." He said after a short pause. "Nicholas finally played his card."

"How so?"

"He took control. He's taken the leadership."

"Surely that's no surprise to you Alessandro. With my husband gone there are no real contenders. And, he was approved to be leader by the Commission at one stage."

"That's true." Alessandro said. He looked at her now more than a little confused. "I'm curious dear friend. Did Gatto not tell you about tonight?"

The woman suddenly stood. She'd dressed simply tonight in dark tailored pants and a fitted turtleneck knit. Her woollen coat and scarf lay across the chair behind her. Her luscious blonde hair was clipped loosely at the nape of her neck by a square tortoise shell bar.

She paced, unbound her hair and shook out the tresses slightly, rubbing at the back of her neck and shoulders. Bice stopped by the bare windows, her figure silhouetted in the frames. She faced the street below as if pondering her next move. Large diamond earrings caught the light when she turned to face him.

"I miss this." She said simply, waving her hand to encompass the space. "You have a very nice room here Alessandro. It's made me realise how much I miss the masculinity of a private space."

He didn't know what to say.

"You know, when Carlo was alive," she began, "I would walk into the room after he'd left. I'd tidy, reorganise and return things back to where they should be. Now, I wished I'd had left them as they were."

She stopped and thought for a long moment.

"A woman's senses are alive when a man is around." She said quietly.

"Bice, I'm sorry for your loss. And here, tonight I talk about Nicholas. Forgive me." Alessandro met her by the window. "But, I thought Gatto ... it's not my business. I'm sorry."

Bice laughed bitterly. "Yes, Gatto. He makes assumptions and demands just like Carlo. He thinks he can step in where Carlo left. My life is not ..." her voice faded away leaving the sentence unfinished.

"I'm not an object to be passed from one to another. But if I say ..."

She faltered, her expression closing at once. He looked at her curiously and reached for her soft, bare hands.

"We are friends you and I. Yes?" Alessandro said softly.

She nodded.

"Do you trust me?" He asked.

She nodded again.

"Bice, are you in danger?"

9

....

tepping away from his hold, she crossed the length of the room. Her mind whirled. To verbalise her next thoughts would invite danger and perhaps remorse, but it would forever change her relationship with this man she'd hardly known yet instinctively trusted for many, many years.

Being in his apartment tonight, alone with his treasures, had enhanced her confidence in telling him. Here was a thoughtful, patient man. Someone filled with integrity and compassion.

However, should she be wrong, she would need to choose her words with utmost care.

"I don't know if I'm in danger." She said at last. Truthfully. Cautiously.

"I'm not even sure if it's Carlo's death or Carnevale that's unsettling me. I mean this is the party to end all parties, is it not? Not to mention, the added thrill of anonymity. One can wander unrecognised in the crowds."

She spread her hands out in gesture.

"But this year it's different. The masks are confronting. Every night I dream of faceless people and sinister acts."

Bice leant against the desk, her back to the framed prints she'd admired not so long ago.

"There's danger about. On that I am certain. And it has nothing to do with the festival. My instincts are warning me and without Carlo to protect me, I'm heeding their warning."

"Who is threatening you Bice?" he asked.

"I don't know. That, I can't tell you. It is a feeling. Everything's changing in my life, in our country. I feel very uneasy." She drew a deep breath and exhaled. "I just feel threatened."

"Has anything happened to make you think this way?" A serious tone injected his voice.

"Nothing has actually happened. I come and I go as before. But I do sense change." She lapped the room again speaking softly as if she was expressing her thoughts out loud for the first time.

"Change is within me. Around me there is danger and I don't know what to do about it. I did sometimes wonder what I would do should Carlo pass away. Whom would I trust?" She glanced in his direction and turned her focus to the floor at her feet. She suddenly felt very quiet and shy. She was at the point of no return now and somehow it had felt easier to make the decision to ask when he was not in the room.

"Well I hope you know that I'm one of those people you can trust." He said, gently lifting her chin to meet her eyes with his.

She faltered. She shook her head. This was stupid. She would leave.

She turned her head away from him and took two steps back, putting physical distance between them.

"Bice? Tell me. What troubles you tonight?"

"It's stupid Alessandro. I'll go now. It's very late and I've wasted enough of your time. It is a fool's errand and I'm a bigger fool."

He shook his head.

"No. Come now friend. Sit with me." He guided her gently towards the chair. He sat, facing her and smiled kindly. "I insist."

She looked blindly at the marine chart on the wall beyond his shoulder.

"Do you ever get tired of it? The double life?" She asked taking a deep breath and looking him straight in the eye.

"I'm not sure what you mean honey?" He said in a careful tone.

"You know, the respectable business and then the other. People suffer. For what? So that I can live a lovely life?"

"Our organisation provides a service." He said simply. "If people suffer it is of their own volition. We provide a framework for honour, tradition and stability in a world that is becoming increasingly erratic. Old values are slipping away."

He shrugged a nonchalant gesture. "We sit outside the law guaranteeing reassurance and structure to those in need."

"Do you ever think about leaving the organisation?" she asked carefully.

"No. To be truthful, never. Life is what it is. I made my choices long ago and I'm content. Are you thinking it's time for you? Is that why you're feeling ill at ease?"

"It's a dangerous thought." She conceded. "I know not much, but enough. To think of leaving seals a death warrant." She said. Her voice wobbled and her eyes filled with tears. "But I feel also, another threat."

"Are you worried about your safety with Nicholas being back?"

"No, absolutely not." Her voice regained clarity. "Nicci doesn't have grievance with me. Carlo did a stupid thing by undermining Silvio in the first place."

"Are you saying he got what he deserved?" Alessandro sounded surprised.

"I'm saying Carlo knew the risks and consequences and he should have known better." She was angry now. "And now he's dead."

"And you wonder what's next for you."

She remained silent.

"Are you worried about Gatto?"

She nodded.

"Our organisation respects those who follow the code." He said. "If Gatto takes liberties he *will* be dealt with by the Commission. Or as with Carlo, directly by Nicholas as a point of honour. He is the Capo and that is our way.

"You and Giuliett will not be taken advantage of during this time of transition." Her worried expression remained etched in the faint lines around her dark eyes at his absolute tone.

"Look, my best advice, for what it's worth ... you're grieving Bice. Don't rush a decision. No one is expecting you to alter one thing in your life. You can travel and enjoy your life, attend events as you've always done.

"*Your* standing remains the same. We're individuals within a family. Loyalty to the family comes first. You've always respected the family and its demands. In turn, you've earned the respect of the Commission and so that will remain.

"With that in mind, the business need not concern you. Mario and I are ensuring that your assets are protected. Gatto and Enrico are in place to *serve* both you and Giuliett, just as they served Carlo."

Bice nodded.

"Gatto. Enrico. Carlo. I'm so tired of those men." She mumbled. She looked him directly in the eye, a shocked expression replacing her worry. She'd not meant to say those thoughts out loud.

Alessandro encouraged her to continue with a curious look.

"Bulls. They're bulls filled with overbearing demands and constraints. When Carlo died, I needed their guidance and protection. Now, I realise it was a mistake. I'll no longer be restrained by the chains of the past."

She looked at him with an expression acknowledging she'd confided too much.

"This is embarrassing." She mumbled to herself, reaching for her coat. She wrapped it around her shoulders.

Injecting false bravado in her voice, Bice stood and smiled brightly at her friend. He wasn't fooled for one moment.

"Don't worry about it Alessandro. It's all okay." She shook her head momentarily, chasing the fears of speaking her truth away. "Let's just forget I was here. Blame it on the season."

She patted him on the forearm.

"Thank you for the drink. And the company. You're a good friend. We are lucky to have you as one of us." She said, collecting her things and striding across his sitting room towards the doorway. She glanced around one last time.

Alessandro was on his feet and met her at the threshold. He kissed her thrice on the cheeks, as was the custom, his warm hands gently cupping under her jawline, fingers splayed behind her neck and reaching into her hair.

"Good bye my dear friend. I will call you tomorrow." He was resolute and concerned. "Although, I'm loath to see you leave tonight. We have unfinished business to discuss, but I respect you need more time to think things through before disclosure."

She nodded in acknowledgment.

"In the very least, let me take you home." He said. "It's quite late. You shouldn't be wandering the streets alone at this time of night."

She smiled sadly, holding his dark concerned eyes in hers. There was something else to say. She closed her eyes in a long blink, her fingers interlocking with his at the nape of her neck.

"Bice, your secrets are safe with me. Please, I'd like to know."

"Sometimes it would be nice to be someone's focus." She whispered at last, her cheeks turning pink as she looked downwards so as not to see the expression change in his eyes.

His thumbs gently caressed her cheek. His eyes gently stroked her face and paused at her lips.

"Like this?" he asked, as she lifted her sad eyes to his and he kissed her tenderly.

10
. . . .

Mid-morning sunshine streamed through the gothic windows and the hustle of well-dressed waiters attending the well-dressed guests filled the room. The blonde strode into the café, confidently seeking the private, permanent table that had been her father's preference, by the window, with a full view of the exterior and interior. She sat in his seat.

Despite herself, she missed him. She mentally sought his guidance. He'd taught her some things well. Today, the most important lesson was in action. Despite inner turmoil, the world would see a confident, young lady; polished, polite and in control.

Giuliett ordered the coffee. She checked her phone for messages and gazed unseeing out the window.

Bice Seta sat quietly beside her daughter. Her elegance and impeccable dress matched only by her daughter. Long strands of honey coloured hair hung in loose waves. Her tailored look, softened by a cashmere scarf she wore loosely draped over her shoulders, and the unfastened pale pink trench coat.

"Come to gloat?" Giuliett asked roughly.

"Giuliett." Bice breathed out her daughter's name in a compassionate sigh. She reached out to smooth a blonde wayward curl in the way a mother soothes a child.

Giuliett flinched slightly and turned away.

"Gatto told me about last night." Bice said gently.

"I bet he did. Tell me was it before or after he..."

"Giuliett!" Bice whispered angrily to cut her off. "Don't be so crass."

The conversation stalled before it started.

"What do you want mother?"

"I want to know how I can help you. With the Commission."

Giuliett raised an eyebrow. "I'm trying to work that out myself. All I know is that last night Nicholas Delarno outplayed me. Again."

"What are you going to do about it?" Bice asked.

"Find Francesca."

"Francesca?"

"Salucci. Francesca Salucci."

"The cop? Why?"

"Because I have unfinished business with that bitch and Nicholas is going to help me. She's his kryptonite, she'll bring him to me and then I'm going to take them both out. The Commission have long memories and their choosing Nicholas over me proves it."

"You need to focus on the leadership Giuliett. Not settling old scores. Francesca Salucci is nobody. Silvio left her for dead. Nicholas is focused on the Commission and so should you. Besides, Salucci is not the right way to go."

"Since when did you care?"

Giuliett clenched her jaw together and glared out the window. After a frosty moment, she turned to face Bice and asked impatiently.

"Alright, I'll play your game just as dad used to when he

wanted to amuse himself. What is your brilliant suggestion mother?"

Bice ignored the hurtful jibe.

"I think you rebuild with sympathisers within the Commission. Not everyone is happy that a Delarno is back in control. Your father had a lot of support. I think you should start there."

Giuliett thought for a moment.

"Pocco? That two-faced Florentine! You can't be serious."

"He has more power than you realise. But you need to learn how to use him right. You're a born leader Giuliett. You're like your father in that way more than you realise. Show *him* Giuliett. You'll get what you want." Bice finished her espresso and placed the tiny cup in saucer. She chased it with a sparkling water.

"I've said this before and I'll say it again only once. Capo is yours for the taking *if* you can prove yourself. But I'll not risk everything your father and I have worked for on a foolish whim. Daughter or no."

The older woman stood. "And get off the gear. It's messing with your brain." She abruptly turned away from her daughter and left.

Giuliett stared out the window stewing over the conversation in silence.

"A beautiful lady sitting all alone is surely in need of company."

She turned to see to Robbie L standing by her table. He looked dangerous. Her instincts prickled. Where the fuck was Enrico when she needed him?

"I might sit." He said and took his place beside her. He motioned to the waiter and ordered in Italian. "I don't think we've been properly introduced. I'm Robbie L. You're the delightful Giuliett Seta I believe. I'm pleased to meet you at last."

He put out his hand in greeting. She reluctantly accepted his gesture.

"What a shame Mr. Robbie L I can't stay. I was about leave. Enjoy your breakfast." She motioned to stand.

His hand snapped out and strong fingers clamped around her forearm, anchoring her to the table. "I think you might like to stay Signorina Seta." He said evenly.

Anger welled in her chest. She glared at him but obeyed. She sat silently ignoring him.

"You might like to welcome me to your beautiful country." He said. "That would be the civil thing to do. Perhaps wish me good morning. Or enquire did I sleep well. That's what people generally do when they meet in the morning."

"Welcome to Venice." She responded coldly.

"Thank you. It is an interesting and beautiful place."

"Yes."

"You know, in Australia, we like to have a nice little conversation before we get down to business. Silvio was always up for a wee chat before instruction. What do you say Giuliett? We might get to know each other a bit. Exchange pleasantries as you Europeans like to say."

"What do you want Robbie L?" Her icy response made him chuckle, but his mood was dark.

Robbie L stared into her eyes. She held his hardened gaze and a slight smile curved at the edge of her mouth. She accepted his childish challenge. His hazel eyes flicked in mutual response. He only glanced up as the waiter brought coffee, water and food.

"Grazie my friend." He said, tucking into his breakfast at once.

Giuliett took the opportunity to observe the intruder she'd heard so much about. His island heritage reflected in dark thick brows framing dangerous, alert eyes. High cheekbones stretched over taut golden skin. A well-kept moustache and goatee emphasised full lips. Two strings of wooden beads and a leather lariat sat lightly around his neck. Behind the facing of his casually unbuttoned business shirt, Giuliett noticed the heavy black colouring of a chest tattoo.

"I enjoyed your show last night." He said. "I thought your strategy was interesting. Not sure if busting balls is the way to go with this mob. Although I did very much enjoy the foreplay with Nero. As did your mate Pocco."

He flexed his biceps and shoulders as she checked him over.

"You should be pissed." He continued. "None of those bastards respect you. You're an outsider. Enrico is a waste of space. He did nothing to help you last night."

"Is that right." She responded, returning her focus to his face. "What would you know about us? A motor bike rider from Australia."

"I've spent enough time with Silvio." He shrugged. "And I took the opportunity to observe unnoticed. Gives a person a clear idea of a situation."

He took a moment to sip his water. "Have you eaten? You look a little pasty this morning." He called the waiter again. "Get the lady the same as me."

Giuliett nodded as the waiter glanced pensively between her and the stranger.

"Why should you care?"

"I don't. Just saying that's all."

"What *is* your point?"

"Geezuz, you're so uptight. For someone who loves a good rumble between the sheets you sure are frigid. What happened? Didn't get any last night?"

Giuliett stared at him. "I beg your pardon."

"You heard me."

He ate in silence and she tried to ignore him.

"Pass the water. Please." He said, placing his cutlery across his plate. "Thank you. Well, that's me done. You haven't eaten much. Scared you'll get fat?"

"No." She leaned into him and whispered. "I don't like you so let's cut the bullshit. What do you want?"

"Nothin'." He said. Her nostrils flared slightly. He looked her straight in the eye.

"Thought I'd have breakfast with a cute piece of fluff. And give your mate Pocco something to think about." He indicated the gentleman with a nod of his head. From across the room Don Poccolini was watching them both intently. Giuliett visibly paled.

"You're welcome." He said loudly, smiled and impulsively kissed her on the side of the head as a parting gesture. "Thanks for breakfast. The company? Well, you could work on your morning after small talk. But ..." He raised his voice so it carried across the room. "About last night? Holy Honey Hotness!"

With that he left her to glare at his retreating back and the dark woolly dreadlocks brushing the back of his collar as he swaggered out of the restaurant.

Giuliett stood, straightened her jacket and strode towards the Don.

11

....

"It's not what you think." She said, approaching the table.
"A guilty response." Pocco said simply. He returned to his
pastries and caffe. "I heard it but I didn't believe it. Gatto
assured me you had nothing to do with it. Now what is this? A
tryst in the hotels café? You should learn to be more discreet
Giuliett."

"I didn't know he was here. *He* came and sat with me. He's
a cunning bastard just like Silvio." She said vehemently. She
nervously licked her lips. "May I?"

Pocco wanted to believe her. He nodded towards the vacant
chair, indicating for her to sit down.

"It's true Pocco. I had nothing to do with him being there last
night. This morning is the first time I've met him. When he
came, and sat at my table."

She waited and when he didn't respond, she added. "I need
your help."

"I'll bet you do." He said smugly, finishing the small pastry
and licking his pudgy fingers.

"You and my father were very good friends. Don't make me beg."

He sighed dramatically, placing the cloth napkin on the plate.
"Walk with me."

They exited the restaurant and strolled together along the
promenade.

After a while he asked, "What is your proposal?"

"I need to go away for a bit. Not long, a week or two. Before I do, I'm looking for someone I trust to help push my cause with the Commission. I'm only asking you Pocco."

"Addressing your addiction. You have my attention now."

Giuliett blushed. "I've never done the initiation. I want to. It shows that I'm serious about our organisation. Would you help me with that too?"

There was a long silence. They'd reached the private berth and paused alongside the waiting speedboat.

"My father is dead. I need a mentor. Of course, I could ask Gatto, but I was hoping it would be you." She said, appealing to his ego.

Pocco wasn't fooled by her game. He looked directly at her breasts. "What's in it for me? Why should I help you?"

"Because we've no other choice. To end the Delarno stranglehold we need to work together."

"*You* have no other choice Giuliett. *I* have plenty. You know I am Nicholas's godfather. Silvio trusted *me*."

"Yes. I know." She said. "I'm not asking you to betray Nicholas on my behalf. I'm asking for your help to teach me the ways of the Commission. I want to learn more about our business to help me understand how I can contribute without further embarrassment to my family or me."

"You think you should be leader." He said plainly. "You made that point very clear last night. Such ambition does not wane overnight."

"I think our leader should be *you*, Don Poccolini. Last night proved to me that I'm not experienced enough. I know now my place is to support you. You helped my father and now, in his absence, it is my desire to return the favour. I want to help *your* cause. In order for that to happen, I need to gain favour with the Commission. *Any* role I can play I would be happy to undertake." She said sounding contrite.

He climbed into his private launch. His party was already aboard, ready for the day's outing.

"Will you at least think about it?" she asked, tilting her blonde head to one side.

Pocco nodded. "Yes. I suppose I will do that." He said dramatically.

"Thank you." Giuliett stepped back from the edge of the pontoon. She stayed there for a long time, gazing into the wake left from the speedboat, contemplating her next move.

12

....

Kintail Station,
Bourke, Western New South Wales, Australia

Reality caught him swiftly and with a start. Sinclair McCrae woke with his thoughts in that fuzzy place between dream and waking. And wept silently in the pre-dawn.

A gentle breeze coming through the open window blew the gauzy bedroom curtains across his leg and he pulled her closer to him. She snuggled into his warmth, and he brushed her hair aside, gently pressing his lips to her shoulder.

Reassured by her even breath and steady heartbeat in sleep, Sinclair closed his eyes, conjuring the troubling dream. It came immediately to him with the subtleness of a Claymore to his chest.

He opened his eyes again to their western farmhouse bedroom, assuring himself she was safe. But as his mind replayed the dream, in the darkness the images became so clear the scene could be real.

"Are you ready?" Francesca whispered against the backdrop of a Scottish Highland night.

Resolute but defiant, illuminated in the pale moonlight, her skin glowed. Dark hair cascaded freely over her shoulders.

Clad in a sheer white gown she stepped closer to him. Behind his silhouette, the Highlands loomed higher and met the deep darkness of a never-ending evening sky. The breeze whipped up and circled around them.

Bustling frozen shafts stabbed at their bare legs and the loch's stony shore. Gentle waves lapped her bare feet. In the fuss, her skirt embraced his calf gently and released at once.

He smiled at her as he drifted again into sleep and became as one the observer and participant that only dreaming can bring about.

Her serene face changed momentarily to a wickedly secretive grin. It met her sparkling eyes.

"Let me look at you, my love." She teased softly. "Dressed in the kilt of your ancestors. If I didn't know better I should think you're from another time: long hair, the ease and build of a warrior and that dangerous look in your eye," Francesca mimicked his father's tongue and reached to touch his face.

"For eternity, I should think I'm the one in danger, my love." She whispered and her eyes locked with his. He held her warm hand to his frozen cheek.

"And I would think you remind me of a temptress of the loch," he said quietly. "Your eyes say you have chosen me. A pledge I shall submit."

He saw himself bow slightly.

Gently taking her hands within his, he brought her fingers to his lips, breathing in her loveliness in the dark night. The loch ebbed against ancient rock and castle. The sky was streaked in heavy layers of cloud and mist. He knew could never love her more that he did at that moment.

"Sinclair." She whispered. "It's time. The children are by the gate. They need their father." She clasped his hands tighter in hers. "Remember, I love you with all of me. As long as you need, I am with you."

He watched a tear slide along her cheek and gasped as she faded before his eyes. A warm gentle air enveloped him.

His heart shattered into a thousand pieces. He called out to her.

"Francesca! Not yet. Stay."

Across the loch, a curious mist returned. It moved beyond him towards the candlelit remains of an ancient kirk. He turned to see Archie and Bella standing by the gate, their mother beside them. Her ghostly hand rested lightly on the little boy's shoulder.

He was racing towards her. "It's not time. Francesca, please. Stay, you must stay with me. I need you."

She'd smiled sadly and the warmth of her spirit rushed through him one last time.

He woke again with a start and grasped for her hand. Heavy emotions breached and his tears shed readily again.

"I canno' do this anymore." Sinclair whispered to the morning star rising in the east. He lay, thinking the unbearable and waiting for sunrise. In the end, he knew what had to be done.

13

....

"When did you think you would tell me? As you boarded the plane to Afghanistan?"

Francesca began the enquiry with a tone that was reasonable enough. However, by the time she'd finished her second question, her agitation at his deceit had exploded through her body and into action, and the documents that had been in her grasp angrily catapulted across the room towards him.

"Were you even going to tell me at all?" she was storming by now and didn't wait for his response. "Re-enlisting is a decision we make *together.*"

"Francesca let me explain. I have to do this …" Sinclair started to say, trying to justify his actions.

She promptly cut him off with another blistering tirade. She wasn't done yet.

"Not only did you go behind my back, I'm to find out whilst sorting through this pile of paperwork and rubbish … cleaning up *your* unholy mess. AGAIN! For goodness sake Sinclair, how hard it is to put rubbish in the bin?"

To demonstrate, she screwed an old chocolate wrapper into a ball and tossed it into the rubbish bucket beside the desk.

Francesca returned to the one last page tightly clutched in her hand and pointed aggressively to the date at the top of the letter of re-engagement and scant details of deployment.

"This letter was sent weeks ago!" she scanned the contents again.

"Look at that! Isn't that nice," she almost sneered. "You're required at the base next week. Pray, Sinclair. When? When were we actually going to have this conversation?"

Francesca sat heavily in a kitchen chair. She threw a cleaning cloth she'd been using across the room towards the sink in frustration. The action triggered a familiar ache in her side. Her body was still fragile. She tried desperately to ignore the pain.

She pinched at her side and hip as the pain increased. Her physical weakness aggravated her more, feeding into her frustration. Fucking gunshot wounds, she swore under her breath.

"Suck it! Silvio Delarno, you dead fucking bastard, and your lasting torment I must bear! Fuck you and all your dead relatives and your mother and your father." She cried out suddenly in Italian in case the children were listening. It did nothing to release another pent up hurt. She clutched her side harder, bending forward in the chair, her elbow leaning on the table as she looked down at the newly polished timber floors.

She was close to tears. Francesca blinked quickly to hold them back. Her brain was exploding under the strain of checked emotional pressure.

Sinclair leant against the kitchen sink. His bulky frame blocked the rack of clean dishes that'd been waiting all day for him to clear away. He held the cleaning cloth he'd caught one handed when she tossed it in his direction. Through the bluff and stormy outbursts, he watched her closely.

She stood. Avoiding his concerned expression, she straightened, stretching slightly to try and get some relief from her healing injury. It was too uncomfortable to sit in those hard chairs anyway. Francesca marched to the windows overlooking the so-called 'lawn' to the red earth paddocks beyond. Did it ever rain in this goddamn place?

"What am I going to tell the kids?" she asked mournfully and then looked at her partner. Her eyes narrowed and her chin lifted. "*You* will tell them. *You* will forever remember their faces as their hearts break with *your* news."

"Are you done?" Sinclair asked. "Is a man allowed to speak yet?"

She whirled around to face him and suddenly paled. Sinclair took three quick running strides reaching her as she swayed; fell into him and her eyes lost their focus.

"Hey. Hey." He said gently, holding her against him. "Take it easy love. Are you okay?"

"Of course I bloody well am." She snapped defiantly but she didn't move from his hold. "Well, I'm waiting Sinclair. I'm waiting for your explanation."

"It's a special assignment." Sinclair responded simply.

And she watched as he visibly closed himself to her along with the emotions around the decision he felt he needed to take. She knew it would do neither of them any good to go over the past again. He was suffering as much as she. He blamed himself for the injuries she suffered during the Delarno combat. And she could not change his mind. Lord knows she'd tried many times.

A conversation about it at this point would not end in a good place for either of them. And it would never be resolved by the time he'd need to leave for deployment. One look into the devastating hurt reflected in his eyes, she knew part of the reason and her anger and shock tempered.

Besides, after a long pause, it became obvious to Francesca that was all the information she was going to get from him.

"And that's supposed to satisfy me?" she asked quietly.

"You know the protocol."

"It's not the protocol I have issue with Sinclair." She reasoned. "It's the manner in which it was carried out. That's the problem right there. You should have discussed this with me *before* you re-joined. As I said before, this is a joint decision, one we make together."

"There was nothing to discuss." He was a closed book. "Your reluctance to move back to Fiji forced my hand. I can't make a decent living for us out here."

Her temper flared again.

"Come on. That's not fair! Don't you dare point the finger at me! Oh, no way mister! I'm not wearing the blame for this."

"There's no blame Francesca. It's simple math." He spoke gently but emphatically. "The department contacted me with a proposal. I accepted their offer. Lots of money in the bank. Two year tenure. End of story."

Weakened by physical pain and exhausted from the continual mental surplus it took to reconcile the dramatic changes in their lives, she yielded. He looked into her eyes brimming with hurt and tears. He held her hands in front of him, drawing her again into his broad chest.

"I'm going to miss you," he said, holding her close and breathing in deeply the scent of her shampoo and the feel of her in his arms like he was committing it to his memory.

"Yeah? Well miss this." She turned quickly and marched towards the back door, slamming it behind her.

14

....

Undisclosed location
Singapore

"'ll have you know I'm in a world of hurt with Francesca." Captain Sinclair McCrae smacked the back of his informant in a bear hug greeting. "She's flat talking to me because of this new assignment. Talk about being wedged between a rock and a hard place. Yours is the friendliest face I've seen in over a week!"

His friend returned the greeting affectionately.

"The infamous Salucci temper! Yep, good luck with that." Nicholas Delarno smiled knowingly. "I'll let you know her father was worse. He always knew how to make an insult reach the next level. It's an art form if you're not on the receiving end."

Sinclair grimaced.

"How are the kids?" Nic asked.

"Great. Missing home. But you know … taking the challenges of outback living with Marnie and Pop in their stride."

Nic nodded. The upheaval of leaving their Fijian home wouldn't have been easy for the McCrae clan. He guessed least of all for Archie. "We need your help Sinclair."

"We?"

"The Guardians. Many lives are at stake."

"Tell me what you know." McCrae dived in, getting straight to the point of their rendezvous.

"Don Carlo Seta. The family-owned transport businesses with networks across Europe including eastern block and Russia. Their cargo shipping enterprise is based in Genoa. Until recently, he was the Capo of the Seta mafia group.

"He operated within the Commission of crime families run by my father. He took it upon himself to oversee the whole European operations for our group, undermining my father with our Italian counterparts and spreading lies about our family amongst Commission members."

"What happened?" Sinclair asked.

"He recently passed." Nicholas responded coldly.

Sinclair raised an eyebrow. "That's convenient."

"I shot him." Nic said. "Twice. One bullet for an elderly dear friend of mine who he tortured and killed. One bullet for Francesca."

Sinclair nodded slowly. "Sounds fair." He said cautiously.

Nic continued. "Seta had a Russian mistress, Anya Frida Volkov. She's the lap dog for his important associates. He shared her for information and favour. Now that he's out of the frame, she's disappeared."

"What's that got do with us?" the soldier asked. "The Australian Defence Force."

"Guns for drugs. Afghanistan poppies." Nic replied.

"I'm interested. Ex Russian military?"

"Australian military issue." Nic said, looking at his friend, before draining the last of his beer.

"What?"

"Decommissioned, but Aussie none the less. Anya is your link."

The conversation paused as the waitress arrived with another round of drinks and a plate of canapés. It gave the soldier time to digest this new information.

"Any ideas where I can find a mob whore?" Sinclair asked.

"A couple. There's a house in Ibiza. Her family also have a large estate near St Petersburg."

"But they've been checked already."

"Yes." Nic nodded. "Some quite specific jewellery has recently appeared in the market. I'd suggest she's cashed up. But where she's gone, is anybody's guess. Alessandro's Guardian team have set up surveillance at some of their favourite haunts."

"What about contingency locations? Would Seta have secured a place for her in the event of things going bad?"

"Carlo Seta was only interested in one person. Himself." Nic said.

"But he may have a hideout – a place he went to when the heat was on." Sinclair pressed. "Or a favoured meeting point."

"Perhaps. But unlikely." Nic remained adamant. "Seta was not the sort of man who'd hide out."

"What about family? Is there a wife? Kids?"

"One daughter. Giuliett. She's a narcissistic, manipulative, reckless piece of work. Has a lot to learn about the business but what she doesn't know, she makes up for in other ways. She's a cunning little wench."

McCrae nodded.

"Bice Seta is the wife. She's a socialite with genuine networks and a real lady. Since Seta's death, a man known to all as Gatto is doing day-to-day management of the business. He was Seta's advisor. He's a wily cat and Carlo trusted him completely.

"Enrico Nero is Seta's brother-in-law and was the Dons' underboss. There's a lot of entitled expectation in him. Nero's assigned himself to Giuliett. Don't be fooled. He's as ambitious as her for the leadership."

"And the wife?"

"Leadership sits with Bice by default. But I'm thinking she'll want to relinquish to Giuliett in the near future. Our kind of business would not sit well with her. Giuliett is certainly making everyone aware she's wants the clan leadership. Gatto is keeping Bice in a tight bind. He's not keen for her to let go."

Sinclair arched an eyebrow.

"Do they know about the Anya Frida?" he asked.

"Yes. They're both very familiar with her role in their lives."

Sinclair nodded.

"They didn't bump her off?"

"I believe not." Nic said. "Gatto is also gunning for the girl."

"I don't get it. She's a high-class hooker. What does it matter?"

"Anya Frida Volkov isn't just another mob whore. She's the sister of the most powerful mafia man in Russia today. Loyalties run deep and long between the Seta and Volkov families. If Gatto is looking, you can rest assured there's a mutual problem."

Sinclair was intrigued and confused.

"I'm still not convinced of my role." He said. "What do you expect me to do about it? A missing chick is not my problem. And I can investigate the guns for drugs using other sources."

Nic nodded thoughtfully.

"That you can, but this way is more efficient."

Sinclair raised his eyebrows again. "Where I come from mate we don't bump people off because they've offended us."

Nic's mouth twisted in a half smile. He nodded once, acknowledging the soldier. "Neither do we."

Sinclair watched his friend closely.

"I see you're not convinced. Let me explain what's at stake." The mafia boss said. "During WW2 when Russia and Italy were at war against each other, the Seta group formed a secret alliance with key members of the Volkov family in a bid to protect lucrative vested interests. Because high-ranking leaders within Mussolini's black shirts were benefitting from the deal as well, transactions were overlooked. As you know, Russia itself was in a state of chaos and corruption, meaning the arrangement easily slipped through at their end unnoticed as well.

"The gesture was never forgotten by the Russians. A life-long loyalty and business partnership was developed and continues to this current day.

"About ten or so years ago, soon after her sixteenth birthday Anya Frida Volkov eloped to Italy with her lover. She was beautiful, rich and wilful. She was a girl who'd never known boundaries. Her family was incensed by her behaviour. Her father threatened to disown her.

"Carlo Seta saw an opportunity to strengthen the family ties. He promptly found Anya, supported and protected her. The young lover conveniently disappeared and Anya fell in love with the much older man. She agreed to help him build his networks and wealth in the way his wife could not. In return, he gave her anything she asked and more."

"If that was my daughter, I'd want to kill him."

"That's because you're Australian. You don't understand. Throughout old money Europe, a mistress is expected. Particularly when she's as vibrant and beautiful as Anya and

Seta is equally as powerful. Both organisations grew. Seta's not stupid. He made sure the Volkov coffers benefitted generously from the arrangements."

Sinclair looked at his friend, lost in thought for a long moment.

"Sounds like a valuable asset. Makes me wonder why he didn't put something or someone in place to protect her. You're sure she's not returned to Russia. To her family?"

"She's not there." Nicholas was adamant.

The soldier leant forward, and spoke in a hushed voice.

"What makes you think she's linked to the Afghanistan opium and gun trade. The country has major issue with Russia. The feeling is so intense, I wouldn't even begin to think how the Russian mafia could infiltrate."

"I have evidence. You will want to find her, believe me. Your country's successful withdrawal from Afghanistan depends on it."

Sinclair leant back in the chair and looked about the hotel's lounge bar. He grunted softly to himself as he made his decision.

"I'm on my way to the base. I'll have a sniff around." Sinclair said. "I can't promise anything. You keep looking for the girl. I'll meet you when I'm done."

Nic nodded. "And the time frame?"

"For me to know ..." the soldier said.

After a short silence, Nic nodded an agreement. "I'll be waiting." He said.

"Send me all your information so I can start a profile."

Nic pulled out a blank envelope filled with papers and photographs from his carryon luggage.

"Done." He said, handing it to the soldier.

15
. . . .

Kintail Station
North West of Bourke,
New South Wales, Australia

"Kintail, this is Victor. Charlie. Foxtrot. November. Delta. Requesting permission to land."

The call sign of a light aircraft using the NATO phonetic alphabet broke the afternoon stillness. It relayed through a CB radio fixed to the wall at the junction of the lounge, dining and kitchen area of the western homestead. V.C. - F.N.D.

Lost in the quarterly figures, Francesca glanced up from the banking spreadsheet, invoices and bank statements she'd laid across the dining table and looked blankly towards the small device. *Was that the radio?* She thought.

"Kintail Station. Do you copy?" the voice asked after a few impatient moments.

Outside the late afternoon sun was dipping behind the stubby stands of eucalyptus and wattle. The tree line formed a dust screen between sheds and homestead. Unannounced company at this time of day was very unusual. And she didn't recognise the call sign. Her eyes narrowed as old suspicions, warranted or no, surfaced.

"Permission denied." She said into the mouthpiece. "This is a private air strip. And it's closed for repair." She added for good measure.

The plane continued towards the homestead. She heard the small twin engine fly overhead and begin a wide circle.

"Archie! Bella!" she called out. "Come inside please."

"Mummy! A plane just flew over our house!" Bella burst through the back door. "It was really low. Is it bringing the letters?"

"I don't think so honey. Not at this time of the day."

Both faces turned to the radio at a repeated request.

"Kintail Station. I repeat. This is Foxtrot. November. Delta. Requesting permission to land."

Francesca prickled. "And I repeat the answer is no. The airstrip is closed for repair." Archie appeared by her side. "Comballala is fifty miles due east. Its landing strip is in good condition. Best you head in that direction." She said pretending to be helpful. "The co-ordinates are ..."

"Kintail Station. This is Victor. Charlie. Foxtrot. November. Delta. I have a mayday situation. I repeat, mayday."

"Frogging hell." Francesca swore quietly. Now she had no choice. "Foxtrot. November. Delta. This is Kintail Station reading you loud and clear. Stand by. I need to clear the runway. Do you copy?" She responded curtly.

"Copy that Kintail. Standing by for instruction."

"Can I do the roo run, mum?" Archie pleaded. "Please? Please?"

Francesca nodded. "Take Bella. Wait for me at the house yard gate. I'm coming too."

Francesca collected a .22 calibre rifle from the bedroom gun safe and hurried out to meet her children in the waiting vehicle.

"Sit beside your brother, honey bear." She said to the little girl. "I need the window. Righto Archie. Let's go, but not too fast mind."

"Who do you think it is?" asked Bella. "Will they stay for dinner?"

"Not sure baby girl. But I do know one thing." Francesca responded, pushing unfounded wariness down. She looked at her daughter and forced a smile. "We're bound to find out pretty soon."

The four-wheel drive utility negotiated a well-worn track over red dirt and patchy clumps of native grass towards the airstrip paddock. The plane passed over them again.

"I saw the pilot!" yelled Archie.

"How about you just concentrate on the road young man." Came Francesca's stern reply.

Soon they reached the end of the airstrip. Archie knew exactly what to do. He stopped the vehicle and faced the dirt strip runway. The young boy turned the utility's lights on and engaged the hazard lights. Next, he placed his hand on the horn and pushed hard. He accelerated through first gear, transitioned into second and headed towards the far end of the paddock in a straight line.

The engine roared. The lights flashed in a click click timing. The horn blared from under the bonnet. And a young boy was grinning from ear to ear.

A small mob of kangaroos grazing at the airstrip's edge looked up in fright at the sound and lights. They immediately took to the trees.

"There's one! Look out Archie!" Bella shouted as a roo doubled back towards the airstrip.

"I've got him." He said confidently. Archie slowed. The small kangaroo passed a short distance in front of the bulbar and continued on across the paddocks.

"Look out for his mate." Bella said.

Archie stopped the vehicle. He looked left and right. When he was sure they were safe to proceed, he continued on.

The sun was sinking lower. Dusk and orange dust lit the sky. Archie reached the southern end of the runway and turned around. He began the return trip in the same fashion.

At the end of the airstrip, he turned a third time. This time, he moved off the runway and drove adjacent to it. About half way along the stretch, he faced the vehicle at right angles to the cleared runway, switched off the hazard lights and pushed the gear stick to neutral. The engine idled.

"Good job Archie." Bella said proudly and clapped her little hands. She gave him a hug.

Archie looked from his sister to his mother.

"Yes, good job son." She said giving him a big smile. "Up." she said. "Windows up."

Francesca reached up to the CB radio mounted in the roof above Archie's head. She released the mouthpiece from its fastening clip. The cord stretched across the interior windshield.

"Victor. Charlie. Foxtrot. November. Delta. This is Kintail Station. Proceed to land. I repeat, proceed to land. Over."

"Copy that Kintail. Over and out." The pilot responded.

A short time later, the plane dipped and landed in front of them. Dust followed in a billowing rage, catching the craft at the end of the runway. The pilot turned into it. A single headlight shone through. Slowly it made its way towards the waiting vehicle.

"Wait in the car please." Francesca said, taking the rifle and hurrying to meet the small plane that was slowing some distance from the family's vehicle.

Francesca looked first into the cockpit window. After a few moments, the door opened.

"All my days." She said gazing in amazement at the person grinning before her. "What in heaven and earth?"

16

. . . .

"Uncle Nicci!" Bella was out of the utility and running towards the plane. She jumped into his hold, her chubby arms wrapping around his neck as she planted a big wet kiss on his cheek.

"What's this Archie? You can't give your uncle a hug?" Nicholas Delarno spoke to the boy, who grinned all the wider and ran into his uncle's arms.

"Did you see me driving?" he asked immediately. "Did you see me Zio?"

"I did son." Nicholas said. "You've been taught very well. Maybe tomorrow you could show me around this vast place you have here."

"Absolutely. That will be okay won't it mum?" The little boy asked, mirroring Nic's dark looks and expressions.

Francesca looked between Archie and Nicholas. At Archie's hopeful face she relented. "Sure, first thing. I'm sure Nicholas will be heading back east before it gets too hot. We're expecting a scorcher tomorrow."

The children turned towards Nicholas. "But you only just got here." They cried in unison.

Nicholas looked over their heads at Francesca's indeterminate expression.

"Well," he said. "Now that I'm here I might stay a couple of days. It's such a long way. And I haven't seen you both in so long. Business can wait. What do you say?"

"Yay!" Bella squealed. Archie grinned. Francesca grimaced.

"How about we get home?" She said. "No point standing out here in the dark." Francesca started towards the utility. "I'll drive this time Archie. You and Bella can squash in with your Uncle. Sound fair?"

It was the longest drive from the rural landing strip to the tired, old homestead of Francesca's life. And quite possibly, the shortest for her two children and the man who remained engaged for every moment.

The noisy exchange between her children and their uncle was interspersed with laughter and storytelling. He'd recently been in Italy. Francesca could tell by the pronunciation of his words and the unintended lapses in his vocabulary from English to Italian.

"Okay," Nicholas said at last. "Where is your papa? Your daddy?"

"He's in Afghanistan." Bella responded in a matter-of-fact tone.

"Really?"

"Yes. He's been gone for three weeks." Archie supplied. "He re-joined the army."

"Yes. And I miss him." Bella cried, mournfully dramatic. "So does mummy. And Archie. And Marnie. And Pop."

"Oh, honey, I bet you do." Nicholas said, giving her a cuddle.

"Your mummy hasn't said much on the drive." Nicholas probed cautiously, looking over the children's heads to her.

"Who can get a word in?" Was all Francesca said.

* * *

It was late. The children were fast asleep. The chores were done. Francesca now showered and changed into the daily wardrobe of a simple tee shirt and shorts, padded bare foot into the kitchen. She chose a bottle of red wine, poured two glasses and joined Nicholas in the sleep out room that doubled as a casual seating area. He was dozing in a single chair.

"Old age catching up." She quipped handing him the glass.

He smiled at her. "Long day. Time zone changes."

"Old age." Francesca responded in a matter-of-fact tone. She plopped in the chair beside him. "You wanted to see Sinclair? You should've called ahead."

"Perhaps." He said. "I really wanted to talk to him face to face."

"Well, more fool you."

Her matter-of-fact response sat heavily on the night.

"How are you?" he asked gently, turning to face her.

"Good." She said glancing from him to the gauzed window that looked out towards a water hole fed by a natural spring. Moonlight skimmed the water. A frog and cricket chorus rang throughout the bushland setting.

"Your injuries are healing well?"

"Yes." She sighed. "I'm all better." She smiled pathetically at him and looked towards the night.

There was a long silence. Many questions hung thick between them. Francesca remained silently pensive; acutely aware she'd rather be anywhere else than alone with him, answering questions about those last hours in Fiji when all hell broke loose and everything since was different.

"You haven't asked me how I am." Nicholas said at last.

"How are you Nicholas?" She asked, glancing quickly at his direction and back to the waterhole.

"I'm well. Thank you."

"Great to know." She suddenly stood, returning a few minutes later in a lightweight jumper she wrapped around her more for comfort than warmth.

Nicholas watched her in silence.

"Have I done something wrong?" he asked. "You seem very agitated with me tonight."

"No." She breathed in and out heavily. "Yes. I wish you'd let me know you were coming … so I could prepare."

"What do you mean prepare?"

"Oh, you know, prepare." She responded in an agitated tone, waving her arms around the untidy run-down house. *Prepare to not be here,* she thought, suddenly wishing she'd moved to Wild Dog Creek when she had the chance.

He looked confused. Francesca changed the subject.

"Would you like a top up?" she asked, offering him the bottle of wine.

"No thank you. I'm satisfied."

"I'll bet you are." She mumbled under her breath and immediately regretted it. She cast him a quick glance. Where was this rudeness coming from? Was it her? Was it is him and the way he thought he could just come and go in her life as he pleased? She'd been completely out of sorts since Sinclair left. Maybe it was just a timing thing. And he'd arrived at the wrong time.

"I'm sorry Nicholas." She said. "That was unnecessary and rude. I don't know what's wrong with me tonight."

He nodded.

"Will you return home?" he asked suddenly.

"This place is our home now." She responded. "This palace in the outback."

She knew full well what he meant and avoided the question. She sounded like a spoiled child and immediately blushed. The McCrae family had opened their home to her, giving warmth and love in her time of need. They lived a simple, honest life.

Had she really drifted so far from her own upbringing to be embarrassed by the outward appearance of her current abode? She glanced at Nicholas again. He certainly seemed at peace in the humble surrounds, despite his obscene wealth and designer tastes.

The observation irritated her more. What the hell was wrong with her tonight?

"To Fiji. Are you returning to Fiji?" he asked.

"Why? Do you want to buy it?"

"I'm not interested in another purchase." He said quietly.

"Besides, what would be the point of returning to Fiji?" she asked, completely ignoring his response. "That place is full of suffering. It's not a good environment for the children."

"Are you sure? I bet Archie desperately misses Tui and the islands." He probed.

"He does." She said her voice edged in sadness.

"Bella and Sinclair must be longing for it too? His practice is still there, giusto?"

"Yes, his practice is there."

"He built it from the ground up. It must've been tough for him to walk away."

Francesca nodded quietly.

"And you?" he probed. "It would be difficult living here

without Sinclair. In fact, I'm surprised you didn't settle at Wild Dog Creek. You always said it was your healing place."

He paused as if he was tossing a thought, evaluating its merit in being spoken.

"I saw you today and it has only made me more determined." He reached out and circled his finger and thumb around her wrist. "Look at you, wasting away here."

He lifted her t-shirt slightly to reveal a bony hip. His tongue clicked sadly.

"Francesca, there's nothing holding you to this place. Now that Sinclair has resumed his duties and you're physically better, you must desire some semblance of your former life. You have a talent for investigation. Now that you've left the police there are other opportunities. Agencies on the right side of the law are willing to pay a lot of money for your skills and knowledge."You've always loved the coastal lifestyle. If you want, we can leave tomorrow. I can fly you and the kids directly to Wild Dog Creek or home to Fiji. Just say the word, love. My only desire is to bring your wishes about."

He looked into her eyes. "Francesca, let me help. Please love. Let me help you."

"Okay Nicholas. You can stop right there with the psychoanalysis and pretence. You'll not dump our situation on me, like Sinclair did and then bail when it gets too hard." Her voice itched in agitation.

"I see what's going on. First Sinclair. Now you. I can't go back to that place. When will you both get it?" She jumped out of the chair.

"My glass is full. Do you understand? FULL! I need to stay here. Away from everyone. And everything. Away from anything that has anything to do with Delarno! And now you've ruined that too, because here you are. Sitting in my and Sinclair's home."

She was raving. She knew it. She didn't care. Anger and pain overtook every rational emotion and she unleashed on her oldest friend.

"And I'm damn sure you didn't come all this way out of platonic concern for my welfare. I've known you too long for that. So, get to the frogging point!"

"No, I didn't." he said. "I wanted to see you and the kids … I've missed you. I needed to see your face."

"Argh!" She cried in frustration. "We've been over this Nicholas. I can't help but think you knew Sinclair was already gone and decided to show up anyway." She faced him accusingly.

"Did you think you'd find me wanting you again? I might be angry at Sinclair but that doesn't mean I'm about to rekindle a relationship with *you*."

In that vehement last word, every hurt and all her frustration mustered as one.

This time Nicholas looked out the window. It was a hurtful blow. "I knew he'd re-joined the department, yes." He said honestly.

His voice hardened. "But let's not confuse things Francesca. I'm not here to seduce you."

"Well then Nicholas, why exactly are you here."

"To take you home."

17

·················

She was momentarily stunned. In the silence her face crumpled as she held back the tears. Nicholas watched her collapse and compose within a single heartbeat.

"You're wasting your time. I've no desire to go there. With you or with anyone else." She said.

"Lover, let me help you. Please." He begged.

"Thank you. I don't need your kind of help." She said, turning her back to him.

He was by her side. He took the wine glass and placed it on a bookcase shelf. He turned her to face him. "I know you better than any man. Mind. Body. Spirit. Perhaps even better than you know yourself."

He gently cupped her face. "Love. Let me help you. That is all I want, more than anything in the world. You and I ...." He faltered momentarily searching for the right words and keeping his own emotions in check.

"We've lost more than most. We need to close that chapter together. It's the only way forward. You *must* feel that need deep within your soul, as I do."

Francesca held her rigid expression, her intense efforts to maintain control radiated through her dark eyes and the emotions charged through her. She felt her lips wobble involuntarily under his familiar intense scrutiny. She lowered her gaze from his dark eyes.

"I know you're scared."

"I'm not scared." She spoke quietly. "I'm goddam angry."

Rage flashed from her eyes towards him. The more she said, the angrier her voice became.

"And you have no fricking right to be here telling me how *you* feel. I've lost everything thanks to you and your family. So you need to back off and leave us alone."

With that she promptly burst into tears.

Nicholas gathered her close, as the frustration she'd forced deep inside washed from her eyes. His shoulder muffled the wails she could no longer control.

Her heart ached. It filled her chest, hard as granite and just as impenetrable. With each inward breath, her chest cavity stung. Surely it would explode. With one hand, she held it. With the other she gripped her forehead as it threatened to peel from her skull.

He pulled her closer, cradling the storm of emotions as he folded her arms into him, encircling her within his own protective strength. Lost in her grief, Francesca subconsciously connected with a place of safety and completely lost control.

The more she grieved, the heavier and harder her heart grew. Foreign sounds emanating from her chest released through her open mouth. Sounds she'd never heard but at the same time she knew well. Here was a hole of the deepest grief. No longer able to walk around it, she entered that dreadful place and stayed there, as her body physically gave way under the pressure.

There was no room for tears. Only sound and Nicholas held it close, against his steady, beating heart and gave her the strength of him to see it through.

He brought her gently onto his lap, like a child. Comforting, tender strokes smoothed her hair, her back and shoulders, soothing her. Finally, the tears came.

Nicholas didn't rush her, allowing the pent-up anger and grief to walk its own path. In time his quiet serenity and patience brought her to him.

In the aftermath of stillness, he hummed a soothing childhood melody they both knew well. Perhaps he'd been humming it the whole duration. Neither knew or cared. The soft melody of their mothers and grandmothers resonated within their souls, touching them both and bringing with it a sense of mutual comfort.

At last he whispered. It was an emotional, affected sound that reverberated around the back of his throat. He wiped his own damp eyes.

"My flower, you see. I'll always come to you, whether you want me or not. I know when you need me like the tide knows it needs the moon."

He brushed her wayward curls gently from her hot face.

"I can't control what others do but I can control my own actions. Long ago I made a vow to protect you. And I intend to keep it until there's no breath left in my body. Don't ever be afraid to share your emotions with me Francesca."

Francesca nodded, her head pressed against his chest. She couldn't speak. Her own throat was closed with emotion and sadness.

"You're strong and resilient. You've endured unmentionable pain. It's forced you to understand the workings, the duplicity in our lives in an unforgiving light."

He sighed. "I'm sorry you had to learn this way." His warm

breath ruffled the wayward strands from her ponytail. He released her hair from the tie and massaged the place where the band had held it. He watched as her dark hair fell about his shoulders and chest. He gently stroked the silkiness of it.

"You're a gift. A beautiful and wise gift. And I'm fortunate to be your guardian."

She nodded, breathed deeply and propped back from his hold. She blew her nose. Wiping the last of her tears with the back of her hand, she smiled weakly, her eyes shimmering and clear.

"Thank you." She mouthed.

"You're welcome." He responded softly and his smile lit his eyes.

She laid her head against his shoulder and her legs across his lap, as she sat in the corner of the wide armchair. There was a peaceful silence between them. He waited for her emotions to completely subside. When her breath returned to normal and her shoulders relaxed, he quietly said,

"Come now. It's very late. That's enough for tonight. Let's get you into bed. Before I lose my head in my own battle of desire for you and you resent me in the morning."

He patted her gently on the arse to push her forward. The unconscious act of familiarity was lost on them both. "Lead the way my flower."

At the doorway to her bedroom, she paused.

"Goodnight Nicholas." She said kissing him thrice on the cheeks, as was the custom. She held him close for a long moment.

"Goodnight my heart." He said.

He brought her palms to his lips. "I'll see you in the morning."

18

....

"Mum. Is Uncle Nic coming to Fiji too?"

"I doubt it Archie. I suspect your uncle has a lot of work in Canberra at the moment." Francesca said, thinking of the many conversations ahead between the fugitive turned informant, the Australian Federal Police and the Federal Immigration Minister. "So, probably not." She glanced at him and smiled. "Are you disappointed?"

"No. I can't wait to see Tui again." He beamed. "The first thing I'm going to do is go to the village, find Chief and give him a big hug and a pat, then Chief, Tui and I'll have a swim and climb in the caves and go exploring ..."

"All right mister. I get the picture. I won't see you for days, maybe weeks. Is that it?" she teased.

"Yep. I'm sorry mum but there's some things a boy has to do." He said sternly.

Francesca smiled. "Well, my darling boy, I'm happy that you're so happy. Now, is that the last bag from your room?" she asked him.

Archie nodded.

"Okay, just the overnight bag from mine and then we're done. I think. Oh look, here comes Marnie and Pop to say goodbye."

Francesca stood at the open tailgate of the Landcruiser station wagon. She waved and smiled as the McCrae grandparents approached the house yard.

"Hello you two! Thanks for popping round." She greeted them warmly, kissing them each on the cheek.

"Good morning Francesca." Alasdair's thickly accented rumble wrapped around her like a warm hug. "How're you this morning love?"

"Well, thank you Alasdair." She said. "And you?"

"No use complaining." He responded wandering behind the four-wheel drive to check the load.

"I believe we're organised." She said. "Aren't we Arch?"

He nodded. "Yep, hey Pop, did you go to the yards this morning to check on the sheep?"

"Aye son, I did. They're none too happy about being couped up. But it's only for a short time." Alasdair pointed to the tightly packed load.

"I see you've been helping your mother out. Great job there, packing everything in too." He said with a smile and a wink.

"Would you like a cup of tea before we hit the road?" Francesca asked.

"That would be lovely, wouldn't it love."

Marnie Rose McCrae nodded. "I'll not be shedding tears, I promise." She said wiping her eyes with a hanky and shoving it back under her bra strap. She hugged Archie close. "I'm going to miss you Archie. It's been good for your grandfather too, having you right next door."

The boy hugged his grandmother and smiled.

"Family is everything." She said to Francesca. "But I don't need to tell you that my dear, do I?"

Francesca squeezed the older lady's hand. "I'm going to miss you too." She said.

Alasdair ruffled the top of the boy's hair.

"Now, where's my little girl?" Alasdair asked, taking great long thumping strides towards the homestead. "Has anybody seen Rosa Bella?" He joked as the little girl danced around his feet. "Where could she be?"

"Here I am Poppy! I'm here." She yelled.

"I wonder. Rosa Bella McCrae! Where are you?" He called out, standing up straight and looking towards the sky. His hands sat on his hips.

Bella's little foot stomped on his riding boot, as was the familiar game. "I'm right here," she said, pulling on his rolled-up shirtsleeve. "Look down Pop."

"Och! Here's my princess." He swooped her in his arms. She was propped high on his chest, above his rounding stomach. "I thought I'd lost you."

"Poppy." She rolled her eyes giggling. "I didn't lose you."

"And what have we here?" he asked, as she waved a white sheet of paper coloured with pencil and glitter in front of his face.

"I made this for you and Marnie." She said proudly.

"That's lovely!" he said.

"You read it Poppy." She said. "I've done funny writing just like mummy."

He looked at the wavy lines that were meant to be what he assumed, cursive writing. "How about you read it to me. Poppy forgot to bring his glasses this morning."

"Silly Poppy." The little girl sighed dramatically. "It says 'Dear Pop and Marnie, I'm sorry but I have to go to Fiji now. I'm going to miss you very, very much. Please come and visit me soon. Love from Bella. Kiss kiss hug hug.'

"And can you see Pop, I've drawn a yellow sun over here and the water and our house. And here is you and Marnie coming to visit. And Archie and Tui. And I'm in the swimming pool."

"That's beautiful Bella." He said popping her on the ground. "Thank you very much. I love it. Do you want to show Marnie?"

"Yep." She raced off towards the two women and her brother who were ambling together towards the house.

"How's about that cup of tea." Francesca said as they entered the kitchen. "Please wash your hands Archie and Bella and then you can help set the table. We're so lucky. Marnie made scones *and* pikelets."

"I'll come too." Their grandmother said and the noisy trio headed towards the bathroom.

"Rose tells me you're heading to Wild Dog Creek first." Alasdair said, buttering the pikelets.

"Yes. I need to collect some documents from the safe. I'd feel more comfortable if they were with me in Fiji. And I'd like to show the kids my childhood home. Now they've seen Sinclairs, I thought it'd be nice to visit mine too."

He nodded. "It's all over now, isn't it? With that whole damn Delarno thing I mean." He leant against the laminex bench to face her.

Francesca blushed.

"You mean the investigation? Yes. Completely out of my hands now. It's up to the Federal Police. Sinclair and I've made our statements. So, I'm pretty certain that's it from us."

She faced him.

"Besides, I don't think Nicholas will be going anywhere anytime soon, now that the Feds have a hold of him in Canberra. Goodness knows how he's going to talk his way out of those discussions. I'm finally free from that family." She said smiling. "*We're* finally free from that family."

"He's is still in the frame though, with Archie. It's a lifetime bond of biological father and son, even if you and Sinclair raise the boy." Her father-in-law didn't mince words.

"Yes, but he's on our side. We've nothing to fear. Archie is safe."

Alasdair grunted.

"Be careful." He said. "Nicholas Delarno is a snake. I know you've been friends for a long time. But there's something about him I don't like or trust. I told Sinclair the same thing."

"I understand. But my eyes are open now." She cocked her head to one side. "You'd never ask, but you know Nicholas visited last week."

"Yes, the kids mentioned it."

Francesca nodded. "I thought he was up to his old tricks, with Sinclair being away and all." She said, her cheeks turning pink. "I told him I wasn't interested in his games. But his coming here has made me think about our family's future in a different way. I'm tired of living in the shadows.

"It's time for me to stand up beside Sinclair. Once, I was strong and independent. I had a great career in the cops. I have my law qualification. I owe it to my children and Sinclair to reclaim that part of me. I owe it to you and Rose.

"Our family was happy in Fiji. I thought I was protecting the kids by coming here. The last days on the island were very traumatic. I thought if we moved away, it would help the kids recover from the disaster more easily. But, it turns out I was only protecting myself.

"Archie needs to be in the classroom. And he misses Tui

terribly. Bella should be socialising with other children.

"Sinclair was right. I have to accept everything that's happened."

Francesca held the older man's gaze. "I don't have to like it, mind." She said.

Alasdair McCrae nodded.

"But," she continued, "As soon as I accept it, I'll heal more quickly, physically and mentally."

She took a deep breath in and out.

"And now I've made the decision to go, you can see how excited the kids are. And Sinclair will be overjoyed to be back in his clinic. Now he can finish this project and do what he loves most in a safe environment.

"Alasdair, I've been selfish. I just wish I'd been able to reach that conclusion *before* he re-joined. In fact, I wish he'd told me about his plans in the first place. Perhaps, it would never have got to this."

She stared pensively into the assessing expression in Alasdair's bright blue eyes. At his silence, she continued to speak.

"I've messaged Sinclair, but I haven't yet heard back from him. Obviously, I'll keep trying. He's involved in some huge operation over there so he may already be offline. If you happen to catch him, will you please let him know our movements? Email is best as you know."

Alasdair nodded. "Of course."

"Thank you." She chuckled, slightly embarrassed. "Old fears, new habits. I put all our flights with dates and itinerary in an email to you this morning. And my phone is activated with GPS locator and in sync with Rose's so you can track me too. Just in case."

He suddenly hugged her. "That'll do." He said. "You're okay Francesca Salucci. We're lucky to have you in our family."

"I'm going to miss you and Rose so much. Thank you for taking us in and looking after us so well." She said and stopped talking as her throat closed over with emotion.

19

....

Wild Dog Creek
Queensland

The family spent the night in the regional agricultural town of Dalby. And after an uneventful drive reached the property entrance of Wild Dog Creek in the late afternoon, successfully clocking up almost two solid days in the car and well over a thousand kilometres.

Any drowsiness was quickly checked as deep corrugations in the dirt road jumped and jilted the four-wheel drive along the last 200 meters of driveway before reaching the homestead entrance.

Everyone was exhausted.

"Archie, would you please text Marnie and tell her we're at Wild Dog Creek safe and sound." Francesca said, easing the loaded vehicle through the last deep washout at the house yard gate. "Is Bella still asleep?"

"No." Came the soft reply. "I'm awake. How much longer?"

"We're here." She said, stopping close to the steps of the homestead's front veranda.

They peeled out of the vehicle. Archie lay flat on the grass, his arms spread out like an angel. Rosa Bella walked in circles and flopped down beside him. Francesca stretched, stiff and sore from sitting. Everything ached.

With arms reached above her head, she breathed the warm salty air, exhaling a deep sigh, before drawing a long slow inward breath. It connected with her chest and stomach and was released with equal control. This she repeated numerous times until her head felt light and the sun rippling through the eucalyptus leaves danced across her mind's eye. She faced the sunlight and warmth, eyes closed.

On the last breath, her eyelids opened to the sky and her surrounds. Arms flopped gently to her side. Shoulders flexed one last time. Peace. Such was the peace and calm familiarity.

Her senses drank the velvet green grass; the painted timber Queenslander home, tall stands of lemon-scented gums and an ancient frangipani. Shallow garden beds ran the length of the veranda, abundant with colourful flowers and green. Vibrant green. Who knew there could be so many shades of it? After months of red dirt, vivid blue skies and constant glare, her eyes relaxed in the muted shades of an east coast afternoon.

Parrots roused high in the trees. Tiny finches darted amongst the lower canopies of tea trees. The river ebbed against its loamy bank. Francesca breathed in deeply again, relishing the smell of rain hanging thick in the air. Everything and everyone was at peace.

She lay flat on her back on the grass with Archie and Bel. The trio formed a windmill shape, heads gently connected in the centre and arms outstretched to meet each other. Nobody spoke as they looked to the sky and watched puffy white clouds move gently across.

Francesca focused on her breath as a familiar calmness

radiated from her. Nowhere to go, no need to rush, after such a long journey it was time to just be.

Nicholas had been right to remind her. A visit to her magical healing place was the exact first step she needed to take before heading home to Fiji.

20

....

ate autumn sunlight beamed into Francesca's bedroom window, and she was already up and tiptoeing about the old family homestead. With a cup of tea set on the floor beside her, she scoured the contents from the living room safe. Statements, photographs and legal documents were quickly sorted and secured in the zipped compartment of her carry-on luggage.

There'd be no time to do that when the kids were up and about. She pulled the envelopes of old photographs from the open safe. Francesca laughed softly at the image of two sisters, standing proudly at the entrance gates of the local show, dressed in what could only be described as the biggest fashion mistake of the era.

"Oh my," she whispered to herself, "what was I thinking with that hair?"

She filed the photos and sought the pre-Francesca era, along with some treasured heirloom pieces. Archie found her wrapped in her favourite crochet blanket and deep in thought.

"Hi mum. What are you doing?"

"Good morning mate. Look! Here's a photo of my grandfather. You're great grandfather." She said showing him the black and white image.

"Why is he wearing that?"

"In those days, the men always wore a coat and vest and the ladies were always dressed."

"Even when they were in the yards?" the boy asked, losing interest almost immediately.

"Even when they were in the yards. Are you hungry?" Francesca was already on her feet, anticipating his response.

"Yes."

"Great, because I'm starving. Let's have a good old-fashioned McCrae cook up breakfast. The kind that daddy likes to cook. Any sign of Bella this morning?"

"She's still asleep. What are we doing today?"

He followed her into the kitchen and sat at the laminex-topped table. Francesca gently brushed his dark, wayward curls from his puffy eyes. He looked tired.

"That's up to you mate. We can go fishing or for a walk up the track. I can show you where I first met your dad and frightened the life out of him."

Archie beamed. "Can we go fishing?"

"Sure."

Francesca turned towards a movement at the doorway. "Here she is! Good morning honey bear. Did you sleep well? Give me a cuddle."

The little girl climbed into her mother's arms.

"What's that you're wearing?"

"I found it on the floor near your cup of tea. Isn't it pretty? Did it belong to grandma?"

The heavy gold chain dripped through Francesca's fingers. She folded them around the shield shaped family crest. So much misery held in the palm of her hand.

"Can I see?" Archie raced around the table to meet them at the kitchen bench. Francesca slowly opened her fingers flat.

"Woah! Is that real gold? Did it cost a lot of money?"

"Yes, that's real gold. It's very valuable. That's why I think we should put it back where it came from. In the safe." Francesca thought she'd dodged the question brilliantly.

Archie took it from her hands and held it up to the sunlight. His fascination was captured at once. He stared at the red cross of St George on the pearly white background, tracing the ruby pathway with his finger.

"It's a hospital cross. Like Daddy's sleeve patch." He said.

"Look Bella, there's a gold lion with wings and he's holding a sword! And there's a girl with curly hair and three legs! What?" He shook his head disbelievingly. He looked again.

"Three legs? And three feet! Can you see that Bella?" he asked. "And there's the top of a castle. Did you live in a castle mum?"

"A castle? Were you a princess? Was it scary?" Bella asked unable to hide her excitement. She wriggled out of her mother's arms. "Let me see Archie."

"Was there a dragon?" Bella asked looking between the pendant and her mother, her eyes as big as dinner plates.

"No. No and no." She said. "None of my family has ever lived in a castle as far as I know. Have you finished looking at it now?"

"How did you get it?" Bella asked. "Can I wear it?"

"No one is wearing it." Their mother said. "I don't know how it came into our family so until I find out, I need to keep it locked in the safe."

It was an outright lie and Francesca would not apologise for it. "For now though, it can sit safely here in my pocket." She drew a sharp breath. A metaphor for the no nonsense full stop.

She opened the snap on her dress. Bella took one last look at the object and put in her mother's pocket. Francesca snapped it shut.

"Thank you Bella. Now, I'm starving and you must be too. Who'd like eggs with bacon for breakfast?"

Francesca grabbed four eggs from the carton and a stainless steel bowl. She whisked the eggs together as briskly as her mind raced, pushing the Delarno family crest and its significance to the back of her thoughts. This was the infamous mafia symbol that guaranteed Delarno protection to anyone who wore it.

That kind of information was on a need-to-know basis. And a three-year-old and a nine-year-old did not need to know that particular aspect of their lives. Not in this time frame anyway.

Seeing Bella with the Delarno pendant around her neck made her sick. Francesca tried to reason with her initial reaction. To be fair, when she'd first laid eyes on the beautiful piece, she'd also been transfixed by its stunning beauty and craftsmanship. That was until its secret message became clear and her world came crashing in around her.

Francesca pushed it behind her. For the hundredth time since he'd left for Afghanistan, she wished Sinclair were there with them.

She got busy serving up breakfast. Sitting between her children at the dining table, she wrapped her hands around the cutlery and said,

"How about we try fishing today? We can take the tinny out on the river and go for a burn up the creek towards the ocean."

Francesca opened the local tide time app on her phone.

"Perfect." She said. "We have a little time until the tide turns."

Francesca looked excitedly between Archie and Bella. She smiled and said,

"I know a secret fishing spot. Who wants to see it?"

21

....

McCrae Compound
Viti Levu, Fiji Islands

"This is the first chance I've had to call. Are you able to talk at this moment?"

"Yes," Francesca responded, walking at once to the locked carry-on bag she'd hidden in the laundry. "Thank you for calling back, Alessandro. I know you're incredibly busy."

"Well Francesca, as we say in Italy, fine words don't feed cats." He quipped in his heavily accented English. "How can I help?"

She silently acknowledged the comment, whilst placing the phone on the laundry bench. "Just one moment." She yelled. "I'm unlocking the bag now."

She held the phone back to her ear.

"I recently found a letter from my father and a number of other items that had been hidden in his bedroom cupboard at Wild Dog Creek. You've called at the perfect time actually. I've just walked in after my shift at the clinic. The kids are still in the village with Tui, so if you don't mind I'll pop you on speaker so both my hands are free."

"Not at all."

"I took the opportunity recently to clean out dad's bedroom cupboard and found a letter amongst his legal papers. It led me to documents that'd been stored in an old shoebox. As well as some photographs wrapped together in a large yellow envelope. The letter is addressed to me. In it, dad says I should call you as soon as possible. He says that I can trust you with these documents.

"Some of the photographs are quite recent." She paused slightly and took a deep breath. "Recent in so far as they were taken around the time he died."

"Have you read the documents?"

"No. I had a quick glance. It was enough for me to know that I wanted to bring them with me."

On the other side of the world, Alessandro nodded. "Did you look at the photos too?"

"Not all. But like the documents, I decided to lock them in my carry-on bag. I'm looking at them again as we speak."

"Do you recognise the people in the photos?"

"Of course. I wish Johnno and I had these when we were investigating Silvio. Here he is with Robbie L and Castello. These men were found in the boat on Sydney harbour; only in this photo they're alive and well. Here they are with our victim. Must have been moments before they killed him. It's dark. Looks like the back of that warehouse we searched. The paint job was very distinctive."

She gasped. "That can't be right." She mumbled, looking at the picture of Nicholas in deep conversation with the two offenders.

"What's that Francesca?"

"Nothing."

"Are there any more photographs?" Alessandro asked.

Francesca put the photo aside, out of the mix, sitting it on the laundry cupboard bench top beside her. She glanced between it and the other photos in her hand.

"Just the kind of photos you'd expect from a private investigator following someone. Documented meetings in café's or on the street. Hmm, that's interesting. Perhaps a different operative took this collection. They're very well documented with time and date.

"Here are some Chi You operatives with Sebastino Nero. It must be Melbourne. Yep, here's a location I know. They're in Melbourne."

"Nothing else?" Alessandro asked.

"Not in the photographic stakes."

"Are you sure?"

"Yes, I'm sure." She was irritated. "I might seem casual in my manner Alessandro, but I'm a very thorough person. Particularly when it comes to work and family related matters." She looked at the photograph of Nicholas again and frowned.

"This is old information." She said, frustrated by the thought that outcomes would be completely different if she'd had this evidence during her investigation. She picked up the offending picture and looked out the window thoughtfully.

"We know about these connections now. People are dead. In jail. Mostly dead." She paused. "If only dad had trusted me with the information. A whole lot would've been different."

"You can't know that for sure."

"For one, my father would still be alive. I could have protected him."

"I'm sorry Francesca, but again I say you can't know that

for sure. Your father was an incredibly independent man. I'm sure if he thought it would help you, he'd have told you of the connection. In the very least he'd have found a way to help with your investigations."

"Maybe. But that would have compromised you Alessandro." She fell silent again and thought about her father and his lifelong friendship with this man, Alessandro Delarno. A man she hardly knew. "Did my father take these photographs?"

"Stefano organised for our friends to take them. It was during the time we were putting together some information around Silvio's new venture and what that might look like."

Francesca skipped through the photographs and put them back in the envelope. She glanced one more time at the last one of Nicholas and put it away.

"I think you and I are out of sequence." She said. "I was meant to find that letter from Dad earlier, before we met. It's very cryptic. I think he wanted you to tell me about his role in the Guardians. My apologies Alessandro, I fear I've wasted your time.

"But, I thought I should call you even though we've been through it. Dad was very insistent in the letter that I understood everything."

"You could be right." He said. "Your father was very proud of his ability to undermine Silvio and his operations. You mentioned some documents. What are they about?"

"Hmm." Francesca went quiet for a moment, as she sorted through the musty papers.

"Bank statements. Insurance. Legal papers. One moment whilst I open this package tied up with an old bootlace. Seems dad was in possession of a number of land titles. Of course, there's our farm at Wild Dog Creek. But he also has the deeds to his Vicenza house, and my mother's family home in Treviso. I had no idea he'd accumulated so much real estate.

"He's very organised and tidy. Each lot number is in its own marked envelope. There's a place in Padua, with 'University Quarter' written on the envelope. And my sister's old flat in London. I recognise the address on the front.

"I remember when he bought that from her. I thought he was doing her a favour because she couldn't find a buyer." Francesca chuckled, lost in her memories.

"Turns out he was being a property tycoon! He told me he'd sold it on. There's also an apartment somewhere. The address looks French.

"It's in Paris, France! There's a holiday we need to have when Sinclair gets home. Maybe we can meet him there." She said dreamily.

"Is there anything else Francesca?"

"Of course, sorry. In the last envelope there is only one piece of paper. It's a newspaper clipping which looks like ... looks like he was going shopping for another place. It's in Italy. He's circled a fine-looking apartment in the real estate pages. It's near the seaside. An address at a place called Salerno? Do you know the city?"

"Yes." Alessandro pounced. "Does it have the address in the advertisement?"

"Yes. I'll photograph it and send it to you. Is that okay?"

"Thank you."

"Do you think he managed to buy it?"

"I'm going to find that out. In fact, I'll go there personally."

His voice softened. "Thank you, Francesca. For trusting me as your father did."

"His lawyer has never mentioned any of this. Would she even know, do you think?"

"Probably not. Usually, my own international lawyers would organise the purchases on his behalf. Now that I know the address, I'll be able to work everything out. Just make sure you send me a copy."

"And here I was thinking I had no money and no prospects." Francesca quipped happily. "Wait 'til I tell Sinclair! This year, Christmas is in Paris and it's on me!"

His tone changed. "I don't think you understand Francesca. You must not tell anyone about this. Not even Sinclair. Of course, Wild Dog Creek is the property you share with your sister. The farm belongs to you both. But knowledge of the other deeds must stay between us."

"Why? I don't understand."

"Because of the nature of Guardian business. Visiting these places, even speaking about them, is completely out of the question. To do so puts a lot of people at risk. I'm sorry."

"Well that sucks!" she said. "And I'm to blindly believe everything you're telling me. Forgive me Alessandro, but there have already been too many lies between your family and me."

"I am not my family." Alessandro said bluntly. "Stefano was a wonderful man and a dear, dear friend to me. Like you, I miss him every day." He paused as his voice wobbled in emotion. "I'm not aware of any grievance he held against me."

Francesca felt his emotion and said nothing. There was a long pause.

Alessandro cleared his throat. "I understand that you might

need proof of our friendly terms." He said quietly.

"It's only natural that you would want to protect your father's interests. I have saved all the messages from your father on my phone. He sent this one to me before his capture. In fact, it is the last time we spoke. I'd like to forward it to you, as well as my response. Would that be okay?"

"Please. I'll wait."

There was a brief pause. Francesca's phone pinged. She read the messages quietly. In-turn she photographed details of the Salerno property and forwarded to him.

Another long silence followed.

"Thank you, Alessandro." Her voice was husky and strained with emotion.

"It's my pleasure." He said. "I know this is difficult. There's so much you've had to learn in a short space in time. Everything you thought you knew has been turned upside down."

"Thank you for your understanding. I'm sorry too." She sighed. "And now I have to keep another secret from Sinclair. It doesn't make for a great foundation in a relationship." She said. "When will you look at the new property?"

"Tomorrow. We've already lost too much time."

"But you don't know that dad actually purchased it. I mean that was years ago. It's probably gone by now."

"Maybe. In any case I need to follow up."

"Would Nicholas know?" She asked.

Silence.

"Alessandro? I know at the time his allegiance lay elsewhere, but now he's a Guardian like you. Back then he may've heard a whisper and simply forgot about it in all that went down. A little chat might jog his memory."

An uncomfortable silence on the end of the phone continued.
"Alessandro?" She thought about the photograph she'd just found.

"He's still on our side, isn't he? Please. Tell me he is." Francesca felt the blood drain from her face. Her gut somersaulted. Had her instincts in Bourke been right after all?

"Nicholas is having a little trouble adjusting to his new life in Italy." He said in a matter of fact tone. "I think our problems and more specifically your fathers, are more sinister than your first thoughts regarding me."

Francesca felt her stomach lurch painfully. "Nicholas would not betray my father. He wouldn't." She stressed the last two words.

Her shaking hand went to her brow. An immediate ache crossed her forehead and settled behind her eyes. Her stomach rose to her throat and sat there. Waiting.

"You are wrong Alessandro." She said forcefully but quietly.

Alessandro sighed loudly.

"There are changes." He said.

"He came to Bourke." Francesca blurted, her mind whirling as she sought reassurance from the older gentleman. "Nicholas came to visit me in Bourke." She repeated as if trying to confirm it within herself.

"When?"

"Three weeks ago. He arrived unannounced."

"What did he want?"

"I'm not one hundred per cent sure. He asked about Sinclair, even though he already knew he'd been re-deployed to Afghanistan." Francesca blushed and chose her words carefully. "I suspect he wanted to reconnect. With me." Francesca felt her cheeks burn. "If that doesn't sound too conceited."

"Of course, I refused." She rushed. "He told me we both needed to grieve and that he wanted to take me home to Fiji. Again, I said no."

"And yet there you are." Alessandro sounded wary.

"Yes." Francesca was flustered. "Yes, it's true we are in Fiji, but of my own conclusion and we're certainly not with Nicholas. The kids. Archie needs to be here with Tui and school. And Bella ..."

Francesca heard Alessandro sigh on the other end of the phone. The more she tried to justify her actions the more colluded the hasty decision sounded. Francesca kept talking and then finally she stopped. She just stopped. And realised how the situation must look from afar.

"And you were hoping he'd join you later." Alessandro slammed his fist on the desk. "When will you both ever learn? Dammit!" He yelled.

"Now just you wait a second! That's not the story at all."

It was time to confess. She laid her claim out straight.

"I couldn't stay out west any longer without Sinclair. That place is not my home. I need to get my family back on track. I need to stand up. I cannot hide from the past. Nor do I want to. For the sake of our future, it's time to heal."

Before it becomes too hard. She thought.

"When Sinclair finishes this tour, he'll come home to the clinic and our life will return to normal. And all the business with mafia, Guardians and death will be behind us, never to return again."

She held her breath waiting for his response. She released it, realising she didn't need his approval to do anything in her life.

"Do you know the remainder of Nicholas's plans? After he left you?" Alessandro asked.

"Yes. He was on his way to talk to the Federal Police and Immigration. Create a memorandum of understanding so that he can come and go I suppose." She laughed and paused.

"Seriously though, I thought wow, if I was him, I'd be pissing off back to Italy, keeping my head down and living a simple life. He could go to jail for a very long time if they find enough evidence to charge him. He still may. Italy and Australia have bi-lateral arrangements for extradition."

"Yes, not a course I would have taken." Alessandro said.

"But, he's always been one to flaunt his authority and push the limits. Well, the Nicholas Delarno of old certainly was. Alessandro, I don't want this again. We don't desire this complication in our lives. I have no plans to seek the path of my father. But I have a nagging fear, an intuition if you like, that Nicholas has another agenda. Should I be worried?"

"Not worried. Be cautious …"

Francesca cut him off mid-sentence. "What now in the name of holy God?"

Movement visible through the laundry window caught her attention. Her mind whirled as she simultaneously shoved everything into the carry on and pushed it back in its hiding spot.

"Francesca? What is it?"

"Oh no! What's *he* doing here?" She thought out loud.

"Who? Francesca, who is there?" Alessandro couldn't hide the panic in his voice.

"Nicholas! Nicholas is here! He's coming from the pirate path with Archie and Bella! He's been at the village. And they're heading my way."

22

....

A quiet settled over the McCrae compound as the Fijian night rolled on, chased by the rising full moon. Waves tumbled against the golden sands on the shore below and echoed in the pirate caves dotting the estate's perimeter.

High tide. She could always tell without looking at the charts. The waves sounded closer, a tremendous noise as they crashed into the rocks. With the constant ocean noise, the surge and flow, Francesca found peace and reassurance.

Nicholas joined her on the terrace with two nightcaps in hand. "Do you mind?" he asked.

"Be my guest." She languidly indicated the chaise opposite.

"It's a beautiful evening." He said, facing the enormous hill, standing like a rear guard, protecting the compound beyond the secure gate. He breathed deeply the mingled fragrance of salty air and damp vegetation.

"I'll sleep well tonight." He quipped, handing her a drink.

"Thank you. The kids went down quickly. You'd better watch out – you'll be on story time duty every night if you're not careful." Her voice was lazy with fatigue.

She stifled a yawn. "Excuse me, it's been a long day. I'm still getting used to this nine to five caper."

After a moment she asked, "How long do you intend to stay in Fiji?"

"A week, if that's okay. I have to be in Rapallo by the 20th of this month for a meeting."

"Rapallo? I thought you'd quit that place."

He looked at her wryly. "Yes, I had decided it was not for me. But, Venice is ... how do you say, not Rapallo."

"I see." She replied, confused.

"Rapallo will always be my home. It is the place I feel most comfortable and alive." He looked out to the night.

Francesca raised her eyebrows slightly and sipped the hazelnut liqueur.

"I must say again Nicholas, it was quite a shock to see you walking up the pirate path today with the kids. Why did you come?"

"I'd already suggested I needed closure." He said tightly. "I don't see why it was such a shock to see me here."

"Yes, but this is my home. Not a memorial site. Courtesy would've deemed you check with me first, do you think?"

"I knew you wouldn't object." He said confidently.

"Perhaps, but this is the second time in a matter of weeks you've arrived unannounced." She pointed out. "I'm not entirely comfortable with it."

"It never bothered you before." He said, looking at her at last. "In fact, I remember you being more than okay with my surprises. Many times we wouldn't make it to the bedroom. You remember don't you?"

Francesca blushed. "That was a little bit different." She said her voice strained in mortification. "And you know it. You're being very unfair, Nicholas."

"Not as far as I see it. Francesca, I'll always feel that way about you."

And she could almost physically touch the sexual tension emanating from him.

"Well you'd better rein it in big boy, otherwise unexpected visits like this are off the table. I'm feeling very uncomfortable in this whole conversation."

"Oh come on Francesca." He teased. "What is a bit of banter between lovers?"

"We're not lovers."

"A man can hope." He said and his expression intensified.

"What are you doing Nic?" She spoke quietly and evenly as her emotion caught in her throat. She knew that look very well.

"Playing with fire."

Francesca pressed her lips together and breathed out her nose. Her head shook slightly from side to side to erase her building tension. There was a clear decision to be made here and she'd not be drawn into reviewing a complicated past. She stared at the stars dotting the horizon.

"What are you doing with your life? Nothing about you makes sense to me anymore." She was quiet, and turned her head to him, trying to quell the intensity emanating from him.

"Why should it?" he said carefully. "You have your life and I have mine."

"And yet you keep trying to drag me into yours."

His eyes never left her face. "I don't understand why you feel so conflicted by that? Our lives are forever interlocked; we have a past, a present and a future. That cannot be denied. Your complication is that you still have feelings for me and for us. Isn't that the truth?"

She didn't respond.

"For me," he continued, "my feelings towards you grow deeper every day as they always have. I am being honest Francesca when I say it is impossible for me to hide or run from them."

"What do you want from me Nicholas?" She asked, trying to shut down the uncomfortable conversation.

"I need for you to trust me and what I'm doing. Things are about to happen and I need to know that I can count on you and your faith in me. That you'll support my decisions."

"Nic, how can I make you understand?" Francesca caught her frustration before it spiralled. "I'm not interested in being a part of the Guardians. I've done my time in the cops. I'm out of the whole shebang. What you do privately has nothing to do with me, unless it affects Archie."

She stood and paced the paved deck area.

"I have two children now. And Sinclair. My job is to be the best wife and mother I can be and to work in this community, helping people. That means being present in our life."

She paused and looked at him.

"Whatever you have going on in your world, I'm not a part of it anymore. And can I just say, it feels damn good to say ... I'm done. I'm out."

She raised her hands in the air to stretch and smiled broadly.

"I. Am. Done." She shouted to the sky. "Do you hear me? I'm done."

Nic jumped out of his seat and came to stand opposite her. His face and tone was serious.

"You're father headed the largest, most secretive organisation whose sole purpose was to undermine the mob and their illegal activities." He said challenging her in the closed space. "I hate to break it to you kid, you'll always be in *and* a person of interest."

Francesca looked at him half expecting a tell that he wasn't serious. It wasn't there and so she went immediately on the defensive.

"Rubbish! I know how these organisations work. I don't poke the tiger, and the tiger doesn't bite me." She drew a deep meditative breath, held it for a moment and let the breath out slowly.

"That's very naive. One word Francesca, 'retribution'."

"For what?"

"Your father's actions have caused significant losses. There's many pissed off, dangerous people out for blood. Sins of the father carry through to the daughter."

Francesca paled.

"That's grossly unfair." She said and paced away from him again. He followed her.

"Unfair? Do you think these people care whether it's unfair for you or not? Francesca, this is a critical time in our organisation. Everything is at stake. Money. Lives. And livelihoods."

He pulled two chairs together and indicated for her to sit opposite him. She did. His forearms leant across his thighs, hands clasped towards her. His face was alight with enthusiasm.

"You cannot see it. But I can, as clear as a winter sky. It's your time Francesca. You are the difference. Destiny is shouting from the rooftops. Fortune favours us to act right now. Don't you see? We have the opportunity to take the organisation forward. Italian politics has never been so ripe for the change we desire. My leadership is secure. Our economic gains and relationships are strong."

"Stop right there." She paused for effect. "There's no 'we' in this discussion."

He looked a little confused.

"Please don't include me." She shook her head gently. "Have you even heard a word I've said? I will not be a part of it. Besides which, I'm a little confused. Are you referring to the mob or the guardians? Because I get the sense you've merged the two."

She looked at him sternly. "You can't sit on the fence here Nicholas. You want to cherry pick the best of the good and the bad. You have to choose a side. There cannot be right and wrong at the same time."

Francesca paused, assessing him for a long minute in the quiet as he stewed over her comments.

"What happened in Venice?" She probed, cocking her head to one side.

His expression closed. "Nothing that I can't handle."

"I can easily find out."

It was his turn to assess her. "Giuliett Seta is gunning for us."

Francesca's brows knitted together. Her mind ticked with questions of why and how she would link them together.

"Because of last year?" she said. "When she saw us at Santa Lucia. She'd assume we were hiding out in secret, I suppose. Why else would we be together in Italy? Why else would we be running from Venice? Does she know about Alessandro? What about Archie?"

"Not as far as I know. Well, nothing confirmed. I guess she has her suspicions. Alessandro has played a very straight bat since that time. I've been running the Guardians in his absence."

Francesca nodded feeling oddly relieved about her father's friend.

"And Archie? Is he still in danger?"

"No. The boy is secure." He said confidently.

She looked towards the sea again, processing this new information.

"She still wants to hurt me! Unbelievable." Francesca said at last. "After how many years? That woman is seriously deranged."

"That she is. She's desperate to turn the Commission against me. It won't work. I can handle her. Unfortunately, you're still in the frame and minds of the Commission. They never understood our love. In their eyes you'll always be a traitor. Salucci's are the enemy."

Francesca was incredulous. "Because she keeps reminding them of us!"

"Alessandro has been trying to temper the rising storm, but unfortunately with the death of your father and other key operators, it's opened up old prejudices. The costly disruption following Silvio's recent death has everyone looking at you. I thought you should be aware." He said.

There was a long pause between them. "And I suppose, you can't defend me to them, without exposing yourself." She said.

It was a bind.

"What can she do to me here? Seriously. That bitch will just want to try." Francesca's commonsense response equalled her bravado. "I'm not a timid fifteen-year-old girl anymore needing protection from her minder."

Francesca's eyes narrowed suspiciously.

"She knows we're not together, right?" she asked.

"My flower," he said, using his pet name for her. "It doesn't matter."

"You never told her? Oh my God, Nicholas! You're unbelievable!" She stormed, jumping up off the chair and pacing in a tight circle around it.

"Honey it doesn't matter because she's stuck in a time when you had me and she couldn't." He said in a frustrated tone. "It's her drug-fucked brain. And that dog Enrico Nero. He feeds her neurosis."

He looked outwards into the night sky.

"Ma poi, Giuliett è sempre stata invidiosa. But then, Giuliett has always been invidious."

23

....

Alessandro's Villa
Treviso, Italy

He sat in the dark. Home at last, away from the curious eyes of Venice, Alessandro gazed through the open windows, relishing familiar privacy.

Just visible in night's dim light, an expanse of manicured lawns, gardens and a stand of poplars framed a circular gravel path. It met a tall brick boundary wall. The latter effectively circumvented the boundaries of his Palladian villa and its private grounds. Beyond the wall, a single vehicle driveway met a winding country road in the distance.

His vision settled on the tall ornate gate, closed and locked, protecting him from the outside. His world was changing. The boundaries of mafia and guardian were increasingly blurred making the subtleties of friend and foe no longer instinctive.

Alessandro found himself living in a faster, more agile environment with players who no longer respected of the ways of the past. They were instead, bent on reaching their perceived rightful place at any cost. Stupidity and ignorance made them consequence averse. And in Alessandro's line of work, that was a dangerous combination.

Of course, right now he was thinking about Giuliett Seta; and to a lesser extent, her mother Bice. Snares were about. Making his relationship with Nicholas fraught with traps and innuendo threatening to expose their most valuable secrets.

He had of course lived this life of in between for decades, but he'd always been able to draw on the wise counsel of his friend Stefano Salucci during times like these, when things became tight.

Unease filled the space around him. Even the still night conjured a slight breeze, creating movement and gently pushing the curtains out into the room. It startled him at first. Then, as he relaxed, the older man breathed in and out with it.

His mind turned to Nicholas, as it repeatedly did after the young man's revelation at the Commission's Venetian summit. Alessandro rubbed his bristly chin.

"Was I right to trust you Nicholas? Or have I made a costly mistake?" he wondered quietly to himself, for the first time in his life questioning his own instincts and honed capabilities.

The older gentleman found Nic's tactical leadership unsettling. After savagely taking control of the group, the new Capo di tutti Capi had physically disappeared a short time later. Again. For a second time his nephew had vanished without a word or explanation. With questions surrounding the previous absence and loyalty lingering on a knife's edge, Nicholas' actions defied belief.

The Commission, if they knew his whereabouts, would demand the end. Of both he and Francesca. But, Alessandro knew Nicholas never actioned without a well thought out plan. And so, he spent this pre-dawn time analysing the facts as he saw them.

The young Capo had been organising business from afar. And he'd thrown bones in the right directions.

The perverse machinations of the Italian government as it tilted and rolled from one drama to the next were in stark contrast of Sebastino Nero's work within the immigration space.

Within the party faithful and across government, the young politician utilised social and traditional media to communicate his messages of hard-line approaches to stem the unsatisfactory and glorify a new golden era for Italy.

His actions were just as decisive and well-constructed. Alleged illegally constructed mafia buildings in Naples were spilled to the ground in piles of rubble at the behest of the people.

Sebastino had taken the fight to known Camorra offenders there.

The scourge of the south, the Nigerians who'd wrestled control in Palermo, were being harshly dealt with in co-ordinated, vigilante raids. Under the guise of a new anti-mafia law, specialist police were heavily financed, and with seeming unlimited artillery and levels of co-operation had begun making headway previously only dreamt about.

The young politician had then taken Italy's immigration overflow woes to the root cause, organising meetings with the militia and leaders of the northern African nations.

Flip the spectrum to his engaging messaging to his homeland community. It was naturally relaxed, thoughtful and family value orientated. And it was cutting through the politically weary population at an extraordinary rate.

Charismatic, articulate and with a witty flare for the dramatic, Sebastino Nero was morphing into a modern-day Caesar right before their eyes. A strong leader who left his political rivals floundering in the shallows.

Giving Nero clear air and bolstering his standing within the commission had brought all but Giuliett Seta across.

The Australian outlaw, Robbie L, remained in Venice. For what reason, other than to bait Giuliett, no one could guess. The biker was an unknown quantity to the firm and Alessandro was determined to get to know him better.

At this point in time, he remained compliant and satisfied, organising the Australian activities utilising his outlaw group on behalf of his new family. Nicholas had insisted that the biker be brought into the fold. After all, it was the wish of his father and respected the traditions, something they were all keen to uphold.

Even Pocco had yielded to Nic's outreached hand, but the Florentine would never be trusted. Both he and Nicholas knew that man would turn for a single gold florin.

Alessandro was one of two, it seemed, who was not fooled by Nic's outward congeniality.

Nicholas was biding time. Always watching. Away from the mix he gained the advantage of distance and perspective. But he was playing a dangerous game with his prolonged absence in Australia and Fiji. It made Alessandro feel very uneasy.

The first of the morning light broke the horizon. With it the birds began to wake. Venice had already joined them. His mind turned to Bice Seta.

The beauty and symmetry of his Palladio surrounds was no balm today for the agitation Alessandro bore this morning as he thought about that woman. And he would certainly not concede it was her imminent visit that had him tossing and turning all night.

She would be here today. In his home. And he had no idea why the thought of it irritated him so. Or what her business might be.

The night transcended into pre-morning light. Alessandro turned his attention to the international news bulletins, something he did every morning. His curiosity was immediately roused by the images.

"Breaking news from Australia." The news anchor said. "We're crossing now to our reporter standing by in our Sydney studio. Katie, what can you tell us about this latest drug crisis in Australia?"

"Good morning, Virginia. The Australian Federal Police have today secured a large amount of cocaine and methamphetamines destined for regional cities and towns throughout the states of Queensland, New South Wales and Victoria. Raids conducted simultaneously across Melbourne, Sydney and Canberra have targeted addresses known to be associated with the outlaw motor cycle gang known as Ares.

"Virginia, evidence found at a Canberra location indicates the Ares group may be part of a larger international crime syndicate. A spokesperson has confirmed that the Australian Federal Police and Customs have been working in conjunction with their respective European counterparts in a covert operation spanning a number of years." The reporter said.

"Police have confirmed that the haul of chemical drugs alone has an estimated street value of $12.5m. Large amounts of cash and firearms were also found at the premise in the Nation's capital.

"A police spokesperson said the haul was a result of a tip off from the public. In fact, Virginia, it hasn't been a good day for the Ares outlaw group.

"In a fortuitist twist for police, evidence was found during the Canberra raid that may lead to solving a cold case that's been baffling the Organised Crime Detectives for eight years.

"Police have amped up their search for Mr. Robin Lark. The leader of the Ares Outlaw Gang, widely known as Robbie L, is now wanted for questioning over the alleged murder of another gang member.

"Mr. Luke Vincent was a chapter leader of the Melbourne-based, Chinese triad gang known as Chi You. Eight years ago, some tourists found Mr. Vincent dead in his car at a remote seaside location outside of Melbourne.

"Based on evidence found within the Canberra residence, detectives are now very keen to talk to Robbie L about the incident."

Alessandro was not often lost for words, but in that instant, he knew exactly what Nicholas was about. And he set about to protect him within the Commission rank and file.

24

....

Operation Laylor,
Mehtar Lam, Afghanistan

Snow spotted mountains stretched as far as he could see.
They touched a clear blue sky in jagged forbidding peaks,
breaking off in shards slicing into steep ravines and valleys.
The floor was a landscape laid out in a patchwork of taupe,
grey and green. Army medic Captain Sinclair McCrae held
his breath at the natural beauty of Afghanistan, a country of
extremes and the war weary people who inhabited it.

Amidst the steady beat of the Chinook blades, he remained
vigilant, scanning that same landscape for potential trouble.
This was dangerous country, particularly in the hand over
phase, and now was not the time to dream melancholy thoughts
of what could be for this ancient culture.

Soon they would land at the Forward Operating Base at
Mehtar Lam, where a skeleton staff of allied soldiers remained
with Afghani military personnel. From his designated spot
beside the door gunner, he quietly observed the team who were
accompanying him on today's mission. He made it his business
to know everything about the key members of this group. He'd

spent the last month travelling with them across Afghanistan, assessing, checking and writing reports in preparation for the next phase of the allied forces withdrawal.

Captain Taylor Grant, keenly alert as always, sat beside her Afghani counterpart, known to all as Iceman. They could be brother and sister, both bearing the same colouring of ice blonde hair, distinctive eye colour and deep olive skin. Both possessed an open-faced expression of expectation, medium build and fit stature.

Their friendship had begun in the drug and criminal intelligence unit of the newly established Afghan Interpol National Central Bureau in Kabul. It extended to the gym where, more often than not, they spent their spare time together challenging each other in the defence facility.

But that was where the similarities ended. Grant, of Italo-French descent, was brought up under a strict regime of army life with serving parents. She duly rebelled against the system in typically French fashion during her teens. After experiencing a life another world away in Asia, she returned to her calling with a renewed understanding of herself and what it takes to be community.

Grant was a unique blend of French independence and Eastern humility. She was soulful inside and out, possessing a calm presence. Meditative, focused and quick thinking, she was aware of herself and those around her at all times.

Iceman was Kalash. His tribe were rumoured to be descendants of Alexander the Great, something the Greeks were keen to feed on. The people of that tribe? It was at times difficult.

On the ground it created a range of problems for this small

community residing predominantly in remote Nuristan, located on the Afghanistan side of the Pakistan border.

The Taliban had declared war on the blond-haired blue-eyed people, their culture and heritage, and anyone who supported them.

Undeterred by the stigma and threats, Iceman set about joining the military and the elite Afghan Interpol National Central Bureau whose officers supported local police with intelligence and access. He'd recently joined the Global Fugitive Investigation Team after graduating with honours in International Law. No mean feat in this country, and his tenacity and humble personality immediately won admiration amongst the troops.

McCrae's attention was drawn to Grant as she bent her head as in a quick prayer. Her lips touched her upheld forefinger tips. She whispered 'My love. Peace.' Thumbs and forefingers formed a diamond, resting on the tip of her nose and under her chin.

Next, she set her thoughts and words into the air, fingers slowly opening first followed by thumbs. She looked skyward and momentarily closed her eyes as her fingers came together again in a prayer position at her closed lips. The deliberate action was over in a moment.

McCrae knew it to be her own reverent prayer to her lover who'd lost his life in an ambush not far from their current location. The French had been slaughtered. The soldiers didn't stand a chance. He breathed slowly out.

Asmaan Banesh flanked Grant's left-hand side and sat directly opposite McCrae. The Afghani national was part of the team providing the necessary link between the Non-Government

Organisations, relevant Afghanistan Ministries and the United Nations Office on Drugs and Crime.

She specifically was a data specialist. Her brief focused on Trafficking in Persons, or TIP, as they were known. Today she was meeting with a case management worker in the town.

Asmaan was a civilian who'd endured unspeakable hurdles. Grant, recognising the young woman lacked basic military training and was unlikely to get it, had personally seen to rectifying it as a matter of urgency. The Afghan woman was already a valuable asset to the tight team. Now she could defend as well as protect.

The remainder of the group were new to this particular mission and included an IED specialist as well as a select crew of Australian soldiers. In all twenty personnel shared the space with supplies.

Grant caught his attention. They were approaching the base. McCrae's game face slipped effortlessly into place as his attention sharply drew to the job at hand.

25

....

Mehtar Lam Forward Operating Base, Afghanistan

smaan found him in the empty barracks, immersed in his thoughts and the messages left behind by the soldiers. He was facing a written quote, coined first by a Vietnam veteran. His hand was clamped over his chin and rubbing the whiskers in a sandpapery sound. A digital camera was gripped in the right, his fingers wrapped around the Canon SLR, as the strap trailed beside his leg.

"Captain McCrae? Pardon me. We need to talk."

"Sure. What's on your mind Asmaan?"

"Take a look at this." She said solemnly, holding out her mobile phone for him to see the image.

Slumped together on one mattress in the dark room, bound and gagged, two women flanking two children stared back at the photographer. McCrae zoomed in at their faces. He paused at the two blonde ladies. Their hair was pushed back from their terrified eyes. McCrae recognised one immediately as Anya Frida Volkov, Carlo Seta's missing mistress.

The army medic looked questioningly at Asmaan.

"Who are these people?" he asked.

"Traffic in person. TIP. Women and children smuggled across the Pakistan border." She said.

"How many?"

"Four in this group. I believe they've been separated from the rest because they're Russian." She paused for a moment.

"Sir, the women are payback for a time when our country was occupied by Russian forces. They and the little boys are rape and torture bait for Taliban soldiers."

"Where are they?"

"My informant says they're being held at Galoch Kala, a village on the border of Laghman and Surobi districts. They're to be moved tonight to Surobi city. As you know it will be very difficult to reach them once they're in that city. I think we need to act now, intercept the traffickers before the victims are moved."

She looked at him as her voice shaking in trepidation at the last sentence.

"And how did you come by this photo and information?" he asked.

"As you know I met with our case management worker in the village today and she has told me of this situation. Her husband heard about it at market and knowing we were coming here today, he made enquiries."

"So this is real time?"

"I trust my team member." Asmaan replied.

McCrae looked at the image again. "You say they are Russian. How do you know anything about them?"

"That is how my colleague discovered it. Because of the war with the Russians, there is no sympathy for them in my country.

The men were talking." She blushed. "One is the grand-daughter of a Russian general and diplomat. This one." She pointed to the first girl.

"And the other?"

"I don't know her." She said.

I do. Thought McCrae. "The young boys?"

Asmaan shrugged. "I do not know Sir." She said.

"We need Grant and Icemen on board. We'll move on it with our team."

"Thank you, Sir."

*   *   *   *   *

Grant and Iceman were in the situation room, poring over a satellite image over laid in part by a topographical map. It was spread across the table, together with a small collection of cartographer's tools. In one hand, she held a mobile phone. In the other, a pencil was flicking back and forth as she looked between the maps and the image on her phone.

Iceman stood.

"Sir." he said. "We have a situation unfolding in Galoch Kala."

"TIP?"

"Yes Sir."

"Tell me what you know." McCrae said.

"Intel stacks up." Grant said. "We've been tracking a person of interest running an underground operation out of Pakistan. The organisation offers men and women the opportunity to work and earn big money in high-risk countries. Whilst the organisation is legitimate, we have reason to believe this one individual has a sideline business in TIP. We've been working for months on a thread linking our POI to the Nigerian mafia."

"The Nigerian mafia?" McCrae asked.

"Yes Sir. The Nigerian mafia are trading persons for opium and guns. Small numbers, high worth individuals." Iceman said. "Interpol intercepted a message between a known Nigerian brother and our Afghani person of interest. Since then we've been following up a number of leads via our internal agencies and informants. This particular organisation was red flagged in another covert investigation. It's running out of Palermo, Sicily."

"The Nigerian mafia is running a human trafficking operation in southern Italy." McCrae confirmed.

"Yes Sir. The Sicilian mafia is 'allowing' the Nigerians to operate in their territory for a cut in the profits." Grant explained.

She pulled an image up on her mobile phone. "This is a photograph of the ladies and the children we believe are being transferred tonight into Surobi."

"That's them." McCrae confirmed.

"Captain McCrae, we can move now. I have the location of where the persons are being held." Asmaan said, glancing up from her phone messages.

26
....

International Military Base
Kabul, Afghanistan

The afternoon lingered in a confined space, a haze of dust and sunshine, colour washed into the pale rendered walls of the government agency compound.

McCrae made his way through the traditional Afghan layout of a courtyard garden, punctuated by rose bushes in full bloom, and headed immediately into a private reception room adjacent to the Minister's office.

Eight days after the high-risk extraction from Galoch Kala, the soldier medic was anxious to bring some clarity to the hundreds of questions running through his mind. The most insistent was how does an Italian mob's mistress become a victim in a human trafficking operation run by the Nigerian mob?

Behind solid timber French doors, a light filled, large, rectangle shaped room was decorated in carved wood panelling. It reached the height of and wrapped across the top of the doorjamb. The intricate pattern continued in a peach-coloured plasterwork frieze to the ceiling.

Along both edges of the longest walls, seating took the form of a single row of large rectangular cushions. Back support cushions were placed at intervals and scattered into the corners of the room. The floors were covered in a coordinating, traditionally patterned carpet.

On a low table, an individual teapot brewed spiced tea. A glass, a bowl of sugar cubes and biscuits completed the afternoon tea setting.

He found her alone, sipping tea and absorbed in a historical paper written by the grandmother of Kabul, Mrs. Nancy Dupree. She was curled up on a tushak, a floor cushion, at the head of the room.

Anastasia was a quietly spoken young woman, of slim build and possessing typically Russian facial features of a high forehead and thin eyebrows. Her eyes were clear and bright. She'd removed her linen head covering and it draped around her shoulders. Her long flaxen hair shone in the sunlight and though pale with tired stress, her face was a beautiful as ever.

Despite her ordeal she emanated an air of peace and tranquillity.

"Excuse me, Anastasia." He said, entering the guest reception room that smelt distinctly of cardamom. "May I have a word?"

"Captain McCrae." She smiled and it met her eyes. "Call me Anna. It's nice to see your friendly face." She immediately stood and the long linen shift fell easily into place, covering her bruised ankles and bare feet. She smoothed the fabric over her thin frame. "Although I can't complain, I'm being very well looked after by your team. Would you like some tea?"

He smiled at her. "No thank you. So, you are receiving the necessary support for your health and mind?" He asked.

"I am. Thank you." She pulled the long sleeves of her tunic

at the cuffs, subconsciously covering the cuts and bruises on her wrists and forearms.

"Alexandra won't be long. She's finishing up with her interview." McCrae said. "After that, I'll take you both back to the barracks."

"Thank you." She smiled and nodded. "Alex and I are very happy we have each other to lean on. Do you know what happened to the two little boys who were with us?" She asked.

"They've been moved to the shelter in Kabul. It's run by a nongovernment organisation."

"Oh." She said. "Have you found their families?"

"Not yet."

"Oh dear." Anna said. "That's very sad." Her eyes welled in tears. "They were so brave, those dear little boys. So very brave."

The room was filled with silence. Sinclair watched her sip the spicy tea, her face wrinkled in troubled thoughts. Her hands started to shake and she placed the cup onto the table.

"I feel terrible for asking but do you know when I will be returning home?"

"That's what I'd like to talk with you about. Do you have plans to return to Italy?" he asked.

"No." she said cautiously. "I have no further business in Italy. I'll be going to Russia with Alex. Her family offered to help me transition in my recovery. They've been incredibly kind."

McCrae nodded.

"Is that what you want?" he asked.

"A woman in my position does not think about what she wants, Captain McCrae."

"Oh?"

"Milan has been my home for many years. But I won't be

returning to it now."

"Because Carlo Seta is dead."

She looked at him in surprise.

"I know your secret Anya Frida. I'll not play games."

The protest gathered in her eyes and McCrae looked at her with determined insistence. It was a silent dual of wits.

In the end he watched her resolve play out in her facial expression. Sadness and resignation replaced the bravado she'd previously shown him and his crew.

"So what's to become of me now?" she asked.

"That depends on you."

"Ask and I will do my best to answer truthfully and to my best knowledge. With Carlo gone I'm nothing anyway."

"Tell me about your relationship with Carlo Seta."

She smiled sadly. "You might say he was a monster Captain McCrae, but to me, he was my light. My guardian. I loved him deeply from the minute I saw him. He took me in when I was quite young and even though there were many years between us, our attraction to each other grew until we could no longer stop it. I became his mistress for he already had a family."

McCrae nodded.

"And you lived in Milan?" he asked.

"Yes. We've been lovers for almost ten years. It's been a lovely life in the shadows. My home was a beautiful apartment close to his business, and we'd often meet in Ibiza for relaxation and mutual company. I loved him very much and I know he loved me too."

Anya Frida smiled wistfully.

"Did you ever meet his friends and family?"

"Yes, I knew his daughter Giuliett quite well." She said in a tight tone that was not lost on McCrae.

"You told my colleagues that you and Alexandra are jewellers. Is this true?"

"Yes. We source jewels for the trade. We buy and sell unique stones and pieces and have done for many years." She said.

"And Carlo didn't mind that you had your own business?"

"No Sir. He was very proud of me. He encouraged me to do better. Sometimes we would source gems together, but mostly the business was done between Alexandra and I."

"Did Alexandra ever meet him?"

"Only as a client. I didn't ever speak about my relationship with him." She said.

"Tell me about your last movements in Italy." He said.

"Alex and I were following up on a lead in Sicily. There was a person who has connections to Afghanistan gemstones. We were organising a meeting with them." She said truthfully.

"Did you meet with the person?"

"I can't be sure. I fear the meeting was a ruse for the Nigerians."

"You were set up." McCrae watched her closely.

"I was betrayed by a friend. That hurts me more."

"And now you seek revenge."

"Now, I want to go to Russia. To my home in the country and take solace in my family."

"In Saint Petersburg?"

"Yes. My brother manages our estate on behalf of my parents who prefer life in Moscow. I want to be close to him."

"What do you know about guns?"

"Do you mean how to shoot them? I have used guns before, as a child in Russia we would go hunting with our father. I didn't really enjoy it. I know Carlo was always armed."

"I'm talking about illegal gun trade." He added drily.

She looked at him. "Oh. I don't know." She said shaking her head.

"Did you overhear any conversation of this type when you were with Carlo Seta?"

"No. Carlo conducted his business away from me. Besides Carlo would not deal in drugs and guns. He owns a transport company."

"Right. He's dead Anya. You don't need to worry about retribution from him. And you don't need to protect his 'good' name."

"It's true Sir. There were drugs at our parties for the clients but he was not a drug cartel or something like that. I didn't ever see Carlo under the influence of or using drugs."

"In ten years he never took a business call in your presence? That's hard for me to swallow." McCrae said.

"He took business calls of course. But I don't recall a discussion about drugs or guns. Never. Why do you keep asking about Carlo?"

"Exploring all options." He said. "Did you hear any conversations regarding drugs and guns when you were captured?"

She looked at him doubtfully.

"Really? You think they'd discuss something like that in front of us?"

"No. I'm asking at any time during your ordeal did you overhear any conversations about guns?"

"No Sir. I only heard words such as Russian whore. I couldn't understand whatever else they were saying. There was a lot of angry shouting." She started to cry. "And hitting and pulling us and machine guns in our faces and knives at our throats."

McCrae breathed out as his frustration grew.

"Okay Anya. It's okay. You're safe here. I'm sorry I have to ask these questions. You understand that don't you?"

She nodded, pushing endless tears from her eyes across her pale cheeks.

"Let's leave it at that for today." McCrae said quietly.

He reached across and held her hand in his to comfort her. She nodded quietly at him and mouthed, "I'm okay."

He stayed with her until she could compose herself again.

27

....

Sinclair spent the early hours tossing about in his bunk. Anya had said something and it rattled around him like an unwanted truth. 'I was betrayed by a friend,' she'd said. He thought about the conversation with Nicholas Delarno in Singapore.

In the four months he'd been in Kabul, there was not a sniff of a whisper that Australian military issue were being traded on the black market for drugs. He'd forensically checked the whole disposal process. He'd even called in a favour from a colleague who conducted her own covert investigation. And they'd both come up wanting.

It didn't make sense.

With the girl turning up in Afghanistan, he'd now been put firmly in the frame with the Russian and Italian mob. He had to tread carefully to protect his reputation and not invite scrutiny into his own life.

Nicholas Delarno may be used to living in the grey areas, but Sinclair McCrae was not. It settled uneasily over him and he rolled again to face the wall.

Sinclair's mind turned to Seta's mistress, Anya Frida Volkov. She was the only piece of the puzzle that did fit with Delarno's story.

So why was Nic so keen to protect the woman? And did

he know she'd be traded for opium? Was he the friend who'd betrayed her and now he was having second thoughts about the deal? And why would he think McCrae would find her? The chances were too remote to even calculate.

The soldier grunted and rolled onto his back. He stared up at the ceiling. He was overthinking it. There was not a way in hell the Delarno reach could filter into the Taliban. And there was absolutely no way Nicholas Delarno could mastermind the capture and release of an Italian drug lord's mistress in Afghanistan.

Sinclair left the suffocating room to watch the sun rise.

"I'm nobody's fool." He grumbled as he headed to the meal room for a cup of coffee. "And I won't play his game, friend or no."

28

Alessandro's Villa

Treviso, Italy

"I want you to take control of the business." Bice Seta left his bed and stood by the window, her back to the estate's expansive grounds and the hills beyond shrouded in autumn sunshine. She wrapped the silk dressing gown around her in a pale green and lilac sheath.

Alessandro smiled softly at her. Her face was alive with determination and her eyes sparkled. He rumbled an incomprehensible response by way of a noise coming from deep within his chest.

She chuckled.

"I'm serious Alessandro." She said. "I want to leave the business and as I am the head of our family now, I desire you to have it."

"Bice." He replied. "It's not that simple."

She came to him and sat beside his prone body. "It's as simple as I want it to be. I make the decisions."

"And Giuliett? Gatto? Enrico? Not to mention the extended family. You think they'll accept that I am suddenly your clan's

Don, without due process?"

She shrugged nonchalantly.

"Let's be clear – you want a Delarno to lead the Seta clan."

She leaned into him. Her face was inches from his. She looked as giddy as a schoolgirl.

"Delarno you may be, but you are not your brother. You're a good man with a fair heart and a strong leader. And, I desire you to take it." Her eyes were smouldering.

"And when you look at me like that, it's hard to say no." He said, pulling her to him.

She giggled. "That's precisely what I want."

He felt her relax into his naked warmth. Alessandro placed a kiss on the back of her head as she snuggled further into his arms.

"It's nice to be out of Venice." She said, looking out towards the rows of grape vines hugging the curves of the hills in the distance. "This home you have made in the country side, Alessandro, is lovely. It's very calming. I didn't realise just how stressed I was, until I walked through your front door today. Everything was suddenly easy and crystal clear. I knew straight away my decision was the correct."

"I haven't agreed yet."

"You will." She said.

"Is that right?"

"Yes." She replied with all the confidence of a person used to getting her own way.

"Alessandro, I first came to you after the Commission met because I didn't dare dream that what I wanted to do, could be done. Now I know more than ever that this is the only way to go forward. I do not care for that side of the business. It never sat well with me.

"Besides, I have more than enough to do. The transport business takes a lot of my time. Then there are the many patronages. I want to travel, explore places and experience new things Carlo would never dream of doing.

"When I married Carlo I made a commitment to stand by him and part of that commitment was accepting the family business. Now that he's gone, I'm not interested in it," she said, adding. "In fact, I'm washing my hands of it."

"And you think I'm the right person? There is structure within the organisation, a legacy to uphold."

"I know. However, you are the very person, Alessandro, who can make it work and this is your moment to have what should've been yours from the start."

"I don't know what you mean." He said.

"Silvio. Your own brother blocked you out."

"Bice, I was happy with that decision. I never sought the Delarno business."

"Forgive me Alessandro for what I am about to say. It's probably just as well. You could not have had it even if you wanted! Goodness me! To try and take that little boy from his mother, that act was the end for me. It was surely his most despicable in a long line of disgusting acts!

"And that Carlo was implicated in his crime as well! Carlo was a bully, but he would never advocate stealing a child! Silvio was pure evil. Pure evil."

Alessandro looked surprised. He propped himself on his elbow. She rolled to face him.

"Like I said to you once before. I know some things but not a lot. I sensed Carlo was changing and so I paid attention. I could piece it all together in the end."

"Tell me what you know." Alessandro said feeling a little apprehensive.

"Francesca's boy belongs to Nicholas. Silvio wanted to bring him into the family business. He was bent on kidnapping the child and bringing him to Italy."

"And you have an opinion on that family?" he asked cautiously.

"Yes. That girl has been through enough. Losing her mother at a young age and then her father's death at the hand of that dreadful consigliere, Castello. Of course there is Nicholas. That young man has played with her heart her whole life. She needs to be left alone with her new family."

"And the child?"

"Stays with her." she said adamantly.

"Even though he has the birth right?"

"This is not a life for children. I've watched Giuliett be destroyed by it. I could not save my child from her father, but I can do something about Francesca Salucci. And I will. It's not right."

"How do you intend to do that?" He was more than curious now.

"By giving you Seta's clan. You are the Don. And you have my express permission to reach out to Francesca and assure her, we will protect her and her family. Now you have the power, the others will fall into line. They would ignore my wishes. Gatto would see to that. The family feared Carlo. None would go against him. But they respect you. They'll follow you at their own volition."

Alessandro was stunned.

"There is a place in Salerno. Stefano Salucci bought it for Francesca as a safe haven. He knew Nicholas would drag her to Italy at some point. Did you know Nicci brought her to Italy to try and persuade her to join him? At the very time when we all thought he was dead?"

"How do you know that?" he asked.

"Never misjudge a woman's ability to find out the necessary information," she said with a wink. "But of course in this case, by chance, Giuliett and Carlo saw them together in Venice. When Carlo found out about the purchase, he had it investigated. He thought the property had something to do with the Guardians. So he interfered and got a hold of the papers."

"After Stefano died, the apartment was left abandoned. I want you to ensure that Francesca knows it belongs to her and that her father wanted her to have it. I have the deeds and legal documents with me today. When Carlo died I took them from his office. I've signed full ownership over to Francesca Salucci, as it should've been right from the start. The apartment is fully furnished. I asked my décor stylist to make it comfortable for the family."

She glanced at his profile.

"You look so dismayed Alessandro." She smiled at him.

Her hands gently clasped his jaw and she bent his face towards hers. She kissed him thrice in the place where the corner of his lips met his cheek. Her nose and forehead touched his briefly and she pulled away. In the confined space between them, her eyes were alight.

There was a quiet silence between them as she gave him time to digest her proposal and the information she'd revealed.

Bice settled in beside him and his arms came protectively around her. Her head rested against his chest. Gentle fingers lightly caressed his forearm, tracing the muscle in abstract patterns and loops as it flexed with her touch.

He spoke to her at last. His voice came from some place deep within in his chest. It was a quiet, emotional rumble.

"Bice, I did not seduce you to take control of Seta group."

A new smile lit her eyes. "And my dear Alessandro, I did not consent to it to persuade you."

29

....

Venice, Italy

A hand pressed hard over her mouth and nose. It was ice cold and she felt scratchy palms press against her lips. It took a moment to realise the act was actually happening. She woke abruptly from a sound sleep, confused and panic stricken. Giuliett tried to scream but with the muffled sound, he only pressed harder.

"Shut up!" he whispered loudly.

She struggled in the darkness, thrashing out from the bed sheets, kicking wildly, her arms flaying at the bands of steel pushing against her chest and the unrelenting pressure on her mouth, pushing her head and neck into the soft pillows. Suddenly she stilled.

After a few tense moments the pressure eased and she let out another stifled scream, biting the inside of his hand.

He chuckled, forming suction on her lips as his palm pressed harder. Giuliett rocked in the bed, banging the bed's legs and frame against the floor and wall before grabbing at anything on the bedside table and throwing it noisily across the room.

Her fingers wrapped around glass. She pegged it in the

direction of the wall. It bounced and hit the tile floor, shattering noisily.

"You stupid wench!" he whispered again loudly, pulling her towards him with one hand and deftly binding a cloth around her mouth, wrists and ankle. She contorted forward, bound like a trussed pig.

In all the commotion, she recognised the faint click of the connecting door between her and Enrico and relaxed a little. He'd heard it too. His momentary distraction eased the pressure on her chest and she screamed another muffled sound against the bindings.

He pushed her into the bed and unable to control the momentum, she rolled onto the floor, hitting her head on the tiles. The last she remembered was the sound of two quick gunshots and a body falling heavily. Next, she was airborne, lifted into arms and hoisted over his shoulder. She passed out.

* * *

The air was sticky and smelt of the sea. Water lapped near her head, but she was dry. It was the first thing she heard. She thought the sunshine warmed her face. She was hot and her face tingled. She was moving forward at a slow, steady pace. A diesel engine quietly hummed.

Her head hurt. A bulging tightness stretched across her cheekbone and eye socket. She tried to hold it, immediately withdrawing her fingers. She pressed again as lightly as she could, her cooling touch relieving the bruising pain.

As her senses caught up, Giuliett realised she was laying on something soft and comfortable. She tentatively opened her eyes, quickly shutting them again as the bright room triggered a blinding headache. She propped a pillow above her eyes, to block the light. Calmly, using her senses to gather information, she tried to make sense of her situation. She instead fell asleep, wrapped in the room's balmy temperature and the constant rocking motion.

The next time she woke, she deliberately kept her eyes closed and listened. It was quiet. The sun was shining. Water slapped against the walls. They were moving more quickly now. She gingerly stretched her legs out. Someone had covered her with soft sheets and light blanket and she stretched into the crisp cleanness and fresh smelling linen. She lay like that for a long moment.

Her arms stretched beneath the sheets. She pulled them up close to her chin, rolled to one side and folded her legs across the bed. Opening her eyes at last, Giuliett found herself alone in a stylish, master cabin of a luxury yacht. It smelt brand new.

Long windows, running parallel with the bed, showed a blue sky streaked in pale pink clouds. She suspected the room was aft, judging by the momentum and the forward-facing layout of the ensuite cabin.

Her bedroom door was closed. She rested on a raised, central king sized bed. American walnut built in cabinetry and off-white upholstery, piped in black, made the room feel elegantly spacious.

She breathed deeply, gently touching the bruise on the side of her swollen cheek. It didn't feel so tight now and the ache in her head had at least dulled. Her eyes rested on the subtle pattern covering a bench chair. It faced a small, leather built in desk creating a perfectly private writing nook.

Slowly she came to focus on the fabric design. To her astonishment, she discovered it was threaded with the Delarno family crest.

Without thinking she sat upright, the action quickly sending her head spinning. Blood drained from her face and she thought she might pass out for a brief moment. Her cheek began to throb. Her hands went to her face and she sat, waiting for the moment to subside.

The room righted itself as bile rose into her throat. This she ignored, her mind now focused on one outcome and one word. Nicholas.

In a fuming tirade, she strode directly to the central cockpit. She faced him from the top of the stairwell. They were under full sail.

"What the fuck are you playing at?" she demanded, challenging the man resembling a modern day pirate and looking all too comfortable at the helm station.

"Principessa!" he responded with a large smile that split his dark features. "How do you like my new boat? She's an absolute ripper! My Ducati on the sea!"

"I asked you a question." Giuliett stood her ground between them, glaring at him as they rocketed in a northerly direction.

He, on the other hand, was having the time of his life, racing the wind along the Italian coastline. His hands confidently held a large, hip height wheel. He was focused, looking straight ahead, completely oblivious to her temper.

His exhilaration was palpable. In fact, his entire body was animated in the joy of the moment.

"No, Giuliett, you demanded an answer." Robbie L's attention was caught by the computerised pad set in the cabinet bench top directly in front of him. His thumb and finger zoomed in the screen.

"Where is Nicholas?" she asked rudely. "I want to see him."

"Nicholas? How should I know! Do I care? That would be a resounding 'Hell No'!"

After a quick glance in her pouting expression, he suddenly laughed.

"That's why you came up here all hot and frothy in your underwear! You can save your time and money honey. I'll tell you right now, he's not into *you*."

He added, "By the way, you're welcome. We'll work out a way for you to thank me later."

"For what?"

"Saving you from that fool Enrico Nero."

"What the fuck are you talking about?"

"A long, sordid story. And you'll get nowhere talking to me like that."

"Like hell I won't. You'd better tell me right now what the fuck is going on."

"You want to watch your mouth young lady, unless you like the taste of Cashmere Bouquet." His tone was terse and he looked at her fully for the first time.

"It's a bit chilly out here, despite the canopy. If you want to stay, my coat is on the chair beside you." He suddenly grinned devilishly at her, a row of white teeth highlighted against his brown skin and shoulder length dark hair. "Or not."

His wandering gaze slid from the top of her glossy blonde hair to her manicured toes in a slow, sensual assessment. Eye candy wrapped in raspberry coloured silk short underwear and camisole, trimmed in matching lace.

"Take a good look." She spat, refusing to move. "It will be the one and only opportunity."

"My, you're a feisty she-devil when you first wake up!" he laughed at her temper. "I'll have to keep that in mind as future reference."

His attention was drawn again to the data feed and electronic map.

"You'll find more suitable attire in the cabin wardrobe, if you so desire to make use of it. Please, be my guest in the master. It has everything you need. Aperitif hour begins at 6pm sharp in the cockpit."

He proudly indicated the seating area and table directly behind him with a sweeping, grand gesture.

"I know what a fricking cockpit is!" She retorted.

"I expect you to be on time." He concluded.

He returned to the sail and his co-ordinates, effectively dismissing her on the spot. And to her own dismay, Giuliett turned on her bare heel and strode back to the cabin without another word or hurled insult in his direction.

30

....

Giuliett appeared on deck at 6pm sharp as requested, dressed in a black pants suit. Her golden hair was loosely pinned and fell in waves to the middle of her back.

Her face, pale and bare of makeup, was sporting a deep purple bruise on her right cheekbone. The colour deepened as it met the corner of her eye. It looked as painful as all get out and he felt, possibly for the first time in his life, a little guilt around the unfortunate mishap.

"Does that hurt?" he asked.

"What do you think?" she sulked. Her bad manners remained despite her princess looks.

She sat on the very edge of the booth, across from him. He handed her a champagne aperitif. She took a long gulp. It had been a crazy day and on an empty stomach, he saw the bubbles go straight to her head.

"Well, if you hadn't have put up such a tantrum, you'd not have hit your head." He said. He reached into an ice bucket beside him. "Here, put this on it."

"A piece of meat?"

"It's rib fillet! And it's wrapped in cling wrap! Don't tell me you're a vego as well."

She looked puzzled. He rolled his eyes.

"A vegetarian. You know, the one's who can't stand meat."

Giuliett shook her head. "No. I'm asking a question. You want me to put meat on my face?"

"Yes silly. It's an old remedy. The meat will bring out the bruising so it doesn't hurt so much." He said. "We do it all the time in Australia. Can't believe you've never done it." Robbie L reached across the table to hand it to her. "Here."

"You're crazy. I'm not putting that on my face!" Giuliett was mortified and then she saw the humorous flicker cross his face.

"Oh ha! Ha!" she said sarcastically. "You're a real joker Robbie L."

"Come on Giuliett. Where's your sense of adventure? We'll use frozen peas instead." He reached into the bucket and pulled out a packet of baby green peas.

"No Robbie L! You're not touching me with any of your stupid home remedies. You're seriously deranged." She laughed for the first time, but she was not entirely amused. "Now, tell me you also have champagne in that bucket of tricks. This girl is getting dry."

He softened a little as he danced like a boxer around her mood.

"Champagne? Yes, I do. But first, let me take a look at that face. I'll be gentle. I promise." He tilted her jaw away from him, so that her head was angled towards her shoulder. He leaned in close.

"Heaven knows I've seen my fair share of broken bones and black eyes. This one's not broken, thank goodness." He said. "But it's pretty bad. I think our best options to help it heal are time and ice. Maybe the first aid kit has that cream that brings out the bruising. It's going to get hella ugly before it gets better. I'll check the kit after dinner."

He felt her relax and as she inhaled a deep, long breath he sensed a wary truce forming. She placed her hand on his linen shirtsleeve, gently pushing his forearm away.

"No need, I'll check it." She said, standing. "But ... This is how we play going forward. I've done everything you asked of me. When I get back, you need to start talking."

Robbie L watched her walk away, the long palazzo styled pants swaying with her hips. When she disappeared below deck, he switched the on-board lights to navigation and filled her champagne glass with mineral water and a slice of lime.

He found some blankets and placed them on her seat.

The distant sounds of life on shore filtered across the water in the indistinguishable noise of town. He'd chosen a secluded bay near the town of Grado to drop anchor. They were protected and anonymous within the lagoon.

Tomorrow he'd push further east along the Italian Adriatic coast, towards the Trieste port. Robbie L was keen to keep moving. In the very least they'd stay in anchorage until that bruise faded and the dust settled in Venice.

The breeze had dropped and the cool night air, dank and salty, left its wet footprint across the decks. In the moonlight, it glistened over the exposed stainless steel.

He looked around his boat with pride. She looked just as magical in the full rising moon. *What do you say Meadow?* He thought suddenly. *You'd have loved being out here too.*

31

. . . .

"All better?" he asked as she sat beside him on the bench seat. "Yes thank you. Much better. You certainly have a unique way of trying to impress a girl." She said.

"I'm not trying to impress you. Let's be clear on that right from the get go."

"What are you trying to do Robbie L?"

"Look ahead." He said.

"Is that why you felt the need to murder my consigliere last night?" She was straight to the point.

"It was always going to be me or him." He was matter of fact. "I won a fair fight. In any case, I did him a favour."

"Is that right? And just why would you think that?" she remained unimpressed.

"Gatto is on the prowl. He's been manoeuvring to push Enrico out of the nest. I saved everyone a lot of time and effort."

"And played into Gatto's hands by the sound of it. I hope that was your intention."

"Not quite. His end is coming too." Robbie L sounded more than confident.

Her eyebrow arched. "That is your opinion, of course. You are no match for Gatto."

"You may be right."

"He'll see you coming a mile off." She said smugly.

"Maybe." He said and he looked straight at her. "But he won't see you."

"You are truly deranged."

"And you're a bigger fool than I first thought, if you can't see what's happening before your very eyes." He was not moved by her insult, and his eyes held an unreadable serious tone.

"Humour me." She said. "Tell me what you think is going down."

"You really have no idea. Wow!" he said, shaking his head. "Did your father teach you nothing?"

"This conversation is over." She stormed. "You are fishing Robbie L and have no idea what you've started, baiting Gatto and the Seta clan."

Giuliett stood. "Not to mention abducting me against my will. You know the outcome for that offence I assume, if Silvio tutored you correctly. I'll take my meal in my room. Don't even think about disturbing me."

He handed her the plate. "Take it."

Waiting until she was just within earshot he commented, "Pocco was right. You have neither the temperament nor the strategic vision to lead. You're a waste of time and energy."

Robbie L cracked a sand crab claw that had been resting on his plate and peeled the shell from the meat. He stuffed the sweet flesh into his mouth.

"What did you say?" she was immediately at his side.

"You heard me." He said before taking a long drink of his beer. He shoved another piece of crabmeat in his mouth.

"What in the fuck does Pocco have to do with this?" she asked.

"There's that word again." He warned, raising the claw to

his mouth and sucking out the juices. He wiped his hands and face on a clean tea towel. She looked at him as if her head was about to explode.

"Pray, Robbie L, what does Don Poccolini have to do with this situation?" she mocked, her diction as deliberate and punctuated as a school mam.

"You went to him to ask for support. Yes?"

She nodded.

He stared at her, authority oozing from him in the one statement. His casual persona switched in the instant. He looked every bit as dangerous as the outlawed motorbike leader he was, and Giuliett quickly sat down opposite him.

"You should have come to me." He stated emphatically.

He took control. The tension notched up between them.

"Gatto and Pocco have been working behind the scenes to cut you and your mother out of the business. Enrico was to be collateral damage to bring you on side with the new terms."

He stared at her for a long moment.

"I bet you thought you were clever. Trying to manipulate Pocco to help you? Sugar, you've been outed. Pocco is a turncoat. You have to know how to play him. And you played the wrong hand. As soon as you met with him, he started calling in favours. He and Gatto are taking over the business right under your cocaine filled nostrils."

He looked at her hard.

"Sugar, you'll never be leader. You won't earn the respect of the Commission with Pocco as your main man. The best future you can hope for in the Commission is the trophy whore, just like your long-time root Anya Frida Volkov."

He saw a flicker of something cross her face.

"Now, if that's what you want, I'll drop you in town tomorrow and you can call Pocco. I'm sure he'll be delighted. And I'll make my merry way back to Sydney on this fine-looking boat to my buddies, who, by the way, have been holding down the fort for me, whilst I've been trying to save your sorry arse."

He'd maintained a steady tone, but as he neared the end of his explanation, his temper rose along with his pitch, beat for beat with hers as she'd listened to him.

He watched her for a long, steady moment as the information penetrated. Her expression tightened into pure rage. He braced himself for her onslaught. The truth hurts. Cuts deeper than any knife wound he'd ever seen.

"This is bullshit!" She screamed angrily. "Non hai capito una sege!"

"I do know my shit, thank you very much!" he roared at the insult. "And what I see is a spoilt little girl wanting to play in a man's world."

Robbie L fed into her immature emotion and finally lost his temper at her arrogance.

"Face up to yourself woman! This is not dress up Gangster Barbie. You're in this business with your eyes open or you go home."

They seethed at each other in the small space of the cockpit.

"If you can't do it, here's my phone. Go on, give Gatto a call." He taunted. "Or Pocco. I don't give a fuck. It's your life! All I know is I've wasted enough of my time and energy helping you."

"Gosh damn and darn it!" He was beyond angry. His fist slammed on the table. "Now I've gone and sworn." He pointed an accusing finger in her face.

"See what you made me do! Because of you, I've broken my

ninety-nine day not swearing streak. Bugger it!"

She looked at the man-child as if he'd grown tentacles from his ears, and shook her head.

"What the fuck do I do now?" she asked.

32

. . . .

"You sit down, nourish yourself and grab on like any normal human would when they're given a lifeboat." He said through gritted teeth, eerily quietly, although his exasperation was still clear.

"Now is the time to explore your options." He said moving the blanket so she could sit opposite him.

Instead she squashed in beside him. "Is that who you think you are?" she sidled closer, flirting with her eyes and her mouth. "Are you my saviour Robbie L?" she asked, pushing her body close to him.

Giuliett paused in the tactic she'd used often to get what she wanted. Robbie L looked her up and down and remained unmoved. Her eyes narrowed at his rejection.

"You think you have the right to make decisions for me?" she retaliated scornfully.

"Don't be absurd woman! I'm giving you an opportunity to have what you desire. You either want the role or not. Action without a plan will get you nowhere. Or dead."

He shoved the discarded plate in front of her. "First things first, eat your dinner."

"I can't tell if you want me to be your lover, your sister or your child?" She eyeballed him from close proximity, trying hard to read his closed expression.

"None of the above." He said. "Eat. It's getting cold. You've had nothing all day. You're going to need your strength tonight."

"Lover." She concluded quietly. "And that will never happen."

Robbie L ignored her assumption with a comment of his own.

"First we address your addiction. This boat is a clean zone. And since we're going to be in anchorage for a long time to come, you'd better get used to it."

Giuliett opened her mouth to speak. Enrico was so much easier to manipulate.

"As you wish." She said sarcastically. "You're the boss, apparently."

"You'll pull your weight around here. I've no time for princesses. You'll be tasked every day with specific duties in the maintenance and running of the boat." He said.

"I'm not a fucking child." She retorted.

"That's it! I'm getting the soap." He said, standing. "You'll clean up your mouth and your act."

"You're going to hold me down now and wash me?" She coiled back.

"If it comes to that," he said, and it was no idle threat. He returned moments later with the bar of fragrant soap and slammed it on the table between them.

"I'd suggest unless you want to suck on that, you'll watch your language." He said.

She looked at him horrified. "You wouldn't dare." She said.

"Is that a challenge Giuliett?" he replied, his eyes glinting at the prospect of bringing her into line.

Giuliett put her head down, staring at the soft-shell crab pasta he'd served for her dinner. Despite its appeal, her appetite waned and her cravings grew as her long-time tonic for facing threats kicked into full gear.

She scowled at his face and to her horror a tear slid down her cheek and plopped on the timber topped table, near her plate.

He didn't miss a trick, despite being occupied with his own meal.

"Tears don't move me." He said. "Particularly when they come from spoiled brats. Eat your dinner and then you'll clean up. After that you can go to bed. I'll do first watch."

33

·················

Paris, France

They could be any European couple, cuddled together in the outdoor café, ignoring everything but each other. Francesca wrapped her gloved hands around Sinclair's. On the chilly spring morning, she brought his bare fingers to her lips.

"I love you." She said, staring into his chocolate eyes. "I'm so happy."

He smiled at her. "Me too. I'm glad you decided to come. I know the daytime is lonely for you."

"But we have the evenings together." She said.

"And maybe we can stay a few days longer. Just the two of us! With Marnie and Pop on extended childcare duty we don't have to rush back. They'll be happy to stay on, it's so beautiful in Fiji this time of year." She concluded with a twinkle in her eye, pressing his cold bare fingers to her cheeks.

"Let's not get ahead of ourselves." He warned. "I need approval from the department to extend my leave."

Francesca was undeterred. "They will." She said confidently.

The soldier medic watched the other delegates enter the government building across the street. "Well," he said. "I'm sorry but I have to go. Duty calls."

She watched his professional distance wedge between them. Francesca refused to let it in. She cupped his jaw within her hands and brought his lips to hers. She held them there for a long moment.

"Good luck today with your presentation." She whispered.

"Thanks." He responded absently. "Text you when I'm done."

She watched him cross the street, his height and hair the colour of dark sand easily distinguishable amongst the delegates. He disappeared into the building and she sighed, feeling instantly alone and missing him more. She ordered another pot of tea and pastry and sat in the grey glow of morning light, waiting for the day to warm up a little more.

The waiter came to clear her table.

"Excuse me sir," she asked. "Do you know this address?"

"Oh yes madam," he said. "It's in the Temple District. Catch the metro to Temple and walk towards the Temple Gardens. Or if you prefer the metro station Saint-Sebastien Froissart is also close."

"Is it a nice area to visit?"

"It's an arts and restaurant quarter, and Le Marais is not far from there."

"Oh. Sounds like a full day out. Thank you."

"You're welcome."

Francesca's heart was in her mouth. Alessandro had specifically instructed she stay away from the property. Nicholas encouraged her participation at every opportunity.

Curiosity and fate are a tempting combination. Feeling safe in the knowledge that Sinclair was not too far away, Francesca followed her wilful heart and ignored her instincts.

After all Francesca, she thought, life was to be lived in the moment. And today, the moments belong to me.

34

According to her maps GPS, the apartment was another five-minute walk. Was she now close enough to satisfy her curiosity? Francesca questioned if she should continue as second thoughts filled her head. It was all well and good to be bolshy in the safety of a café, miles from her current location. Quite a different matter to be in the very precinct, where she was told, that a mere visit would put lives at risk.

She entered the park's green space, the Temple Gardens and stopped. It was almost the point of no return. She punched key words into the search engine on her phone.

A little history lesson always settled the nerves and put her world into context. She sat down on a nearby bench and followed the digital information trail. It led her to the Knights of the Templar. Francesca marvelled that she was indeed present in their very space, albeit centuries later.

The more she read, the more her imagination absorbed her thoughts, creating the balm that calmed her nerves and shifted her focus. What might their days look like? She thought about the brutal training they'd have undertaken and the boys who turned into men in this very place. It must've been an incredibly noisy neighbourhood, with the pounding of metal on anvil, markets and leather workers, cloth merchants and maybe even jewellers. Her mind turned to the dreadful massacre that ended their tenure.

From heroes to villains on the whim of a king and she sent a silent prayer for their souls.

A wayward children's ball bounced in her direction and tapped her on the leg. Her mind quickly returned to the present. She kicked the ball gently to the child and looked around her. The area was now filling with tourists, families and musicians.

Fortune favours the brave, she thought. So with her heart in her hands, Francesca conjured the spirit of the Templar Knights, found her bearings and forged ahead.

She crossed Rue de Bretagne without so much as a glance at the designated building. A row of boutique stores and cafes perfect for window-shopping lay ahead. It wouldn't be the first time she'd use one as a covert observation post.

"Where are you?" She mumbled to herself as she stood, pretending to be absorbed by the menu options on stands outside the café and the window displays of pastry goods. In the reflection she studied the buildings around her, searching for the correct building number.

Every now and then she'd check her phone. The GPS indicated the apartment building was directly behind her. Francesca resisted the urge to turn around and stare. Instead, she strode into the café opposite it and took a seat near the window. Her heart was pounding in her chest.

This is crazy. She thought. She removed her outer coat and laid it over the seat beside her. Francesca looked at her phone again like it would magically reassure her and licked her lips nervously. *What do you think is going to happen?* She asked herself. *You're a tourist. Act like a tourist.* And she looked around the busy café, pulled out a pen and journaling book as well as a tourist map of Paris.

The waiter came to take her order. She gazed out the picture window to the busy street, people watching and settled into the location. Every now and then she'd write in her book and flick through her phone.

She took a photograph of the menu, the wooden bench that was her table, the ornate iron decor and the way the light came through the window and highlighted every indent of the hand-blown glass of her water carafe. And she hoped that was enough to convince anyone on lookout, she was just another star struck tourist fascinated by all things French.

By now, she'd really settled in, and concluding that her anxiety was more about post-traumatic stress relating to Silvio Delarno, rather than giving up a Guardian hideout, she relaxed into the Parisian café scene. She grabbed a French magazine from the stack nearby and flicked through the fashion pages. She came to the real estate section.

Francesca imagined her father house hunting in Paris. It was not an easy task. How could it be only moments before she could all but see the Crusaders riding through the streets, and yet to imagine her father buying an apartment in Paris, she simply couldn't reconcile that part of his life?

"You think you know someone." She said to herself.

Across the street, an attractive looking, well-dressed blonde exited the target apartment building. She crossed the street and strode confidently into the café. The staff greeted her warmly and a quick conversation was followed by laughter.

Francesca caught herself daydreaming about the woman's life. What would it be like, living here in such a volatile, historically rich place? She laughed at herself. She'd been living off grid for too long. Was that not her entire formative years with Nicholas and the Delarno clan? A life filled with extended family summer vacations in Italy and Spain?

Within moments, the woman was returning towards the door, goods packed carefully in a string bag that dangled off her forearm and two cups of take away coffee in china cups. Her stride broke slightly at the sight of Francesca sitting in the window. Their eyes locked momentarily and Francesca smiled as she always did, and looked out the window in the direction of the gardens.

The woman smiled tentatively back and kept walking. She let herself directly into the building without a second glance.

With nothing but pure fantasy to back her claim and in an act of pure naivety, Francesca concluded her father had chosen well. The neighbourhood felt safe and friendly. People could come and go in their new lives and be anonymous.

Nothing to see here, she thought.

With that, the guilt of being a busy body snoop resumed. Her order arrived, making her visibly jump and Francesca decided as soon as it was consumed, she'd hightail down Rue whatever to get the hell out of there and walk towards Le Marais.

She'd satisfied her curiosity. It was never her intention to visit the actual apartment. Francesca just needed to know the location. Get the visual and feel for the kind of place her father would've chosen for the victims of crime. Somehow it made her feel closer to him and this part of his life.

Francesca finished her coffee and stood. If life was a moment to be lived, despite her earlier thoughts, this was not her moment to be sleuthing around places she had no business being in.

Besides which, Sinclair would almost be done with his

presentation to the World Health Authority Summit. Maybe he could meet her in the famed district for some overdue relaxation.

And then her mind changed.

"What in the hell is this all about?" she said out loud, watching unbelievably as Nicholas and Sinclair arrived together at the apartment building and went immediately into the foyer entrance. Francesca sat down dumbfounded. She could not even think straight for a full five minutes.

35

· · · · · · · · · · · · · · · · · ·

Panic set in. With it came emotional indecision. *Do I stay or do I go?* She thought. Weighing her options, she looked at her phone again for some hidden inspiration. She fiddled with the teacup and spoon. The detective in her was definitely ready to stay. The abiding citizen was pushing to leave.

"Wouldn't it be nice if all the secrets were out."

A voice inside her spoke up. It seemed so clear and loud that Francesca actually turned around to see if someone had joined her.

The café was humming at a busy pace as visitors filed in for a late morning snack.

And the former detective and the diligent citizen sat by the window and waited, scolding and consoling each other in turn, terrified and curious at the same time, feeling the guilt of knowing what she couldn't tell her husband and wishing she'd just done as she was supposed to do all along. Go shopping.

Her phone rang, vibrating in her hands. It was Sinclair.

"Hi babe." She tried to sound natural. "How did you go this morning?"

"That's what I'm ringing about. I know we agreed to meet afterwards, but something's come up and I need to be in meetings all afternoon. I'm sorry. I know we talked about doing the Louvre."

"That's okay." She said. "Are you still at the venue?"

"Yeah."

"Oh okay, I might go shopping or something. Will I see you tonight?"

"Sure thing. Looking forward to it. I've got to go. Love you."

"Okay, love you."

Francesca hung up and her decision was made. She was definitely staying.

Almost immediately, the blonde from the café, Sinclair and Nicholas exited the building. She looked in the direction of the café before climbing into the front passenger seat of a black SUV. Nicholas slid into the driver's seat. Sinclair opened the door of the passenger seat, behind the woman.

He checked the surroundings before climbing in, a visual sweep of the location. Francesca examined his manner. He was ready for combat.

The car pulled out into the traffic. Brake lights showed and they stopped. Sinclair turned back towards the café. Francesca ducked behind the alcove near the window.

He climbed out of the car and headed towards it. Francesca ran to the waiters.

"Is there another way out?" she asked, glancing towards the front door.

They handed her a key to the toilet, indicating it was located behind the building. She smiled, "Merci."

Francesca found herself in a back alley and leaving the key in the door, she hightailed it down the narrow-paved street, took a left-hand corner down another narrow gap between the buildings and entered Rue de Bretagne in front of the waiting vehicle.

She stayed protected at the juncture, glancing behind her and listening intently for the sound of footsteps following her. She was seriously out of practice and out of breath.

It crossed her mind that she was now behaving beyond ridiculous. She could appear, as if out of a shop and pretend she'd never seen them. After all, she was meant to be shopping. And she had every right to be there.

But she was as hopeless liar as she was curious cat. Now, because of her actions and despite having told Nicholas she wanted out, this former detective was well and truly back in the middle of the clandestine world she so wanted to avoid.

Peeking around the corner, she saw Nicholas watching the street ahead. Every now and then, his eyes would dart to the rear view and side mirrors.

Francesca watched Sinclair cross the road and climb back into the truck. It merged with the traffic. She waited. She knew Sinclair would still be on watch.

All traffic was heading in a one-way direction and Francesca stepped out onto the pavement to hail a taxi. And then she stopped herself. It was a physical and mental decision.

She was not doing this. She simply was not going to be dragged back into that crazy life. She'd made a commitment to herself.

Tonight at the Hotel, she'd talk to Sinclair in a logical, thought out way to find out what today was all about. Skulking around behind his back was not the answer to a healthy relationship.

"Seen enough?"

"Oh!" Francesca visibly jumped.

"I'm begging your pardon monsieur?" She stuttered in French, turning to face the direct glare of Sinclair's angry expression. She instantly looked between him and the street ahead.

"Sinclair! But how?" she said. "Oh honey, this is a nice surprise!"

"Hmm." He replied sternly. "You're a terrible liar Francesca Salucci." He grabbed her by the elbow. "We need to keep moving." He glanced around, another quick reconnaissance and hailed a cab.

"Not a word." He warned as they climbed in.

36

········○········

She didn't speak until they'd arrived in the bedroom of their apartment. That was a full taxi ride to the hotel located across town, through the foyer, up the lift, along the whole length of the corridor and into the apartment room they'd rented for their week together in Paris.

It was time to face him. But by now Francesca had worked through so many emotions and questions she was mentally exhausted. Every one of those feelings had played across her face as she stared out the window or straight-ahead avoiding eye contact with him.

She opened her mouth and shut it again.

"I can't speak." She said, putting her hands up to him palms open, and headed to the bathroom. Next, she did the only thing she could do at such a moment and ran a bath. She plied it with an unnecessary amount of body wash and shampoo to create the right amount of bubbles.

She undressed, walked out to the small kitchenette, grabbed a bottle of champagne from the fridge, one glass and returned to the bath, shutting the door behind her.

Her toes touched the cold cloud then sunk into the warm abyss. She lay, shoulders disappearing under the rising warmth. Her head relaxed against the padded rest. Francesca took a great swig of her champagne, refilled her glass and then lay back fully, shutting her eyes.

After a long while, she heard the door open. He sat on a plush, single armchair and lit the fragrant candles. He closed the white shutter blinds, creating linear sunlight beams that streamed across the tub and white walls.

Francesca waited for his explanation in the silence. The tension between them grew, filling the space, crackling like a pent-up fire. Francesca sunk further backwards, sliding down into the cooling water so that it slopped at the back of her head. She swirled the waning bubbles.

She looked at him directly and sensing it, his head raised upwards from examining the floor at his feet to meet her gaze.

"I wanted to tell you." He said. "I don't like secrets between us. It's a covert mission."

"Involving Nicholas and Defence? I find that hard to believe. But then, with him, why should anything surprise me at all." She said. "He can make even the stupidest idea seem logical."

"The woman is a high value target. I needed to ensure she was safe, and that the handover to her family was secure. She had been expatriated to Afghanistan against her will. My team happened across her on another mission. We organised her safe return to her family."

"So tell me how the Australian Defence Force is now working with a crime boss of the highest order." She asked.

"They're not."

Francesca thought for a moment. "He's compromised you. Hasn't he." She said. "That's why you can't look at me."

"The only compromise is my knowledge of who she really is and how I know that. Our relationship with Nicholas Delarno is not something I usually disclose for obvious reasons."

"I'm going to kill him." She said.

There was another long silence between them.

"Is she the reason we're in Paris?" Francesca asked.

"In part. When I saw the opportunity to talk at the summit I made arrangements to accompany her, her colleague and two other targets. Defence came on board with the suggestion. It solved a little diplomatic problem for them as well."

"I only saw one woman."

"The others were extricated yesterday utilising French operatives."

"And how in the hell is Nicholas involved in this? You let him take the woman?"

"She requested that he accompany her back to safety. There is a family connection. I'm sorry Francesca. I can't tell you anymore than that. To do so compromises the mission."

"Yeah, well we wouldn't want that." She said sarcastically. Francesca knew Nicholas's family. That woman was not part of the Delarno family.

"Christ! You'd think I was the criminal!" He said. "Why don't we have a little talk about you?"

"What about me?"

"Funny you were in that exact location all morning. Funny that you happened to be in the café directly opposite a Guardian safe house."

Francesca squirmed. She let the plug out, stood and he handed her a towel. She wrapped it around her.

"If you must know, I knew it was the place my father had chosen as a hideout for victims of crime. I wanted to see it for myself, to shut the lid on what the hell my life has been about for all these years."

Francesca felt the emotions come forward in a rush.

"I wanted to be closer to him. To better understand that part of his life I never even knew about. I'm tired of being told about it. I wanted to see it for myself.

"But, never in my wildest dreams did I think I'd find you there with another woman! Is that where you scampered off to yesterday as well?"

"I didn't sleep with her! She's a victim of a crime. I went yesterday to check in with the French agents who were on watch!"

Francesca almost face-palmed. "French agents?"

"Yes honey. French agents. Did you think I'd let a real potential threat escape so easily?"

Suddenly she felt so very foolish.

His phone pipped with a message. *Sir, wheels up at Le Bourget. Cargo secure.*

"Can we stop arguing now?" he asked. "I didn't suggest we meet in Paris to fight. You've been teasing me for long enough in that bath tub. I'm only a man … in desperate need."

37

Naples, Italy

"Minister would you like to comment on the acceptance of the humanitarian ship docking in Sicily today?"

Sebastino Nero smiled at the reporter. "Yes of course Signorina."

"I will continue to work with the governments of our partner nations so that the load of suffering will be shared with Europe. Italy cannot and will not stand alone in the war against human trafficking. It is a shared responsibility in our region.

"I will continue to talk with our security forces to ensure that the perpetrators are brought to swift justice. And I respectfully ask again, that governments from the affected regions of Northern Africa and Syria put human lives above their thirst for power. Our region can thrive economically and socially when we all work together.

"To my fellow Italians, the people about to dock in Palermo will not be staying in Italy and draining our economy. I've been able to negotiate with our friends in Canada and Germany, who I'm happy to announce today, will be taking the majority of the displaced peoples."

"Thank you Minister. Can you tell us what brings you to Naples today?"

"Thank you, yes Signorina," he said with a devastating smile.

"Of course, I've come to Naples today to visit the Castel dell' Ovo and discuss plans to rejuvenate Naples; to continue to make Naples strong. Naples is the engine room of the south. Thank you."

He smiled for a photographic opportunity and excused himself from the journalists.

Sebastino strolled the wide stone walkway bridging the mainland waterfront, the Caracciolo, and the islet Megaride. Long ago, a thin strip of rock once connected the two.

The politician held his phone up and began a live feed for his thousands of followers. He watched as they each joined him on the walk. It was a glorious summers day in the port city of Naples and he was delighted to show this part of the city in all its glory.

"Welcome all. Today we are in Naples. Legend says this tuff island is the final resting place of the mermaid Parthenope." He began. "The islet itself is a narrow and long rock tuff, and the villa that once stood here was built by General Lucius Licinius Lucullus who returned to Naples after making his fortune in Asia. In fact, some of the columns of the original villa were used in the construction of the castle we see today.

"Castel dell' Ovo has been a villa, a monastery, a fort and a prison. It's had many names since the Middle Ages. Can you guess two others?" He asked his legion of followers on the live.

"Yes, that is correct. I see two names coming up on my feed. Castrum Lucallanum and Fortezza of San Salvatore. Bravo tutti."

"Did you know there are many stories about this location? The most famous legend is the story of the magical egg. In this story, the ancient Roman poet Virgile took the first egg of a chicken and placed it in a vase. Next, he placed the vase in a gilded cage and hid it somewhere within the foundations of the original Villa.

"Virgile said that the caged egg had protective powers and whilst ever the egg is intact, Naples is strong. Some people treat this story as a joke, because we suspect Virgile wanted to laugh at the people of Naples."

He turned the camera around to show the shoreline and panoramic views of the ancient city.

"I say, look at this place. Look at her beauty and her strength. Regardless of your feelings towards the story of the powerful egg, I tell you that Naples is ripe for another revival. And that is not a joke.

"I can deliver for Naples because my voice is heard loud and clear in government. Change is coming for Naples. I am bringing it and with it, comes jobs and money for the people of Naples."

In true Sebastino Nero style he interwove historical facts and political ideology in an engaging commentary, feeding on the heartbeat and desire of the people. Wit and insight into his personal life provided the hook. Creating suspense kept his followers coming back.

He stopped at the large entrance. "We enter this castle directly from the walkway. Beware, first we have to pass directly in line of these forbidding cannons." He zoomed the camera up towards the battlements, and then to his face showing a wary, respectful expression.

"Now we are at the entrance." He turned the camera around. "This picture depicts the castle during Renaissance times," he said. "And you can see I'm not alone in my appreciation for this culturally significant place." He moved his phone around the stone portico, showing the visitors gathered in the castle entrance at the end of the walkway as they smiled and waved.

"And so, now, unfortunately, it is time for me to say goodbye my friends. It's time to go to work for the people of Italy. Thank you for joining me on this lovely walk towards Castel dell' Ovo in Naples. Ciao tutti."

Sebastino posed for a few photographs and after a few moments, excused himself. A concierge appeared ushering him towards the prestigious Italia meeting room within the castle itself, via a small room that was once used as a private chapel. He left the politician alone and shut the heavy timber door behind him.

The stone cavern with high arched ceilings was lit by rows of candles. The room was cool and dank. Religious fresco paintings and the smell of burning incense reminded him of the monks who once resided here.

A small stone altar, bare of any decoration was in the centre. To the side, a kneeling stool faced rows of thin candles embedded in shiny brass holders. Three timber benches in a row faced the altar.

"Nicci, my brother," he said, stepping into him at the Capo's extended hand and gave his friend a great bear hug. "It's good to see you again."

Nicholas Delarno smiled at him. "And you, my friend. You have them eating out of your hands." He squeezed his compatriot high on the left shoulder.

Sebastino shrugged. "All in a day's work." He said. "Now, what can I do to help?"

"We found Anya. I've just hand delivered her to Sergei safe and sound."

"Thank God. Does Giuliett know?"

"Not from me. But I made sure the Volkov family knew exactly who served their sister up to the Taliban. I don't think we'll need to worry about Giuliett and Enrico interfering any more in our business."

"I wouldn't give Enrico a second thought, full stop." Sebastino said. "Robbie L finished him in Venice. Gatto and Pocco are out for blood. Although, I can't be sure that they're all puff and no action. Makes you wonder, particularly for a man like Gatto."

"Should I be worried?" Nic asked.

"I don't think so. Robbie L's got Giuliett. It's between the Seta family and him. Robbie L works alone, you know that. Besides, it takes the heat off us."

Sebastino paused for a moment. "Can't say I'm surprised he made his move with her. I've been watching him sniff around that family like a bitch on heat."

"Take out the weakest animal in the pride." Nic said in agreement.

"Si, si. And it plays out well for you my friend." Sebastino smiled.

"How do you figure that?"

"I hear that your family has increased its holdings." Sebastino said.

"Oh?"

"Bice has given the business to Alessandro."

"When did that happen?" Nic glanced at his friend in surprise.

"The very day Robbie L broke up the Seta clan. That's where it doesn't look good for the Delarno name."

"Hmm." Nic nodded. "And Gatto has confirmed his allegiance to my uncle?"

Sebastino shrugged. "Who would know, but Gatto and Pocco are working together, that is certain. And maybe Robbie L is part of their group too."

"Some might say it's an extremely fortunate event." Sebastino said drily. "Timely, in fact, given the recent demise of Carlo Seta at the hand of a Delarno."

"What are you inferring Sebastino?"

"Well, let me see. It's now three Delarno at the table."

"There has always been the three of us." Nic said.

"Yes, but Alessandro was impartial. And now with taking hold of Seta he brings that cause across to Delarno way of thinking. And if Robbie L brings Pocco as well."

"You think there's an imbalance of power. Who's to say Robbie L is on board with us? You and I both know that Pocco is a turncoat to the highest bidder. And Gatto will never come to us. I don't see it as a problem, yet. We wait and see what rolls out after this shakedown. And we wait until Volkov makes his move."

Sebastino nodded.

"In any case, we need to settle on a new advisor sympathetic to our cause." The politician said. "I'm thinking Bruno Moretti. He shores up the middle where Pocco flips and flops. Pocco likes him too so he won't see the appointment as a threat."

Nicholas thought about it for a moment. "Castello will be pissed."

"Another from the North? We can't afford it. I think we risk dividing the group. We need a central or southern family."

"I'll approach Moretti and smooth the way with Castello. We don't need them shoring up Seta. Let's keep that family isolated for the moment and wait for Volkov." Nic said, making his decision swiftly.

Sebastino nodded.

"You really didn't know about it before hand?" he asked.

"No. I didn't." Nicholas looked concerned. "Not this time."

Sebastino straightened up. His voice lowered in a stern warning.

"No-one could find you. It was a huge risk Nicholas, to disappear so soon after the takeover. You're lucky Pocco was so caught up with Gatto's scheming. If he'd known the truth of your whereabouts, Pocco would've invoked the trial in absentia. You know what he's like.

"And I don't know if we'd have had the numbers to protect you. I speak as a friend, give it up Nicholas. She will literally be the death of you. For what?"

Nicholas looked surprised. "I've been trying to secure Anya."

"In Australia and Fiji?"

Nicholas began to protest.

"Don't worry I kept it to myself. But if I can find out, so can the others. It's a dangerous game for a bit of fluff."

"I know we're like brothers," Nicholas warned, "but you'd better watch out Sebastino. You'll not talk about Francesca that way. Ever."

"Santa Madre di Dio! She's with that soldier. Leave her be." Sebastino was unapologetic.

"Yeah, well that soldier found Anya, and he knows her story, so we need to keep them close."

There was a short tense silence between them.

"Your father was there when I took the oath to protect Francesca." Nic said. "He took a hell of a risk going against Silvio that day. Christ Sebastino, we were children! Who knew back then she would turn out to be a cop?

"On your father's life and for me right now, it's a lifelong commitment, whether we want it or not." Nicholas said. "I have to abide by the tradition. It's what separates us from the anarchy of Seta."

Sebastino sighed loudly, knowing it to be the truth.

"Si, si. Our family has a legacy, aligned with the Delarno clan." He said. "That intent remains today. I have your back but I say again it's a foolish act to keep her so close in the picture. The Commission will not stand for it."

"Thank you, friend. I appreciate your loyalty and that of your family." Nicholas said.

"How do you want to play it forward?" Sebastino asked.

"We need to protect Alessandro. Let me talk to him to see what support he might need. Robbie L has the ego to handle Pocco and Gatto. Giuliett will go with him because at this point she has no choice. Plus, as I said, I don't want to be close when Volkov strikes."

"I agree. What about the Nigerians? What do you want to do there?"

"This government continues to roll from one disaster to another. Yours is the only voice cutting through at the moment. Alessandro and I've been setting up a private enterprise linked with the maritime insurance business.

"Keep sinking their refugee boats so the aid ships feed the news cycle. Also, I want their income sabotaged. We want to cause as much disruption as possible for them. We'll take a hit, but the gain for us will be worth it in the end." Nic said, lowering his voice.

"Make sure you let key operatives in your team know so they're not caught in any crossfire and can prepare for combat and retribution. I have a solution for the government and you're going to deliver it." Nic said.

"Sebastino, be sure to let your operatives know they'll be duly compensated for their financial hits when we're done."

"When do we start?" The young politician asked.

"A matter of weeks. The Nigerian brothers' days are numbered."

38
....

The Adriatic Sea
Mathraki, Greece

"Got more cheek than a bitch with a face lift ..." Robbie L rapped the words to Avi Chenza's hit song.

Camped up on deck, his iPod belting out a diverse playlist, the biker relaxed in the canvas swag looking skyward. The night was clear and mellow. The moon was high and full.

"Catchy lyrics." Giuliett commented, climbing the short staircase to the upper deck of the luxury cruiser.

"Principessa!" he shouted happily. "Welcome! Join me on the fore deck."

She looked at him, shaking her head in bemusement. "Really Roberto," she said, "It always sound like you swallowed a nautical terminology dictionary when you direct me around your boat!"

"Oh, come on honey, that's a bit rough. Why don't you love my pleasure craft?" He grinned at her. A mutual truce had been achieved during the last week as they slowly cruised south along the Adriatic coast. It had to. It was either work something out or kill each other.

Differences had been laid to rest, and he'd given her the time, space and direction she'd needed to push through the addiction withdrawal.

"Come and grab a slab of moonlight with me." He said, patting the space beside him. "How are you going with those patches?"

"Oxytocin is meant to be the love drug. So why am I not feeling that much love at the moment?" She asked plopping down on the canvas and cotton bedding he'd rolled out on the deck.

"You'll get through it. Not long now."

"I think so too. I definitely feel calmer overall. But sometimes, my feelings are very intense. And I keep dreaming about my father. There's a lot of emotion coming up every time I think about him."

"I could be a smart arse and say don't think about him, but that's probably not the answer you're looking for. Sorry, I can't help you sister. Daddy's not doing their bit is not my area of expertise. The drug can bring up negative emotions too. So it could be that."

He drummed out the beat of the song with his fingers on his hips. His feet twitched in time with the rhythm.

"Maybe."

He filled the short silence with a comment on the evening.

"Do you ever stop talking?" she asked. "Or moving? You're so amped up all the time."

"Just part of the natural charm I guess." He said. "My name's not Robert by the way. Robbie is short for Robin."

"Oh. I beg your pardon." She said. "I apologise. I just assumed it was Robert; you Australians seem to shorten every word."

"That's because it's so hot over there. The less you have to say the better."

There was another awkward pause. He'd noticed a change in her today. The differences in their upbringing and lifestyle were clear and obvious in their early days on the yacht.

So, he'd pushed her physically and mentally all the way to Greece, breaking down the barriers and attitudes between the haves and have-nots. And conquering the challenges was beginning to be the making of her.

"I've been wondering Robbie L; you never talk about your family."

"There's not much to say."

"Well, you know I'm an only child. Do you have any brothers or sisters?"

"My sister's dead. There's just me and my crew and that's the way I like it."

"What about a girlfriend? Do you have someone special in your life?" she probed.

"Are you sure those patches aren't making you horny Giuliett? Because, I have to tell you, you're not my type. To be sure, if you were, I'd have jumped your bones in Venice."

She blushed. "No. I was just making conversation."

"Now look who's doing all the talking." He said.

He glanced over at her. She was looking directly skyward.

"I have someone in my life." He said quietly.

"Do you miss her?"

"Every single day."

"What's her name?"

"Meadow."

"That's a pretty name."

"What about you? Who's your special someone?" he asked.

"I don't have one."

"That's not true. I wasn't born yesterday."

"I don't understand that comment." She said.

"You can't fool me. What's her name?"

Giuliett looked at him surprised.

"Anya. Her name is Anya." She said quietly. "But she is lost to me now."

Giuliett sighed. In the moonlit night she lay staring skyward, fighting the troubled emotions bubbling away just under the surface.

Robbie L's playlist turned to Lenny Kravitz. He sang along with the lyrics.

"Your turn." He said handing her an imaginary microphone.

She shook her head. It didn't bother him. He didn't skip a beat and sang to the starry night and moon above.

At the end of the song, Giuliett propped up on her elbow and faced him.

"Make love to me." She said. "Up here, on deck."

"You don't know what love is Giuliett." He said gruffly.

"Have sex with me then. Make me feel alive, Robbie L. You, who never gets any closer than a scratch at the edge of emotions, have nothing to lose."

"What's that supposed to mean?" he asked.

"Every time we get close to an emotional conversation about feelings, you back down, change the subject or become just plain annoying." She challenged. "So, what's your go Robbie L?"

"I don't have to explain myself to you." He said, starting to stand.

Giuliett gently placed her hand on his. "Please. Don't go. I'm sorry. It must be the patches." She smiled sadly at him. "I could really do with the company tonight. It's just that, you know so much about me. I've been thinking I don't know very much about you."

"It's better that way. What you don't know can't hurt you." He lay beside her.

"Can I chose a song from your list?" she asked.

"Sure. Take a pick."

She chose a country ballad. He looked at her surprised.

"You didn't strike me as a country chic." He said.

"I'm not. But it's nice and quiet and evokes the kind of emotion I'm seeking. And I know you like it. It's the first song you choose when you want to play your music."

Her big eyes looked at him. And in the moonlight, on the deck of his beautiful yacht, Robbie L gave into his lonely desires and kissed her tentatively.

He suckled the hollow of her neck. She groaned softly, clasping her hands over his. His kiss deepened as rough hands slid between her thighs. Heat vibrated through the flimsy cotton of her flowing skirt. He caressed the supple skin of her stomach, and his warm hands filled the space, fingers gently rubbing the delicate skin at her hips.

Her back arched to his touch. He pushed the skirt up and finding the string tie of her bikini bottoms, he pulled. Pent up passions released an urgent whisper close to his ear.

"Don't stop."

His eyes rose to meet hers and that beautiful face. She smiled shyly at him.

He felt her fingers slip along the side of his naked torso, scarred and marked in tribal paint. She sought the hollow of his back, tracing the band of his board shorts to his hips. Gently sliding back and forth for a few moments, she traced a long winding, trail from his hips to his shoulders. The action continued in one fluid motion, ending with her arms resting, fingers clasped above her head, deliberately vulnerable to his touch.

"I've wanted you from the second I saw you." She said. "Satisfy your need Robbie L."

39

. . . .

The biker woke to the smell of fuel and something not right. Water lapping against the hull at the stern alerted him to movement at the back of the boat. His eyes opened to the dark night. A small sound behind him and he instinctively turned his body portside as the back of the tommy hawk axe skimmed his right shoulder blade and slammed into the deck.

Robbie L grunted loudly, springing to his feet and pushing the offender as they came crashing onto the deck of the luxury yacht. The smell of fuel grew stronger as they wrestled, and the biker could almost taste it on the assailant's hands as his fist punched the air between them. Robbie L danced around him.

Below deck he could hear Giuliett engaged in her own scuffle.

There's only two. He thought, circling the attacker again and wasting no time.

Robbie L took the fist to the side of his torso and brought the offender in close with the follow through. Pulling him downwards, the momentum brought the assailant towards the biker's hip. The attackers face connected with a satisfying crack.

He let out an agonised cry. Next an upwardly mobile knee met his jaw and the biker's fist slammed into the side of attackers head. With that, Robbie L cartwheeled the attacker overboard and hurried towards the boat's interior access point.

Two people were huddled together on the ground. Giuliett was between the small bar and lounge.

Robbie L roared. The sound reverberated around the cabin, echoing into the quiet cove they'd selected for safe anchorage. He thundered towards the intruder who pulled the girl up as a human shield. He held a gun to her side.

She looked as white as a sheet but her face and mouth were set in a determined line and her eyes darted taking in the situation, quick as a whip.

Robbie L stood, facing off the offender in the small space.

"You won't get her out of here." He said.

"Who said I want her?" He taunted. "But we all know you do."

Robbie L resisted the urge to dance a fistfight circle with the offender in the confines. One step closer and he'd reach the pistol hidden in a pocket at the chart table. Robbie L stepped forward and to his surprise, the pocket was empty.

The intruder held his ground. He laughed and dug the gun's nozzle into the soft tissue below her ribs. Giuliett winced.

"Put your hands where I can see them." he shouted.

Robbie L brought his hands up.

"Let her go." He said.

"Or what?" the intruder taunted, bringing her closer to him. She was almost within reach. "Walk." He said, directing the biker away from the only exit.

Mid stride, Giuliett was pushed violently towards him and in her surprise at the action, lost her footing. She fell heavily.

The biker lunged forward, grabbing her upper arm with one hand, breaking her fall inches from the floor. His injured shoulder dislocated with the sudden outward movement. He cried out as it gave way under the strain.

Twisting, he took her weight across his upper torso, saving his shoulder and sliding her down his left arm. He let her gently onto the ground.

Continuing in the one perpetual movement, he quickly stepped over her prone body and finding his balance, shot his left leg out towards the intruder in a full leg extension.

The turning kick caught the attacker off guard, as the biker's foot slapped him powerfully towards the steps. He tripped, clipping the top step with his elbow in the scramble to escape.

"Enough!" Giuliett commanded in a clear and direct tone. Both men stilled. Robbie L's missing pistol was held in the ready.

"How do you say in Australia, take a load off and sit!" she directed.

"That's my girl." The biker said proudly, his eyes remaining on the offender standing warily at the bottom step. Robbie L felt Giuliett close behind him and then the nozzle of the gun dig into his back.

"I'm not your girl." She said. "I'm taking back what belongs to me."

Next she spoke directly to the intruder, who Robbie L realised, was her team member.

"Tie him up. Burn the boat. Good bye Robbie L."

40

Florence, Italy

Giuliett smoothed the silk-georgette Red Valentino dress from her ribs to her hips. Her eyes traced the outline of the pale green, pink and black butterflies and garden insects of the designer fabric, following the line of the skirt along her thigh to where the silk fell away at her bended knee.

She checked her face and hair in the pocket mirror and slid the compact into the open clutch placed on the leather seat between her and Loris Moretti. He glanced sideways at her fidgeting and looked out the window as they passed another tourist bus edging slowly up the steep hill.

"We're almost there." He said to her.

Giuliett nodded. "Game on." She said. "Pocco won't know what hit him."

Their black sedan entered the large square of the Piazzale Michelangelo, turning into the tourist traffic and the centrally located replica of Michelangelo's David. In the late spring afternoon, the views from the lookout across the River Arno to the city of Florence and north towards Fiesole were ripe for toasting.

Clearly visible, Brunelleschi's dome rose high above the

terracotta tones. The outer ribs, lantern and copper ball of the fifteenth century gothic cupola were glistening in both the sunshine and the attention. As intended, it dominated the space between the river flats and the purple hued layers of the Monte Morello and La Calvana mountain ranges.

Her driver dismissed the tourists as much caught in the views as they were lacking spatial awareness with a steady outward breath, and took the winding driveway towards the Romanesque styled Basilica di San Miniato al Monte. They were now at the highest point of the renaissance city.

"Signorina, during the celebrations, I will be waiting here." Her driver indicated a place in the vast paved courtyard adjacent the Basilica's entrance. "I will be looking out for you."

"Thank you, Elia."

He turned the car, employing an exit strategy, quickly surveyed the area around them, before taking his place at the back passenger door. He respectfully opened the door for her. Loris met her at the rear of the sedan. His pistol, clipped in the shoulder holster, exposed momentarily as a quick burst of breeze caught his jacket. Subconsciously Giuliett touched the small Beretta stowed in her simple clutch.

"Leave it." He said gruffly noticing the small movement beside him. His eyes were everywhere.

On cue, the bell tower chimed a welcome to the exclusive group. Most had gathered in the cloisters. Only Don Poccolini remained outside, greeting his guests on the steps outside the geometrically patterned marble façade, reminiscent of the infamous cathedral of Florence.

"His men are next to the Pharmacy, at the staircase and behind us." Loris said quietly. Giuliett nodded.

"Gatto?"

"Haven't seen him yet."

She nodded again and smiled as they approached the aging Florentine Don.

"Giuliett! It's nice to see you!" His disingenuous smile didn't reach his pug like eyes.

"Good morning Pocco. Thank you. You remember Loris Moretti, don't you? Don Moretti was kind enough to lend me one of his best until I can secure another companion." She said smoothly.

"Of course," he lied. "Welcome to you both. May I offer my condolences for your recent loss, Giuliett? A terrible business that," he said dramatically. "A great loss to the Seta family, to lose Enrico Nero."

"Yes." She said. "Thank you. The Seta family appreciates your considerations and support."

She placed her hand on his forearm and leant in close. "Don Poccolini, shall we not concern ourselves with sadness on this beautiful day and lively occasion?"

"Of course," he replied.

"After all, fortune has restored balance," she continued at once. "A death for a birth."

Immediately Giuliett turned from him and strode into the Basilica and the christening of Don Poccolini's first grandchild.

41

....

Curious eyes followed her the length of the centre aisle. Despite the whisper encore, Pocco's wife embraced her warmly and indicated for her to sit with the family. Giuliett obliged. Gatto would have surely witnessed the show. *Now*, thought Giuliett, *you have the short ceremony to stew over your future.*

Loris Moretti positioned himself observing the proceedings, Pocco's personnel and her. His internship was a show of solidarity towards the Seta clan, and she'd asked that Loris be well briefed in his role by Don Moretti.

Giuliett reflected on the swift and precise negotiations between her and his uncle. The Moretti heartland sat between the Tuscan capital and Venice. Two historical powerhouse regions and the clan were well versed in negotiating between them, as they had done over centuries of leadership battles and powerful alliances.

With Pocco disrupting the middle heartland in his usual Florentine style, it was only a matter of time he'd be out of favour. And luckily for her, that time was now.

The ceremony ended. Gatto came to her as she separated herself from the Poccolini family.

"Giuliett!" He leant in to kiss her thrice on the cheek and she turned her head away.

"Hello Gatto." Giuliett greeted him coldly. "Shall we walk?"

The pair headed towards the belltower, between the outbuildings to the historic cemetery behind the Church in silence. It was quiet save for the birds singing and the distant thrum of small tractor. They passed the small plots overlooking the River Arno and left the pavement, following the wide, decorative cobblestone driveway towards the ornate mausoleums.

Death had never looked so beautiful and tragic. Life size angels and bronze statutes were raised on steps above the buried, amidst rows of ornate death houses. Marble slabs and decorative crosses complimented the intricate iron and stonework of the mini cathedrals. Ancient cypress, date palms and gardens contained by forged iron gates and fences, punctuated the serene colour wash of aged marble, verdigris patina and sandstone.

"It was a nice ceremony for the family, don't you think?" He began as they strolled along the wide crushed granite walkway. "You look extraordinarily well considering your ordeal."

When she didn't respond he asked, "And Robbie L? What became of the biker?"

"He sunk with his boat." She replied. "But you know that already."

There was another long pause.

"Have you spoken to your mother recently?" He asked, chastened by her cold manner towards him.

"Yes. I am aware of her proposition to Alessandro Delarno."

"And so I think we need to ..."

"We will be doing nothing." She said, cutting off his words abruptly.

They'd reached a wide crossroads marked by two young olive trees in large terracotta pots. The cross shaped layout was outlined by narrow garden beds of rosemary, oleander and perennial herbs. Giuliett turned to face the man who had been more like a father to her than her own.

"Let's cut the bullshit Gatto. What you're really wondering is, am I clean? Do I have the capacity to negotiate with Alessandro?" She said. "And most importantly, do I know your secret? And the answer is yes to all of the above."

She waited a long moment.

"I have engaged Loris Moretti. You're services are no longer required by me or any member of the Seta clan."

"You can't do anything without me!" he spluttered, visibly unnerved by her controlled demeanour.

"I can and I will. You have betrayed me. By engaging with Pocco to undermine our business, you have betrayed my family. Such a disloyal act ends in death. You are familiar with the old ways, no?"

"You wouldn't have the guts." He taunted.

"Not the correct answer." She said calmly. "Gatto I'm disappointed in you. Interfere with my business again and I will see the block and blade beside you *and* your new friend Don Poccolini."

42

....

Delarno Estate,
Rapallo, Italy

Nicholas pulled the cover sheets off the family sized, rectangular dining table in a dramatic, cinematic moment. A cloud of fine dust filtered into the air, caught in the thick shards of sunlight beams coming through the vast windows of the formal dining room.

He sneezed and rolled the offending cloth into a ball, placing it at the end of the oversized table. Lesson learnt, he rolled the remaining covers from the chairs together and gathering them to one, he carried them to the laundry room.

Next he opened the home to the northern Italian summer. Blossoms from the climbing jasmine trellised along the front façade of the Italianate mansion filled the rooms with a heady scent.

Nicholas breathed in the childhood memory. He'd missed this place. And the realisation smacked him with melancholy loneliness. At any other time, Maria would have prepared the home for his arrival, or any member of his family or guest.

The old woman always greeted him with a warm hug, a cool

drink and time to sit, bursting with gossip on the town's latest news. She'd say he was too thin, too fat, too tired and in great need of her care and attention over the coming weeks. Then she'd set about rectifying what she deemed needed fixing in her own, uncomplicated ways.

He missed her kind gentleness as much as he missed his mother. The pain of losing both hurt. He wandered through the large rooms, opening doorways and peeling off covers. He stopped in the library.

The memory of Francesca filled this space. In fact, the ghost of her happiness haunted his entire house. He could not look at an object or walk into a room without her being forefront of his mind.

In his mind he saw her, sharing her desires and secrets as they sat together on the single leather armchair. She'd trusted him then, blindly, wholly, without question. And naively he'd trusted the process, loyalties and traditions of his organisation.

Everything changed that night. As he held her close, his rebellious challenge to Carlo Seta brewed with sinister consequences. The ambitious Don's cunning play to out manoeuvre Silvio Delarno for the leadership was exposed. Nicholas knew the risks. It was a planned strategy. But even he could never have foreseen the vile vitriol that followed.

He remained caught in the moment. It was the sole reason he'd never returned after that fateful day in Coolum, so many years ago. But like everything in his life, change was inevitable, disruption part for course. He would learn to adjust and accept again as sorrow and hope walked side-by-side, holding hands.

The three most important women in his life, taken from him by circumstances he could never control, were linked and bound together at this house. His house. His home. It was the right decision to return to Rapallo.

Nicholas stepped out through the library's French doors, onto the wide, tiled portico. He strolled the length of it stopping at the place where he could clearly see the protected bay through the lush foliage of the estate's gardens. Sun's light was sprinkling diamonds over the clear waterways.

This place was his soul's home, his healing place. Surrounded in spirit by the three women he loved more than his life and his happiest childhood memories. It was a compelling mix. A persuasive thought.

The realisation brought a sensation of overwhelming peace. And with it, at that precise moment, to his utter amazement, a single white feather floated down from the sky and landed softly at his feet.

43
·················

Sunshine and gentle breeze, the smell of pastries baking and fresh coffee wafting through and Nicholas woke feeling somewhat cramped and more than a little tired.

His eyes opened and he found himself on the leather chesterfield lounge, where he'd fallen asleep. He unkinked his neck and unhinged long legs, and as his feet found the floor his movement was accompanied by cheerful burst of laughter.

"You look like a praying mantis trying to walk along a narrow stick!" she said in deeply accented French. "Good morning Signor. I've brought your breakfast on a tray this morning."

She placed the tray on his desk and pulled the linen curtains across a little so the bright morning sunshine didn't shine directly into his eyes. It became obvious to him she was quite familiar with the home by the way she moved about the room, and the confidence of her service.

She gathered the remainder of dust cloths he'd discarded in the corner, straightened his chair at the desk, surveyed the rest of the room and when she was satisfied, stood facing him.

She had the colouring of the southern Italians. Glossy dark hair was tied back in a makeshift ponytail and her black cotton blouse was tucked into black tight jeans. She bounced around soundlessly in a pair of brogue detailed, leather joggers with an elevated white sole.

Her eyes sparkled with unspent energy and expectation.

"Good morning. Thank you Signorina." Nicholas felt more than a little confused and disoriented. "And you might be?"

"I am Marionetta Phillipa Maria Castello. But you may call me Mari. My great aunt served you for many years, and it will be my pleasure to do the same." She said. Her speech was thickly accented in French.

"Your great aunt was very special to me."

"I know Signor. We all know what you did for her and our family. And you may be assured that she loved you as a son as well. She spoke about you all the time in a loving way."

"How did you come to be here this morning?" he asked.

"Nonna C, that's my special name for her by the way, had been teaching me to take over from her. I received a telephone call that it was time for me to take up my new calling. I do apologise Signor Delarno, I have been in transit and didn't realise you were coming home to Rapallo so soon. I would have made sure that everything was in order as I've been shown."

Nicholas accepted her apology with an invitation of his own.

"Would you like to join me Marionetta? I'd like to know more about you and it would be rude of me to eat alone in front of you."

"Yes. I'll get my tray. One moment Signor ... you may start without me."

Nicholas watched her leave and smiled at the young woman's combination of youthful brashness and diligence to service. She returned promptly with her own tray and a large pot of coffee.

"It's a beautiful morning, shall we eat on the porch?" she said and without waiting for his response, she exited the French doors to the small table overlooking the garden.

"Sure." Nicholas said as to himself.

He sat opposite her. She smiled cheerfully.

"I love this time of year." She said her energy bouncing around her. "Don't you?"

"Yes." He said, taking a sip of his coffee. "Why don't we talk about you for a bit?"

"I'm twenty-six years. When I was sixteen, I moved to Paris to finish my schooling and to learn French. I love children. I've been working in orphanages throughout France, Germany and Italy. I am fluent in Italian, English, French and German." She said proudly. "Nonna C asked me to come home to help her out and so I did. Now here I am."

"And you're happy to give up your passion to work here?"

"Signor Delarno. Of course, I miss the children, but this was her wish and I'm happy to oblige. Nonna C always knew what was best for our family."

"I can attest to her good judgement." He said.

There was a short silence between them. Marionetta ate her pastry quickly, looking out to the garden and interspersing the quiet solitude with comments on the bird species singing that morning, the meals she'd prepare for the coming week and the occasional piece of town gossip, just has her great aunt had done.

After a long silence over the last of the coffee she turned to face him and her demeanour changed.

"I know we have just formally met Signor Delarno, but may I say something?"

"Go ahead."

"May I please thank you for making things right after Nonna C was hurt." A dark cloud washed over her youthful features. "It was a terrible thing and your swift action saved my uncle and my brothers from entering a war with that family."

It was the last thing he expected to hear from her and he looked at her carefully.

"You're upset with me now. Nonna C said I was always too quick to put my feelings out. It's a problem." She sighed dramatically. "I like people to know so there can be no complications."

"You misunderstand." Nicholas said. "I'm taken a little by surprise."

"We are a very close family Signor Delarno. Nonna C, mother and I, we share a lot of secrets. We are one. I know you took care of the business and that saved my uncle and brothers from having to take action. Retribution for her death would have certainly fallen to the men in our family and rightly Don Castello, my uncle would have sought it. Because you stepped in, the leader of all our families, you have elevated our family status in the eyes of the Commission. But you already know this and for that I thank you. "

She eyeballed him in the intense manner of the southerners.

"As I said, you have nothing to fear from me and everything to gain. Nonna C, mama and I are of the same mind and action as we have been invited to do. One thing you will learn about me Signor Delarno is you will always know my feelings, but you will never know my secrets unless I wish to tell." She said revealing the coded sentiment of the Guardian pledge.

He suddenly smiled a ridiculous broad band of happiness, filling his cheeks and face. It met his eyes.

"Well in that case Marionetta, you'd better start calling me Nicholas."

44

....

Zanda Apartments,
Milan, Italy

"Pocco's leaning on the Commission to organise a meeting. He's counting numbers. But not everyone's invited. I suspect he's trying to invoke a trial in absentia." Mario Zanda sat back in the comfortable single chair. He adjusted his black bow tie and thoughtfully swirled amber liquid in a large balloon glass.

"Against who?"

"Giuliett."

"Of course he is. You know why don't you?" Alessandro asked his long time friend and colleague.

"Yes. I do." He put the glass on the side table and reached for the antipasto plate. He handed it to his friend. "Pocco will not be satisfied until he has brought us all down."

Alessandro sipped the aperitif.

"Between his vanity and Giuliett's addictions, they'll be white noise for five minutes." Alessandro said confidently.

"I'm not so sure." Zanda said. "She's clean. Robbie L sorted her out. Before she tried to sink him and his boat, that is."

"Really?" Alessandro was shocked.

"I'm surprised friend. I thought you would've heard. He reached out to one of my colleagues for some repair work. You know he bought an Amel 60?"

"Yes, I was aware. He asked my advice. So it's true. I'd heard a whisper but it seemed so unlikely I admit I ignored it." Alessandro said. He scolded himself, shaking his head. "Due diligence Alessandro. You always say due diligence."

Zanda reached out and tapped him reassuringly on the arm. "Alessandro, you can't be everywhere. This new proposal to government between you and Nicholas has been your focus. As it should be."

Alessandro looked at his friend thoughtfully. "I might reach out to Giuliett." He said. "You know Bice offered me the contract."

Zanda nodded. "Yes, she came to me for advice. I told her that it was a brilliant idea, to give you control of the business that is. The other realisation she came to of her own volition." He looked knowingly at his friend.

"It's a small world we operate in," the gentleman said wryly, almost blushing. "Do you know the terms? Actually, I don't mind discussing this with you, if you don't mind, because I'm really in need of some advice myself."

"I don't know the details." Zanda replied, leaning forward taking a canapé from the plate.

"She wants me to let Francesca Salucci know that she has Seta group protection. Carlo's actions, and those of Silvio, incensed Bice no end. She's an incredible woman. Do you know she's already spoken to some of the families in the clan to pave the way? But she desires I reaffirm her stand."

Alessandro looked at the Commission Chairman.

"I don't know what to do." He said. "For me to promise protection to Francesca Salucci of all people! If I show her favour, the Commission will have my nuts on a platter. Can you imagine? First Nicholas. Now me. I will be the one on trial in absentia." He laughed at the irony. "And then there's Giuliett. If she's cleaned up as you say, she could be a great asset to our organisation."

"It's a tricky one." Zanda took a sip of his drink. "So you think if Giuliett is on track you can convince Bice to give it to her, as it should've been all along, and stop the carnage with Pocco."

"That's where my head is at after hearing your news, yes."

"But?" Zanda prompted.

"But can we trust Giuliett? And you know the years of drama we've had with that love triangle. Nicholas, Francesca and Giuliett. Imagine Giuliett pledging to protect Francesca! It will never happen. Why do my troubles always come back to those three names?"

Alessandro looked at his friend.

"I've never sought the position of leader. I'm very happy being an Advisor to our group. With the added complication of Bice and now with Nicholas coming back ... it's a lot."

"Perhaps you could offer to be Giuliett's mentor." Zanda said. "After all it is the reason she went to Pocco in the first place. She was looking for guidance. Now I know for certain she's just engaged Loris Moretti. At last it's a good step in the right direction for her. Moretti won't put up with her shit."

"Maybe. Do you think she'll buy it?"

"There's always persuasion." Zanda said. "Speaking of which, here comes my beautiful influence now. You're ready my love?"

The gentlemen stood and Mario Zanda stepped forward to greet his wife with a kiss on the cheek.

He wrapped his tuxedo jacket around his thin shoulders.

"Hello dear Alessandro." Lucia Zanda greeted him with a smile and a hug. "It's nice to see you again. You're looking extremely well."

"Thank you!" he smiled at her. "As are you my dear friend! It's a lovely night for a gallery opening, would you agree?"

She nodded. "Yes. I hear Bice is joining us as well." She said with a twinkle in her eye.

Alessandro blushed for the second time that night. "Yes, that's true. And Nicholas too, so it will be a family affair! Well, not that Bice is family and affair is probably not the right word to use. Goodness, for an apparently older and wiser man, I'm no good at this at all."

He looked completely uncomfortable and the more he spoke the bigger the hole he dug for himself.

"Save him Mario, for goodness' sake." Lucia laughed, looking at her husband who seemed to be enjoying his friend's discomfort a little too much.

"No!" he said. "It's good to see him lost for a change. It puts him on a level stage with the rest of us! The unflappable Alessandro Delarno does have a soft heart after all!"

45

....

"I wanted to thank you for saving my daughter from that fool Enrico and helping her through her addictions."

Bice Seta slowly circled the large sculpture, a single rectangular shaped chain link made from expelled bullet casings. It extended five metres high from a two-metre wide short end. Inside the hole defining the interior space, a single pendant light bulb shone. Arabesque shaped patterns of light and an occasional rainbow, formed by the gaps between the shells, reflected onto the grey gallery walls.

"A deal is a deal." He said.

"I know she can be a handful sometimes." Bice looked at him briefly.

"I've had worse."

"Keep the boat. A bonus for the extra trouble she caused and I'll cover the cost of its repair." She said.

"Thank you. She's a nice little piece that."

This particular room of the gallery started to fill with guests. Bice wandered into the next.

"Champagne madam?" the drinks waiter stood at his station.

"Thank you."

Robbie L walked in a few seconds later, drink in hand and they stood beside each other discussing the artwork painted on a large wall panel.

"You have to see the magnificent watercolour in the next room. She's a fabulous artist. One of my favourites." Bice asked and they left the quiet room and the waiter.

"What are your plans Robbie L?" Bice asked when they were alone.

"Might head home I think. My job here is done and some connections need my personal attention."

"There's always work here if you need it."

"That's nice but I like my own space."

"Robbie L, it's not really my business, but I feel I should ask." Bice said. "You've seen the news haven't you? Coming from Australia."

"Yep. I know. The Feds have issued a warrant. It wouldn't be the first time. And I'm damn sure it won't be the last. Some bastard has set me up. I want to sort it out."

He walked through an immersion piece using digital technology combining light, sound, smell and touch.

"What about the leadership?" Bice asked.

"I don't want it. Never did. I'm happy in my patch. I just came to see the show." He said. "I'm keen to get home now. Having said that, I might take a little detour via Fiji and visit an old friend."

"Well, be sure to give her my regards."

"You know my friend?" he asked.

"That girl is more than a daughter to me." Bice said. "That's why I put her under Seta clan protection."

"Since when?" he asked, facing her for the first time.

"Since I bought you and your services to sort out Giuliett." She said and walked slowly towards the exit and the main reception rooms.

She handed him an envelope from her clutch.

"You'll notice also a key and an address. Let's just say it's a place you can call home, when you're away from home. Every man needs more than a cave to lay his head. It's safe, secure and discreet. One day you'll need that kind of protection."

Robbie L shoved the envelope into his jackets inside pocket. "Thank you. You've been more than generous."

"Prego. Now, I must go, I'm late to meet Alessandro. Keep in touch Robbie L. You're one of the few I do actually like."

"I don't understand you." He said watching her carefully.

"You don't have to Robbie L." She said, holding her ground with him. "All you need to know is that I'm putting right that which my late husband fucked up."

46

....

"**N**icci!" Lucia greeted him with an extended hug and three kisses. "I'm so happy you decided to come! Let me look at you." She said taking a step back and holding his wrist in her hand so he could not escape her inspection.

"Lucia!" He said warmly, relishing his favourite cousin's attention as they picked up where they'd left off. "It's been a very, very long time. You're looking exceptionally well tonight."

"Thank you. It's my new hair colour. Do you like? Mario says now I look too young for him! But I know for certain he likes it!" She said smiling secretively. "Did you come alone?" she asked, looking around for company.

"Yes. I'm still the bachelor. Some things don't change." He laughed.

"You can walk with us. Avoid the gossipers! Mario will not mind I'm sure." she said. "Let's go this way. Bice tells me there is a sculpture made from bullet casings I must see. She says I should buy it and put it in our garden at the estate. Imagine that? Bullet casings, for goodness sake! Mario will think I've gone mad! So, tell me, what's news?"

"Busy, busy. You know what it's like." He said.

"You know what I mean. How's Francesca?" She whispered.

"I wouldn't know." He said.

Lucia propped mid stride at the threshold between the

sculpture and the front room. Her eyes grilled him.

"Oh come on Lucia, don't give me that look!" Nic exclaimed.

"Surely you were hiding out with her? Where else would you disappear to and make us think you were dead! It's very dramatic. Very romantic." She said swooning and steered them towards the sculpture.

"Although, I should smack you for what you put your poor mother through. Oh I could never smack you!" She said pushing her hand through his crooked elbow. "So, do tell. Spill the beans Delarno. What were you doing all that time?"

"I had to sort out a few things. Yes, I did reconnect with Francesca. It's not going to work for us, she found somebody else." He said, glossing over the most difficult time of his life with surprising ease.

"Rubbish! You two are peas in a pod. To hell with everybody else! Love is love. It sits above everything else. There's no one more right together than the two of you." She said.

"Apparently there is."

She looked at him unconvinced.

"Did you hear about Giuliett?" she whispered.

"Yes. Crazy behaviour." He lowered his voice. "Speak of the devil's mother at one o'clock."

"It's made from shell casings apparently." Lucia said, raising her eyebrow slightly at Nicholas as Bice and Alessandro joined their circle. "A statement about the effects on the family structures when the war stops and families try to reconnect in fractured communities.

"It's quite a powerful piece actually when you put it into context. More than I expected." She said, her voice drifting away.

"We've lost Mario I'm afraid," Bice said, embracing Nicholas. "I think he's caught up with a Senator from Five Star."

"That man never stops." Lucia rolled her expressive eyes. "I swear I can't take him anywhere! He's literally always working! Politics. Business. Finance. Well, history dictates he'll be while, so we might as well enjoy ourselves. Who'd like champagne?"

Lucia and Bice led the small group through the gallery, stopping every now and then to discuss favourites but mostly they gossiped about the latest news from Milan until it was time to say good-bye.

47

. . . .

"In all it was lovely event." Lucia said rounding out her continual commentary that lasted from the time they left the gallery until they walked through the front door of the apartment.

"Gentlemen, I'm going to bed." She announced, yawning loudly as she finally drew breath. "You may now have your cards and brandy in peace."

"Goodnight lovely." Nicholas stood and gave her a hug. "Great summation of tonight's do. I swear you didn't leave out one single detail!" He teased. "I'll see you in the morning."

"Goodnight love." Mario kissed his wife on the cheek. "I won't be long." He said to her retreating back. She waved the comment away.

She climbed the stairs slowly and stopped at the top balustrade. Lucia turned to face them from the juncture of the stairwell and the mezzanine walkway connecting the bedroom zone to the lower library and sitting room in the elegant loft apartment.

"It's good to have you back Nicci. I've really missed you. Tonight reminded me of the old days, when we were kids. It's like the old gang is back together." She smiled warmly at them both and trundled off along the hall, taking her shoes off one step at a time as she went. "Mamma that feels good!" she said shutting the bedroom door behind her.

Nic laughed. "She never changes. One hundred per cent crazy." He said. "Do you remember the mad water fights? And the twenty four hour board games she made us play?"

"Yeah, you'd think age would hold her up a bit more, but no. Sometimes I feel our life is just getting started." Mario said, smiling happily. "In our fifties mind."

"Fifty is the new twenty, so they say." Nicholas said. "How did you go with the Senator tonight?" He said changing the subject.

"He'll come round to our way of thinking."

"Sebastino is on board." Nic said. "He's ready to push the button when we say go. Have you ever seen him in action? I caught up with him in Naples last week. He has them eating out of his hands down there."

"Yes, he's come a long way from the early days. I like him. He can be a bit hot but he's a valuable asset." Mario said. "How are you doing my friend? There's a lot going on at the moment."

"There's always a lot going on." He said ruefully. "I'm across it Mario. My mind is clear and focused."

"I'm not talking about the business. I have no worries there." He said.

There was a long pause. Nicholas sighed loudly. "It's a lot. It's like I never left and sometimes it feels a lifetime has passed." He replied. "But I think, I'm coming out the other side. I'm not afraid to say I've had some very dark days."

"In recent times?" Mario leant forward towards his friend. "You know you can always count on me when you need to talk."

"Thank you friend. I was thinking more about the past." Nic grimaced. "I had no choice." He said. "To leave like I did. And disappear. I couldn't talk about it, even to you."

The younger man had an anguished, far-away look on his

face. "I had to disappear or risk letting us all down. I wasn't in the right frame of mind to clearly analyse decisions. Mistakes lead to exposure. I made a vow I'd only return when I was sure my actions wouldn't jeopardise our group."

"There is always a choice." Mario said, bringing Nic back to the present moment. "Your choice was to step aside and sort out your shit. Some might say it's a fool's temperament, others might applaud; but it was a choice you made and now you have consequences to deal with."

Nic acknowledged the comment with a slight inclination of his head. "True. And many are centred on me earning everyone's trust. My greatest personal regret is that I didn't get to say goodbye to mum and Maria. It used to haunt me knowing what my mother went through because of me."

He was quiet and still.

"But I feel her spirit has returned to me now. The permanent return to Rapallo was the right decision. Mum is happy, Maria is happy and I am quickly learning that when the spirits are happy, life is easier." He laughed, trying to lighten the heavy mood.

"Well those amongst you who are living and love you as a brother are happy you're back in our part of the world. Venice is not a good place for you to stay long term. Your home is and always will be in Rapallo."

"I agree. Now, that's enough about me. Tell me about Pocco. I hear he's trying to call a meeting?"

"Yes. He wants Giuliett out, but in his usual double-handed way he wants it to look like a Commission decision." Mario said.

"He's a problem. Does Giuliett have the support to take him on? She'd be entitled to after his collusion with Gatto."

"You know about that?"

"I do try to keep up with the family machinations. Yes."

"So you know about Robbie L?"

"I hear he bought a boat, tried to dry her out and she tried to sink it with him on board." Nic said in a bored, matter of fact way.

"Do you know what he's up to now?"

"No, I'm assuming he'll be gunning for her. A man like that won't settle until he's avenged his ego."

"Why do you think he tried to sort her out?" Mario asked curiously. "I have my theories but I'd like to hear your thoughts."

"I think he wanted to form an alliance with Seta group ... two outsiders working together. Maybe he thinks he can see something there that we can't. We all know she can talk the walk."

Mario nodded in agreement.

"And your thoughts on Giuliett?" Mario asked.

"Well," Nic said looking across the top of his glass at his host, "She does have a habit of shitting in the nest."

He shrugged. "To be honest Mario, I haven't tried to dissect their relationship status. My mind has been on Pocco and Gatto. Do you know what Robbie L's fascination is about?"

"Not yet. Like I said, I have my theories. But I'll be finding out and when I do, you'll know too. I think we need to keep an eye on them for the simple reason they have no regard for protocol or tradition. That's dangerous for the rest of us."

"I see your point." Nic rubbed his chin absently.

"Be assured I'm not afraid to cut them out if I think the rest of us will be exposed." Mario stated emphatically. "We would have Commission support on that."

"I knew I always liked you the best, Mario Zanda." Nic's attention was caught by a message on his phone.

Mario watched as the colour drained from his friend's face. Nic looked at him. His mouth opened and shut. He checked the message again.

"What's happened?" Mario immediately stood and grabbed his coat from the back of the lounge.

"Bice's dead. Alessandro is in surgery." He said. "Car accident. Police are looking for the other driver."

With a dark expression, Nic looked up from the phone, stood and was striding out the door in one movement. "Smells like Gatto."

48
....

Robbie L poured another whiskey, swirled the peat coloured, viscous liquid and watched as it skimmed the glass lip and then subsided. He took a long sip, a deep sigh and laid his head against the headboard. His legs stretched out under the sheets and his toes massaged the crisp, clean cotton.

He sighed again. Perhaps he should've sailed tonight. In the very least he could have made Genoa and the *Sea Meadow* moored in a private marina there. Between his fingers, he flicked Bice's secret apartment key, twirling it round and round, from end to end.

A new passport, mobile phone and wads of cash completed the little package she'd given him earlier that evening.

He punched the new address into a digital map for the third time. The indicator pointed to a location on the outskirts of that ancient port city. More than a little curious, he'd decided the place was best visited in daylight. That way he could easily scope out the unfamiliar neighbourhood before setting sail to Sydney.

Too tired to sleep, he flicked on the television. It launched straight into a local news bulletin. The regular program was interrupted by news feed footage of a car wreck. A black Mercedes sports car was a mangled mess, having been T boned in a city street intersection not far from the gallery.

Two people he knew well were pictured. The biker outlaw turned up the sound.

"Police are looking for this man who they believe can help them in their enquiries." The reporter said as a black and white picture was shown. It looked like a still from the gallery's security camera.

"Fucken what?" Robbie L yelled, looking in disbelief as his self-portrait splashed across the television screen.

"Witnesses say that the man had been in deep discussions with Signora Seta at a fundraiser gallery opening earlier tonight and he had left angrily after a dispute."

"Fucken not true!" He yelled at the television screen. He stormed to the open window and looked out to the street below. The familiar wail of the police sirens rose up to his fifth storey suite as three cars pulled up in unison at the entrance to the hotel.

Robbie L quickly grabbed his things and left, taking the stairs to the restaurant on level two and then the service elevator to the ground floor. He exited the building into the alley car park behind the hotel and found himself on the road to the port city after all.

It was early in the morning when he reached Genoa and he headed directly to the Cristoforo Columbo International Airport. Knowing his car would eventually be traced to the city, he dumped it in an overnight car park and checked in to the next direct flight out of the country.

Thankfully there weren't too many people around at the hour and as he stepped out from the airport arrivals section and into the night air he hoped he'd left enough of a trail to nowhere for the cops.

It was time to disappear. He punched the address into the

GPS on his phone and hailing a cab, chose a location in the city centre. It was time to backtrack to his new residence and calculate his next move.

49

· · · · · · · · · · · · · · · · · ·

Standing forlornly in the doorway of the hospital suite, Giuliett watched the man who'd always meant too much to her and would be, for most of her adult life, her greatest torment. He was broken. Nicholas Delarno sat with his hands in his head, looking at his feet and the floor, his body shaking softly in grief stricken tears.

She saw the desolate child in him. And despite her grief, her heart broke.

Sensing her there, he turned and immediately stood, bringing her silently into the private room. He couldn't speak. She understood that depth of sadness. The gesture washed away all their animosity. A simple sharing of grief and shock and in that moment they were as one.

"Giuliett, I'm so sorry." Nicholas found his voice first, embracing his long-time foe, holding her close as her tears fell.

"I can't quite believe it." She said in a bewildered tone. "The police say it was a deliberate act. They said that Robbie L was driving the other vehicle. Do you think that's right?"

"Do you?"

"I don't know. I kind of doubt it. I left him in his yacht in a not so disastrous state." She half grimaced. "If he was half the man he says he was, he'd easily have survived. And his retaliation would be directly against me. Not through my mother. He's more single minded in that way."

She sat on the lounge chair.

"Please." She said, indicating for him to sit as well.

"Yes, I heard about that." He said. She could tell he was not amused.

"But I haven't seen or heard from him since." She turned her body towards him. "Not an inkling or threat. I just assumed he returned to Sydney like he said he was wanting to do."

There was a short pause.

"He knows mum and I weren't exactly close." She burst into tears again and Nic wrapped his arm around her. "So going after her doesn't make sense. There are a lot of other ways he could get to me if he wanted to take that path."

She looked at Nic. "Right?"

He nodded. "Yes. I've known Robbie L for a long time. I agree. Revenge is more literal for him. Straightforward eye for an eye." The accusation against Robbie L didn't make sense to Nic either, despite the boat episode.

"God, all the terrible things I said to her. All the accusations! About dad and about Gatto. About everything that was wrong in my life. But deep down, I always knew she had my back, you know. Despite this, she loved me more. I wish ..." she quietly sobbed against his shoulder.

They sat together for a long time saying nothing. Through the glass observation window, they could see Alessandro, out of surgery and hooked up to every machine and monitor. Nurses fussed around him, their faces focused and their voices hushed.

"How's Alessandro?" She asked following his gaze into the private intensive care room.

"Not out of the woods yet. He's fighting. The doctors are

happy with the surgery. Now we just have to wait." He sighed heavily.

Giuliett wiped away the tears gathered under her eyelashes and looked straight into his dark, rimmed in red, wearily black and blue eyes. Unable to bear the pain she saw staring back, she looked away.

He turned back to Alessandro and after a few moments she glanced at his profile. Away from the anger of the Commission meeting in Venice, she took a moment to really look at him again after his years of absence.

His hair was beginning to turn an early salt and pepper, just like his uncle's. It also appeared in the stubble sprouting above his top lip and along his chin.

He turned to face her. Giuliett put her hand up and pressed it against his cheekbone, her fingertips gently rubbing the tension building behind his ear, at the back of his head. A subconscious action, brought forth from her childhood, and one her mother often did to soothe her only child in times of distress.

"It's going to be alright." She murmured absently, just as her mother had done.

"I know." His eyes scanned her face. *For the first time in her life*, Nicholas thought, *this girl is actually being real.*

"You know they were dating." She said quietly, her hand dropping to her lap.

He smiled at her with his eyes. "I'm still trying to get my head around that latest development. She must be a special woman, your mother. Alessandro's pretty set in his sea dog ways. How did you feel about it?"

"It's her life." Giuliett shrugged. "I've always liked Alessandro. He struck me as someone who was inherently kind. Or is, I'm sorry. I don't mean to talk in the past tense." She said. "I can see why mum was drawn to him. He's the complete opposite of my father and Gatto."

"How did Gatto take it? The news of your mum and Alessandro."

"How does Gatto take anything he can't control and disagrees with?" There was a slight pause. A moment. A skipped heartbeat.

"Oh God!" she suddenly exclaimed, pushing her hands up to her cheeks and across her forehead. She suddenly stood, propelling herself into the middle of the room. She faced Nicholas.

"It wasn't Robbie L who was driving. It was Gatto!" She spoke through her fingers that were now resting across her mouth. "I bet you Robbie L was nowhere near it."

He watched her carefully. It happened in slow motion and Giuliett literally felt the expressions change on her face as her thoughts sifted through and sorted all the knowledge.

"He killed her because she gave Alessandro the business." She said. Her face crumbled. "And because I told him to stay away ..."

There was a knock on the door. They looked at it in unison.

"Yes." Nicholas said. "Come in."

"Excuse me Signorina Seta." A local police officer stood outside the doorway beside a hospital orderly. "When you are ready, it's time for you to identify the body."

Giuliett looked at Nicholas and the colour left her pale face.

"Would you like me to come with you?" he offered without waiting for her to ask. Giuliett nodded.

50

· · · · · · · · · · · · · · · · ·

"I had nothing to do with it."

Robbie L jumped up from the bed and walked again to the bedroom window. Between the half-closed shutters, he looked out over the Genoa Harbour and the cargo cranes working in the distant horizon.

He scanned the street below, the people going about their business and looked up and across at the shabby buildings surrounding the apartment complex.

His apartment was a simple affair decorated in nostalgic Italian flair. One bedroom sat behind a small sitting area and balcony. A separate kitchen and small bathroom connected along a short hallway to the second bedroom. Entry into the third-floor unit was through the small dining area via an exterior U shaped staircase.

The rooms were light, clean and pleasant.

"I know." Nicholas said. "That's not why I'm calling. Giuliett needs your support."

"Piss off! So she can set me up again with the cops, no thank you."

"She says you were with her that night. The two of you had a very nice, very private rendezvous after your visit to the gallery." Nic said. "The cops believe her."

"Why would she say that?"

"Ask her yourself."

"Hmmf."

"Don't be a fucktard! Look Robbie, I know we've had our differences in the past, but this time you and I are on the same team. I'm offering support if you need it. I can get you safely to Giuliett."

There was a long, silent response.

"Are you sulking?" Nic asked incredulously.

"No! I'm thinking."

"Well think about this." The Capo said. "I could reach out and grab you by the balls right now if I wanted to. Your illustrious dreams of grandeur are over. I'm extending the olive branch for the good of our organisation. If you don't need my help, that's fine. But you will call Giuliett and the two of you will sort it out."

Nicholas hung up the phone. *And get back to work or go home,* he almost added.

He looked at Alessandro and encircled the old man's hand within his. "Come on my dearest. You can do this." He said.

*   *   *   *   *

Alessandro Delarno opened his eyes. The first he saw was Nic's head bent forward, resting on one hand and the other reaching out over the blankets, closing the space between the younger man and his uncle. Next, was a place unfamiliar to him but recognisable as a hospital room.

Alessandro squeezed his fingers. Nic raised his head slowly, looking at the hands clasped in his. Alessandro squeezed his nephew's hands again. He focused on squeezing as hard as he could, but was suspicious the action was in fact quite slight.

Nic looked from his hands to Alessandro. Relief reflected in his face.

"Zio."

Alessandro smiled weakly. He tried to talk. "Bice?" The name was just audible and he mouthed it a couple of times before the raspy sound came out.

Nic shook his head sadly. "I'm sorry." He said.

The older man shut his eyes. He rested again for a long time. When Alessandro opened his eyes again, Nic was asleep in the single lounge chair positioned alongside the bed.

Alessandro whispered his name. "Nicholas."

He roused quickly. "What do you need?"

"Gatto knows. About us." Alessandro said quietly.

"How can you be sure?"

"Bice. She wasn't always accurate. But close enough to the mark for me to know he was gathering evidence."

Alessandro patted his nephew's hand reassuringly at his alarmed look. "It's okay." He said. "It's why she gave me Seta clan."

"Does anyone else know?" Nic asked.

Alessandro closed his eyes and gently mouthed 'no'.

Nicholas thought for a moment. "Gatto can't prove it." His hand rubbed the overgrown stubble on his cheek and chin thoughtfully. He stared at the patterned linoleum covering the floor.

"Go to our safe." Alessandro whispered, indicating the secret safety deposit box they shared in a private hotel room in Genoa. "There you will find the documents from Carlo and more. Protect Francesca."

"Francesca? What in the world does she have to do with this?" He asked, looking at his uncle in surprise.

"Gatto drove the car." Alessandro said. "Bice. Alessandro. Francesca. Nicholas." His fingers moved indicating each of the four names, from his chest to Nicholas as he listed them.

His eyes closed and throughout the room and nurses' station, every alarm started beeping at once. Two nurses rushed into the suite.

"What's happening?" Nicholas asked.

"Your uncle is going into cardiac arrest." One replied ushering him out the door. "Mr. Delarno, please wait next door. You can still be close to your uncle from there."

In a daze he went to the adjoining room, watching helplessly through the glass window divide as the doctors joined the team surrounding his uncle.

51

. . . .

Grand Hotel Savoia,
Genoa, Italy

A djacent the central train station and a short distance up
the hill beyond the Piazza Aquaverde and the Cristoforo
Columbo monument the iconic Grand Hotel Savoia was
open for business and pleasure. But neither was on Nicholas
Delarno's mind as he entered the hotel's polished foyer.

Set amongst the rabble of the unkempt and worn out that
was the historic centre of Genoa, the 1897 Belle Époque hotel
upheld its reputation of luxurious comfort, security and privacy.

Values the Delarno family revered, having enjoyed possession
of an executive suite within, for their exclusive use, for the
hotel's entirety. Alessandro's personal guests frequented the
landmark, as well as Nicholas himself when necessity kept him
overnight in Genoa.

An unexpected lump rose to his throat. Embraced by its
gentile nature, he was abruptly reminded of the stark contrast
witnessed just a few short hours before. The plush warmth of
familiarity gushed forward, replacing the sterility and trauma
of his uncle's hospital bedside.

"We are very sorry, Nicholas." The concierge of the Savoia met Nicholas solemnly. "To hear about the loss of your uncle and our dear friend."

"Thank you Antonio. It is a terrible thing ..." Nic's words drifted away.

Antonio nodded kindly. "Alessandro was a good man. A gentleman. We will all miss him greatly."

"Thank you."

"I see you are tired, Sir. Your room, as always, is ready. Is there anything more you desire?"

"Thank you friend. I'm happy to see to my own needs tonight."

The pair briefly embraced.

"If you change your mind, please call. I'm on duty this afternoon and all of tonight."

Nicholas nodded. "I will."

In the intimate space of the Delarno suite he immediately relaxed in the soft colours, surrounded by the vintage keepsakes and his family's personal collection decorating the room.

He placed his bags on the floor, opened the window to the fresh salty air and collapsed on the bed, too exhausted to move. And, many hours later, this was exactly how Francesca Salucci found him.

Fast asleep, fully clothed, his peaceful face etched in deep lines and the dark stubble a great deal more than a five o'clock shadow filling his cheeks and chin. Long thick eyelashes brushed high cheekbones and even in his slumber, the black circles of fatigue were fiercely evident in the soft red light of dusk lighting up the room.

"Nicholas." She gently whispered. "Nicholas."

Francesca gently touched his forearm before linking her

hands in his. "Nicholas." This time her voice was a little louder.

He woke with a start, looked around and at her. The surprise of seeing her made him sit straight up, before he was fully awake.

"Francesca?" His voice was thick with sleep and he spoke in Italian. "Am I dreaming?"

She smiled at him. "No. I came as soon as I could. I'm so sorry my love."

She sat beside him on the bed. "Lay down love, until you fully wake." She gently guided him back against the pillows. "Don't jump up before you're ready and hurt yourself."

He let her fuss and shut his eyes. Francesca bent forward to kiss him on the forehead and brushed his wayward hair from his face.

"I heard about the accident and was preparing to come." She began in a quiet melodic tone. "Paul and Angel met me in Rome and brought me to Genoa. They've gone to Arenzano.

"I wanted to give them space in Alessandro's place, so they suggested I stay here. I'm sorry love, we didn't realise you'd be here. We thought you'd head straight to Rapallo to organise things. But then I should've known you'd stay close." She said, smiling sadly.

Her hands stopped stroking his head for a moment. "Actually, why are you here and not at Alessandro's apartment? Or on the yacht?"

"Alessandro told me to come here."

She looked at him a little confused. "Alessandro? Told you come here? Are you sure?"

He sat, now fully alert and present. Francesca's hand fell away to the space between them. Nic looked at her and shook his head.

He opened his mouth but couldn't speak. He gave her a hopeless look. His lips trembled and his whole face squashed in together.

"It was the last thing he said to me." Nicholas gave into the tears he'd been holding on to since he left the hospital in Milan. His whole body shook as his hands came up to shelter his face.

"Oh love." Francesca pulled him close to her. "I'm so sorry." She said holding him tightly to her.

As the sobs waned, she looked quietly around the dark room. The reflection of the sun had sunk away and the night sky, lit by the glow of distant stars and a thousand lights, had darkened to cobalt blue.

Francesca looked out into the beauty of the blue of a northern Italian sky at night saying, "It's a bitch, this pain. Together we will learn to walk along-side it."

52

·················

In the soft glow of the sitting room lamps, Francesca flicked through the menu of Tralalero Trattoria Genovese and scrolled through the selection of dishes.

Nicholas emerged from the bathroom, fully shaved with those wayward dark curls brushed back. A fragrant combination of soap and aftershave burst from the steamy room and wafted towards her. The former detective breathed the Armani aftershave deeply, smiled and looked up at him from her seat at a small desk.

Dressed casually, he padded bare foot across the parquet floors towards the location of his leather satchel. He dug around the interior, paused and looked around the room and out the window.

"I'm ordering dinner." She said. "I suspect you've not eaten for days. Well nothing substantial anyway. Any requests?" she asked.

"You know what I like." He said, his attention returning to the satchel.

"It all sounds so good. I'm thinking octopus salad to start, fish ravioli and potato gnocchi with pesto. Or would you prefer the Genovese ravioli? They do an amazing Tuccu sauce. Then to finish, I'm thinking Panna Cotta with rose syrup and a plate of mixed berries. And wine. We definitely need wine."

"Go with the meat sauce. Get whatever you want."

"Done." She said after a few moments. "Think I'll jump in the shower whilst we wait. It's a long way from Fiji to Genoa."

"Okay." He said distractedly. "Whatever you want. Make yourself at home."

She looked at him sitting on the sofa looking through her. She felt him distancing himself from her. He walked into the bedroom and she followed him.

"Nic, I'm going to book another room. I don't think it's a good idea we stay here together. I think you need some space to think and process."

He was standing in the middle of the room conjuring a dark distant expression.

"Hmm? Okay love, whatever you want to do is fine with me." He said and moved to a bedside drawer.

"Righto, I'll do that now. I'll try and get on the same floor so it's easier if you need me to help with the organisation of things for Alessandro."

"Sounds good." He said.

"I'll come back and have dinner with you though. Is that alright?"

"Sure. Like I said, whatever you want to do is fine with me." He looked up avoiding her gaze and walked out to the lounge space. Francesca followed and gathered her bags near the door.

"Where are you going?" He asked abruptly, looking at her bags. "I thought we were having dinner."

"I just said I'm going to book another room."

"Why would you do that? You need to stay here with me." He looked at her for the first time since emerging from the shower. "Weren't you having a shower?"

Francesca giggled softly and shook her head. "Well I can't say you weren't listening because clearly you were! The information is just taking a while to compute. Are you okay? This is not like you at all Nicholas."

"Of course I am." He snapped. "I'm just looking for some paperwork." He sounded mildly insulted.

"Proceed then." She turned her back on his closed expression. "In the meantime, I'm taking a bath, then we can have dinner and discuss the room situation. Right?"

He ignored her and turned back to his satchel.

Francesca emerged from the bathroom to an empty suite. "Where the heck could he be now?" she asked herself, standing in the middle of the room. There was a knock at the door. Francesca let the room service waiter inside.

"Good evening Sir," she said. "Let's put it on the table here. Thank you. The sweets can go on the side table, right there. Beautiful. Thank you."

He briskly laid out the tablecloth and items, setting the table in quiet efficiency.

"Would you like me to pour the wine?" the waiter asked.

"I can manage that." Nicholas said, entering the room.

"As you wish, Mr. Delarno. Will that be all?"

"Yes. Thank you. Have a good evening."

"And you Sir." He nodded to Francesca. "Madam."

"Good night. Thank you." She replied.

Nicholas walked him to the door and shut it quietly behind him.

"This smells delicious." He said returning to the small dining table full of enthusiasm. "I didn't realise how hungry I was until I walked in to the aroma of good food."

"Well, take a seat Mr. Delarno. Let's make an immediate start. I thought we could share the octopus and potatoes salad." She said, removing the lid from the plate in the middle of the table between them and placing it on the side table with the others. Francesca sat opposite him.

"This is nice." Nicholas said, reaching for her hand across the table. "Thank you for coming."

Francesca smiled. "I had to. I know how much Alessandro means to you. And to my father as well."

He smiled sadly back at her.

Letting go of her hand, he started to eat. She watched him for a moment over her glass of wine.

"Nic, I want you to know that I know you've always tried to show me only your strength as a way of protecting me. As your friend I appreciate you letting me see you um, opening your emotions ... oh heck what am I trying to say?" She thought about it for another moment. "I'm sorry, this all sounded so much better in my head!"

He looked at her quizzically.

Francesca took a deep breath. "Please don't pull away from me now because you're feeling vulnerable. I value our friendship more than ever. I hope you feel the same way." She finished in a rush and the colour rose to her cheeks.

"I do." He said. "Nothing has changed for me Francesca. I'm sorry you had the impression I was pushing you away." There was a quiet moment of reflection. "Now, I need to ask a question."

"Ask away." She said.

"Does Sinclair know you are here?"

"Yes. He sends his thoughts and deepest sympathies from

Afghanistan. Archie and Bella send you 'big cuddles and lots of hugs and kisses' from Fiji." She said.

Nicholas visibly relaxed. They finished the meal in quiet camaraderie.

Over coffee Francesca was the first to speak. "Okay, it's time to address the elephant in the room."

"What's that?"

"The sleeping arrangements. I still believe I should get another room."

"Absolute nonsense. You're staying here with me." He said.

"Where? Is there a pull out bed?"

He looked at her. "Seriously?"

"Well? Is there?"

"God Francesca, when did you become a prude?"

"Since we are not dating and I have a solid partner and kids."

"Please. I think you are quite safe. Besides we have too much to discuss."

"Oh? Okay then." She looked at him expectantly.

"Yes, we do. But any discussions will have to wait until the morning. I'm completely exhausted." He moved to the more comfortable lounge area, stretched and rested against the back.

"That's a good idea. You need to rest." She stood and took his empty coffee cup. Francesca cleared the table and placed the empty dishes outside the door in the hallway. "We do that here don't we?" she asked him mid movement, unsure of the hotel's protocol.

"Yes," he laughed. "You can do whatever you want."

"Righto." She clapped her hands together, scanned the room and deftly tidied their things. Plumped the cushions, straightened the curtains and rearranged the dining chairs. She shut the windows only to return a few minutes later to open them wide again. She looked out and scanned the night sky and street below.

Nicholas watched on in amusement.

Next she went to the bathroom, rattled around in there and came out with a pile of laundry she promptly put in a bag for the hotel staff to sort out in the morning. She put it by the door.

"That's all done ready for tomorrow." She plumped another cushion. "Now mister, it's time for you to go to bed." She quipped.

"Are you talking to Archie or me?" he asked, leaning back against the lounge chair and folding his hands behind his head. He ruffled the edge of the carpet rug with his foot to watch her straighten it out. She caught the amused look on his face and giggled.

She shrugged. "I'm nervous okay."

"Nervous! Mamma Mia! About what?"

"About being here alone with you. It's weird. Don't you think it's weird?"

"No. I don't feel weird or nervous. I feel the same I always feel when I'm with you." He said.

"Well, I feel weird." She said. "Awkward."

He gave her a funny queried expression.

"Look, I'm on edge and sad. It's a lethal combination for me. Makes me do stupid shit."

"Like sleep with the enemy?" He asked.

And from her expression she knew he knew that's precisely how she felt tonight.

She looked at him genuinely perplexed. "So you go to bed and I'm going to sit up for a bit, gather my thoughts and star gaze out the window. I'll be as quiet as a church mouse so I don't disturb you."

"So that's why you didn't bite!" he said, grinning and jumping up from the chair. "I was thinking I've lost my touch."

He paced the small room excitedly, saying, "I thought for sure you'd latch on to the bait. Hook line and sinker. Where did I go? What was I doing? What do we need to discuss?"

"Everyone's a comedian." She laughed. "Of course I'm curious. But I'm trying to think of you Nicholas. And to be honest I thought it was your other business, so best for me not to ask."

He stopped pacing directly in front of her. He looked her straight in the eyes and smiled lovingly, "You'd make the best mob wife ever, Francesca Salucci. Did anyone ever tell you that? If only I could have persuaded you all those years ago."

"Who said anything about years? Six months ago you were still asking!"

"Touché, my flower, touché." He smiled at her, knowing he would ask her again tonight if he knew he could persuade her to accept and she'd not regret it in the morning.

"Okay," she said grinning, because they both knew she did desperately want to know. "I'll play your silly game and be the curious cat. Where did you go earlier tonight Mr. Delarno? What did you do? Whom did you see?" She pressed her fingers under her chin forming a small platform, bent slightly forward from the waist and fluttered her eyelashes at him.

"I went to the gift shop."

"The gift shop?" That was not the answer she was expecting. She stood up straight.

"More precisely, the jeweller."

"Oh no. Nicholas, what are you doing?" She knew that look

and stepped back from him.

"I bought you this." He handed her a small black box, embossed and wrapped in a black grosgrain ribbon. "Unwrap it my love."

"What is it?" She asked feeling trepidation and the warmth of excitement both at once.

He shrugged slightly. "Open it little one and you will find out."

Francesca carefully pulled at the ribbon bow and lifted the lid. She pulled a small, rectangular metal box from the velvet lining. It was decorated in red, white and gold. The lid was a simple design of rubies and diamonds set in a floral pattern.

She gasped, exploring the texture of the raised stones with gentle fingertips.

"It's stunning! Look at the detail." Her eyes searched his. "Thank you."

"I had trouble deciding." He said smiling and his brilliant dark eyes embraced her. "That's why I took so long. Saint Matthew the Apostle is the patron saint of Salerno, but you are from the north. Our patron saint is Saint George. So I chose the red and the white. Open the box."

He came to stand close to her and their heads bent together over the gift. "You slide it."

Inside a key was attached to a ruby, heart shaped pendant. Its glowing scarlet lustre caught the subdued lighting of the suite. She gasped again.

"Oh Nicholas! It's beautiful. Thank you. I love it." She said searching his face for a clue. The air shifted between them.

"You've gone all quiet on me." He said softly, smiling down at her.

"I'm trying hard to understand. I confess. I'm a little confused."

"This is what we need to discuss. You'll have a lot of questions. And I'll try to answer them as best I can. The key is for a property in Salerno, a little town on the Amalfi coast. Your father bought it for you before he died."

He was right. Francesca did have a lot of questions. "Why did my father buy me a property in Italy?"

Nicholas smiled. "Future proofing your safety, my love. Think back. At the time we were courting. He knew I was trying to win you over and had Castello and Carlo Seta not stepped in, we may still be together now.

"He was protecting you from me, because he knew, you would eventually find out about our business interests and that you would run."

He waited a moment for her to think about it.

"Little did he realise the turn of events that would have me come to your side." Nicholas said quietly. "And now I have to be sure to protect us in other ways."

He caught the light bouncing off her auburn hair, sitting in a curl across her shoulder. Despite his need to feel its softness between his fingers, his hand kept close to his side.

"He was right about the running bit." Francesca said, looking directly at him and seeing his need reflected in his eyes. She looked away. These moments were difficult for her to navigate.

"This is the missing property that Alessandro was looking for?"

"Yes. The documents were in Carlo Seta's possession. In short, Bice discovered them, gave them to Alessandro to pass on to you. She also placed you under Seta protection to stop any potential threats from Giuliett, Gatto or clan members." He said. "But now, I'm thinking, you'd best stick with me."

"Why would Bice care about me? I haven't seen her since I was a child. Plus, I'm out of the picture now. That's all in the past."

"I did try and warn you." He said. "Francesca, Gatto knows. About the Guardians and Alessandro and me. He murdered Bice and Alessandro. It was not a random car accident. An unfortunate event, as the police have reported. Before he died my uncle directed me to protect you. I can assure you, you're still very much on the radar, well, Gatto's anyway and that is dangerous enough."

"What about Archie?"

"Our boy is safe. Bice made sure of it with the people who matter. Gatto learnt that lesson about the same time as Silvio and Carlo Seta. Besides, he has no interest in our son. As far as he's concerned, I've left my boy to be with you and Sinclair. So, in his eyes, he is of no value to me."

"But you're so calm about it."

"I'm angry as hell." His temper flared. "Don't underestimate the damage I'm about to do." He walked away from her and stood facing the open window.

Francesca looked at his back solemnly.

"Let me be clear." He said. "Gatto wants you so he can go after me. Along with those we've worked so hard to protect."

Nic turned to face her.

"You are the daughter of Stefano Salucci and the cop who couldn't be bought. Stefano had a lot of supporters in high places, people you don't even know. Your resilience against Silvio won a lot of favour.

"I don't think you realise just how close you came to almost bringing down the whole organisation. You might think you're done with it, and maybe in your mind you are. But in our world, determination like that never wanes and it's intergenerational.

"Gatto will say you have influenced me to betray them all. On that alone, the Commission would support his actions towards you and me."

Francesca bit her lip and spoke solemnly.

"I should never have come."

53

Milan, Italy

Gatto knew he'd stirred the hornet's nest and was now very much alone. And to his surprise he realised he was more than satisfied operating on the outer circles of the corrupted group. It gave him perspective and opportunity to see things others couldn't.

He walked on in the dark, taking the back, dimly lit streets of one of the most beautiful cities of the world. But he was not there for the fashion and the culture. Or the dingy night time activities claiming souls in the back streets.

He'd find a way to prove his theories beyond the hearts and minds of the Commission. In the meantime he'd seek refuge in the comfortable lodging no one would even think about checking. Carlo Seta had kept a place in this district for Anya Frida Volkov.

Seta's one time mistress, lost in the Afghanistan mountain ranges in some Taliban camp, was putting up more than he could even imagine. It was a grisly end for the genteel woman who, for the best part of her entire life, had stood by the mob boss.

But what Giuliett wants, she gets. Gatto knew it was a rush

of blood that put wheels in motion she'd no clue about, egged on by Enrico Nero. He wondered if the heiress regretted the action now.

Despite his abilities, Gatto had to be careful. He'd used and influenced Pocco as much as he dare. He knew the self-obsessed Florentine mob boss would fold at the first sign of pressure from the Commission. Gatto had been careful to load the bullets and let Pocco fire the gun.

But with Giuliett now being mentored by the Moretti family, her knowledge may be his eventual downfall. He shook off the ill feeling. Gatto knew how to play her. Pressure turned her head to her vices. Any credibility gained would soon be lost.

He was the only choice to take control. The Seta clan may be in a leadership crisis right now, but he was not yet in the position to take the lead. Not until he sorted out Delarno and his association with the Guardians. And the way to do that was through Salucci. Nic would do anything for that bitch. Even give up the leadership if the Guardians secret could not be found. It was a win-win situation for Gatto. He just had to be a little more patient.

The consigliere reached the plush apartment complex and scoped the area. Nodding at the doorman, he took the elevator to the fifth floor. He let himself inside.

The entrance opened to a parlour that looked out to parkland and the city lights of Milan. He flicked on the rooms only light, a crystal and coloured glass chandelier, commissioned in Venice by Carlo for his mistress.

"Hello Gatto." Giuliett greeted him icily from a single lounge chair positioned in the corner of the room. Loris Moretti stood beside her.

"Giuliett!" He bent to kiss her cheek and hide his surprise. "On a terrible night such as this, I see you too are seeking comfort in a private place we both know well."

Giuliett looked through his lies.

"I'm so very sorry to hear about Bice. We're all suffering with her loss. I still can't believe it. It's devastating. Please accept my deepest sympathies. I am at your loyal service if you need anything."

At her continued silence he added. "I'm an old and simple man Giuliett, I don't know what else to say to you to ease your pain."

"I bet you don't." She said.

The older gentleman turned to her consigliere. "Good evening Loris. Thank you for being with Giuliett at this difficult time."

The henchman nodded.

"I didn't know you were in Milan." She said to Gatto.

"I've just arrived back tonight." He lied.

"And you thought to yourself, I'll breeze on in to Anya's home and settle in until things blow over?" Giuliett asked.

"I'm not sure what you're implying Giuliett." He said. "But I confess I do wonder at you being here."

"I thought I'd made myself clear." She said. "Stay out of Seta business. And yet here you are. Right in the middle. I've run out of patience with you Gatto."

Gatto was not prone to panic. Nor was he used to being questioned over his loyalty. He looked for a way to turn the tables back on the girl he'd always thought of as his daughter. He gnawed at her pinch point.

"Now Giuliett." He cautioned. "Don't make the same mistake you made with Anya."

"I beg your pardon." Giuliett paled, despite her outward show of strength.

At that point Gatto knew he had her right where he wanted her. It was a huge mistake for her to confront him in Anya's home at a time and place she'd feel most vulnerable and emotional. She was walking straight into his lead and was too stupid to realise.

Loris on the other hand, aware of all the nuances, remained prepared.

"I know who hurt your mother." Gatto said smoothly, like he was reassuring a child. He glanced at the stony-faced Loris Moretti.

"And you know this because?"

"Bice discovered the family secret."

"What are you talking about?"

He had to be careful here.

"She confided in me before she came to Milan. I know how to remove the Guardians once and for all."

"I'm all ears." She sounded sarcastic but Gatto knew her well enough. Her ambition ran as deep as her hatred of the Delarno family.

"Alessandro is playing both sides."

Giuliett laughed. "You've got to be kidding me. I've never heard such garbage. Next you'll be telling me that Silvio was the leader."

"Don't be absurd." He said. "I just need time and a place to work up some leads. Then you can confront Nicholas at the next Commission meeting with all the evidence. And the leadership will be yours."

"You must think I'm a fool." She said, shaking her head from side to side.

"I do not." He said. "I also know the risks. We are on the same team, even if you don't believe so at the moment. Carlo installed a safe here in the apartment. He had been building a case against Alessandro. Only he, Anya and I knew about it.

"It holds the proof we need. There's a tangible link between Alessandro Delarno and Stefano Salucci. I know it. I think Bice discovered it after she'd handed the leadership to Alessandro. So Delarno engaged Robbie L to murder your mother."

Giuliett thought for a long moment.

"Alright." She said. "Let's take a look in the safe. I assume you know the combination."

"Yes."

Giuliett motioned for him to go to the safe situated in Anya's bedroom. He punched in the combination and went to open the door.

"Stop!" she said. "Step back. I'll open it. We wouldn't want any surprises now, would we?" Loris was one step ahead of her and held Gatto under the constant supervision of his pistol.

Giuliett pulled out the contents. She emptied everything on the bed.

"I see a lot of beautiful things here," she said, "But I don't see any evidence of Guardian relationships as indicated by you."

"Look at the passports." He said.

"Fine." Giuliett held them up. "Anya the Russian. Anya the Italian. Anya the American. Carlo the American. That's it."

Giuliett walked up into his space. Her eyes and mind were clear.

"Do you know what I think Poppa Gatto? My mother did not confide in you and Robbie L did not hurt her. I think you couldn't stand that my mother chose another man. You are a murderer and traitor of the highest order."

It was smallest of glances behind her, more an intuitive, non-verbal communication between them. Loris shot the former consigliere without a second thought. Life was over in a moment.

And without a second glance, Giuliett turned on her heel leaving her long-time friend and advisor slumped and dead on Anya's bed, surrounded by all her treasures. Loris Moretti was by her side, in close step with his new boss.

"There's a mess upstairs that needs cleaning up." Giuliett said to the doorman at the unit block's exit. "Let it be known, traitors will not be tolerated."

54

Genoa, Italy

Delighted to be on board the Sea Meadow at last, Robbie mapped the course to return to Sydney as quickly as possible. He wasn't running away. He was getting back to business.

He'd said goodbye to Bice Seta at the Milan Cathedral. Hidden in the upper reaches, he had the mental capacity and truth on his side to face off the emotional Italians, but why tempt fate when there was another, more familiar life waiting for him in Australia.

He came and saw. He'd done what he set out to do. That was to learn the business utilising his own skills, eyeballing the operation, rather than relying on Silvio's tainted versions.

And from the shadows the experienced man manager had worked out whom he could trust and who wasn't worth the space. His job was done and now it was time to go home.

Well, that's what he was telling himself as his cell phone rang unexpectedly early one October morning.

"I hear you're moving out soon." Her voice was husky with emotion and the sleepless strain of the last fortnight.

"Giuliett! Yes, I'm leaving tomorrow."

"Without a goodbye?"

"Well, honey, the last time you said goodbye you tried to sink my beautiful yacht, so I'm sure you'll forgive me."

He felt her smile on the other end of the phone.

"At the time, Signor, I felt I had little options available to me. I want to thank you for coming to Bice's last day with us at the Cathedral."

"My deepest sympathies extend to you and the family."

"Thank you." There was a slight pause. "You're not staying for Alessandro's ..." her voice trailed away. "Delarno is your family now. It would be expected."

Robbie L thought she sounded tired. Like it was a struggle for her to speak. Her voice was quiet and soft, as she chose her words carefully in short, direct sentences.

"Look Giuliett, I think the last person anyone needs to see is me. And granted normally that wouldn't faze me, however, I have my own business to run at home. I've been away too long." He said.

"Despite the warrant for your arrest?"

"Pha! What's new about that?" He said laughing off the far away threat.

"A modern-day pirate to the core." She mused. "I want you to stay."

It was the last thing he expected to hear.

"Well now, why would I want to do that?" he asked.

"I need your objectivity and distance to help me work through a problem."

"And here I was thinking you wanted my body!" He quipped. "Sorry sister, flattery will get you nowhere."

"What do you need done to make you stay?" she asked and waited.

"It's that serious?" he asked when she didn't elaborate.

Robbie L thought for a moment. "It's going to cost you. As I said, I have my own business to run, not sort out Seta group problems."

"Name your price." She said. "I'm willing to pay double."

"Give me the day to think about it."

55

. . . .

"I'm glad you changed your mind." She said, as he followed her into the sophisticated apartment by the sea. "You remember Loris Moretti, don't you?" Giuliett indicated her new consigliere, standing by the window and scanning the busy street below.

"Is this some kind of weird joke? You're the clown who tried to kill me on my boat." Robbie L faced them with both angrily. He turned to Giuliett. "You really take the cake you know."

"No sir, this is not a joke." Loris Moretti stepped forward and reached out in a friendly gesture. "I meet you now in different circumstances."

"And that's meant to be okay?" Robbie L glared at Giuliett. Regardless, he shook the man's outstretched hand.

"Come now Robbie L," she said. "It's already been an upsetting and long week."

Robbie L looked between her and Moretti.

"You will see my advice was correct. It was wise to attend Alessandro's service." She said. "You're part of the Delarno clan, so by taking a place alongside me, shows those who matter, that we are all one. It puts Pocco on the outer even more. Particularly now you've extended your respect to the clans and the remaining Delarno family.

"Nicholas and Paolo embraced you. You may think it's

nothing, but in our family, such gestures have meaning and are not forgotten."

"Like I had a choice." He mumbled begrudgingly, despite knowing she was right. "Did you see Pocco's face when we walked in together?"

They nodded.

"He knows, we know. It's a matter of time for that two faced Florentine. But I know how to manipulate him. We'll have no more trouble from that clan." Giuliett said.

"I hear you set Gatto straight." Robbie L said.

Giuliett nodded and paled as the colour washed from her face.

"There has been too much talk of death this week." She sat on the gilded, turquoise coloured chaise lounge.

"Loris, you must be exhausted too." She said, looking between the two men standing before her. "How about we meet again tomorrow morning? Do you mind Robbie? I'm sorry I know I promised you a meeting. All of a sudden ... I suddenly feel very fatigued."

Robbie L looked at her taut face and the deep dark circles she couldn't hide with makeup. "No problem. Can I get you something? Caffé? A drink of water?"

"Thank you, no. I just need a quiet afternoon. Loris you make a time with Robbie." She stood unsteadily and wandered into the bedroom.

"I'll be next door, Signorina." The consigliere said. "If you need anything just call."

She shut the bedroom door. He took his cue and walked out with the outlaw biker. They stood in the entrance threshold.

"One of us is staying right." Robbie L said. "She doesn't look good."

"I agree. Do you want to take shifts?"

"How about I stick around tonight and you can do the day stint." Robbie said. "You look like you could do with a decent afternoon off and a good night's sleep yourself."

Loris nodded. Sensing the consigliere wanted to ask something else, Robbie L said, "It's alright. I know in your country, Dons don't do this kind of thing. But where I'm from, we don't mind getting our hands dirty. I've certainly done more than my share of dogwatch over precious cargo. I'm good as gold."

He opened the door for her man.

"Okay, thank you Signor. Call me if you need assistance. Good afternoon."

"Buon pomeriggio Loris. I'll see you tomorrow at 9am. And not a minute before."

56

. . . .

"First things first." The outlaw biker said as he walked back into the main salon of the quiet suite. He slipped out of his dark suit jacket and threw it over the back of the chair. Next he unbuttoned the wrist cuffs and first two of his shirt collar. He slid the necktie lower so it hung like a pendant in the middle of his chest.

He took a deep breath, walked to the opened window and looked out beyond the harbour into the Ligurian Sea. His mind traced the route. Sail set to starboard, and he's heading to Barcelona, via Ibiza. Choose port side and he follows the Italian coast all the way to Sicily, around the toe of the boot to Greece and into the hotbed of the Mediterranean Sea where it meets the Suez Canal.

Stay right here, and he's entering a hotbed of his own. God only knew what was on Giuliett's mind. But she had the guts to take out Gatto and she's clean. Robbie L thought it prudent to hear her out. And he'd negotiated a nice little percentage of her clan's income for it.

He sighed. All the same, it would be nice to be on the Sea Meadow and charting a return journey to Sydney. At a noise behind him, he swung around.

"You're up again. Can I get you a drink? Paracetamol?" He asked.

"I heard a noise. I thought someone was in the apartment."

"Surprise! I volunteered to stay on duty. Loris looked like he needed an afternoon off."

"I don't need a babysitter." She said, but there was no sting in her comment. "But thank you for staying. I'm just so tired. I don't understand it."

"Well, go and have a nap. I'm good. I'll watch television or something. You won't even know I'm here. I'll even be extra quiet."

"I suppose it's easy for you." She said suddenly. "I bet you've lost a lot of friends. Some perhaps by your own hand. I always think that kind of thing is easier for a man."

"Because we don't have feelings?" he asked. "It's never easy Giuliett, to take another man's life. Are you sleeping?"

"A few hours here and there. It's easier to just keep on working."

There was a slight pause.

"Did you ever have to take the life of someone you thought was on your side?" she asked.

"Yes." He said solemnly. "It's difficult. You trust someone and then they betray you in a way you didn't think possible. What Gatto did to your mother and Alessandro is an unthinkable act of dog arse treachery.

"The prick deserved to die. And I'm not just saying that because he tried to plant the stitch on me."

"You did it again." She said with a tired little smile.

"What's that?"

"You swore again. How many days is it this time?"

"Oh," he laughed. "I didn't notice. It must only happen when I'm alone with you!" He smiled knowingly at her and their private, shared joke.

"Giuliett, we don't have to talk about this now. I've made the commitment to stay to sort out whatever you need. I've put a solid leadership team in place back home. Go to bed and have a sleep. We'll chat when you get up. Hell, we'll chat all night if you're up to it."

Giuliett looked at him and he wondered if she'd even heard him. Her expression was real. Her baby blues, red with unspent tears, shimmered. Her sad stillness washed over them both as they stood, facing each other in the midday heat filling the apartment.

Robbie L sensed he should reach out and yet he doubted she would even register his touch. He did anyway. His hands gently clasped hers. He brought them together and up to his heart place, so she could feel his life filling her.

She watched the motion, observing as if from afar. He held her sadness in his breath.

"When you look into your soul and you see nothing." She said quietly, her eyes searching his. "And you look into your heart and it sits like a rock in your chest. And so you search through your emotional toolkit as you've been taught, looking for anything to help you. You look for that which used to bring joy.

"And no matter how hard you try, all you find is the deepest abyss. So you look towards the habits that used to bring you down, and then realise you're too far gone to be bothered with them. What do you do then?" she asked.

"What do I do then?" she repeated.

"I ... I've been there too." He said, his emotions in check. "When I lost my sister Meadow. I can tell you all the things that don't work. And believe me I tried a hell of a long list.

"Time. Giuliett. Time is your friend and guide. Learn to sit with those terrible feelings. Quietly. Peacefully. Accept the feelings and allow them to move around and through you. A bit like that breathing thing I've seen you do when you're stretching."

She nodded a quiet acknowledgment.

"You're a good man, Robbie L, despite what they say." She said, placing his hands by his side. She turned away from him and headed towards the bedroom.

"What do they say?" He called after her. "Aww crap, Giuliett, don't leave me hanging!" But he was only teasing and they both knew it. He already knew what they said about him.

57
....

Hours later, after watching all the television he could stomach, calling his team to check in, checking the weather outside and eating and drinking until he couldn't anymore, Robbie L wondered what else he could do. He looked around the apartment in the expectation that new entertainment would jump out of the highly decorated, painted plasterwork.

He quietly checked on Giuliett, fast asleep in the dark room and paced the floor of the entire suite. Finding a radio in the lounge area, he tuned into a music station. He sat on the chaise and scrolled through his phone, searching the world wide web for anything and everything that caught his attention in an eclectic range of topics and eventually gave into the boredom.

Three sets of fifty push-ups, squats and crunches and variations thereof, he decided to take a shower. He checked on the sleeping beauty again and satisfied that all was in order, he stepped into the bathroom.

Sunlight streamed through the open window, its angle high and to the west. It lit the shower box and as Robbie L stepped into the tepid water streaming down, he caught his reflection in the polished glass of the shower screen.

It took him by surprise, to see his reflection this way, undistorted by mirrors and showing his torso as he really was, half lit in the sunshine. Yet he could see all of him in the shadows as well. All the imperfections, the freckles, the ink of his tattoos were completely visible in both light or shade. He focused on the memorial mark dedicated to his sister.

In the direct sunlight and at such close proximity the detail was more evident. Adding to his wonder, his image fitted in the sun's light bath perfectly framed in angular shards of shadow. He moved and the light shone on his centre chest bone and the springy dark hair sprouting from there. He could observe every detail, segmented and brought into focus by the sun's light, factually correct and so very clear.

He moved to centre the attention on the left peck and Meadow's tattoo. He noticed there was no warmth from the sun. Only the light highlighting slabs of his body in its own objective will, creating a pure, visual experience. His attention was caught further as the water trickled over his pecks and the intricate design he'd created just for her. This was the first time he had seen it in this meditative way, faithful to her, without emotion. It took him by surprise.

A sound and movement of the connecting door opening turned his attention to Giuliett. Without a word, she stepped into the shower space with him. Her eyes said everything she couldn't.

Under the streaming water she brought his head down to hers. She pressed her forehead to his, gently nudged his nose and kissed him. Her passions released in their mouths and he steadied himself, placing his hands either side of her on the tiled surface above her head.

She lifted her head slightly, nuzzling his neck in the soft place below his ear and returned to his lips. Her forearms wrapped around his neck, holding his head close to hers. Robbie L lifted her hands above their heads and turned her on the spot towards the sunlight. He stood behind her, pressing her bottom to mould with his hips.

The shadow cut a line, highlighting her left eye and breast and a soft, creamy décolleté. Behind her, he too was caught. The light did not discriminate.

He gently traced the shadow line across her, from the top of her head until he reached the exit point at her hips. Her eyes closed, she moved in the sunlight as his fingers traced the definitive path between light and dark. With his inquisitive touch, her movement altered. Mesmerised by the sensuality of her and her instinctive sunlight dance, his desire grew.

Her breast was now fully exposed to the sunshine. Every tiny bump, every shade of colour of her hardened nipple and the tiny goose bumps of arousal were there, magnified in daylight and uninhibited in the glass reflection.

He watched it change. He wanted it. He touched it. He couldn't resist, entranced by the play of shadow and light and her reaction to the slightest touch of his fingers as they traced over her. He breathed deeply in and exhaled slowly. Her desire grew. Evident as her skin reacted to his soft, warm breath.

He ached to taste her. His lips touched her shoulder. He bit her golden skin gently, tracing the supple path to her neck. He watched her reflection as she reacted to him. The tiny bumps of arousal covered her breast and as her lips parted, those pearly whites bit down into pink softness. Her head moved back to him exposing her neck and the freckles splattered in the hollow, shimmery and damp, above her collarbone.

His attention turned to her beautiful face. Eyes closed, she moved lost in each sensation. Her highlighted forehead and those silky black eyelashes pressed downwards in the light. The water bounced across her, falling in a delicate stream along her jaw, trailing her neck to find the path between her breasts. He traced it gently with his fingertip, stemming its flow and tracing its new path.

She pressed into him as her hands slid along his thighs and moved to the small space between him. She let them linger and as his yearning grew, he found that place, soft and supple on her neck and suckled until the temptation to turn her to face him subsided.

She reached behind him, pulling him closer to her before sliding her hands along his buttocks to return to his thighs and the space between their legs. She waited and lingered there, caressing them both until her finger tips followed the contours of her body to fondle her breasts. She sought his arms, shoulders and eventually his head forcing his lips deeper to her throat.

He focused on the long blonde strands pressed in waves across the indent and rise of her collarbone as it shifted and moved with her breath. Extending across the top of her shoulder, golden strands of honey coloured hair were dipped in sun filled droplets.

He pinched them together watching the droplet squeeze through his fingers and run down his thumb. He brought the watery thumb to her lips and she opened her mouth to him.

And for all the time, the sensuality of skin pressing against skin, naked and wet. Craving for precious fulfilment in touch. Robbie L bent his head to kiss her again. He watched himself in the reflection, closing his eyes as his lips met the side of her neck and travelled towards her wanting mouth as he at last spun her to face him.

She cried out as he sucked the breath from her lips. It was

the only sound she made. He made love to her in that sun filled shower room, directed solely by the play of light and shadow. When she was ready, he carried her to the bed and he loved her again with all the tenderness she needed for as long as she needed.

58

Delarno Estate, Rapallo, Italy

When Nicholas drove into the estate driveway and parked the sporty black Mercedes in the vast garage, he didn't immediately enter his home's interior. Instead, he wandered to the edge of the property and the lover's seat set in the centre of a semi-circle shaped pergola shrouded in a blooming climbing rose.

Through a wrought iron fence, the small harbour below was clearly visible and the viewer was protected both from probing eyes and unsavoury winds.

His mother had planned this space. He remembered she couldn't decide on the ivory, the mauve or the coral, so she'd chosen all three and a combination thereof, and planting the rose bushes randomly, had now achieved a rich scented wall as unique as her taste.

As a child he'd been impatient to leave the nursery, having been tasked to help with carrying the purchases. Impatient to get to the water or the sporting field or whatever held his interest that day; anywhere but the place rank with the smell of fertilisers and earth and damp.

Today, he'd give anything to be following her amidst the endless rows of flowers.

He watched the serene scene before him and let the emotions of the day drain away. He was tired. Exhausted in fact. Emotionally. Mentally. Physically. Saying goodbye to Alessandro this morning had been harder than he could ever have imagined. It was as if today he'd said goodbye to three at once – Maria, his mother and the uncle who meant more to him than his own father.

And so he sat, his body shaking in grief and tears, in the sunshine and the patchwork of haze and flowers, tiny singing birds and buzzing insects as that gentle breeze lifted off the harbour and found its way to him.

"Thought I'd find you here." Francesca came to him some time later, joining him in the private space, handing him an icy drink and a damp cool towel. He wiped his face and hands.

"This my favourite place to be when everything is too much." She said quietly, standing behind him. She rested her hand on his shoulder and his hand came up to rest on hers. "God bless Cristiana." She continued. "I'm so grateful she cherished this little spot too and had the vision to make it even more special."

She rubbed his upper chest and shoulder gently, leant forward and kissed him on the top of the head near his temple.

"Do you mind?" she asked.

"Please." He said.

She sat close beside him. He reached out and placed his hand on her thigh.

"I need you Francesca." He looked at her for a long moment

and turned again to the harbour.

"I need you more than I've ever needed you in my life. But I know that's not what you want. I wish you could have been there today with me as my wife. I wish you could have been there with all our family. I wish things could be different." He said to her. There was another long pause.

"This is too hard. I can't be just your friend. Not at a time like this. I need more from you. I need you, completely, wholly." He concluded. "I need us to be one."

"I know you do. It is a battle for me too. To know this and to try and give my family the truth it needs. I'm realising now that my being here is a huge mistake. Not only have I upset you, I've put you under more pressure. That's the absolute last thing I want to do.

"When I heard about Alessandro, I had to be with you during this time; to show you love and warmth. And cherish you. And I couldn't even get that right. I've been incredibly thoughtless. I'm sorry Nicholas."

He didn't answer.

"I think the best I can do for you is to go back to Fiji, where I belong." She said. "And give you the time you need."

"I think that's a good idea." He said.

He reached for her hand and brought it to his lips. They sat in a silence together.

"Robbie L and Giuliett have formed an alliance. I trust her less each day." He said. "Pocco is unreliable as ever. It's too dangerous to stay in Italy at the moment anyway."

"Robbie L?"

"You're infamous Ares Outlaw Motor Cycle Gang friend."

Her mind ticked over.

"There's a blast from the past." She said, quietly stewing as her thoughts churned.

"Fricking Robin Lark, hey? I don't believe it. Johnno and I have unfinished business with that prick. What's he doing here?" She asked.

"He took over where I left off. He runs the Australian operations for us."

Francesca looked incredulous.

"What?" He asked.

"Nothing." She said. "I just thought ..."

"You thought what?"

"Nothing." She repeated in a stronger tone.

"Francesca, I do have a business to run. And he is a great operator, despite being a pain in my arse."

"I've been out of the loop too long obviously." She said wondering how she felt about this latest knowledge and the reality of Nic's duplicity slapped her in the face once again. She sat quietly beside him, staring out to sea, mulling over her potential options for action or not.

"You can always come back, you know." He said quietly. "From a business perspective, I could use you well."

"Use me well?" She turned to face him.

"You know what I mean." He said. "I've always championed your abilities. Bring your talents, Francesca. You'd be helpful *if* we could get past the whole Salucci Guardian business that's putting you in this awkward juncture with the Commission and fucking up our lives."

"Yeah well, I've gotten by pretty well so far without the added complication of working in secret with the Delarno's and the Guardians, thanks very much." She looked out to the harbour.

"Who said anything about in secret?" He asked.

"Well, I'm assuming that's the only way." She mumbled. "Isn't it?"

Gently reaching for her wrist, he pushed the sleeve of her pink day dress towards her elbow revealing her forearm and the cross hatches of defensive wounds, the pink lineal scars of the knife, inflicted during her altercation with Silvio. Silently his hand wrapped around them and held her. She felt the warm energy of him flow through her and the irritation of damaged nerves that surfaced every time her forearms were touched. She pulled her arm away, mumbling, "Don't touch it."

He caught her hand and she stilled, trapped in his eyes filled with sadness and something more. Instinctively, Francesca felt her fingers uncurl slowly in his palm, the familiar action filling her with comfort.

When she was ready, his attention returned to the exposed forearm. She swallowed her racing heartbeat, following his silent stroke with anxious eyes as he travelled a direct pathway from her wrist to her bicep, to linger at her shoulder.

In a trance, absorbed in a mixture of conflicting feelings, she blinked slowly when his touch reached her heart space, opening her troubled eyes at last to meet his. He filled her vision and at that moment, Francesca realised his attention had never left her face as his touch remembered and his mind felt.

Her shirtdress unbuttoned another. The warmth of him spread across her chest and damaged shoulder. Her eyes closed again savouring the safety of his healing gentleness.

Next, his thumb sought the hollow below her lips and his fingers splayed out across her cheek and jaw. Francesca rested her head into them.

He gently massaged the meridian point at her chin and paused for a moment. Francesca tasted him. Her lips pressing against his skin and she gently suckled. She felt his sharp intake of breath.

The loving caress traced a pathway to her cheekbone and temple. He smoothed her hair behind her head, down the back of her neck and returned to her heart. Francesca opened here eyes and heart to him.

Her fingers remained caught in his grasp. He brought them to his lips in the same tender way, held them there for the longest of moments, but not long enough. Soft lips pressed against her palm. Next he enclosed her hands fully, as if he wanted her to hold that feeling, keep it safe and never let it go

With each measured touch, she watched the emotion ebb and flow as his soul remembered. Her energy tumbled inside, in tune as it always was, with each rise and fall of his emotion.

He placed her hand in her lap, buttoned her dress and rested his hand on her thigh as it had done before. His heat burned through the fabric of her skirt where his leg touched hers, and her own desires bounced around them. He'd joined them together in a similar way last year in Venice. A symbolic joining of heart and soul, and combined pain, reminding her of the trauma they both shared as a result of her connection to the Guardians.

All manner of heaven and earth, she wasn't made of stone!

"Oh yes, so far so good." He said huskily. "This is the outcome of secrets."

"Well, aside from that." She said, her voice disturbed and caught in her throat.

She sat for a long time reliving his silent demonstration in her mind and fighting the longing desire to kiss him and push all that hurt away.

"The only way to solve this problem once and for all is if I declare my allegiance to the head Capo. The boss of all the bosses." She said at last, her voice full of emotion. "Or you."

"Would certainly solve a lot of problems for you." He said looking ahead to the harbour. "And for me come to think of it. I could visit the kids without fear."

He faced her.

"They could holiday with Zio Nicci in Rapallo. You know how much fun that would be." He said dreamily. "You remember, don't you?" he asked feeling nostalgic.

"I remember." She said quietly. "It was a beautiful time together."

There was another long silence between them.

"It would never work. We shouldn't even be thinking such things. We're both too vulnerable at the moment to make a solid decision." She said.

"You're probably right."

Nicholas lent forward, his elbows resting on the tops of his thighs. His shirt fluttered open in the slight breeze. In the air between them, his masculine scent combined with his Armani perfume.

It was a combination so familiar to her. Francesca breathed in. She knew everything about him. His tastes. His faults. The parts of his soul he only shared with her.

"I'm not made Nicholas and I'm not about to begin the process of joining the mafia now."

"No-one said you had to be made Francesca. That's the path you take when you desire leadership roles." He said. "Giuliett's not made."

"Sinclair would kill me. Not to mention your operations are

highly illegal! We've gone through so much trying to protect Archie. To turn around and commit to this organised crime outfit so that it's easier for us? It's a crazy idea. I might as well watch the last shreds of my integrity walk out the door now."

"You wouldn't have to do anything you didn't want to do." He said. "You just have to prove your loyalty to me. Which, by the way you've already done through your actions towards me, Paolo *and* Alessandro. And you'd never have to worry about Archie and Bella's safety ever again."

"You make it sound so easy." She said.

"I'd be there every step of the way. You're already under protection thanks to Bice Seta. It's up to me to act on your behalf and convince the Commission you're on board."

She closed her eyes to him. She was so conditioned to pleasing him.

"I'm not making any decisions now. My brain and my emotions are too caught up in this." She said truthfully, her hands doing a wide circle around them. She looked at him to see his reaction.

He turned to smile at her.

"Don't Nicholas! I'm not making any promises one way or another."

"I'm not doing anything." He said in mock defensiveness.

"Stop looking at me that way. Don't think you know the answer." She laughed. "Because you don't."

"Nothing ventured, nothing gained." He joked. "And that's all I will say on the matter."

"Do you think anyone else knows about the apartment in Salerno?" she asked.

"Hard to say. Are you thinking of heading down for a bit?"

"It's one option available. I mean, I should like to see the place my father has left me. If I can, I might as well whilst I'm here in Italy. Who knows when I'll be back this way?" Death was bringing with it nostalgic feelings of her own.

"Curiosity killed the cat." He said.

"Nothing ventured, nothing gained." She said, smiling back at him.

59

．．．．．．．．．．．．．．．．

"What the fuck am I doing?" Francesca said out loud to herself. "This surely has to be the stupidest idea I've ever thought. Sinclair is going to kill me. I don't need to worry about the Commission. *He* will literally kill me."

In a one-way conversation with herself, as her hire car zipped through the Cinque Terre tunnels on route to Salerno, she countered, "I haven't actually made the commitment. I'm just thinking about it."

She checked her side mirror and the rear view as she came up at speed behind a slow-moving truck.

"Yes, but you're seriously thinking about it." She said out loud. "And we all know where that will lead. Sadness and anxiety make you take stupid risks. Now we've already established you're feeling sad and that your anxiety levels are through the roof."

On the inside lane she over took the slower vehicle in a highly illegal move and then had to cut him off as the lane suddenly merged. Her actions were accompanied by an abusive sounding horn. Francesca cringed.

"Brain! For fuck's sake, shut up!" she yelled to herself in the empty car. "You'll make me have a fricking accident!"

She took the corner too wide around another tight bend.

"Okay that's it. I'm out." Her common sense chimed in. "If

you don't slow down around these corners Francesca, there will be a terrible accident. What is the rush anyway?"

And she eased off the accelerator and sat in the slow lane to gather her breath and her mind together. The truck passed her with a barrage of abuse and the horn blazing.

The trouble is Francesca Salucci is that you want your cake and to eat it too! There is only right and wrong in this space. There is no grey area. She thought.

And for a brief moment her heart and mind agreed.

Unless, of course, I swear allegiance to Nic, and only Nic, regarding this one outcome with Robbie L. That way I'm protected from further illegal activity. I'm safe and so is my family.

"So let me get this straight. You're going to cross the line. Join Nicholas Delarno in his illegal activities to bring down Robbie L and then go back to being Miss Integrity? It's not going to work. You're just like Nic. You want your cake and to eat it too!" She said emphatically. "You can't pick and choose assignments. Once you're in, you're in for life. You're a fool if you think it's going to work any other way. End of topic."

An instructional sign at the exit of the tunnel and the numbered highway route she was meant to be following came into view and focus. Francesca took the opportunity to quickly glance at the water glimpses. It was almost decision time. Soon she'd near the exit to Rosignano Marittima. Would she stop for a quick break or keep driving?

She decided to push forward and turned on the radio hoping the distraction would block out her thoughts. Francesca sang along to the songs she knew until she was sick of her bad tone and the playlist.

Perhaps she should have stopped. After the distraction of

decisions around stopping or not was over, her mind started to wander again. And to Francesca's astonishment, it picked up where she'd left off.

And therein lay the hypocrisy. She was an ex-cop joining the mafia. And her ex-lover was the Don. She'd heard the old saying; sometimes you have to join them to beat them. The tried-and-true ways she and Johnno had taken had brought negligible results. Perhaps, for all her fighting against it, this actually was the only way forward. The realisation of that sat a little too easily in her for her liking.

Well, I'll just have to find a way to negotiate out after we apprehend Robbie L. She thought. Nic will understand. I wasn't even thinking of it until I heard about Robbie L. A long time ago I swore an oath to protect and serve. That internal commitment never leaves, even if she did physically leave the police force. Her mind's eye drifted to the boy she found in the dumpster all those years ago, his body broken and bent, a result of his brutal initiation ceremony of another organised crime outfit, the Chinese triads known as Chi You. One that he'd failed at and as a result died a lonely, painful death. He was a child, not much older than Archie come to think of it. Her stomach churned violently.

Somewhere, a mother grieves for her lost son. Francesca had made it a personal mission to bring dignity to that boy and the many like him. And Robbie L had brought those cruel bastards into his fold; hidden them, protected them and promoted them within his leadership team.

I may not be in the cops anymore, but I still have my law qualifications. I'm going to get the evidence I need, re-engage Johnno and the Feds and we can finish that business once and for all. And if it means joining the enemy, that's something I just have to do.

And so, somewhere between Rosignano and Rome her mind took the emotion out and she started strategizing how she could temporarily 'join' the mafia and satisfy her need to bring closure on that matter, keep her family safe and bring the Australian Federal Police on board. And then there was Sinclair. That was a conversation that was going to need some rehearsal.

60
....

Salucci Apartment,
Salerno, Italy

"You want to do what?" he yelled into the microphone and she could see on the laptop screen his incredulous face of thunder.

"Hear me out Sinclair."

"No! After all we've been through. All your ranting and raving and tears and promises, this is the way forward for you? Let it go Francesca. You'll never be able to achieve this goal. Not in a hundred lifetimes."

"You're not even going to let me finish are you?" She tried to speak calmly and quietly.

"How long has there been war in the Middle East? Governments and armies have tried to solve that for decades. People supposedly on the right side of the law. I see human suffering every day. Organisations controlled by crime bosses are always going to be one step ahead and do you know why?"

"Enlighten me, because according to you I have no idea about organised crime." She responded sarcastically.

"Because Francesca, they don't care – about people, safe

communities, family ... values. About what's fair! They only care about themselves and their power over others. It's the same with Robbie L. He doesn't give two shits about Chi You. He doesn't give two shits about the people who suffer as a consequence of his criminal acts."

His eyes bore through her in utter outrage.

"He only cares about the power and influence he has over others and sure as hell, you're dead if you try to go on-board with Delarno and bring this fucker in. Nothing in life is fair Francesca! Can't you see that? You don't get merit points for bringing in fuckers.

"This is an ego driven decision, some high and mighty attitude that has no merit whatsoever. You want to make a stand for your kid by bringing down Robbie L? Bring in Delarno. He's the prize. That one's the golden ticket! But no, you could never do that because of 'family loyalty'. Hell for all I know, the way you rushed off to be by his side, you've probably re-ignited your love affair with the prick."

Fully agitated, he rubbed his hands through his hair. "Fuck!" he yelled and slammed his closed fist on the desk beside him. Francesca felt the vibration through the speaker on her laptop and the image jumped as the laptop bounced across the desk.

"It's hard for me to believe that the same person who has all this mystical insight into crooks of the worst kind could never see what was right in front of her nose!" he said. "Delarno is the bad guy - a manipulator of the highest order. You grew up with the family and you want me to believe you never, ever had an inkling that they were an organised crime family."

"What are you saying Sinclair?"

"I want to know once and for all if you've been lying to me

about your knowledge of them. I want to know the truth."

"That's not fair Sinclair. I have always told you the truth." She retorted indignantly.

"Well why do your actions tell me a different story? When will you come to terms with the facts? He is an organised crime boss and has had his fingers in that business his entire life. You're not bringing him in means only one thing as far as I'm concerned." He paused slightly to draw breath. "You're in bed with the prick."

She sat back in her chair overwhelmed by his anger and accusations. He looked straight at her retreating expression and silence and took it as an expression of guilt. His face contorted in pain and hurt.

"*This* is the last thing I need to be thinking about when I'm over here dodging bullets *and* trying to make a living for *our* family. I've never been so angry in my life. I can't talk to you right now."

With that he disconnected their signal and Francesca sat looking at the empty screen. Tears streamed down her cheeks. A message flashed up on her phone. It read,

Do this and we are over. I can't and won't do this anymore with you on this merry-go-round of stupidity. Don't bother coming home if you decide to stay in Italy.

Francesca's hands caught her gasp as they came up to cover her mouth. She burst into tears.

The laptop chimed with a Face time call. She wiped her eyes and answered, expecting another barrage.

"Mummy!"

"Archie! It's nice to see your beautiful face my darling."

"Why are you crying?" he asked.

"I'm not." She lied. "I'm just tired. It's a long way over here and I'm just sleepy. How are you?"

"I'm good. When are you coming home?"

"Well, let me see ..."

"Bell and I miss you. I wish you didn't have to go to Italy."

"What's happened honey?"

"Nothing. I just want you to come home." He said.

"I know. Hopefully everything will settle down again now. And daddy should be home soon! That's something to look forward too, isn't it?" Her voice caught in her throat.

"I suppose so."

"My flight is Friday afternoon. It takes a long time to get to Fiji. So I'll see you on Sunday. How does that sound?"

"Good. It's still a long time to wait."

"I know! It's a long time without a hug from my Archie." She smiled at his piteous face. "I have a good idea. Marnie can find me on her phone. Remember I set it up when we were travelling from Kintail to Wild Dog Creek? Why don't you ask her if you can have a look? That way, you'll know where I am all the time. How does that sound?"

"Okay."

He looked mildly happier.

"In fact, if you look right now, I bet you'll be able to see that I'm in Italy, at a little town called Salerno."

"Okay."

"Are you sure there's nothing else honey bun? Do I need to speak to Marnie or Pop about something?"

"No. I'm going now."

"Okay mate. I'll see you Sunday. Don't forget to tell Marnie so you can pick me up from the airport!"

"I won't. Bye mummy."

"Good bye mate, love you. Love to Bella and ..." and the connection dropped out "and Marnie and Pop. Thanks for the call." Francesca finished saying to the black screen.

She sat at the small writing table and plopped her hands in her head, realising she had one more task to do. She responded to Sinclair's message.

It's foolish. I'm sorry and pressed send. Francesca shut the laptop and her eyes to the last, exhausting twenty-four hours. Sadness and anxiety. That lethal combination always tested her decision-making skills and her resilience. And now she had pushed the limits of her relationship at a time when the one she most loved needed her unwavering support.

61

. . . .

The morning was brighter and Francesca woke to the sights and sounds of the ocean. She lay in bed and looked out to the blue, planning a quiet morning before heading to Rome, the airport and the long flight to Nadi.

It had to be said that Bice Seta had beautiful taste. Francesca admitted to herself the style suited her own personal tastes, stepped up a notch or ten. The interior of the Salerno apartment was completely done in a fresh and uncomplicated way. Perhaps the magazines would call it 'relaxed sophistication'.

Whatever it was, the peaceful interiors had a logical, clean way that appealed to Francesca's free spirited and eclectic method of interior design. Bice however had brought every item into a glamorous focus. Just as a designer holiday home on the Amalfi Coast should appear.

Its location was superb. Francesca had the option of using the adjoining hotel's concierge services or being completely self-reliant. The apartment had its own private and secure entrance and she could come and go as she pleased.

Everything was at her fingertips outside of the building complex. From inside, harbour views stretched as far as she could see. It was quiet. Dreamy. Relaxing. And the sensually sumptuous, understated luxury brought all her feelings to the fore.

She poured a hot tea and pulled a chair to the edge, in the

space between the open terrace and the interior. The transition point. Not in and not out. And it was precisely how she felt.

Her head and heart said to go home. But her gut, her gut wanted justice. Sinclair's accusations spun around her head. *Perhaps you still love the prick.* Well, perhaps she did. One can't ever really turn off those feelings, can they? She'd spent more than half her life nurturing them.

It was inevitable that sometimes circumstance would trigger her feelings towards him. Not that she had any plans of actioning any pent-up desires. But she'd certainly come close this visit. Francesca put it down to grief. Seeing him so vulnerable and so in need. To comfort him without that wall she'd built between them, would certainly have seen her in his bed.

She thought again about his strange silent reminder of their shared pain over the Guardians. And how his touch had ignited in her the many lost feelings she felt for him.

To action any strategy around Robbie L and be bound to Nicholas she was certain would see that wall come crashing down. Because without the support and love of Sinclair, she knew it would only be a matter of time before Nicholas would find a way back to her heart.

She thought about it for a long time. In the end, her decision was made. She would not forgo her children and her relationship with Sinclair on the chance of bringing justice to a cause that was bigger and better than her.

Despite Guardian blood running through her veins and generations of law enforcement making up more than a fair share of her DNA, Francesca chose again to turn her back on that world to focus on her own reality. A life in Fiji with her kids, the clinic and eventually her man, God willing he made it home safe and sound.

Then her phone rang.

"Francesca! How are you sis?"

The warm greeting from her old policing partner filled her with comfort. He was also Sinclair's brother. That was not such a comfortable co-incidence.

"Johnno? He's rung you, hasn't he? I'm very well thanks and I don't need a lecture from you too. I've made my decision."

"Well honey, I think it prudent you follow your gut. You always had good instincts for this kind of thing."

"Thank you! That's what I was trying to tell him but no, he went all Scottish on me!"

"So I hear you've come close to that prick Robbie L."

"Yes. He's mixed up with the Seta clan. Not sure if you've heard of them. I don't think they were in the mix when I was working with you on the Silvio Delarno matter."

"I'm across that group. So, you wouldn't happen to have an idea where he's holed up would you?"

"As a matter of fact I do. That's why I was so keen on sorting this out right now."

"Great! So where is he?" Johnno asked.

"In Genoa. With Giuliett Seta."

"Genoa?"

"North west Italy." She said.

"Well I want you to stay put. Don't move. Don't do anything rash. We've issued a warrant for his arrest. I'll organise for the locals to go and pick him up and a colleague to interview and lay charges. You'll be pleased to know we've just linked him to the death threat you received."

"What threat?"

"What are you truly this vague now? The one against you silly." He said incredulously.

"Johnno, where do you think I am right now?" Francesca asked stepping into the apartment and shutting the door to the patio.

"In Fiji. With the kids, and ma and pa McCrae." He said.

"Not quite. I'm in Italy." She said plainly. "And I don't know anything about a threat. But Archie does. He rang me out of the blue."

Francesca felt her heartbeat winding up to her throat. "Tell me Johnno," she said. "How do I get the feeling something is up via my pre-teen son, before anyone from your office has tried to contact me?"

"Isn't that why Sinclair called me in a flap?" he asked, immediately on the defensive. "Mind I couldn't make heads nor tail of what he was raving on about. I heard Robbie L, well, it doesn't matter what I heard. Maybe we'd better start at the beginning."

"That might be handy." She said and she was clearly getting uptight.

"A week ago we intercepted a communication from a person of interest regarding your welfare. Francesca, you should know it's an old Chi You operative who crossed over to Ares. And we believe the order for the hit came from Robbie L. Do you know why he is suddenly interested in you again?"

"I could hazard a pretty decent guess." She said. "He's settling a personal score on behalf of Giuliett Seta. Giuliett and I grew up together, of sorts. Well, holidayed together when I was sent away with the Delarno's for summer break."

"And why are you in Italy?"

"A dear friend passed away. I came to his funeral and to support the family."

"And that's where you saw Robbie L and Giuliett?"

"I haven't seen either of them. I've heard from a reliable source, he's in Genoa." She said, closing the subject.

Johnno knew better than to press. "And so what were you talking about with Sinclair that got him all hotted up?"

"Err. I can't say precisely," she was too embarrassed to mention it. "But it was along the lines of bringing in Robbie L and those remaining Chi You operatives." She knew she sounded too coy and yet, she for the life of her could not muster a stronger tone.

"Francesca," Johnno warned. "You and I go way back. Long before Sinclair came on the scene. I know that tone. Were you about to do something really stupid?"

"Everyone needs to relax! I'm going home to Fiji tonight like a good girl." She said. "You're a fine one! So much for your big talk supporting me and telling me to follow my instincts! You're both the same."

"Well, after all we've been through together, I think we're best to stick to the legal avenue." He said.

"According to your brother, that never works. Sometimes you have to cross over."

"He said that?" Johnno was incredulous.

"Mostly he was just negative, negative and … well I'm not going to talk about it anymore. Rest assured no-one is crossing over to the dark side."

"Well I'm pleased to hear it. Listen send me your location and flight details. You know the drill. Leave Robbie L to me and when you get home we can sort out this other stuff. By then, he'll be in custody and hopefully so will the operative."

"Righto." She said. "I'll catch you on the roundabout. Oh, Johnno … it's just me isn't it? Not the kids? Or Sinclair?"

"Yes honey, in this case the threat is against you. And we'll have him in the dock before you can say Robbie who?"

Francesca nodded. Her next call would be to Nicholas. To be frank, in the case of Robbie L and Giuliett Seta, she had more faith in invoking the protection protocols of the mob than the long distance lawful actions of the police.

For all intents and purposes, Francesca Salucci was already under Capo protection at the request of Bice Seta. And there was nothing anyone who followed the code could do about it.

Nevertheless, she was an uneasy bedfellow in this new, complex relationship. She didn't even fully understand what it was about. She did know though, this time there were too many variables to take the well-trodden path.

62

· · · · · · · · · · · · · · · · ·

Delarno Estate
Rapallo, Italy

"What is it that you want?" he asked.

Francesca was used to his no nonsense, business-like tone, but never in such a way as was directed at her. She felt ill.

"I want assurance that no-one attempts to harm members of my family going forward." She said tentatively into the mobile phone.

"And what does the organisation receive for this protection?"

"What do you mean?" she asked, confused.

"You have to give me something Francesca. We cannot put this in motion without compensation."

"Bice Seta put me under protection." She said. "It's her will. Surely that's enough."

"No. That's not how it works."

"This is bullshit Nicholas and you know it."

"This is business Francesca. You want my help, you have to give me something in return."

"Nicholas." She pleaded, almost tearful. "This is me you're talking to."

"I need something in return." He was adamant. "What can you offer the Commission on your behalf?"

"This is not how I thought the conversation would go."

She wanted to back out. He remained silent on the other end of the line. He could almost hear her the machinations of her brain as she thought through his proposal.

"Would you like to think about your due for a little bit?" he asked. "Usually I set the payment, but in this case, I'm willing to allow for flexibility."

"That's your favour to me?" She was incredulous.

"Take it or leave it. You can always take your chances with the police."

"Let me think about it."

"Okay. I'm a reasonable man." Nic paused for effect.

"But don't wait too long." He warned. "Outcomes tend to occur more quickly than you imagine."

Great. Francesca thought.

"I only have me and my word." She said quietly. "There is nothing else I have to offer."

"You're offering to pledge yourself to me?" He kept the incredulous tone from his voice. Just.

"That's what it sounds like doesn't it." She was in disbelief at the very words she was hearing coming out of her own mouth. Her mind wandered to Sinclair's reaction and she shut the inevitable stoush out of her thoughts.

"And this is your decision?" He confirmed.

"I suppose it is." She said gloomily.

"Let me talk to the Commission." And he abruptly ended the phone call.

63

....

"Call off the hit against Francesca Salucci."

"I can't do that. It's out of my hands." Robbie L sounded defiant.

"Bullshit! You'll do it right now." Nic was in no mood for games from the second-rate crime boss.

"Why should I?" The biker asked.

"Because, if you don't you'll provoke a not so pleasant experience for yourself. The Commission is tired of your challenging ways."

"The Commission is tired?" he asked. "Or you? Anyway, who here gives a shit about Francesca Salucci? Aside from you, that is."

Nicholas ignored his taunt.

"Bice Seta." He replied. "Salucci is protected. And to be clear, you and anyone else tied to this organisation will not touch the entire family. Understood."

Silence. Robbie L's lack of commentary prompted a scathing reaction from the Capo as he realised protocol had again been ignored by the outlaw.

"You already knew and you went against Bice anyway." He said.

There was another short silence and Nicholas knew he'd hit the mark.

"Giuliett really has you by the balls." He provoked in a deliberate tone. "You want to be careful Robbie L, where you put your dick and your trust."

"Is that right?" The biker ground out the words between clenched teeth. "Tell me, has your little prick teaser made her choice yet? Or is she still blowing you and the soldier?"

He let the words sink in. "Bice's dead." Robbie L said after a few tense moments.

"I'm aware of that." Nic sounded matter of fact. What he really wanted to do was jump down the phone and smash the bikers head into a concrete pylon.

"So nothing she says counts."

"Everything she says counts." Nic said. "Because her wishes were ratified by the new boss."

"Alessandro's dead too."

"He is." Nic's suspicions were confirmed in those three sentences.

"So I don't hear Giuliett supporting this notion." Robbie L challenged.

"Giuliett is not the Don of Seta Clan. I am. And I'm supporting Bice's wishes until we can all settle down and get the spotlight off our organisation. And that means you and Giuliett towing the family line, whether you like it or not."

Nic suspected the words sounded like a thunderclap in the biker's ears. Gatto might have done the deed, but a man like Robbie L had spent a lifetime making good of someone's misfortune.

He imagined the opportunistic biker's illusions of grandeur in the new leadership structure slipping through his fingers like misty clouds on an early foggy morn.

"Now, you'll call off the hit or you'll have more than Interpol to worry about." Nic sounded smug.

"Interpol? I don't give a shit about them."

"You'd better. You have thirty seconds to get your bare arse out of Giuliett's bed or risk being hauled off to a cell somewhere in Siberia."

Nic heard Giuliett's phone rang in the background.

"You can thank Salucci later for the heads up." Nicholas said. "Call off the hit." He growled threateningly and hung up on the outlaw biker.

Robbie L's 'you're not the boss of me' attitude had the Capo at a pinch point. Perhaps it was time he and Zanda made a little one on one visit to the Australian crime boss and explain the machinations of working within the organisation.

Maybe it's time I take matters into my own hands, he thought. Pocco. Giuliett. Robbie L. *These little agitations needed overdue attention.*

He thought about Francesca's offer. He'd keep that one to himself for the moment and the few he trusted within the organisation. For her sake he certainly wouldn't ratify it with the Commission just yet. There was a lifetime of commitment and pain unlocked in that one motion and more compromising than she'd ever experienced living on the fringes.

But he was no fool. Nic vowed to do everything he could to make her believe he had, so that when the time actually came, she was ready and had the support she needed. He'd spent a lifetime protecting her. He wasn't about to throw her to the wolves.

I only have me and my word. Her words resonated within him. It was time to test her sentiments.

Leonardo da Vinci Fiumicino International Airport Rome

"Swings and roundabouts Francesca." She consoled herself. "You'll get him on the flipside. You can be sure of that." Remorse left a bad taste in her mouth. The sooner she was back in the safety of her Fijian home, surrounded by her family, the better.

Nicholas is a prick. She thought although she was angrier with herself than him and wondering what she'd become to betray her own principles in such a way.

She plodded through the customs line and as she approached the electronic body and passport scanner, she noticed a familiar figure and his entourage pass through the express security gate and into the area for duty free shopping.

She watched him stop for a photograph with a fan. Francesca lost him in the moments it took to look into the facial recognition monitor and passport scanner. She stepped through the full body scan and then directly into the shopping space of the terminal.

Francesca quickly skirted the fragrance and make up section and found him pacing around the store as he spoke on the phone. His ever-vigilant minders waited patiently. She wondered if she'd see him in the airline lounge area, the place she was headed to until her flight time.

The ticketing hostess said to go through the terminal, up the escalator, turn left. Give yourself about twenty minutes to get to the gate, she'd said. Francesca wandered through the busy airport interior, casually taking in the sights and sounds.

The busy hub dissipated as she entered another restaurant precinct. She looked up to the mezzanine floor, towards the entrance to the exclusive lounge area. In this quiet area of the terminal, unease crept up on her and the fine hairs on the back of her neck rose.

She dismissed it as a hangover from the betrayal she'd just dished Johnno and Interpol. But as she entered the lounge, an anxious reaction rose again. Her senses were warning her, but of what?

Francesca always trusted her instincts. Even at a time when others might second-guess and dismiss the feelings. She carefully glanced over the seating area, trying to appear nonplussed and not focusing on anyone in particular.

Her eyes swept over the figures as she moved on towards the buffet. A man and a woman. Francesca stopped at the food and the wait staff at the oval shaped bar. She poured cold water from the dispenser and wandered to the buffet section.

Glancing up from that on offer as if she was trying to decide, she walked slowly around the display twice, placed a few items on a plate and found a seat near the exit.

Francesca pulled out her phone and texted Sinclair. *Heading home from Rome tonight. At the airport now.*

She held the phone up slightly and grabbed a quick, silent shot of the couple with time and date.

This is the access code for my phone. She wrote and sent it in a text to Nicholas. Francesca stood to leave. They made direct eye contact with her and a ripple of trepidation rushed through her.

They knew, she knew and her time was up.

Behind her Sebastino Nero strolled into the lounge. Francesca fluffed her hair, and approached him.

"Signor Nero," she gushed. "I'm such a fan. May we have a quick photo please? For my socials and my mum. She loves you as much as I and she will be so happy to see this photograph as a sign of our friendship."

His entourage stepped aside to give them room. Sebastino looked at Francesca and she noticed the recognition flick through his eyes. He shut it down quickly and smiled at her.

"Of course, Signora." He said smoothly.

"Anything for such a fan." He joked.

She stepped in close to him, wrapped her arm around his waist and held her phone out at arms length. "Let's make it a selfie." She said before an advisor could step in to take the photograph.

"Of course." He replied, dismissing his team member.

They smiled together at the lens. She quickly snapped a couple at varying angles and moved the mobile phone slightly to include the small crowd gathered behind them.

"One more." she said pivoting them both to capture the couple preparing to escort her to their colleagues waiting by the door. "This is a better background view."

"Beautiful!" she said. Francesca extended her hand to his and shook firmly. "Thank you very much. I wish you all the luck, Sir. Italy needs you to be our voice at the decision table Signor Nero. It is your time."

"Thank you. The pleasure was mine. Enjoy your flight." He said, covering up his curiosity with a wry smile. As he turned to leave, Francesca dropped her mobile phone into his suit pocket and leaving the lounge area, stepped straight into back up waiting for her.

65

....

'm safe as long as I do as they ask without a fuss. It was the naive mantra Francesca said on repeat as one foot numbly went in front of the other and she approached the door. *Being under mafia protection must account for something,* she thought.

False confidence presented a calm, serene, almost outer body experience guiding Francesca along the upper walkway from the airline lounge, down the escalator and towards the exit accompanied by her small and terrifying entourage of five.

And the rhetoric of high value targets, good negotiation outcomes and her wellbeing rattled around her head until the fear caught her up and she almost screamed.

Can't anyone see I'm here against my will! She almost yelled as fellow travellers milled around and about her, busy in their own schedules and last-minute shopping.

She imagined throwing herself into the arms of the first law enforcement or security officer who happened to come along, pleading for her life. If only she was not so wooden with panic. If only there was one to be seen.

She brought her fear in to focus on the here and now. Focusing on her breath, her mind opened to her surrounds and opportunity. She was not out of the terminal yet. That brought with it hope. She knew Sebastino would realise it was her phone in his pocket. He just had to tap it to reveal the photograph on her locked screen showing the four smiling faces of her family.

In any case she knew he'd call Nicholas to recount the unusual meeting with the Australian Don. She was confident that together they'd realise she was in trouble.

The mobile phone was Plan B in a list of outcomes she'd utilised from the outset. The text messages to Nicholas and Sinclair another. And by chance, the locator tracking system with Sinclair's parents would raise alarm bells when she wasn't en-route as planned.

Despite this Francesca settled in to accepting it could be days before anyone knew she was missing and that she could be anywhere by then. And hopefully not dead.

Francesca had learnt during her years as a detective investigating and prosecuting organised crime outfits to rely on her own wits and common sense. And to do that, she needed to think calmly. She breathed in and out. The best time to escape is in the first moments of capture when the enemy is vulnerable.

Her mind turned to what was before her as she drew on her intuition and the knowledge she'd gained walking both sides of the law with the Delarno family. Francesca guessed these people were eastern European in origin. Their strong faces, manner and build reminded her of such. They were armed. They were calm and their eyes were everywhere.

The gentleman in the lounge was their sergeant. She didn't trust the woman as far she could kick her and there'd be no sisterhood sympathies extended to Francesca as far as she could gauge. She turned her attention to the other gentleman in the group. No telling tattoos, limps or specific outstanding traits amongst them. They formed a silent cage around her, always moving forward and Francesca felt herself being carried along in a wave, like she was caught in a tidal rip.

Look harder Francesca. She prompted herself. *There must be something.*

The envoy reached the gate, stepped through a small corridor enclosed in glass and steel and directly onto the tarmac. Francesca scanned the surrounding infrastructure for possible disruption opportunities. She weighed up her options in this unusually quiet area of the airport.

One by one, they unbuttoned their jackets, and as the breeze tufted out their coats, she glanced at their firearms, revealed and strapped to their person.

She tried to pick the weakest link in the group, and decided he was behind her and to the right. He was new to the outfit and was agitated and uncomfortable. And she felt it was making him second-guess his place. Perhaps he had a point to prove.

And foolishly or not, he became her target.

They were walking towards a hangar now and the small jet stickered with Air China livery warming the engines. The reality of what she'd have to endure before she was negotiated out caused her to stop walking mid stride.

"Is there a problem Signora Salucci?" the gentleman from the lounge asked in abrupt, modified English.

"No. What could possibly be wrong?" She asked, stepping forward reluctantly. She slowed her pace putting distance between the leaders of the group and herself. Here eyes blinked rapidly as she mentally practiced her next move.

She'd have to outgun them all. Every action movie scene of fantastic escapes and close shaves ran through her mind in that millisecond. In all her fantasies and actions and by every stretch of her imagination she was no Jason Bourne.

And so, swallowing her fear, she opted for 'negotiation' and what that might look like.

66

....

They reached the short staircase leading to an open door. Three of the entourage immediately climbed the steps and the gentleman from the lounge indicated for her to step up next in a short, concise motion.

"Thank you." She said trying to sound confident. The whole fifteen-minute jaunt from lounge to tarmac had been conducted in silence apart from those three short sentences. Careful to not give anything away, the outfit had focused on the task at hand.

The silence between them unnerved Francesca, who in previous policing work had operated in the continual tune of Johnno's commentary.

Back in the day, it'd almost driven her mad. But right now, she'd give anything to hear his take on the situation.

She glanced up and took the first tentative steps. Right behind her, two stood looking outwards. The others were on board and the doorway was clear.

In that split second it was her moment. Francesca grabbed the handrail and felt it give out sideways under pressure. It was about a two-metre drop to the ground. Drop. Roll. Run. Hide.

That's when she heard her whispered name and turned to see Angel at the doorframe. In the millisecond instant their eyes met, her friend both reassured and warned. The girl didn't break stride and headed towards the cockpit area.

Francesca's target at the base of the stairs broke protocol and yelled at her to keep moving as he looked between the ground and the rail and her position on the stair. Caught in her curiosity and escape plan, Francesca stumbled back in surprise.

She gripped the flimsy rail and swayed. She took another step back to steady herself.

He was at the side of the short staircase like a shot and Francesca grabbed onto his shoulder to steady her balance. She turned to thank him and was surprised to feel his retaliation of a sharp, direct smack at her ankle with the nozzle of his pistol. She cried out in pain.

His superior came and slapped him twice across the side of the head.

That in turn prompted a terse conversation between them of which Francesca understood not one word. But by the look on his face as he glared sullenly at her, now she was his personal target. She grimaced and limped up the stairwell into the jet.

67
....

Pocco sat facing the door, his pudgy expressive hands clasped around a tall glass of iced water. "Ahh, Francesca, welcome to our little party. So pleased you could attend."

"Signor Poccolini." She said with a quick, sweeping survey of the operatives accompanying them today. "It's been a long time since our acquaintance. Time has favoured you, Signor. You look as lively as ever."

"Thank you. I think we last met in the summer you turned sixteen. The second year we were in Spain together. You were there one minute and then you just disappeared. Poof!" He said just as expressively with his hands. "But, whilst you may have vanished physically, you were never far in our minds.' He said and Francesca understood exactly the inference.

"I believe you may know my friend Li Wei." Pocco said smugly, indicating the man sitting opposite him.

"How do you do?" Francesca asked, swallowing her gall and politely bowing to the Chi You Commander. The triad groups Dragon head.

He nodded at her, his soulless eyes connecting with hers and she felt fear run up her spine. She stared back at him hiding her emotion, as the vein pulsed wildly in the base of her neck, hidden by the collar of her blazer.

"Please take your seat beside us. Three makes a nice number

don't you agree?" Pocco asked.

"Sure." Francesca responded, taking her place in the chair across the aisle and facing them. They sat in a triangle, with small personal tables beside each chair. It was a strange configuration with Pocco and Li Wei facing the front and rear respectively, and Francesca positioned on what would have been the aisle, with her back to the wing and facing centre.

If it was meant to put her off, Pocco had seriously misjudged.

The Don had afforded her and the Chi You operative at the rear of the craft, the best positions on the jet plane to observe everything and everyone. Francesca suspected the Florentine wasn't even aware of the insult he'd dealt the triad Commander by seating him backwards.

This will be interesting. Francesca thought, running her eyes again around the aircraft interior. Pocco's consigliere and another from his team were placed directly behind him, seated close, squashed together on the bench seat.Two Chi You operatives protected their boss. One sat beside Francesca. The other was at the very rear of the plane and constantly watched the crew and the other operatives.

Her unwelcome entourage rounded out the front and rear of the aircraft.

Angel appeared from the cockpit. She nodded discretely to Pocco.

"Angel, tell the captain we are ready to depart." Pocco commanded. "Buckle up everybody."

Francesca watched the Don closely. If she didn't know any better, she'd suspect he was apprehensive as her. She honed in on her intuition and chose her next target.

68

....

"Y ou're very quiet Detective." Pocco commented breaking
a forty-five minute monologue he'd shared with the Chi
You Commander by way of conversation.

"Is something troubling you?" he looked at Li Wei expecting
a nod of approval at goading her. It didn't come.

"Not at all Signor Poccolini." She said. "I'm naturally a very
quiet person."

"Are you not a little interested in where we are going?" He
prompted.

"Of course, I'm curious, as one would expect. I'm hoping,
though Signor, when you are ready, you'll tell me what is in
store and expected from me." She said calmly.

Pocco laughed. His small, fat hands clapped together.

"I expected much more from you Detective Salucci. You
always seemed to have such a fire under your belly to right the
wrong. Gatto and Giuliett spoke about you in such glowing
terms – how your passions drove you to do such outstanding
deeds. Yet you sit here meek as a kitten."

"I'm a little surprised to hear that Signor. I didn't realise I was
held in such esteem." She said.

At this he laughed again.

"You have no idea." He said. "Maybe Silvio did finally sort
you out before he drew his last breath." The Florentine blessed

328

himself, watching her like a hawk.

Francesca held herself in check. She would not let him see just how much that man had taken from her.

"You see Li Wei, as I said to you. We have nothing to worry about with her. Even raising Silvio cannot get a rise from her. Her will is broken and lost. She will comply."

The Chi You Commander looked at her with his silent black eyes and made his own assessment.

"Tell me what brought you to Italy." The triad boss asked in an unexpectedly quiet voice. They were the first words he'd spoken since she'd boarded.

Francesca felt the heat rise to her chest and her heart rate quicken.

"I came to visit an old friend." She said faltering. "To pay my respects."

She steadied her gaze upon the most dangerous man in the room and laid her old fears down. If ever there was a time to think clearly and be concise, this was it.

"And this friend. Tell me how you know him so well." He said.

"Sir, I spent my childhood and teens holidaying in Italy and a gentleman I knew very well recently passed. I wanted to attend his funeral as a matter of respect to him and his family." Francesca said.

"And have your actions always respected this man, even when he was alive."

"Yes Sir, I believe they have. I have honoured our friendship throughout my life as best I could."

Pocco was leaning forward in his seat and he guffawed loudly.

"Did you attend Francesca? Did you attend Alessandro's

funeral? Because I did. And I didn't see you there." Pocco interjected.

"No Signor I did not. After I arrived in Genoa, I realised my being present could be misconstrued and bring more pain to his family and so I grieved in solitude." It was the truth.

She looked plainly at the triad crime boss as she spoke. Not that she expected him to care about family values. To her surprise he sat back in his seat and folded his hands across his lap.

He glanced calmly at his operative standing at the rear of the plane and the slightest change in his facial expression alerted her to prepare.

Pocco missed the whole thing, rabbiting on about the accident and how it was a terrible loss to the organisation to lose both Alessandro Delarno and Bice Seta. At the same time he was assuring his companion that he, Don Poccolini, was in control of the Seta situation until a Commission meeting could bring in Giuliett. His attention turned to Robbie L. He brought Francesca into the conversation again.

"You know Robbie L don't you?" he asked.

"Very well." She said, beginning to get a sense for why she was on board.

"Tell us about him." He asked. "From your point of view."

"Robin Lark and his sister were adopted by a professional family when they were quite young and were brought up in the family business." She said launching into his biography. "Robbie L was a clean skin when he joined the Ares Motor Cycle Gang, and was very much on the fringes when his sister was murdered by a police officer in a shoot-out at an outlaw motorcycle gang compound in central Queensland.

"Meadow, his sister, had made a statement days prior to a specialist officer that she'd been assaulted and raped by the police officer who was stationed in their small town. This had been medically confirmed and the department were preparing to lay charges against the officer.

"In the meantime, the officer stirred up the local population, planted some evidence and was executing a search warrant when things went pear shaped and an all-out assault occurred. Meadow was killed in the crossfire. Robbie L always claimed she was murdered first, before the incident, but a fire in the barrack where his sister was taking shelter destroyed any evidence of that."

Francesca paused, looked at Pocco who was salivating at the dramatics.

"So, Robbie went on a rampage to avenge his sister and hasn't looked back. Ares have elevated to one of the most feared and revengeful outlaw outfits in Australia. He has a take no prisoner attitude and it filters down to his team. They deal in drug manufacturing, money laundering and prostitution.

"He was co-opted into Silvio Delarno's organised crime outfit some years ago. I believe the Australian Federal Police have issued a warrant for his arrest after recently confirming his involvement in the murder of an Australian Chi You operative about eight years ago."

She looked between Li Wei and Pocco.

"Do you know he's in Italy?" Li Wei asked.

"I am aware of that information yes." She said.

"Do you know his current status with Silvio Delarno's businesses?" He asked.

"No." She lied.

"You know he's looking for you."

"Yes, I am aware."

"And here you are."

Francesca shrugged. "Two of us here have issue with Robbie L." She said and turned her attention back to the Florentine.

"Signor Poccolini I don't know where you fit into this picture. I wonder, what is your story about Robbie L?" She paused momentarily. "Perhaps you are our escort and guide to destination unknown." She said. "I can't imagine the biker is crazy enough to try and penetrate your Florentine fortress. Even someone as devious as Robbie L."

"You flatter me!" he gushed. "But it is true, my standing is secure."

"So, what *is* your Robbie L story Signor?" Francesca asked Pocco innocently. "What has he done to you to warrant such a turn?"

He glared at her.

"I fear he is trying to misrepresent the Seta clan with the Commission." He said after a short while. "And I do not agree with his presence in our cause."

"I see." She said. "Even though Silvio, your Capo, brought him in to carry the organisation forward when we thought we'd lost Nicholas."

"We can't always agree with the Capo, Francesca."

"But the terms of your organisation, from my understanding, is that you do not interfere in Capo decisions. Is that not right?"

"It is true, Francesca, we meet and discuss but ultimately the Capo decides. The Capo is like the Chairman of the Board." He said by way of explanation to Li Wei. "He has responsibilities to the members and directs the organisation."

"I assume Robbie L would have fulfilled his obligations." She said, "I mean Silvio did not suffer fools. If Silvio wanted him there, he must have had a vision for him. Perhaps you haven't had the opportunity to see it bear fruit?"

Pocco thought for a moment. Francesca angled to keep him talking and make his own sorry bed, because she sensed he was too caught up in his need to impress and simply too stupid to realise he was digging himself a hole in the eyes of the Chinese crime boss.

"I've seen what he is capable of." Pocco said after a few moments.

Francesca laughed. "I've seen it too! That's why I'm a little surprised you're unhappy with him in the organisation. Although he's an abrasive kind of character and prone to taking liberties where a more mindful person would think twice."

Pocco nodded. "He has a nose for an opportunity, I agree."

"So then perhaps you disagree because he's not Italian leading an Italian enterprise?" she asked, knowing the loaded question would now pitch him against Chi You and the Russians who were eavesdropping. "That is the code right?"

"Yes, it is the code." He said. "He does not possess Italian roots so he has no right to be an equal member of our group. All leaders must be born in Italy. In our businesses, everyone else is second. Robbie L must sit back with everyone else."

Francesca let that one slide and Pocco was too caught up in his own thoughts. She daren't look for a reaction amongst the other men.

"And perhaps you have concerns for Nicholas, Signor." She probed. "Bravo. That's very laudable. But I think Nicholas will not stand for Robbie L to interfere too much. He'll surely challenge and take back what belongs to Delarno."

She was circling like a shark. Francesca had to keep her wits to expose his prejudices. From here on in she'd have to wing it.

"Silvio would be happy to hear he has a friend in you looking out for his son, I'm sure. Supporting him in his efforts to take back what belongs to him. That shows true leadership and loyalty." Francesca cringed. She thought she'd overdone it but this man's ego knew no bounds. He lapped up her praise.

Pocco beamed. "Yes, it is true. We had a good working relationship. With Silvio and Carlo Seta. But we have lost both of them now and Nicholas has stepped into the role. You're correct Francesca. Nicholas will not let Robbie L take from us."

"Silvio. *And* Carlo Seta?" she asked.

"Yes," he said eyeballing her and suddenly the cards flipped. "Nicholas took matters into his hands soon after he dealt with his father. In Fiji I believe that was." Within his pudgy eye sockets, his black eyes gleamed like polished stone. "You didn't know Nicholas was responsible for Carlo Seta's death?" He asked but his question was loaded with sarcasm.

"No." She said, trying to hide her surprise. "I did not. I was completely unaware." Her voice faded away.

"And then he took the leadership in Venice. It was all very dramatic." Pocco sounded bored. "But *I* was not surprised. When I saw him, I knew it would happen. That Nicholas Delarno would take control."

Francesca looked at him.

"Oh yes Signora. Nicholas Delarno is the ultimate leader of our merry band. He is the Capo who killed in cold blood. He murdered his father and another to take the role he'd once been promised."

Pocco sat back in his chair and looked at her across the small space between them. He gloated at his skill in taking her by surprise and all but said 'Checkmate'.

Francesca refused to panic. She'd been too comfortable leading him along. She couldn't process Nicholas' motives now and the pledge she'd just made to him. Nimble as ever, her honed skills came to the fore and she changed tact. Bice dead. Carlo dead. That left a void in the leadership. Giuliett was the kind of person who'd no doubt choose the sparkly alliance offered by another outsider. And someone as ambitious as Robbie L would let her, much to the distaste of the old guard.

"Surely Seta Clan has a structure that would forbid someone like Robbie L taking more than he is due." Francesca said.

"They do." Pocco said. "But Nicholas's erratic behaviour is causing as much concern as his father's did. And with Robbie L as part of the Delarno clan, you can see it is imperative, to keep us on track, I am required to step up to support Giuliett and the Seta Clan so that there is stability."

"Yes, it sounds like Giuliett is lucky to have you to rely on Don Poccolini." She said.

There was a short pause.

"Let's talk about Silvio. There is something I never understood. Signora perhaps you can enlighten me." Pocco said, breaking into her thoughts.

"I'll try."

"Why did a son turn on his father?"

"You'll have to ask Nicholas," she said smoothly. "I cannot talk for him."

"He must love you very much to kill for you."

"I don't know about that Signor! Of course, I'd never ask or suggest such a horrible deed. So, as I said, you'll have to ask him yourself."

"Silvio was at your property though, in Fiji."

Francesca felt the air get sucked out of the room. "Yes, Signor. He was."

"Why?"

Francesca thought long about her answer. She would not give them Archie, because to even speak about her son in this company, would bring her emotionally undone.

"He came to kill me." She said plainly.

"Why?"

"The answer to that Signor, I don't know. We didn't discuss it."

"Nicholas knows."

"Maybe. I've never asked him and I suggest to find the answers you seek, you'll have to ask him yourself." She said.

A long silence filled the air. Francesca knew Pocco would not be able to stand it and would press to talk. So she asked, "How is Giuliett?"

Pocco who'd been watching her closely, shifted through a range of expressions.

"She has lost both her parents now. I understand that feeling." Francesca said kindly. "Do you know if she has someone to lean on during this time?"

"Are you offering Signora?"

"Not at all, we could never see eye to eye. But Signor, I was thinking perhaps you could step into that mentoring role. I suspect she has her father's men, but speaking from experience, she may need support."

"She did come to me, that is true." He said melodramatically.

"I have offered to help guide her." He looked at Li Wei. "I am guiding her. But it has been a difficult process. Gatto and Enrico did their best to help too, but she turned her back on them."

"Who are Gatto and Enrico?"

"More casualties I'm afraid."

"Of Nicholas?"

"No."

Francesca nodded. "Giuliett has turned to Robbie L. I see your determination and frustration towards the biker has come full circle." She said. "The Seta Group is a mess!" She looked pointedly at Li Wei. "Exposure is a high risk borne by all. And creates mistrust and trepidation in business interests."

Angel discretely signalled again to Pocco. Francesca caught the movement at her peripheral and was careful not to acknowledge her.

"Well, we are preparing to land very soon. You still have not asked for our destination Signora."

Francesca glanced at her watch. They'd been in the air about three hours.

"Am I correct in assuming you'd like the sport of me guessing, Signor Poccolini, since this is the second time you've commented on the matter." She asked, to which he smiled and nodded.

"I expect we are heading east or north east because to head west would not necessitate the air escort I've witnessed accompanying us for the last hour and a half."

69

························

Volkov Family Estate
St Petersburg, Russia

Three black Hummers were waiting at the airport. The group was split between the cars and as Francesca eased into the back seat, she was relieved to be accompanied by the person she assumed to be leader from the entourage that had escorted her from Rome and not the assailant who'd whacked her ankle with his pistol.

Despite his scrutiny she found she could relax. Now that she was away from Li Wei and the anguished emotions he brought forth in her, her anxiety slid to a more manageable level.

Fear and anxiety. Her own lethal combination to do stupid things had kept its head and she'd survived intact. Overall she thought she'd managed well enough on the flight despite almost landing in a hole a couple of times. But there was no time for self-reflection.

She looked out the window and saw her solemn expression staring back. The windows were so heavily tinted there was little chance of hazarding a guess which direction they were travelling.

She discretely checked the compass on her watch.

They'd been driving for about fifteen minutes when the vehicle came to a sudden stop. Francesca heard the screeching tyres and the smash of what sounded like two cars colliding up ahead. Her driver started yelling as the vehicle began spinning wheels wildly on the spot before catapulting backwards. The gentleman was yelling directions as they veered towards a roadside bollard at speed. Her heart went to her mouth.

"What's happening?" she asked.

"Ambush." He said, opening the window and firing his semi-automatic pistol into the snow slush and pine forest.

He yelled again at the driver. Francesca searched frantically for the button to drop the screen between the driver and the back seat. She squashed into the space between the driver and the shooter.

She looked out the front windscreen to the scene ahead. Cowboys. Absolute cowboys. She swore loudly, deciding she'd rather take her chances with this crew.

"This way." She yelled to the driver, pointing. He slammed the gears into drive and they lurched forward. The car spun out and they somehow avoided an oncoming vehicle. She reached across and pulled the steering wheel hard right. It railed on two wheels, crossing an intersection into a two-lane road.

The action forced the cowboys to follow behind them. The gentleman gained the advantage shooting at them through the back left hand window. Suddenly he reeled backwards into the car, his face covered in blood.

Francesca yanked the gun from him and pushed him flat across the back seat, she took his position, balancing herself on one knee wedged between the bench seat and his shins.

"Keep moving!" She yelled, directing the driver, who was watching her in the rear vision window. They weaved in and out of the traffic at a hectic pace. Francesca turned towards the front. Ahead a small gap in the concrete bollards lining the median strip loomed.

"Turn right! Into that gap! There! There! There!" She screamed, grabbing the wheel again as the concrete nosily scraped along the side of the vehicle. The Hummer dipped down sharply, bounced as they hit bottom of a slushy ditch and fishtailed up the steep embankment. The wheels lost traction in the mud.

"Mate, give it to her!" Francesca yelled. "If we stop we're dead!"

She watched out the back window. The cowboys were caught between a truck and a delivery van. A gap was opening up ahead.

"Drive this baby!" she yelled as the tyres eventually gripped the tar. The Hummer bucked and fishtailed again. "Hang on to her now." She encouraged. She quickly checked the assault rifle that'd seen better days, mumbling to herself "Come on old reliable."

"Okay." She instructed as they completed one large block to face their original direction. On the opposite side of the road, the cowboys were gaining momentum to cross the muddy ditch as they had done moments earlier.

"Good job." Francesca encouraged her driver. "Ease off now, I'm in range."

They were now parallel with the offending vehicle. She leant out the vehicle and shot out the tyres and windows. The vehicle slid into the slush, taking out a timber pole and bringing the power lines down onto the occupants of the enemy target.

"Go! Go! Go!" she yelled to the driver. "Don't stop whatever you fucken do."

Francesca squashed again into the space between the seats. Ripping her t-shirt up the middle, and pulling it off under her blazer, she pressed the fabric against the gentleman's ear.

He looked at her with glassy eyes.

"It's okay." She said and her adrenaline pumped so hard her hands shook. "Look at me. That's it." She clasped his hand and looked out the back window. So far, so good.

She checked the sides and twisted to face the front. They were coming towards a set of iron property gates with armed personnel each side.

"Don't stop." She warned. "Keep pressing forward. They'll move."

The men watched the vehicle approaching warily as it careered left and right. Francesca felt it sway from side to side and looked out to see a tyre roll off towards the pine forest at the road's edge.

They were so close. The driver was manic, yelling into a two way, his arms waved wildly and the vehicle slipped and slid like a show ground ride. Francesca checked the rear window again. Company was coming.

And it was coming quicker than they could get into the safety of the gate.

She looked at her patient again and shook him. "Wake up friend." She yelled. She pressed the cloth harder against his head. "We're nearly there now."

Time stood still. They practically limped through the gate and kept going forward. Francesca watched the scene unfold before her eyes through the back shot out window. From nowhere a tractor with a front bucket t-boned the oncoming vehicle. The armed personnel stationed at the gate made short work of the remaining offenders.

She relaxed. With her right arm she reached behind and patted the driver on the shoulder.

"Don't know if you can understand me. You did well my friend." She said. She turned to the gentleman. "We're safe now. We'll get you some treatment straight away."

She pulled the t-shirt away for a quick check and again pressed her hand hard to stem the blood flow. With her other, she clasped his hand in hers.

70

· · · · · · · · · · · · · · · · · · ·

They stopped on the front drive of what she could only describe as a palace fit for a Tsar. Men dressed in black combat gear came streaming out of every hiding place she could imagine and surrounded the vehicle, their weapons raised.

Francesca felt her heart sink into her stomach.

The driver raised his hands and spoke. He opened the door and stepped out. He spoke. They listened. Asked some questions. He spoke some more. More questions were asked. Then slowly he stepped to open the back door and pointed directly at her.

Francesca came face to face with the soldiers, her body splattered in blood and trying to explain that she needed medical help. She spoke slowly and clearly, indicating the injured man lying across the back seat.

Close to her, the passenger door opened. One soldier pointed a gun, whilst another grabbed the rifle at her feet.

On the opposite side, the driver stepped away. A soldier came to inspect. And then the rush of assistance as she was pulled out of the car and the men carried him into the home, taking the driver with them. She stood there in the flush of slushy snow as daylight quickly faded, waiting for her instruction from the team leader.

He looked at her up and down. Francesca pulled her blazer

closed and buttoned it at the only closure at her waist in a bid to maintain some modesty over her bare skin exposed by the torn t-shirt.

Her matching tailored shorts were fractionally longer than the jacket and she suddenly became all too aware of her lack of clothing and grotty appearance now that the drama had stopped and she had time to assess her situation.

Out of the blue, she respectfully saluted.

She pushed her heels together, straitened her spine and engaged her core. As she'd learnt in the police academy, she looked ahead with her right elbow cocked, fingers straight and extending from her outwards facing palm. Her hand and wrist remained rigid and angled at the height between her eyebrow and her hairline, at the place where the brim of her police cap would've been. She held the respectful gesture.

He came within her visual range with the intent of catching her eye. He looked more than a little shocked and his bright blue eyes twinkled in bewildered amusement for a moment before resuming his controlled commanding demeanour.

"At ease soldier." He said in perfect English. "Please come with me."

Embarrassed, she didn't say a word, simply nodded and followed him up the sweeping concrete steps and into the building's main entrance hall.

Francesca stepped back in time to the Romanov dynasty. She paused in the foyer of the cavernous reception room. Everywhere was gleaming in gold. And painted plaster in shades of yellow. And buttery creams and turquoise blue. And the most gorgeous faded shade of deep red she'd ever seen was everywhere.

Visible through an open double width doorway were furnishings rich in velvet and silk. A full-sized replica of the complete tapestry collection known as the Lady and the Unicorn adorned the salon walls. She paused gazing at them.

"Lady and the Unicorn." She said out loud in obvious appreciation.

Also visible from the foyer, a warm, crackling fire encased by a gold and marble fireplace was quite simply enchanting. She gazed up to the ornate plaster ceiling and the antique chandeliers dripping with crystals and coloured glass.

The soldier stood at the base of a magnificent staircase. Marble steps and elegant carved marble balustrading formed a sweeping arc to a large landing resplendent in gilded arches and columns. Wide hallways spread in two directions from this open room and large square windows framed the back wall of the upper foyer area.

Her eyes travelled back to the soldier via the decorative frosted glass sconces lighting the walls from the top landing, down the steps to the ground floor.

Francesca lost her senses. She giggled as a broad smile spread across her face.

"Oh my." She said, bringing her hand to her chest. "This is the most astonishing place I've ever seen. I don't know where to look first."

She down looked at her feet and the exquisite parquet flooring.

"I'm sorry." She said, clearing her throat. "Please excuse me. It's been a hell of a day. I think it best I speak to the Australian Consulate."

"You like my home?" He asked.

"What's not to like?" She gushed, taking the opportunity to gawk again at the interior. "It's magnificent. A Russian masterpiece."

He smiled at her. "Let's get you cleaned up. And then we can discuss the next steps. I noticed your awareness at the tapestries. Perhaps you might be interested in the Fabergè room?"

Francesca's eyes opened wide.

"You mean like the Romanov's had? A whole room of Fabergè Eggs?"

He chuckled but Francesca sensed he was pleased. "And other beautiful items my sister has collected and sourced." He said proudly.

She made a quick assessment and followed him up that magical staircase, careful not to touch anything with her hands covered in dried blood and muck.

At the top of the stairs, along a long wide hallway and passing by a number of closed doors he at last opened a door for her. It led into a reception room bigger than her first apartment in Sydney.

"This will be your suite during your stay here." He said, walking into the room and flicking on the light switches. "The bathroom is this way."

He walked the length of a room with furniture arranged in the centre and where, along one wall, an expanse of glass windows overlooked a fir tree forest. Through an impressive door a smaller dressing chamber was furnished with a large mirror, chaise and round timber table placed in the centre.

Francesca followed him through the doorway into an extravagantly feminine bedroom suite. He indicated a second door coming off the room beside the dressing chamber.

"There is your bathroom. If you would like to freshen up and change, my sister has some items of clothing stored in the cupboard. You'll find something to change into I'm sure, until we can launder your clothing."

"Thank you." She said, absorbing the degrees of wealth and grandeur surrounding her.

"I'll meet you downstairs in the salon. The one you admired when you came in." He said. "If you still wish to call the consulate, you can do so from there."

"Thank you." She repeated.

"My name is Francesca." She said, extending her grubby hand and promptly pulling it away to hide behind her back.

"My name is Sergei." He said, smiling. Holding out his right hand to clasp hers in a handshake. "It's okay. I don't mind. I'm pleased to meet you Francesca. Thank you for saving my friends."

She shrugged, taking in the features of the man standing before her. Closely cut brown hair, penetrating blue eyes and a jaw that so defined Russian men. When he smiled his small ears lifted slightly. They were slightly pinched to a point at the top and flattened out to an angled point about halfway down, making him look a little like a mythical pixie.

His black woollen beanie had been removed when he entered the grand home and was tucked loosely into the thigh pocket of his long combat styled pants.

He stood head and shoulders above her and was just as wide, reminding her of a brick wall. But Francesca wasn't fooled by his size, having witnessed his agility only minutes before during the stand-off in the truck.

"That's okay." She stumbled. "All in a days work."

"Perhaps." Bulky arms crossed high over his vast chest. "I'll leave you to attend to your needs. Take as long as you like. There is no rush tonight. The consul has no after hours answering service and will not act until Monday."

71

....

Gowns, gowns and more gowns. Guess I'll go with a gown. Francesca thought as she flicked through the limited number of items in the walk-in robe. She checked the drawers and shelves, which were empty and concluded that this guest room must be the overflow room for Sergei's sister's gown collection.

She chose luxurious black velvet. A Saint Laurent wrap dress, embellished with lace and tied with a ribbon on the side at her waist. It was comfortable and just the balm after her day. She returned to the bathroom to dry her hair. With no pins to style it she let it bounce down her back.

Francesca assessed her reflection in the mirror and hardly recognised the pale, tired face looking back at her. She searched the vanity drawers of guest toiletries and found a new sample size lip-gloss.

"That will have to do." She said, mentally chastising herself for such vanity at a time like this. Five minutes later she stepped out of her room and into the ornate hallway that would take her to the Salon.

Tantalising aroma of hot food met her at the door and Francesca realised she was not only dead on her feet tired; she was also incredibly hungry for some nourishment. Sergei greeted her as she entered the large room.

He'd changed out of his day attire and into a black dinner suit. Francesca thought he looked to be somewhere in his forties. It was always hard to guess the age of European men.

"Are you hungry?" He asked.

"Famished." Francesca responded. She met him at a long side table.

"I am too." He said. "It's a help yourself affair tonight, I'm afraid. The staff have Friday nights with their families."

"That's okay. It smells delicious." She was salivating. "You're certainly a man of many talents!" she said in a cheeky tone.

Sergei laughed. "I would like to take the credit, but my cook has prepared for me and I simply heated it." He indicated her place at the fully laid table set in a traditional Russian table banquet. "Let's start."

"This is potato and cauliflower soup. There is some bread here. Next we have baked pork and cabbage with fennel and pearl barley, some root vegetables and there is chocolate cake with cherries for sweets. Finally, strong tea to help with your digestion and hand-made chocolates by an artisan in our city. A simple but wholesome meal."

"It's divine." She said. "Please Sergei, let me serve you as my way of saying thank you for your incredible hospitality."

She stood and bringing his plate to the fine china soup tureen, filled his soup bowl as he watched closely. She unwrapped the warm bread rolls from their cotton cloth and brought them to his plate.

"Thank you. Do you prefer vodka or wine with your meal?" He asked.

"Wine please."

He selected a bottle from the many placed on the table beside him and poured her glass.

"Thank you. It's definitely a day for vodka but I don't dare. As it is I fear I may eat my dinner, drink my wine and like a big fat goanna on a hot day, look for a place to curl up and fall fast asleep!"

"That will be okay too." He said.

They sat opposite each other and ate in silence, Francesca taking all her cues from him and listening to the fire crackle. After their meal, he poured himself a wine and they moved to individual armchairs, facing the fireplace.

"Does the wine not appeal to you?" he asked looking at her full glass.

"It's lovely thank you." She took a sip.

"You don't have to drink it Francesca." He said. "I have other drinks to offer."

"It's lovely." She looked embarrassed. "I'm sorry, I don't mean to offend. I thought ..."

Sergei suddenly laughed. A bear like roar that came from his boots.

"You thought what exactly?" He asked, his bulky frame leaning towards her expectantly. "That I might drug you? The bad Russian would poison the good Australian?"

"No. Actually I was thinking more along the lines of custom. You didn't drink during dinner. So I didn't either." She said embarrassed.

Suddenly she smiled nervously at him. "How funny. You thought I was being polite and I thought I was being polite but from two completely points of view. And in the end we almost ended up upsetting each other. You see Sergei! This is exactly how disputes start! Simple misunderstanding."

"Agreed." He said happily. "A toast 'To no more misunderstandings between friends.'"

He clinked his glass with hers and they both took a sip.

"Why did you bring me here?" Francesca asked tentatively, testing the new truce immediately.

"It's a very long and complicated story." He said turning to her face lit dramatically by the firelight. "I'm happy to tell you, but I think you probably need to call your family first? So they aren't worried and to let them know you are safe."

"Am I safe?" she asked. "I have no idea where I am. I'm assuming Russia but I can't even be one hundred per cent sure of that."

"You're very close to St Petersburg." He acknowledged.

"How long am I delayed from going home?" She asked feeling forlorn. She was well beyond anxiety now and her emotions were completely dried out.

"That depends on you, of course, and how things occur in the future. I think for now you can tell your family there was a problem with your flight and you now have to wait until another seat becomes available. You don't have to. If you prefer you can tell them the day as it happened to you and invoke more worry for them."

Francesca sighed. As predicted she was getting too tired to argue. Even her seeming endless adrenaline had reached its end. Now all she wanted to do was sleep. She borrowed a phone and texted a quick message to Sinclair's parents. She closed her eyes in a long blink and rubbed her forehead.

"You look very tired." He said. "I think our conversations can wait until morning."

"How is the gentleman?" she asked, closing her eyes fully at last in the dimly lit room. The room had reached the temperature that brought her to sleep. The fire, invitingly warm, was sucking all the available oxygen from around her. She was too comfortable to move, and the soft velvet dress wrapped around her like a warm hug.

"The gentleman?"

"The fellow who accompanied me from Rome. I nicknamed him the gentleman because of his behaviour towards me."

"Really? You know he is one of Russia's most feared."

"Oh I was terrified, don't get me wrong." She said seriously. "But he respected me."

"He will live. His ear, though will not. He has a lot to thank you for. You're quick thinking saved a lot of lives."

"They said it was an ambush. The other two, Poccolini and Li Wei, where did they end up?"

"Poccolini didn't make it. Le Wei is staying with a friend of mine. I don't want to complicate my business with him."

Francesca thought back to the look she'd witnessed between Li Wei and his consigliere. She shuddered.

"Are you cold Francesca?" he asked, getting up to stoke the fire.

"No." she said. "Do you know who organised the ambush?"

"Yes."

"Who?" She asked.

"The biker from Australia, Robbie L."

"What?" She promptly stood. "This is bullshit!" she said. She lapped the room and came around to stand directly in front of him.

"What's your surname Sergei?" she asked.

"Volkov."

He watched the colour drain from her face.

"Son of a bitch!" She said to the room, reeling in the revelation. She turned her back to him.

Francesca paced another lap of the room quietly mumbling in the most abominable language under her breath and promptly left him to his endless cups of tea and chocolates without uttering another direct word to him.

72

. . . .

Sebastino Nero's Hotel Apartment,
City of Paris, France

"**M**amma! Nicholas! You're taking a hell of a risk!" Sebastino
Nero took the first appropriate opportunity to censure
the Capo. By now his initial curiosity had subsided and
his bad temper had reached boiling over at the airport lounge
encounter with Francesca.

"What risk?" Nicholas asked.

"Salucci! I thought we'd already had this conversation over
you being more discreet."

"She came for Alessandro." Nicholas defended her.

"That's a bit rich don't you think?"

"No."

"I didn't see her at the church." Sebastino pressed.

"She didn't go. She thought it would compromise us. She
stayed in Rapallo. Anyway, where did you see her? I thought
she'd be back in Fiji by now. She left my place at first light the
morning after the funeral."

"In the airport lounge. She posed for a photograph. And then
she left. It was a stupid day that one. Somehow I ended up with

a second phone. As if one isn't enough."

"What day was that?" Nicholas sat forward in his seat.

"Yesterday afternoon. When I was on my way to Paris."

"Friday? I got a message from her yesterday afternoon! Some code for her mobile phone. I just ignored it. I thought it was meant for someone else."

"Mamma! It's her phone. I bet you a thousand. Where the fuck did I put it? I'm putting you on speaker."

Sebastino scoured through his papers and overnight suitcase.

"Wait, I have to tip everything on the bed. It's somewhere in all these papers." He heard something slide across the interior surface and found it in an internal pocket.

"How much shit do you have in that thing?" Nicholas asked impatiently.

"Got it. Mother! It's flat. I'll have to plug it in."

Nic heard him rattling around with cords and plugs. He heard the phone chime as the power connected to it.

"Come on! Fuck me, how long does it take to get organised?" Nicholas was agitated.

"Alright settle down old man. It belongs to her all right. There's a photo of the whole family." He said as a picture lit up the home screen. "What's the code?"

"324598. Go to the last messages and then the photos." Nic said.

"Si, si. Last one was to you. It's the code. One before was to Sinclair telling him she's heading home from Rome. Christ, what an argument! Mama, you're in trouble! He's told her not to come home if she decides to stay any longer in Italy. I told you this would happen, but no, you wouldn't listen."

"Sebastino! I'm warning you now, don't even think about

reading our messages. Stick to the task."

"Si. Si. Relax. As tempting as it is, I'm not about to put my nose in your secrets lover boy." He said. "I do have some morals! The other messages are irrelevant anyway. The days don't match up."

"You mentioned some photos." Nic said. "Could you forward them to me?"

"Sure." He opened her digital photo application. "I'm in the photo album now."

He saw the album marked Family, and scrolled up.

"Is this her boy?" Sebastino asked. "Mamma he looks like you!" Then he gasped. "The resemblance is uncanny. He even has your mannerisms. Have you ever seen him? Seriously this boy could be yours Nicholas."

At Nicholas' silence the penny dropped. "Mamma mia! You're kidding me! Is it true?" Sebastino asked.

"He's ours." Nic said proudly, smiling at the end of the phone.

"Fuck! I'm sorry man I didn't know. Congratulations! So that's why you disappeared."

"Yes," Nic said. "Don't make it public. The old man nearly fucked it up for all of us over our boy. He lives with his mother and that's how it's going to stay. Meanwhile, Mr Busy-body, where are the photos from the airport?"

"I've forwarded them." Sebastino went back to the main album, selected the appropriate images and pressed send.

"If I know Francesca like I think I know her," Nic said, "she'd have worked out that something was amiss, she'd have sent the text to me and as luck would have it, you've walked in. Knowing you'll ring me at some point and assuming you'll realise it's her phone, the background will be more important than the subject.

How am I doing so far?"

"You're either on the money or she's suddenly a shit photographer because this one looks like she accidently hit the button and in this one, she's only caught my shoulder."

"Bingo! Recognise any of those people?" Nic asked hopefully.

"Sorry."

"Neither do I. But I'll be finding out." The mafia boss said. "You're in Paris you say?"

"Yes."

"As it happens I'm all but there now. I'm taking a quick detour before I catch up with Volkov this afternoon. Can you private courier that phone to Le Bourget for me please? I'll collect it from my locked box at their depot."

"Sure thing."

"I land in ten minutes."

73

....

Volkov Family Estate
St Petersburg, Russia

"She's here?" Nic asked incredulously.

"Upstairs in the bedroom suite." Sergei said. "We had a lovely dinner last night, just the two of us. No interruptions. She's a special lady. I can see why you hold her close. We developed a nice connection. I could get used to having her around."

Nicholas looked at his Russian counterpart. He couldn't be sure if he was joking or not. He stalked around the ornate room serving as a study to stand near the windows.

"I'd hoped to rekindle our friendship this morning before the business day started." Sergei continued. "But the staff have told me she's come down with a terrible headache."

Nic looked abruptly at his counterpart. The Russian wasn't joking.

"How's Anya?" He asked tentatively.

A smile split the Russian's clean-shaven, chiselled features. His face lit up with open joy. "She's much better thank you. Again, I thank you for finding a way to intercept and for bringing her to safety."

"Always happy to help a friend." Nicholas said.

"She's visiting her friend Alexandra at the moment to break up the loneliness of being here and to begin new connections for their jewellery business. And I think she is tired of my spoiling her from head to toe with anything she desires." He smiled.

"Has she been able to talk to you about her ordeal?" Nic asked.

"Yes. We've opened up." Sergei closed the conversation around he and his youngest sister's emotional reunion.

Nic paced the masculine room and stopped again by the window reaching the vast ceiling height and in a grid of square panes as wide.

"How the fuck did this happen Sergei?" Nic asked, raking his fingers through his hair. "How could she be safe one minute and then in danger the next? We have protocols."

"Francesca was intercepted by my team when I learned that Poccolini and Li Wei were coming for a visit. They form a nice little group don't you think?"

Nic glared at him.

"Russian men cherish and value their women. It's our duty to protect them from known and unknown danger and our women expect it."

"I thank you for keeping Francesca safe." Nic said not missing the pointed remarks. "I want to see her. Now."

"I thought you might." He said, making his way across the foyer to the grand staircase. "Francesca is this way. I sense suddenly you're in no rush to leave here my friend. We may just resolve this issue with the Chinese after all."

74

. . . .

"Nicholas!" Francesca burst into action. "You fucking traitor. You fucking set me up! You're a prick of the highest order! I nearly died because of you and your stupid tests!"

She launched at him, wildly pushing him in the chest, forcing him backwards, and he sprawled across the dressing room's centre table. She followed through with a second shove at close range. He regained his footing, yelling,

"Wait! Francesca! Stop! I don't know what you're talking about?"

She punched him hard in the ribs with a closed fist uppercut, followed up quickly with a second jab, which he effectively deflected. She danced around him, stepping in quickly when she thought she had a clear shot, utilising her police combat training. Even if she was a little out of immediate practice, her adrenaline and anger was making up for lost time on the mats.

He darted around her. He wouldn't fight her. But he wasn't about to be her punching bag either. He watched her furious expressions closely, looking for her tell in the split second before she struck out.

In a well-practised movement, he grabbed her wrist and then the other as she came in for a blow, crushing her hands together in his strong fingers and pushing her arms in a downward motion. He took her out swiftly in a leg sweep.

She fell forward into him and taking advantage of her momentum, he swivelled under her, lifting her over his shoulder caveman style and carried her towards the bed, the only soft surface in the room that would safely break their fall.

He flung her roughly downwards off his shoulder, promptly rolled her face first into the downy blankets and pressed his knee into the middle of her back.

"Fuck you!" she swore. "Fuck! You!"

"Are you going to listen to me?"

"Do I have a choice?" she screamed.

"Yes."

She thought about it. Seriously thought about it.

"Go fuck yourself." She said her face planted in the soft coverings of the bedspread.

There was another long silence as she struggled under his hold.

"Are you ready to listen yet?" He asked, pushing her harder in the kidneys.

"News flash from a lying bastard? I'll hear what you have to say."

Nicholas rolled her under him and sat across her hips, his knees bent under him. She inhaled the charged air between them in deep gulping breaths. Not quite trusting her yet, he clamped her arms out from her body and his fingers dug into her biceps and the inner flesh of her elbows. Her auburn hair wrapped in chunks across half her face, although beneath it he could see her eyes, dark with fury, glaring at him.

He knew it was taking every bit of her control to not spit in his face. Slowly his grip on her arms lessened, as in time and patient quiet, he sensed her ease down.

"Let me look at you." He said at last. His face was twisted and pale in anguish. His eyes welled in emotion. Gently pushing the hair back from her face, he brushed the frustration away from her wet cheeks gently with his thumb.

"Christ I've never been so scared in my life. I thought I'd lost you. My light." His voice was gravelly. He desperately wanted to bring her up to him, hold her in his arms and not ever let go. Unspent tears filled the corners of his eyes.

"Are you hurt my flower?" He said, his concern wandering over her, checking every bruise and mark. He paused at the dried blood trapped under her nails and cupped her hands in his.

"No. What the fricking hell is going on?" she demanded, pulling her hands free from him.

"Sergei holds the ace." He said.

"He said Robbie L ordered the ambush." She countered. "Is that true? I thought we had a deal."

"What ambush?"

"The one that bumped off Pocco and nearly killed me as we were being brought to here. Assuming this was my end destination."

"I spoke to Robbie L. Told him to call off the hit." Nic responded tightly.

"Well one of you is lying." She said unconvinced. "I don't need your concern Nicholas, I need the truth. And you'd better start talking."

"How about you tell me what happened right from when you left Rapallo."

Francesca recapped the last twenty-four hours, including her hunch that Li Wei had something to do with Pocco's death.

Nic listened intently. Every now and then he stopped her

recount to check on details. In the end he stood and walked to the window, looking over the fir forest spread out below. He reached into his pocket.

"Here's your phone. Sebastino delivered it this morning." He said, handing the device to her.

"Thank you. Did Angel tell you I was here?"

"Angel? Where does she fit in?"

"She was our flight steward. I don't think they realised we knew each other. And I certainly didn't inform them."

"Pocco must have engaged Alessandro's plane and team."

"No, it was stickered with Air China."

"Where's she now?"

"I have no idea. I assume she's gone back to Rome or she's waiting at the airport for further instruction."

"I'll message Paolo. He'll have to get her out. I want her gone from this place." He said texting his younger brother as he spoke.

"So how did you know I was here?" Francesca asked.

"I didn't. I'm here for a meeting with Li Wei and Sergei." He said. "We're finalising the details for ... it doesn't matter."

She realised at that moment she could've been Sergei's unwilling guest for a very long time. At once feeling vulnerable, she sought immediate comfort and came to stand close beside him.

"I think another item has been added to your agenda." She said.

He didn't respond, lost in his thoughts.

She reached for his hand. He looked down at her fingers interlinked within his.

"Did he touch you?" He asked, looking down.

"Who?"

"Sergei." He said.

"Touch me?"

"You know ... touch you." He looked out to the trees, unable to witness the shame in her eyes.

"Oh. My. God! That's all you can think about right now?" Francesca cried. She pulled her hands out of his grasp and put some physical distance between them.

"He told me, no, he inferred the two of you were intimate."

"So what if we did do it?" She was incredulous. "Last time I looked sex was not illegal."

"I need to know." He said, turning to face her, searching her eyes. "Because if he's hurt you, I'll have to kill him." He was serious.

"Christ Nicholas!" She said. "Haven't you done enough of that lately?"

"It's our code." He said grimly. "When a man's property is damaged in that way or there is direct proof of a traitorous act, the Capo orders the hit or the person disrespected carries it out himself if the offence is serious enough."

She went pale and shook her head side to side slowly.

"And as of this week and your sworn oath to me, all of you belongs to me."

75
· · · · · · · · · · · · · · · · · · ·

"Nicholas and Francesca! I see you kissed and made up."
Sergei said and he was in quite the jovial mood when
they walked together into the Salon. Li Wei was present,
looking tetchy and Francesca eyed him cautiously.

"Vodka?" Sergei asked as he handed them each a shot in a
crystal glass from a silver butler tray. To Francesca he seemed
oblivious to the tension in the room. *Perhaps he doesn't care,*
she thought.

"To your health!" He said, holding up his glass to toast.

"To your health." Francesca and Nicholas responded curtly.

"I thought we might eat first. Business can wait." Sergei said
indicating a large rectangular table set out with the entire
spread of food and drinks, as was the Russian custom.

The Russian led the conversation to the end of the elaborate
meal. Li Wei reluctantly participated in the discussions
when asked, contributing the bare minimum so as not to be
completely impolite. Nicholas seethed at this new turn of events
for the entire duration. Francesca watched them all. Nic glanced
at her pensive expression often. When his shoe lightly touched
hers under the table she knew it was time to prepare.

"Talk to me about Don Poccolini." Nicholas said, addressing
his first concern.

"The Florentine." Sergei said distastefully. "A more deceitful man I never did meet. His duplicity would always be his downfall."

"I'm not talking about his character." Nic said.

"I invited him." Li Wei interjected, getting to the point quickly as was his preference once the social necessities were done. "I thought he might be useful."

Everyone turned to face the Dragon head.

"How did that work out for you?" Nic asked.

"Quite well." The Chinese triad boss said, looking at Francesca.

She held his gaze and rather than be a pawn in his game, quickly put herself into the frame.

"Did you kill Pocco?" She asked him directly.

"Does it matter?" He asked. "He is dead."

"Yes." She said calmly. "There is a code. He belonged to a group who follow certain protocols."

He looked at her. Not impatient, not upset. Rather like she was a child under his tutelage who asked too many inconvenient questions.

"You operate under a code, but I am not directed or bound by it." He began, focusing his attention on her. "Deal with his death amongst your group as you wish. The outcome does not affect me or how I run my business."

"Did you kill Pocco?" She pressed again. Her voice was calm and clear.

"Yes." He said, challenging her to object.

"On what grounds?" Francesca enquired in a professional tone.

"He outgrew his boots."

76

....

Sergei sat back in his chair the meal finished, and satisfied himself with tea. He didn't say much during the verbal interchange but his manner certainly did. Francesca already knew the Russian didn't trust the triad boss, a truth he'd confessed to her the previous night. She didn't realise it until now, just how important that little piece of information would turn out to be.

"I can't argue with that." She said, surprising everyone.

Li Wei almost smiled at her.

"So, we are agreed Pocco had to go and that is the end of that." Li Wei said, looking at the assembled group.

Sergei however, was in no hurry to finish the conversation. "What are your thoughts Nicholas?" He asked drawing the Italian into the discussion. "You are the Capo after all."

"I'd like to know what injury he brought to you, Li Wei. It must be some indictment to warrant taking a fellow comrade's life."

Li Wei looked at him and as his anger grew at the veiled challenge, his features and manner reminded Francesca of an unfurling Cobra. His snake like eyes glinted for a moment, in a rare show of emotion.

"Would you discuss your business dealings with me?" Li Wei asked.

"No. But if I had trouble with one of your operatives, I would let you know my intentions." Nic said.

"Well then you are a fool!"

Francesca looked at Sergei who was watching the two men intently. She breathed in and out slowly. If Li Wei felt he was being ambushed, she knew the consequences would be swift and dramatic.

It dawned on her that she also held an ace. Using her knowledge of the organisation's traditions and values, combined with information gained during the recent flight with Pocco, she might be able to mitigate his building discontent. So, she stepped in.

"May I?" she asked Li Wei quietly.

He indicated for her to go ahead.

"Pocco had been speaking out of turn on behalf of Seta clan, giving the impression that he has control of the entire Seta business. He'd been making business deals and promises on their behalf that he could never honour. One of them being Giuliett would soon be named Capo de tutti Capi." She paused. "And he was the person who could make that happen."

"I think Li Wei is suggesting that the death of Signor Poccolini was a matter of honour and trust amongst gentleman." She concluded, looking at Li Wei and then at Nicholas.

"Is that true?" Nic asked the triad.

"She's your girl." Li Wei said as if to confirm, because as Francesca suspected, he would never admit he'd been duped by the silver-tongued Florentine.

"We are done on the topic." The triad boss said to Sergei.

"Are you satisfied with the outcome Sergei?" she asked him gently, being careful with her tone to not offend.

He looked at her, and she caught the momentary surprise in his eyes and curve of a half-smile.

"Yes. I believe we have cleared the air on that matter." He said.

"Good. Next item on the agenda." Francesca said mildly.

77

. . . .

Nicholas looked at her like she had three heads. She shrugged her shoulders and mouthed 'What?'

Sergei laughed out loud at the not-so-subtle interchange. "Next item on the agenda, Madam Chair ..." He began to say.

"Is something that doesn't concern you!" Li Wei interjected, in a hurry to finish the last of his business and leave the country.

She raised her eyebrows and smiled at Sergei. "Allora, if you gentlemen don't mind, I might take a turn around the Fabergè room. I've been longing to see it. Sergei, do you mind?"

"Of course not. I did promise that last night. And then we became distracted with each other." He looked pointedly at Nicholas, who responded suitably irritated. "This way Francesca."

Nicholas knew there was no point rushing the final deliberations with the Russian. Particularly when he was in this kind of mood. He resigned himself to the fact that patience was indeed a virtue in this country in business dealings.

"We'll continue without you." Nic said irritably and Sergei waved his hand indicating to proceed with the protracted details around the immigration proposal for the Italian government. Sergei already knew his price and there'd be no compromising. As did Nicholas.

"I was trying to give you privacy to discuss your business

without my presence." She said, apologising after they were out of earshot. He didn't respond.

"Shouldn't you stay with them?" she asked, propping in the middle of the grand foyer. He propelled her forward as his hand gently touched her lower back and waist.

"No." He said.

An awkward moment passed between them. Francesca changed tact.

"I hope you'll delight me with a history talk as well," she said. "Then I can put all the magnificence surrounding us into context. Starting with the Romanov jewels and those precious diamonds, sapphires and emeralds that never appeared for sale in 1925, despite being in the 1922 photographic catalogue."

"The Russian Diamond Fund! Yes, that tragedy is one of the world's greatest unsolved mysteries." He said happily, immediately stating his version of the events.

78

······················

McCrae Compound
Viti Levu, Fiji

"I tell you something isn't right." Alasdair McCrae said. "Read me that text again."

"It says 'A problem at the airport. Have to wait for another seat. Will let you know new flight details. Love you.' And that's it." Rose McCrae looked at her husband worriedly.

"Nothing about the kids?" He asked. "That's very unusual. It's not her kind of language at all. It's not even her phone number. Look at the previous messages from her, every one is an essay."

"That's what I thought too. Do you think we should call Johnno? Or maybe Sinclair?"

"Sinclair is due home any day now." The older man rubbed his head, his hand running back and forth on the short stubble that was the remainder of his hair. "I'm going to talk to both of them. Something doesn't ring true."

He looked at Rose. "I know it's been a rocky road for a bit with that girl, but I really thought she was coming round. Whatever she may choose for herself, I know she would rather die than hurt those kids."

"I agree." Rose said. "She's changed a lot since the accident. She even ... I'm such a fool! She and I are connected with that app. I'll be able to find her or at least her phone."

"Well what are you waiting for woman?" He said, leaning over his wife's shoulder so he could see the phone face.

"Okay, if she is on the Internet this should work." Rose opened the app. It zoomed in to their location in Fiji and marked it with a blue marker. "This is us." She said. She clicked on Francesca's icon. The map moved, opening up to world map and zoomed in at St Petersburg, marking it with another icon.

"Russia!" They said in unison. Alasdair's hand came up to his head again. "What's she doing in Russia?" He asked. "This is definitely not right. I'm calling the boys."

79

....

"I know what this is about." Sinclair said in an urgent three-way family phone conference with his parents and Johnno.

"Is it something you want to discuss or something the two of you need to sort out, love?" Rose McCrae asked.

Half a world away, Sinclair rubbed his forehead. He took a deep breath. "Delarno's got into her head."

"Oh dear. I'm sorry Sinclair." Rose responded. She glanced worriedly at Alasdair.

"I told her to be wary of him. She assured me he'd changed his ways." Alasdair said. "But, I still think something's not right, Sinclair. She'd never hurt those kids."

"Yeah, well Dad, one thing I've learnt out of all of this is that things never change. Our life together runs on a perpetual Nicholas Delarno treadmill."

"Mate, I agree with Dad." Johnno said. "I spoke to her when she was in Italy. She was heading home. I know it's been a while since we worked together, but she clicked straight into professional mode when I told her about the threats. I'm not entirely sure that Delarno has anything to do with this."

"The threats?" Sinclair asked, sighing heavily. "One of her former targets has re-engaged." Johnno added.

"Should I be worried Johnno?" Sinclair turned his frustration onto his brother. "I thought this was all behind us."

"We have it under control." He said.

"So you've apprehended the person?"

"No, he's in Italy. We're tracing his last known." Johnno said casually. "It's fine. If he moves, we'll know about it."

"Forgive me mate," Sinclair said sarcastically. "Seems to me he *has* fucking moved because he's no longer at the last known! Do you want to get your head out of your arse for a sweet minute? Did it dawn on you this situation might have to do with the perp you're currently after?"

"No, because he's in Italy and you just said you know what this is about!" he said defensively.

"Well what if I'm wrong? Has anyone tried to call her?" Sinclair asked.

"Yes love. I tried. It goes to message bank." Rose said. "What will I tell the kids Sinclair?"

"Tell them there's been a hold up in Italy and she'll be home as soon as she can." Sinclair said. "I'm home next week. If this situation is simply to do with Delarno we can work it out then."

"I'm sorry son, I knew the minute he stepped foot in Bourke, things were going to go cock-eyed." Alasdair said.

"Delarno went to Bourke?" The soldier asked.

"Yeah, mate. What would you say love? It was about three weeks maybe four after you left. He went to see the kids. Then he went to Canberra. Francesca said he told her he had meetings there with the Government."

Rose nodded.

Sinclair did the math from the date of his deployment.

"Son of a bitch." He swore. "I'm going to fucking kill him with my bare hands."

Everyone remained silent whilst Sinclair gathered himself.

There was a quiet sob as he caught his emotions.

"Where did you say she was?" He asked, exhausted by the whole situation.

"St Petersburg, Russia. That's where the icon is marking on the map love."

"Can you zoom in to a location please mum? Send me some screen shots. I need street names or something of interest close by maybe a park, or business name, a highway number, anything that comes up when you zoom right in and around. It will be in Russian but don't worry about that, we can translate it here. I'll make enquiry through our channels if I think it's warranted. Otherwise, I'll see you in a fortnight."

He breathed out heavily into the phone. "Man I need to get home and hug those kids. Thanks mum. Thank you dad. I'm sorry this has to impact on you too."

Rose looked at Alasdair.

"Don't worry about it son." He said. "You just get home safe and sound and we'll do what we can here."

"Wait! Before you go, you said Francesca sent a text, but not from her number?" Johnno asked.

"Yes, that's true." Rose said. "Who's phone number do you think it is Johnno?"

"Some random perhaps. But send it to me in any case. I want to cross check it with our database."

"That's a good idea Johnno. But, what if it's Delarno?" she asked.

"Then we'll know, won't we?" Sinclair said bitterly.

"I hope you're wrong son." Alasdair said.

"Well between the maps and Johnno's follow up I'm sure we'll come up with something. I'll let you know if I have to detour via Russia before I come home."

"Do you need support bro?" Johnno said, smelling a retrieval operation was about to happen.

"No. I'll see to it." Sinclair said. "I'm pretty sure I know what this is about."

80

....

Volkov Estate,
St Petersburg, Russia

"You are more than Nicholas gives you credit."

Sergei watched her, lost in wonder at Fabergè's exquisite Summer in Provence collection he'd recently acquired to celebrate Anya's return to the family fold. The treasured pieces of turquoise, emeralds and diamonds, literally took her breath away, but it was the egg pendant in white gold, diamonds and pearls that had really captured Francesca's imagination.

Her right hand had moved and settled to her heart, and her eyes glazed over in delight. She'd swooned at the delicate trinket displayed in a square shaped glass cabinet, mounted on a black marble plinth. Her face was alight with dreamy enchantment.

This gallery style installation of delicately lit jewel filled boxes arranged within the dark, velvet-lined Fabergè room never failed to excite him or the few he invited into the intimate space.

He knew she'd heard him by the way her brow had slightly knitted after the comment. In time, Francesca reluctantly drew her eyes from the treasure and looked directly at him through the glass.

"I'm not sure I know what you mean." She said.

"I know what you're doing."

"What do you think I'm doing Sergei?" she asked, moving onto a Fabergè egg of emeralds set within gently folding gold and diamond encrusted ribbons.

"You're poking him. He needs it. He needs to wake from his slumber and act on all that's happening around him."

"Do you think that's fair, Sergei? He's just lost Alessandro, a man who meant more to him than his own father. And in such circumstances too. It's a big hole." She paused. "In fact, the last twelve months have been very taxing."

"Fair? Nothing in life is fair Francesca. That organisation is a disaster." He said. "His leadership is questionable."

"I don't understand." She said remaining in front of another stunning sculpture. Sergei watched as her attention was caught of burnished gleam of sinister eyes, looking directly at her from a side profile. She moved slightly but her visible unease remained and she looked back at the eyes following her.

He'd had the same feeling the first time he saw it too.

Two golden snakes, bodies coiled back and forth upon them, with long necks rounding up formed the arch. Their angular heads faced each other in a tug of war combat. Jaws open and wide, gripped an amulet containing a single pearl. It faced outwards and was set in a gold, deceptively simple, rubbed over setting.

He watched her shoulders rise as her shoulder blades came together. Her chin lifted upwards as if someone had physically pinched her in the back of her neck. Then her whole upper body rolled as if to shake off the unpleasant feeling.

He supposed at that moment, she felt like that pearl. Another feeling he'd experienced recently.

Francesca moved on to another piece, but sensing the

unsettled feeling followed her, he moved in front of her by way diverting her fear and holding her full attention.

"He's in two places at once." Sergei said. "Since his return to us he's very different."

"His father saw to that." She countered crisply. "Nic was left to sort out Carlo Seta. A lot of emotion and duty is wrapped up in that one action. Again, it's a lot to deal with. It's not a simple business when someone does you wrong in such a personal way. It's a deeply felt resentment."

"He's not enough Francesca." He said, pressing his point. "You knew the man before. Tell me, do you think he's changed? Can he be an effective Capo?"

"Yes, I think he can. He's arrogant. Ruthless. Those traits will never change." She said quickly and truthfully.

"He's angry Sergei; mostly at the Seta clan. They betrayed him and their lack of consideration for the rest of the group makes him feel exposed. From what I'm hearing, a lot of people are concerned by that family."

She looked squarely at the mob boss with eyes the colour of the palest sapphire.

"Life has taught him to wait, for but a moment, to digest and consider." She said confidently. "He *will* act. On that you can be sure. Swiftly and as necessary. A little like yourself Sergei."

The mob boss sighed wearily.

"There's no doubt the Italian Government will sign off on this immigration solution and if he's not careful ..."

"You're worried about exposure because you think he's inept." She bluffed; completely unaware of what he was talking about. "You make business decisions every day. Are you in or out? If you want advice, from the outside looking in, it's as simple as that. With any new start, there's always complications."

"We can't afford complications." He said. "Who is in charge of Seta group?"

"Nicholas."

"He is? Now you have my attention. And Giuliett is on board with it as well as the other families?"

Francesca shrugged. "I don't know. And I'm not going to speculate. You'll have to resolve that with Nicholas."

"It's a one sided discussion. I have my own issue with that group."

"Namely Giuliett?" she asked.

"Yes. You know what happened to Anya Frida."

She nodded. "I hope her recovery is going well."

"Thank you. She is doing the best she can, given the circumstances."

There was an awkward moment.

"Francesca, I didn't want you to come here. I thought it was the wrong decision."

This time she propped, taken by surprise.

"Who then?" She asked.

"Li Wei. He insisted. On you and Pocco. I just made it happen so you wouldn't get hurt. I owe it to Sinclair McCrae to protect you. I will never be able to repay my debt to him for saving my sister."

"Why are you telling me this?" she asked quietly, feeling the room gush around her.

"Because I trust you. I find myself desiring to confide in you. I've watched you interpret things that others can't, and hold it safe. That's a good heart." He said, lightly touching her chest with the palm of his hand. "And I know you will do the right thing by my family when you need to."

81

. . . .

Francesca held his gaze in that close proximity. Behind the danger and reputation of the Russian mob, she saw the humanness of him. Here was a man struggling to deal with the turbulent emotions of his sister's recent fate and his own inherent desires for retribution. More worrying still, she saw a man impatient to take matters into his own.

She placed her hand on his forearm.

"Look Sergei. I understand you. I understand your need to make good for your sister. But do we have to go to war over it?"

"There is no other way." He said and turned away to leave.

Nicholas Delarno watched the interplay intently from the doorway threshold.

"Nicholas." The Russian acknowledged. Instinctively Francesca took a step back at Nic's black expression. Sergei strode towards him.

"Keep your hands off Francesca." Nic growled.

"Or what?" He said calmly, eyeballing his friend. "Threaten me again and I will take your precious Francesca for myself and everything else you hold dear."

The Russian turned to face her from the doorway. "I have enjoyed our little moments together alone. I hope you did too, sweet Francesca."

She smiled awkwardly at him and said quietly. "Thank you Sergei."

"Aperitifs are served at 8pm." He said to Nicholas, heading towards the grand staircase. Francesca strode towards the doorway.

"What's your problem?" she whispered angrily. "You want to start a fight with him and get us both killed?" She went to push past him. Nic grabbed her on the arm, his fingers digging aggressively into her flesh.

"You're playing with fire, sweet Francesca." He menaced.

"Says you." She responded tautly. "I heard what he said. I've no desire to live out my days in Russia. Smarten up honey and put it back in your pants before you start something you can't finish. Whatever you may think, I don't belong to you like some object to be controlled and passed about."

"What did the two of you discuss?" he asked suspiciously, his eyes narrowed.

"You! And if you're not careful, this whole Anya Frida and Giuliett thing will spin out of control and you can kiss your leadership goodbye. It won't be the Guardians or the Commission you'll fear. Focus on that!" She hissed.

She yanked her arm free. "Now, I need to have a bath, find a gown and get ready for dinner." She said, storming off towards the staircase.

It wasn't enough to leave it alone for Nicholas. He followed her into her suite.

"What now?" she turned to face him.

"You're nothing but a little prick tease." He taunted. "Robbie L was right. You do slut yourself around to gain advantage. My eyes were opened today."

"I beg your pardon!" She was indignant.

"McCrae. Sergei. Me. You promise to blow us all and give nothing."

"Nicholas. That is not true." Francesca went as white as a sheet.

"Prove it then. Prove you haven't betrayed me!"

She looked at him sullenly.

"I said prove it!" he yelled at her so loudly she visibly jumped and his voice echoed around the sitting room chamber.

"Nicholas." She said calmly, her heart was beating hard now. "I know you're angry. Please calm down."

He strode towards her and she stepped behind a lounge chair for protection.

"Prove your loyalty to me Francesca." He yelled again. "Because you are being played for a fool. He has you eating out of his hands like a little lap dog. You want to be mobster's lap dog Francesca? Does that turn you on?"

He rounded the lounge and she stepped just out of his reach.

"Maybe I'll buy you a nice diamond choker from Fabergè and you can be my little lap dog." He taunted, steadily approaching her.

"Stop it now!" She cried. "Nicholas you need to leave!"

Suddenly he lunged at her, catching her fingers. He pulled her into him and as she fell forward the force pushed her ribs into the timber edge of the lounge. Francesca gasped as the hard surface wedged momentarily under her rib cage. She cried out in pain, doubling over holding her side and covering her face from his open hand. He pushed her to the floor at his feet.

"Get on your knees dog." He said, shoving her head into his groin. "How do you like that?" He yanked her hair back and stared at her tear-stained face.

"Ahh! You're not worth the fuck." The Capo yelled and pushed her away. He stormed out of the room.

Francesca didn't show for dinner and hid behind the locked the door of her suite. For hours she lay curled up on the bed, reeling between nausea and shock.

He was a man walking at the edge of a ledge. She'd seen it before but never had his temper reached such heights of aggression and never had it been directed at her. His insults whirled on repeat.

In the early hours after midnight when she was sure everyone was asleep, she opened the hallway door and crept from her room. The long wide walkway was dark, lit only by a full moon gleaming through large windows ahead. She padded quietly along the carpets, tiptoed across the marble and stopped at the top of the grand staircase.

Here she sat, unable to descend and clutching the marble balustrade. Panic gripped her. Before her, in the bright moonlight, the large foyer gleamed in moonbeam hues. In the shadows, macabre shapes tricked her weary eyes.

Somewhere behind her a door softly opened and shut. Francesca froze. Footsteps pressed gently along the hallway in her direction. Quietly another door opened and shut and the noise was gone. Francesca breathed out.

She stood. Taking the outer curve of the stairwell, she tiptoed towards the grand foyer and crossed the floor to the salon, where she and Sergei had met on her first night at the palace.

Francesca breathed again when she entered the room and made her way to the chair in front of the fireplace. Stoking the embers, she placed another log onto the fire and watched as it caught, filling the room with the soothing crackling sound and a soft glow.

She pulled her feet under her and covered herself in a cosy blanket she'd found in the upstairs suite. She stared into space, trying to find a way out of this latest mess.

"Thought I might find you here." Francesca visibly jumped as Sergei entered the room. "I didn't buy Nicholas' story at dinner. Besides, I heard the shouting. What can I do to help?"

"I want to go home." She said, looking at him.

"I can get you to Anya tonight and then we'll get you home. Does that suit?"

Francesca nodded. "Thank you Sergei."

82

· · · · · · · · · · · · · · · ·

Leeuwarden, Netherlands

Finding herself stuck between a rock and a hard place, Francesca couldn't shake that dreadful feeling she'd landed directly in the lion's den. Anya Frida was sweet and beautiful, as Francesca discovered, but she also functioned to the heartbeat of her brother, who seemed in no rush to orchestrate her exit from the Netherlands apartment.

And so with no means to action an escape and too proud to reach out to Johnno or Sinclair for support, Francesca thought about the foolish decision she'd made to pledge her allegiance to Nicholas Delarno, who, as she'd belatedly found out, was in fact the Capo of the whole organisation.

Despite their long and protracted friendship, she could not forgive him for his treatment of her on that night. His repeated phone calls went unanswered and his messages erased. Until the last when, tired of being a Russian pawn, she realised she had enough strength to face him and he would have no other option but to get her immediately home to her family. They met in his car on the quiet residential street.

"I can't forgive myself." He began. "So I can't expect you to forgive me. I have no excuse for my actions. I am wholly and utterly ashamed of myself. There are many adjectives I can use to describe my disgusting behaviour and only four words I can say. They will never erase the repulsion you must feel towards me but I hope, one day we can meet a little closer.

"I am sorry Francesca. Truly and most irrevocably sorry I hurt you in such a demeaning and hideous way. It will never happen again. I promise you that. Please accept my deepest, most humble apology."

Francesca remained stony faced. Her hand came up to rub the space between her eyebrows and smooth the tightness there.

"I don't know Nicholas." She said looking forward. "I'm extremely hurt. I accept that you're regretful. I know you're grieving. I understand people sometimes hurt the ones they love most when they're in the worst kind of pain.

"But fuck it! I'm hurting too! I'm beyond angry with you right now. I've supported you through everything, in and out of every goddam nightmare your family has thrown at me and this is what you think of me? A lap dog? A prick tease? Worse, you put faith in Robbie L's opinion of me?" She turned in her seat to face him.

"Fuck! I've never been so humiliated in my life! And then I hear from Pocco that you're the frigging Capo! You couldn't tell me yourself when I was grovelling to you to protect my family! That really takes the cake. I need time and distance from you. Your actions towards me are barely forgivable. I want to go home. And I want to go now."

He nodded solemnly. "This is more than I had hoped and deserve. I'll make sure you get home."

"I mean what I say Nicholas. I want to go home today." She said.

They sat in silence, her not wanting to stay and him not wanting to leave. Outside it started raining. Francesca watched it drip downwards beating steadily against the windscreen. She opened her mouth to negotiate her way back to Fiji.

"I'd better get you in before we get stuck in this downpour." He said as if suddenly aware it was raining. He looked at her, his eyes damp from tears. "There's an umbrella in the back seat if you want to grab it."

He checked his side mirror before opening the door.

"What the hell? Don't move." He said, continuing to look in the mirror. His hand slid down into the storage pocket in the doorframe. He brought the 9 mm pistol stored there within easy reach.

"What is it?" Francesca asked.

"Not what. Who. Giuliett just walked up the steps of Anya's apartment building. And she's not alone. Where's Anya?"

"She's in the centre, running errands. Has anyone seen us?"

"Not yet. Message Anya. Find out where she is and we'll swing by and pick her up. She needs to call Sergei. We have a situation."

He waited for a moment. "They've gone inside. I can't see Moretti."

"I can. To the right and back."

"Are you armed?"

"No."

"There's a second in the glove box and a spare round." He said, starting the engine and casually leaving the curb.

Francesca's phone pinged. "I have a location. I'm punching it into my GPS now."

83

·················

Montmorency, France

"Alessandro's jet, on board with a crew I trust, will be available in forty-eight hours." Nic said. "They'll take you from Paris direct to Nadi and escort you home. Just to be sure I'm going to leave a small outfit in situ for a week or two. In the meantime, we just have to sit tight."

"Thank you Nicholas."

"I know this place isn't much, but we'll be safe here. I suggest you try and get some rest. You probably feel like you've been around the world."

Francesca smiled wearily. "Rome to St Petersburg to Amsterdam to St Petersburg to Paris. More like a game of ping pong."

"Are you hungry?" He asked.

"No. I don't think I could eat even if I was."

"You're probably wondering why we didn't stay the night at Palace Volkov after we escorted Anya to the rendezvous." He said.

"I'm kind of happy we didn't to be honest." She said. "I had a nagging feeling we'd never get away from them if we stayed much longer. I felt like the air was slowly being gently squeezed out of me in that place. And that is how it would stay until Sergei got what he wanted from us."

"My thoughts too." He said. "He's getting ready to pounce and I won't let you be collateral. I've known that family for a long time, and unfortunately that was precisely the final outcome for you."

Francesca grimaced. "Is that why you lost your shit over Sergei?"

He nodded. "It's why he intercepted you in Rome. And yes, that's why I lost my shit. I could see you being manipulated against me without even realising it. Why do you think Anya left all those years ago?"

She shrugged. With no counter story, she had to believe him, although her mind remained open. She tested this new place they'd landed.

"Nicholas, something's been bugging me from the minute we were ambushed in Russia. I haven't told anyone. I've been trying to process it myself before I confided."

"What's that my flower?" He asked, feeling pleased she was willing to trust in him again.

"The weapons. The gun I used was modified Australian military. I wonder how did it end up with the Russian mob?"

"I have a hunch but I can't prove anything. The Guardians have been working on it too."

"Is this the kind of thing they do? Gather information and then act upon it with the proper authorities?" she asked.

"Yes. As well as moving people around when needed. Provide protection and cash. What did you think they did?"

"I had no real idea to be honest." She said. "I just felt it was well funded and well resourced."

"Sometimes." He said. "Depends on the operation."

Francesca walked to the small kitchenette and opened the double height painted timber cupboards. They were empty. She opened the small retro looking bar fridge set under a timber bench. It was empty too.

Next in line, simple black brackets secured open timber shelving to the wall. An assortment of fine china and crystal glassware were set in place above a small farmhouse sink with a polished brass gooseneck tap. She rubbed her hands along the white handmade tiles that formed a backsplash to the height of the ceiling.

A quirky looking kettle, a coffee pot and a small toaster oven could be found on the oiled timber bench top of a lime washed credenza. It ran along the length of the wall opposite the sink and cupboards, forming a wide galley style kitchen.

A small round table sat in a nook near a large picture window. In between the kitchen and dining table was the exterior doorway to the apartment. It was made of solid timber and had a wrought iron security gate on the exterior. Access to the apartment was by shared external steps through a lovely walled garden where at the end of a stone path, another wrought iron gate led to the street below.

As guests entered the interior of the apartment, the dining space was immediately to the left. Looking towards the back wall, a loveseat lounge and a single armchair shared a large carpet rug covering the wide timber floorboards.

A fireplace with a white marble surround was adjacent the armchair and could also easily be enjoyed from the large bed hidden from the front door by the short kitchen wall. A lovely cottage style bathroom was there also.

Such was the setup, that guests could stay in bed and enjoy the fireplace burning brightly on a winter's night.

The entire room and cabinets were painted the creamy white of a typically French palate. Three iron and glass chandeliers hung from ornate plaster ceiling roses, high above.

He watched her familiarise herself with the room. Touching the tactile surfaces, the buttery dark leathers and the patina of the aged timbers, sensing the room through her fingers as her eyes drank the textures.

"There's a small tavern downstairs. I'll run down and get us something if you like." Nic offered.

"I'm not hungry. Just looking. And thinking." She said. "Might have a tub, if you don't need the bathroom."

"Go right ahead."

At the sound of running water, Nicholas ducked out to get some supplies, locking her safely inside.

A cotton robe hung on a hook on the back of the bathroom door, and in the absence of anything else to change into Francesca sniffed it, checked it and wrapped it around her. To her relief, despite the lack of food, the apartment was freshly prepared for short stay visitors.

She opened the door and the aroma of soapy freshness met baked items, fresh herbs and garlic and her stomach growled loudly.

Nic was crouched by the fireplace, and the crackling of kindling filled the room as the musky smoke lingered. He stood and stepped towards her. Francesca flinched.

His head bent towards the floor and he turned away, scolding himself quietly in Italian.

"I'm sorry." She said.

"Don't be." He said. He indicated the dining table.

"When you were in the shower, I took the opportunity to get some food." He said.

"It smells delicious. Thank you."

"It's not grand but I think it will do the trick tonight. It's been a long day and we need comfortable food. It's ready if you'd like to start. I'll join you in a minute. I want to add another log here and get this room warmed up a bit." He rubbed his hands together.

Francesca lifted the casserole lid to reveal baked chicken, potatoes and fresh buttered beans. Steamy hot bread was wrapped in a red and white tea towel and two chocolate tarts were plated together on an oval dish with dollops of fresh thick cream. In a trio of small tins fresh coffee grinds, tea and sugar completed the meal.

"Wine or mineral water?" she asked, looking at the bottle of the local, light red.

"Both." He said. "I'm working on the premise of a full stomach, relaxing glass of wine, hot bath and a comfortable bed means we'll both have a good rest."

"I hope so too." She said.

He came and sat opposite her.

"Tuck in my flower," he said. "Don't wait for me."

"I need to message home." She said. "Let them know what's going on and when to expect me."

"Sure. I think that's a good idea. They'll be very worried about you."

"Sinclair is due home soon too. I haven't spoken to him since Italy." She said. "I need to reach him before he's in transit."

"Absolutely." Nicholas said. "Do you want some privacy? I can disappear."

"Yes. I do." She said. "But my head's all over the place. So let's eat and I can work out the time differences and we can do it after that."

"Okay. Whatever you need."

84

....

Nicholas returned to the room sometime later, finding Francesca sobbing quietly. He knelt beside the sofa where she curled up in a tight ball and gently comforted her. His head rested against hers, her soft hair lightly touching his forehead.

A man like Sinclair McCrae would take some convincing to take another direction when his mind was made up. And based on the conversation Sebastino had revealed to him from her phone messages, Nic assumed the news from the soldier medic was not good for her.

"I can't blame him." She said wiping the tears from her eyes. "I'm sick of my life being disrupted like this too." She sniffled loudly.

"He's just upset." Nic said. "He'll come round. Once we get you home, you'll see. It's too hard to explain on the phone."

"I hope you're right." She said. "But he's pretty adamant. That's not a good sign for me."

The sob caught in her throat.

"I can't help it. This situation was out of my hands. I *have* been trying to get home!" She wailed and dropped her head into her folded arms resting on the chair end. "Does everything that happened sound far-fetched to you?"

"Oh Francesca." She reminded him of a lost child. All elbows and knees and long matted hair as she curled on herself in a tight, hot, damp ball in the crook of the lounge.

"I know it's hard honey." He crooned calmly. He stroked her soft hair, catching the end length in his hand and gently wrapping it between his fingers. "Like I said, once you can sit down and eyeball him, he'll see and know."

"Do you think?" Her whole forearm rubbed across her blotchy face.

"I don't think, I know." He said soothingly. He stood and put another log in the fireplace. "Shove up." He said to her. "I'm too old and rickety to crouch beside you all night."

"You know what the worst bit is?" She said looking at him in the closeness of the double lounge. "When I was talking to him, I was trying to solve the puzzle. I was trying to explain how things happened and my brain started working on a tangent. I think he realised that and that's why he's so angry with me too."

"Why would he be angry about that? You have to process things."

"Because he knows I won't let it go until it's resolved. And he doesn't want me to resolve it."

"Resolve what my flower?"

"He knows about the guns. When I told him, he went ballistic. You don't think he's part of the chain do you?" She was as white as the French room's wall colour.

"Do you?" Nic asked cautiously.

"No. He's too straighty-one-eighty. But after this last week, who knows anything about any-o-n-e. Oh gosh. Oh no."

She jumped up and started pacing the room.

"Li Wei didn't want me dead. Well, not at that particular time. Not like last time our paths crossed. He's using me to provoke Robbie L." She said.

"What are you talking about?"

"Sergei said to me that he didn't want to make any more business with Li Wei. That's why he was installed at another residence on the estate. He also said Li Wei insisted I come with Pocco to Russia. Don't you see?"

"You've lost me."

"You're right about Sergei and I'm right too. It's all interconnected. I bet if we conducted a fresh search warrant on some of Silvio's holdings we'd find enough. And whilst that punk is spreading his love in Italy, I bet sleeper triad operatives who've planted themselves in Ares businesses back home are gearing up.

"Along with some good old fashioned military stock placed in all the correct places. It's too smooth, too obvious. A random tip off after all these years is one thing, leading to hard evidence and a warrant so quickly is another. I'm not buying it. Someone knows the details and they've talked. I need to talk to Johnno."

"You need to talk to me. You're not making any sense."

"Do you remember when Silvio brought Ares aka Robbie L into the fold?"

"Yes."

"And he brought in the triads as well."

"Yes."

"He had you running around Italy trying to sort out Carlo Seta and me."

"Yes."

"Silvio was brokering a deal with Li Wei and Robbie L to supply the Russian and Chinese black markets with deregistered Australian military issue firearms. He knew the Russians were ripe for the taking because Carlo Seta told him. Ares was already well entrenched in the law enforcement administration – military stores, the audit team, the criminal justice systems. That's why it was so hard for us to bring them in. Johnno and I suspected it at the time; particularly when we discovered a key victim was an undercover cop, Clyde Fletcher. A former defence part-timer, he was also secretly and heavily engaged with the triads.

"Wei is smart. He sent us on the hunt, looking at mafia and traditions and Ares. Whilst we were running all around the place, he was busy in the background troublemaking. Wei was pressuring Silvio to get me out of the picture before any deal was done. Naturally our focus turned to Silvio. We couldn't find the right evidence to prove the big picture. So we had to go piece by piece.

"When we disrupted the triad systems in New South Wales and Victoria, Ares finished them off, took the stragglers and confiscated their business interests for Ares' own coffers.

"Almost simultaneously everything went pear shaped for Johnno and me. Our team lost control of the investigation because the commanders stepped in and brought on another squad. I fell pregnant to you; my team lost confidence in me. Then Johnno was 'promoted' off the case. As we got closer to trial, dates were pushed back and evidence went missing. A conviction was beyond our reach.

"The Feds brought Silvio into line and had him under constant surveillance. His hands were tied and his once strong operational structure was damaged. You weren't there, Castello was dead and Robbie L made himself more and more valuable to the operations, giving Carlo Seta free reign in Italy with Volkov in tow and Ares gaining all the benefits in Australia."

"So you're telling me that during that time Li Wei has rebuilt his team and has eyes on Robbie L?" Nic asked. "And Sergei knew about it, which is why he brought you in close. Because?"

"Because with me in that situation, comes you ... the leader, the Capo." She said. "Sergei wants to wipe the floor with the Seta clan, namely Giuliett, because of what she did to Anya in Afghanistan. But that's it. He doesn't want to start another revolution. His focus is retribution."

"I think I understand where you're coming from now." Nic said. "All the connections and assets in Australia belong to me. Even though at the moment, Robbie L is in control of my father's interests." Nic said.

Francesca nodded.

"Volkov is pressing you to take care of the other business – the triads and the bikers." She said. "He wants the firearms, I know because I've seen it with my own eyes. But, he has loyalty to you because you brought Anya back to him and me, because Sinclair found her and brought her to you. He told me he owed it to Sinclair to protect me."

"So I think Sergei is struggling and making decisions within his own moral compass regarding loyalty to your organisation. Nobody is really sure where Robbie L sits with you, and that is a problem. Li Wei is pressing for action and as you heard in Russia, he doesn't care about your protocols. Chi You won't mark time waiting for you to sort out your shit. Li Wei is ready to act. He's organised his crew and firmed up his options."

She looked at Nic.

"The triads will take over the Ares operations. And that means all the business Robbie L inherited from your father is in jeopardy. I'd be surprised if Wei hasn't already absorbed part of it. Unless you give a clear indication of where your loyalties lie regarding Robbie L, you're unlikely to get support when you need it."

"We thought I was the target because of the threats made to me." She said. "But now I believe Robbie was aiming for Li Wei in that Russian ambush. And I believe Sergei is trying to step away from the Chinese, not move closer. And as the lynch pin for all their ambitions, I was collateral, as you so eloquently put it."

"I have a question." Nic said.

"Ask away."

"You were on that plane. Where does Pocco fit into this?"

"I sincerely believe he doesn't. He was big noting to the wrong person, in the wrong place at the wrong time. And he was too stupid or too vain to realise he was a triad target on that trip. Wei suffers fools less than your father ever did and is far more ruthless. I was fortunate that Sergei protected me, otherwise I'd be in a morgue in Russia right now too."

85

....

They sat together, each lost in their own thoughts and listening abstractly to the silence as the machinations in their brains worked on processing Francesca's hunch.

"So my question is, now what do we do?" Francesca asked him at last. "I know the moral road I'd like to take."

"Can you prove any of it?"

"Not in a court of law. No."

"So why start a war when it's circumstantial?" he asked.

"I don't want to start a war. But I feel an obligation."

"Why?"

"Don't you?"

"Not necessarily." He said. "Francesca it's good for us to understand the landscape, because now we can act to protect ourselves. That's it, end of story."

She thought about his comment for a while.

"Don't you think we should tell someone?" She asked.

"First question is who do you want to tell? And second, you want to give up our ace? No wonder you were never good at card games." He said.

"All the same, I'd love to talk it through with Johnno."

"I think you should keep it between us for the moment until you can substantiate your claims."

"I suppose so." She said.

There was another long silence. The fire crackled on. Francesca poured two wines. She handed a glass to Nicholas.

"When you brought Anya to Paris, you used a Guardian safe house. Why?"

"It was the only safe option at the time."

"But now it can't be used as a safe house anymore."

Nicholas rubbed his head. "I know. I stuffed up. Alessandro warned me it would be difficult to juggle both interests. That's why I decided to buy this apartment in Montmorency."

"What will you do with the other?"

"Air BnB" he said.

"You're joking?"

"No. We'll make a fortune in that location."

"My father chose that place." She said. "He bought it for the Guardians."

"Do you want to share the profits?" He asked. "We could set it up for Archie and Bella? Our first business venture together."

"Yeah ... it's a great offer but I don't think Sinclair would approve somehow."

"He can't say anything if I build them into the business model." Nic said.

Francesca shrugged. "I suppose not."

"How can I keep you safe from Li Wei?" He asked, returning to their previous conversation.

"You can't. He's his own law." She said. "There's no love lost between us, believe me. That's why I was trying to make myself useful in Russia. I felt like I was at a job interview the whole time I was with him on the plane and at that meeting. It was sickening."

"And then I stepped in a fucked it up." Nic said.

"Yes. You did."

"I did have my reasons, as we've just established. But again, I'm sorry."

"What's done is done." She said. "Funny, I've always felt in order to protect myself, I ought to learn as much as I can about an offender. Helps me dissect their motives and understand how they operate. Puts me in a position to know where to start looking for the most effective conviction." She took a great gulp of the wine. "And then something happens and I'm just as far away as I was before I stepped into the ring."

"This really matters to you." He said.

"Bringing down Chi You?" She asked, assessing him carefully. "I spent my whole police career in that grey area between being absolutely terrified of Li Wei and trying to understand him, so I could build an iron clad case. Unfortunately, Johnno and I were never really successful because we had to operate within budgets, policy and biscuit eaters."

"And the law."

"Yes, of course, that too." She added vaguely.

"Talk to me about it."

"You really want to know?" she asked feeling more than a little curious by his motives.

"Yes, I do." He said honestly. "It's important to you so, yes I want to know."

"He's circle walking around Ares," she began, "creating and building up pressure by using opposing forces to generate an eruption. It's the same MO he used with Johnno and me. I can see it clearly now. In this case he's working the leadership team of Ares."

"I don't understand." He said. "What's circle walking?"

"In any type of conflict a solid attack has three phases. Right? The first move is all about provoking your opponent and getting them to react to your advantage."

He nodded.

"I think Li Wei oversaw key personnel installed within Ares leadership. Robbie L's vanguard is a former Chi You operative who's risen through the ranks and proven his 'loyalty' to the biker.

"Triad sympathisers have worked themselves across key positions – operations, executive, within the head kickers and the good time Charlies of the bike gang."

"Why would Robbie L allow that?" Nic asked.

"He's an ego maniac. He thinks he threw the sucker punch in the first hit. Li Wei enhanced his belief through 'contrition'." She said.

"Next more pressure is put on Ares by corrupting and exposing evidence, involving the police and using partners to do some of the dirty work so there's an arms-length between act and discovery."

Nicholas nodded. "I understand." He said.

"Whilst the pressure is on from external sources, Li Wei offers assistance using language and action along the lines of 'We're friends, in this together, I know somewhere you can hide, store etc; someone who can help you ... I'll help with the cops, judges' and so on. In other words classic manipulation.

"Ares is grateful. At the same time, Li Wei is levering up the costs and favours until money is now owed to the triad boss and there's problems at customs, problems with supply and before he knows it, Robbie L is in bed with Li Wei and he's looking at huge problems in his day-to-day operations. He doesn't know who he can trust."

"Sounds like the mafia to me." Nic said.

"Yes, but in this case the steps are getting tighter and tighter, the circle is getting smaller creating concentric forces. Building pressure with each step creates more attack opportunities and more effective strikes."

"Robbie L is not stupid, he must guess he's being double crossed." Nicholas said.

"Maybe." She said. "Maybe not. This kind of operation is a slow, steady process. It takes years to achieve. Patience, balance and business agility are key to its success. Something Robbie L lacks. He's a bam bam kind of personality. Instant gratification is the name of the game for him. And he backs himself that his decisions around his leadership team. That they are loyal only to him.

"I have absolutely no doubt team members within the Ares businesses are driving and feeding into the pressure. Strikes against the Ares group are almost always effective. There's no wasted energy because Wei is the ultimate Dragonhead. Wei has the advantage of distance and like a puppeteer can pull the strings knowing what he says goes without question and is acted upon with ruthless precision.

"The Australian triad operations may be askew for the moment, but that doesn't mean that his world network is suffering. Robbie L lives in his own bubble of influence. Your father opened his eyes to other opportunities but I feel the biker is so self-assured in his safe zone, he thinks he's untouchable." Francesca concluded.

Nicholas nodded, remembering his encounter with Carlo Seta in Ibiza years before. "I know what you mean." He said.

"I think Robbie L is sensing things are closing in around him." Francesca continued. "It's not visible to him as such, but he's suffocating and then pop!"

"The ambush." Nicholas said.

She shook her head. "No. The first pop was to get Robbie L out of the country. Fortune or favour or winds of change, however you like to look at it, the changes in leadership in your situation created an opportunity for Robbie L to escape the pressure he'd been feeling, as well as providing Li Wei with an opening. Now Ares are wide open for attack."

"Which leads me to phase two." She said. "Robbie L's head is filled with learning this new entity. He sees an opportunity with Giuliett and the now unstable Seta clan. He seizes it, thinking he'll buddy up and build a bigger fortress. I don't know if he even realises why or if it's greed or ego, but I do know subconsciously, he'll be thinking I need to get bigger to wipe out this pressure back in Australia.

"In fact, I bet he's hearing rumblings from Ares team members. And you have to look at it from their point of view, simplistic as it is. They're being hammered by the cops, relying more on their relationships to get their regular business moving. Meanwhile pressure is mounting for some kind of reprieve in the outlaw camp."

She stood and stretched and walked a lap around the small space.

"Robbie L on the other hand is over here living it up with his new squeeze, free as bird and you know yourself, when you're not on the ground, there is a sense of removal and without eyes on, things can be cocked up through misunderstanding or misinterpretation or just plain old laziness and wrong skillset."

"Someone on Li Wei's team let Robbie know there was a meeting in Russia and framed it so he had to act to prove to the boys back home he was addressing the damage." She said, rubbing her eyes.

"You could be right." Nicholas said.

"My question is do you want Li Wei to finish Robbie L?" She said, coming back to sit in the single chair opposite him. She snuggled into the butter soft leather and pulled a cashmere blanket over her legs and bare feet. "Or are you going to back the biker in?"

"That's a good question. And worth exploration ..." He said. "I know my immediate response. What is your take?"

She yawned and shook her head. "I suppose it depends on who you can manipulate best to suit your needs, Robbie L or Li Wei? Robbie L is annoying but he's mostly on the team. Would you want to give more power to the triads?"

She took a deep breath to stifle another yawn.

"You need to go to bed." He said.

"I can keep going. A cosy fire always makes me sleepy. It's something to do with my body and the room temperature and the lack of oxygen." She rambled. "Anyway, I want to keep talking about this; my brain is going one hundred to the dozen. But every time I open my mouth I have to yawn."

He pulled her out of the chair and steered her to the bed. Pulling back the quilt, he waited for her to climb in saying,

"We have time. Let's sleep on it and explore some options going forward tomorrow." He breathed out heavily, brought the bedcovers over her and wandered back to the lounge with the cashmere blanket and a spare pillow.

"See, once someone starts with a yawn, that's the end for

everyone. Good night my flower."
And she was already asleep.

86

....

Francesca woke later, tossed and turned and despite a bed like a cloud, fresh and clean linen and a cosy crackling fire, she could not sleep. It was still dark outside. She looked at Nicholas sprawled across the lounge.

Men! She thought. *They could sleep on top of a pumpkin.*

She climbed out of bed and tiptoed to the sink and a glass of water.

"I'm awake." He said, making her jump.

"It's my restlessness isn't it? I just can't sleep tonight." She said coming over the lounge with the last of the chocolate tart and cream.

"Maybe tart might help. Would you like to share?" She said giving him little opportunity to object. She wedged in the corner next to him, forcing him sit up even if he didn't want to and with her back resting against the side armrest, draped her legs over his thighs.

"Why not." He said relenting because he knew it was pointless to argue.

"What's keeping you up?" she asked fully alert, leaning slightly forward to feed him. She in turn, took a small mouthful.

"It's nothing." He said.

"Tell me. It's obviously bothering you."

"I have something to tell you." He said. She stopped with the fork halfway to his mouth. He gently guided her hand to his before cream dipped off and all over him.

"Oh. Okay."

"Sinclair went ballistic about the guns because I told him. I arranged to meet him in Singapore before he went to Kabul."

"Why would you do that?"

"Because I knew Sergei and Wei were at odds over it and I stepped in because I want the Chinese to help me with another project."

"The one that Sergei doesn't want to be involved in anymore but he's already half way in?"

"What makes you say that?"

"Because rather than sit at the negotiating table he took me around the egg room. It wasn't hard to work out." She said.

She placed the fork on the plate noisily. "Why oh why did you involve Sinclair? He's completely hopeless at this kind of thing. He nearly tore himself apart over Anya."

"You know about that?" Nic asked.

"Of course I do. I was there at the safe house when you were moving her. Lucky you weren't in range. I could've kicked you in the shins at the time."

Unexpectedly Nicholas blushed. "That was you in the café?"

"Yes."

There was a long quiet silence, save for the clack of the fork on the plate and the fire crackling.

"What was keeping you up tonight?" he asked.

"I don't really want to talk about it," she said.

"Fair's fair, you made me tell my secrets."

"Alright then.' She said gathering herself and launching straight in with all honesty. "Two things. How to wrap Robbie

L and Wei together in a nice little package and hand them over to the Federal Police. And complete bewilderment and wonder at how easy it was for a biker and a Russian mob boss to manipulate you against me."

He sighed. It was the sound of a person irritated by another's persistence.

"The last year hasn't been easy on either of us." At any other time it would have been an apology, but she sensed he meant anything but. She prepared to move away from him. A difficult manoeuvre, as her legs were prone across his thighs and the remainder of the lounge. Sensing her retreat, he held tightly onto her legs, one hand each side of her knee, effectively changing her mind for her.

"My flower," he said his eyes set on the fireplace and glistening black like polished iron ore. "Many times since our altercation at my father's house I reached my absolute mental limit. In those darkest days I turned and faced myself. I understood who I really was. To survive I had to change in order to lead this organisation, as it needs to be led."

Francesca watched him closely. Her body tensed for a quick reaction.

"Have you heard this old belief said often in the north of our mother country? If the serpent wants to become a dragon, it must first eat itself." He asked quietly. He turned to face her.

"No. I have not." She said, trying not to gulp. He nodded and looked back to the fireplace.

"I tore myself up over what I've done and could've done better. The lives lost and costly mistakes. I sunk to the deepest lows. I tormented myself, faced my defeat, reflected and as a result do you know what I learned?' he asked.

"No." She squeaked, looking at him expectantly.

"Despite itself, the serpent needs the white spirit as much as night needs day, as good desires evil."

He turned to face her and his intense eyes full of past feeling shone brightly.

"You, Francesca, have been my constant. My light. My compass. There has never been a moment when your welfare hasn't been at the core of my being. *But ...*"

He paused for a long moment. "If you try to arrest Robbie L or Li Wei, you will also bring unwanted focus to my organisation and me. You understand that don't you?"

She nodded. Her eyes never left his and she was captured in his snake like guise.

"My message to you then, should you pursue that path, please do so with vigour and endurance, because those actions will put me in a public, untenable position. We'll forever more be at odds.

"Of course, it gets complicated because you've now joined us. As you've pledged yourself to me, by taking on Robbie L as you wish to do, you will go against the code. As much as he irritates me, the biker is one of us and as such, enjoys the binds of our organisation. If you break the code, you become a traitor. I will not pursue you, but I will not protect you as I've done in the past."

He paused. The reprimand, delivered in a measured quiet tone was shouting loud and clear. Francesca would be a fool to test his patience. She moved uncomfortably beside him and she was sure he could hear her heart pounding. At the next sentence, her face turned bright pink with emotion.

"However, I cannot and will not guarantee your safety from others within my organisation."

"Geezuz Nicholas! Stop talking." She said, jumping up quickly from the lounge to put some distance between them. "Stop! You're frightening me!"

"My flower, this is a serious decision." He said, sounding as cold as a villain in a vintage movie. "We have discussed this."

"No, you said it was better we understood our circumstance. I said I felt we had a moral obligation to let Johnno know. I am a cop, Nicholas. Retired or not I pledged an oath to serve Queen and country. I can't help who I am, even when you threaten me."

"And yet you betrayed Johnno when you told me of the impending arrest of Robbie L in Genoa."

"You're an arsehole." She countered, stung more by her indiscretion than his comments.

"That I may be, but I speak the truth. Will you at last open up your eyes to the world I'm living in? I need you to know and fully understand the consequences of your actions. People's lives are at stake."

"Yeah, mine." She said glaring at him for a long, tense minute.

"And many more." He remained unmoved by her temper. "For now, you can stop staring at me. I'm not going to throw flames from my nostrils and hide you away so your hero can come and save you."

87

·····················

"God help the Guardians." She said challenging him, refusing to be bullied by him. "Maybe I should take my father's role. Live out my destiny, as you tried so hard to persuade me, for the sole purpose of prosecuting you and your team."

"Don't threaten me Francesca." He warned. "Unless you really want that fight."

"Maybe I do." She said. "Someone needs to remind you that you're not the centre of the whole damn universe! In fact, here's a thought. Li Wei is poised to strike at the heart of your organisation and you can't even see it."

"Rubbish! The Commission would never allow it! *I* would never allow it."

"Really. You did SAS training in Australia when you were under Alessandro's care. When is the ultimate opportunity to make an offensive strike?" She asked.

"When the enemy is in chaos." He said simply.

In the short pause between them, Francesca was tempted to fill it with a satisfactory grunt.

"Nic, none of you will see him coming." She said in a matter of fact tone. "Instinct tells me triads already have a firm grip on the Delarno holdings in Australia. Volkov is all but out of your latest collaboration after decades of support. Poccolini is dead. Giuliett and Robbie L are working together. Take out one

416

and he takes out both."

"That's very melodramatic don't you think?" He said dismissing her. "We are not in chaos. When Carlo Seta was in charge? Definitely. But not now."

"Why? Because suddenly the famous Nicholas Delarno is here to save the day? If you think Wei hasn't already planned out a strategic, focused outcome you are fucking kidding yourself. His eye is on the prize, and the prize is the whole damn operation. Wake up Nicholas! Your world has changed."

"Why should you care? We are an organised crime outfit! I thought you'd be happy if... Che cazzo è?" He cut her off with an obscenity a his phone lit up. He raised his fingers in a silent gesture to be quiet, effectively snapping the tension in the room into a thousand splinters.

"What?" she asked at his crass language. "What's happened?"

"It's a video." He landscaped the image and zoomed in, scanning the surrounding scenery.

"Of what?" she asked, leaning over his shoulder to watch it.

"I'm not quite sure I believe what I'm seeing." He zoomed right into the picture to read the name. "Come my flower, sit beside me." He patted the seat and drew her in close, instinctively encircling her in a protective embrace. The tension between them dissolved as they became engrossed in the image that would force them together again.

"Fuck. It's the Sea Meadow!" He said. "Robbie L's new boat is on fire in Genoa Harbour. It's all over the news. They won't be able to save that. There's fucking firecrackers coming out of it! I'm waiting for the explosion. Oh ... there it is!"

"Who sent it to you?" She asked.

"A friend of mine. Your arse might've just been saved. Just as you were winding up for an interesting battle too! You won't be arresting Robbie L. He's a marked man. It's on."

"Has to be Wei. Absolutely he's behind it." She said confidently.

"Who fucking cares as long as they don't involve me and they keep it tight."

"You're going to sit back and let them go at it?"

"Do you want to get into the middle of that? I'm staying out of the circle dance, or whatever you called it. That biker made his bed. Now he has to lie in it. You're wrong about Wei and our organisation. The only person he's interested in is Robbie L."

"Unbelievable! Not five minutes ago you were threatening me if I went to the cops." She said incredulously.

"That was different."

"Yeah? How?"

"Because that action would've put you firmly in Wei's focus and because I made a deal with the Feds over Robbie L. I'm untouchable in Australia. In the meantime they can sort each other out and I'll be there to pick up the pieces. Wei is not the only person with a long term goal. I'm willing to make sacrifices whilst he cleans out the Australian ops. I don't give a fuck how long it takes. So I guess you would say I'm circle walking now just like your triad boss."

"You're so infuriating." She sulked, realising the sting had gone out of him as he was only trying to protect her from the Chinese warlord. "You could have said that at the start instead of some raving speech about loyalty and fucking snakes and serpents. Not to mention scaring the hell out of me."

"Serpents and dragons." He corrected. "*That* still stands. I meant every word. Your actions around law enforcement are forever changed."

Seeing his face turn towards her in her peripheral vision, she said, "Doesn't mean any of this is right." She pointed at the phone.

"There you go again. Miss Integrity Righteous." He said. His awareness roused at her leaning into to him, pouting at the mobile phone with her head pressed back against his shoulder absorbed in the images. She snuggled in close as he moved his hips against the back of the lounge to a more comfortable position.

"So white light, I sense a truce. Are we getting any sleep tonight?"

It was a deliberate loaded question and Francesca ignored the double meaning.

"You take the bed." She said. "I'm not tired anymore." And she left him and walked to the kitchen table.

"Suit yourself." He said, climbing into the cosy space she'd left. No sooner had his head hit the pillow his breathing became regular and deep. Francesca listened to him sleep, watched the fire gently simmer on and thought about how much had changed in him.

Sergei had asked if she thought Nicholas could lead. Of course she'd defended him. It was an automatic response. For her entire life she'd found a way to justify his actions.

Tonight of course, she actually realised he could. Perhaps not in any way she was used to. He'd developed a new methodology and the parameters had moved. Francesca wasn't sure she could commit to following that particular path with him. Although, she was quickly realising, it was a little too late to have second thoughts about her circumstances. She'd made a commitment to see this project through.

Now, that perpetual, exhausting dance with him would never end. She, trying to bring this new Nicholas in close to her to protect him from his vulnerabilities and vices and he, in a constant struggle of pushing her away and wanting her by his side and in his bed more than he'd ever done. Everything wrapped up in a blur of doing right and wrong, in the guise of commitment and loyalty when really it was about love. A love they held so tightly. The deepest kind of love shared between them. And they're overwhelming instinct to protect each other above all else.

It was confusing and fluid. Francesca hoped time and distance would help them find a new kind of friendship they could both live with.

She tuned into the news footage on her own device and watched the boat sink in the harbour. Around 5am the former detective drifted off to sleep as the birdsong called in a new day outside the apartment window.

88

Francesca woke mid-morning, disorientated and alone. Stretching, she strolled to the bathroom and then to the kitchenette where Nicholas had left a note, a small bunch of flowers and some fresh pastries from the deli café downstairs. The restaurants empty dishes had been returned.

She smelt the flowers, flicked the kettle on and opened the envelope.

Dearest Francesca, I was happy to see you did eventually fall asleep after such a restless night and I hope you feel a little more refreshed today.

This district is very safe and I highly recommend a walk around this charming city to break the boredom of being in the apartment.

I suggest using cash should you wish to make any purchases and as such I've left for you to use as you wish. Please accept as my gift to you. Enjoy Montmorency. See you tonight. Nicholas xxx

Francesca looked at the wad of cash that was more than Sinclair's monthly wages with Defence and thought *well I'm not going to starve to death.*

Next her phone rang. "Pronto?"

"Good morning my sunshine." He said. "Did you get my note?"

"Yes thank you. The flowers are beautiful. The cash, though very generous is completely unnecessary."

"Take it. Spend it. Think of it as recompense for inconvenience. How are you feeling this morning?" He asked.

"I'm not long up and still unkinking from the sofa. When did you leave?" Francesca put the cash in his carry-on bag. She wouldn't be bought.

"Seven thirty. My first meeting was not far from our apartment. I'm in the city proper now. I wanted to call to make sure you were okay."

"I'm good." She yawned. "Thanks for ringing and for everything else. Hope your meetings go well."

"Thank you. Enjoy your day my flower. See you tonight. Oh, Francesca, watch the breaking news from Australia and tonight you can tell me if you still want to get involved." And he hung up the phone call.

It was civil war at its most caustic as an internal battle for leadership and control within Ares Outlaw Motor Cycle Gang raged across the island nation. Chi You had raised its bull head and Li Wei was unrelenting. Francesca hugged herself in the safety of the Paris apartment and thought of her colleagues trying to end a war that had no end. She thought about Nicholas's comments. Did she really want to be there in the middle of it?

89

················

With scarce minutes to take off Francesca felt like a child on the last Friday of school term before summer holidays and couldn't hide the skip in her step as she crossed the tarmac to Alessandro's private jet.

After a harrowing forty-eight hours in Paris she was more than ready to leave the drama behind, get that Fijian sand between her toes and hold on to her family and not let go for a very long time.

Within Australia a series of rolling, targeted battles at Ares compounds dawned to a new day of quiet relief. But the former detective was sceptical. Key media outlets had stopped reporting the carnage so more police resources could focus on bringing the tensions under control. On that she was sure.

Li Wei was raging and she couldn't help but feel until Robbie L capitulated, it was unlikely rest would follow.

Nicholas came so far as to see her onto the plane.

"Well my love," he said in a business like fashion. "It's been a pleasure as always. Give those patient children a hug from their Zio Nicci."

"I will. Thanks Nic." She said softly and kissed him thrice on the cheek. "For everything. And please be careful. This war is just beginning. I want you to promise you're going to lay low until they sort each other out."

"I promise. Besides, I have my own battles to fight." He winked and smiled at her. She watched him unravel before her eyes. "Now you look happier than I've seen you in a very long time. Give me a good long squeeze. It's got to last a long, long time."

He kissed her briefly on the lips, which surprised her. He pulled away moments after she responded and cupped her cheeks gently in his hands, his eyes searching hers as if he needed her to understand his thoughts. He bent his forehead to hers and kissed gently her on the tip of her nose.

"Francesca, I adore you. I love you more than my life." He said in a low voice. "This feeling is mine alone to overcome. I understand now this time is not for us. My beautiful flower, there will be another time. And that will be ours to share. In another life."

His lips pressed against the top of her head for a long moment. He released her. When she looked at him, the tortured emotion caught in his dark eyes and in his expression brought her to tears.

"Nicholas." She whispered, holding his jaw and cheek softly in her hands.

He sought her lips again, hugged her close and pulled away from her.

"Go on, get going before I lose my mind." He said quietly, sadly. "Saying good-bye is always the hardest part." And he waited for her to take the few steps into the private jet.

From her window, she saw him drive away to meet his chartered helicopter and return to Rapallo. A tear slid down her cheek. Saying goodbye was indeed the hardest of all when he was so desolate and she was so happy to be going home.

Four hours into the scheduled flight and Francesca's mood dramatically changed.

"Excuse me Ms Salucci. I've been asked to let you know we're being re-routed to Warsaw." The hostess said apologetically. "We have a situation unfolding and Mr Delarno has requested we attend immediately. Mr Delarno has asked me to specifically express his sorrow, knowing you will feel disappointed."

"Oh for fucks sake." She grumbled angrily. "Of course he has."

"I'm sorry Ms Salucci. I know it is a terrible inconvenience."

"It's not your fault." She said. "I'm sorry, I'm just feeling frustrated. Thanks for letting me know." Francesca tried to smile and thought immediately about Sinclair and his growing intolerance of her situation.

And as she sat looking out the window, alternatively sulking and cursing and vowing to take the next commercial flight out of the country, no matter the risk, the hostess interrupted her again.

"Please excuse me Ms Salucci, I have Mr Delarno on the phone for your briefing."

"Thank you." Francesca responded totally confused. "This is Francesca. Wait. Nic, I can't understand you. There's something wrong with the line."

"I need your help." She heard him say and the line went dead.

90

. . . .

Delarno Estate,
Rapallo

"Nicholas, we have guests." Marionetta Castello greeted her boss at the entrance to the expansive Rapallo family home. "They've been here for some time. I made them comfortable in the library."

"I see. Thank you Marionetta."

"Signor Zanda and Senator Nero are here." She said.

Nic nodded.

The Capo opened the double timber doors of the library room. His young housekeeper, being the niece of Don Castello was well versed in the ways of family hospitality and expectation, and after serving their meal, had dressed the side table with coffee, sweets and fruit. The exterior French doors to the garden were opened to the sea and light breeze rising up the hill towards the home.

As Nic entered the room, she was one step behind him, silently closing the double timber doors and leaving them to their privacy.

"Gentlemen." He said, greeting the executive members of the

Council of Ten. "How can I help you?"

"Nicholas, we are sorry to come on short notice, but you will understand this is a matter of urgency," Mario Zanda began. "In short, this unrest has to be stopped. Have you seen the newspaper reports today?"

He threw the latest copy of Il Fatto Quotidiano onto a table between them.

"Everyone is demanding answers." Sebastino Nero said. "It won't be long until they start connecting the dots."

"It won't happen." Nicholas said.

"Do you see this photograph?" Mario Zanda said. "Socialite Giuliett Seta has been linked to the alleged outlaw motor cycle leader with the romance rumoured to have begun in Venice during the city's famous festival, Carnivalè."

"Let me see that." Nicholas said, looking at recent photographs of them together at Bice's funeral, sunbathing on the Sea Meadow deck off the coast at Portofino, shopping and dining out in the renowned celebrity destination. "Fuck!"

"I am doing my best with the editors Nicholas, but in this age of digital media, anyone with a camera phone and Internet connection can create a story." Zanda said.

"It's an internal battle in Australia between the triads and Ares." Nic said. "I took a briefing on it last night."

"We need to move him back to Australia then." Zanda said.

"I agree."

"I can't be anywhere near it." Sebastino said. "This immigration report is due to be tabled next week. I have enough on my plate satisfying the needs of my colleagues on that. I'm happy to make generic comments supporting an extradition but I have to be at arm's length."

"I don't expect you to do anything friend." Nicholas said, patting the politician on the shoulder. "We have bigger fish to fry. I know someone I can talk to in the Australian Federal Police. A trusted person who will help."

"Salucci?" Zanda asked.

"No. But as a matter of fact she could be helpful." Nicholas said. "She knows us and she's had dealings with Wei and Ares."

"Have you lost your marbles?" Nero interjected. "She'll betray us all."

"Melbourne was a long time ago Sebastino. A lot has happened between then and now. I think if I lean on her she'll be happy to cut a deal. And she'll be able to convince the Australian Police of it too. Our organisation's protection in exchange for Wei and Robbie L. It's a good exchange." Nicholas said.

"Do you think she'll agree?" Zanda asked.

"I think she'll be happy to step into the negotiations. Would you like me to contact her on our behalf? I would normally make these decisions on my own gentleman, but in light of our history and her relationship with the Guardians, I won't act unless I have your approval on this matter." Nicholas said.

"What are our other options?" Zanda asked.

"I can use my contact in Australia, but there are no guarantees with him." Nicholas said.

"There are no guarantees with Salucci either," Sebastino grumbled.

"That is true. But I think we have better odds with her. And she has more to lose in failure than a distant police operation." Nicholas said.

"I want to be there when you meet her to discuss this." Zanda said.

"That's a good idea." Sebastino said, looking at Nicholas knowingly.

"Of course. We'll meet in Warsaw tomorrow afternoon. It's neutral ground and no chance of newspapers." Nicholas said. "I'll forward you the time and details."

Sebastino looked at his watch. "You will please excuse me, I have another engagement in Genoa this afternoon."

"Of course, let me walk you out." Nicholas said.

"No need. I know the way. Keep me informed so I can direct the media's language in our favour."

Mario Zanda sat back in the armchair and sipped on a fresh caffé. He watched Nicholas closely as the younger man made a coffee.

"Lucia sends her love." He said gently.

"Thank you." Nicholas said, sitting beside his oldest friend.

"How are you doing?" Zanda asked.

"Not good." The Capo confessed. "I miss Alessandro so dearly. It's been a hell of a year and now this. You know it all comes back to Silvio. Serves him right. I hope he's rolling in his grave knowing that we now have to ask a Salucci for help to resolve the shit he created."

"But it's not all bad for you Nicholas, surely." He said with a wink.

"It's worse. She doesn't want me. She's doesn't want this." He waved his hands around the room, taking in the whole estate in one large sweeping motion. "She's made that abundantly clear. So, you and Lucia should lay off because you're not helping." Nicholas looked sternly at his friend. "This is a business decision and a business negotiation. And you will see for yourself that is the case when you see her tomorrow."

"Okay!" Zanda's hands gestured upwards. "We give up. No more talk of romantic liaisons with the opposition." He teased and smiled. "Don't let Sebastino get under your skin. I know we can trust Francesca. She would've had our balls years ago if she was that way inclined."

"I agree." He said.

"Well my boy," he said standing, "you have work to do and I have to get back to Milan, so I'll see you tomorrow in Warsaw. I'll make my own way there so don't worry about co-ordinating our flights. Go when it suits you and I'll do the same."

He looked worriedly at Nicholas.

"And get some rest my friend. You look like hell. Tomorrow we can begin to resolve this disaster or in the very least, move it on to Australia for their disposal."

"Thanks for your support, Mario. It means a lot. Once this is done, I'd like to meet with the Commission again."

"I think that would be wise. I'll organise on your behalf once I know the outcome of tomorrow and I'm satisfied with the terms."

"Thank you." Nicholas hugged his friend tightly. "See you tomorrow."

91

. . . .

Warsaw, Poland

Francesca watched the endless rows of traffic tail-lights from high through the full-length window of her senior suite in the city centre hotel. She sat on the back edge of the lounge, the long skirt of her vintage white leather gown folding in fluid lengths against the modern black sofa.

The bodice was strapless and modest. Her hair was temporarily fixed in a low loose bun and pinned at the back of her neck. At the moment she remained bare foot, stretching her toes and arches meditatively as she watched the city buzzing below and waited for Nicholas and Mario Zanda.

Across the back of the lounge beside her, a velvet cape draped.

Nicholas entered the cloistered surrounds of her suite first, dressed in a black tuxedo, his hair damp and wavy and at the length of his youth.

"You look ravishing." He said, smiling as he greeted her with three kisses on the cheek and held her hand briefly in his.

"Not so shabby yourself," she said back at him in a bored, pissed off tone.

"Again, I apologise for dragging you all over the place. I

promise you will get home." He said. "But I was thinking of you when I suggested this way forward. It was an opportunity too good to pass up."

"Really." She remained unconvinced.

He linked her hand in his. "Yes. Really." He bent his head and with his mouth close to her ear, he whispered. "Take this job and satisfy your hunger."

Francesca turned to look at him her eyes wide and his determined, expressive eyes filled her vision. "Excuse me?" she said.

"Business, you told me Nicholas. You will see Mario, purely a business negotiation. I'm not sure everyone will agree with the way you soften your business partners Nicholas, but then, who am I to argue with the Capo?" Mario laughed as he entered the room. "Nice to see you again Francesca. It's been a long time."

Francesca blushed a deep shade of crimson. Nicholas' eyes twinkled and she stepped forward to greet her old friend. "Mario." She said smiling. "You know Nicholas is incorrigible!"

"Only ever with you my dear." He said warmly, hugging her close. "Only ever with you. We've missed you kid. Lucia was only reminiscing the other week about our mammoth water fights and card games at the Rapallo house. Do you remember? It was a long time ago but you haven't changed a bit."

Francesca laughed. "I remember! Good times. And I'll take that compliment any day of the week! How is Lucia?"

"I could say that she sends her love, but she'll tell you herself shortly. We're meeting her at the restaurant." He looked tentatively at Nicholas. "I couldn't get out of the house without her when she knew I was meeting up with you." He said to Francesca with a wink.

"Now, down to business. Nicholas has briefed you?" He indicated that they all take a seat.

"No, he was very mysterious." She lied. "But I think I know who it could be about."

Zanda's brows knitted together briefly and he glanced at the Capo.

"You've been keeping up with events then." He said. "How soon can the police lay charges against Robbie L?"

"Charges have been laid. There's an extradition order in place." Francesca said, looking between the two men.

"So what is the problem?" Zanda asked.

"The cops can't find him.' She said looking at Nicholas. "He's disappeared."

"Well his Chinese friend isn't having any trouble. Flush him out! How hard can it be?" Zanda asked.

"I think they've tried." She said.

"He needs to leave Italy." Zanda said firmly.

"I know. I absolutely agree with you. This problem with him and Chi You needs to be sorted out at home, where there is scrutiny in the procedures and the law courts can't be corrupted." She said, adding. "No offense." And she blushed again.

"None taken. You know both of them better than any of us, how would you approach it?" Nicholas asked.

Francesca looked at him and wondered if it was a loaded question. She had to tread carefully here to not expose Nicholas's links with the Guardians. With no briefing and unaware of his dialogue in the face of Commission members, she was flying blind. She leant forward, her forearms leaning on her thighs.

"Talk to me Nicholas." She said, focusing on him in the tight space between them all. "You said you needed my help. I'm coming into this discussion against my better judgement, alone and completely blind to the landscape. But, I'm not a complete fool. I won't be making any assumptions."

"Simply," he said, "there's too much heat in Italy and too many questions around the Seta clan and the recent deaths of Pocco and Alessandro. We have to step right out of this one."

"Can't you do something about them under the radar? That is your business after all." She said, looking between the two Mafia men.

"Our hands are tied." Zanda said emphatically. "The media and government are all over the story. It's too risky."

"So you want me to be the bunny?" she asked, her eyes fixed on Nicholas. Francesca sat back in her place and placed her arms across her chest. "I've spent my life trying to pin those two. What makes you think I can do it now?"

"Timing. Opportunity. The right kind of support." Nicholas said. "You're the perfect choice. You understand them better than anyone. Besides, they are so focused on each other, this time the police have a fighting chance. Francesca the only way to resolve this matter is inside the law. The Australian law."

"You mean, this time we'll have a chance without interference from you." She said pointedly to Nicholas.

"How do I know you're not setting me up? It'd be real handy for your organisation if I were out of the way. Make life a lot easier for you Nicholas now you are the Capo. To have me dead."

Nicholas almost choked.

"Francesca, please." He said, faltering. And possibly for the first time ever she saw his soft underbelly in a negotiation, when his guard completely fell away. He composed himself quickly.

91

"There'll be repercussions in Australia." She said unmoved.

"I know. I'm accepting of that fate."

"*If* I do this I'm going to need support." She said.

"I have a small reliable team you can use."

"I mean I want Johnno on board. He's the only one I fully trust at the Feds who won't pursue this beyond the parameters." She said glancing between the two of them.

"You're putting a lot of faith and trust in me, and I want to ensure you understand I'm trying to repay that sentiment. But, you need to understand the results are out of my hands. There are no guarantees. I'm not a sworn officer anymore but I do know the law and all those pieces of paper I've earned account for something. Still, there are no guarantees and I'll not be held responsible if it gets bigger than me."

"We understand." Zanda said.

"Sergei Volkov is in the loop." She said. "Offer him immunity from prosecution if he helps me out. I can organise that with Johnno on his behalf."

She looked at their surprised expressions.

"No. He's not an option." Nicholas said bluntly. "That's a deal breaker."

"I'll tell you why." She ignored his comment with a blink of her eyes and leant forward again towards Mario. "I know for a fact he has my back. I trust him. If everything goes to shit, I'll need a safe place to land until Johnno can get me out."

She looked directly at Nicholas. "And seeing as Rapallo is out of the question because it's too hot, Russia would be a good option for me."

"I don't agree with that." Nicholas said. "You have to come to Rapallo. I can protect you there."

"No. She's right Nicholas." Mario said, breaking a hole in the tension building between them. "It has to be out of Italy. At least until we get this project through government. We don't want Wei suspecting we're supporting this."

"That makes up the terms, Nicholas. Take it or leave it." She said eyeballing him.

"Have it your way." He said but he wasn't happy.

"Whilst we're on it, my family will need protection."

"You have it." Nicholas said straight away. "Always."

"That's a given Francesca. Day and night for as long as it takes." Zanda confirmed.

Francesca stood and paced the small room in silence.

"I get Ares and Wei out of your hair *and* into the hands of the Feds *and* uphold my oath. Win. Win. Win." She mumbled. The former detective mulled it over. The risks were huge. But the outcome was doubly enticing. She felt like an addict being given the golden key. The tiny voice of reason screamed no.

She lapped the small, silent sitting room again. She stopped in front of Nicholas.

"I've worked out Wei's weakness." Francesca said, taking command of the room. "I know how to play Robbie L, but success hinges on one thing."

"What's that?" Nicholas asked standing at once.

"Knowledge is the best way to draw those bastards out. The Guardians sought to disrupt more than Italian mafia. I need to find out from them if there's intelligence on the triads and Ares that I can use." She looked steadily at Nicholas. Not wanting to give up his secret. Not breaking eye contact.

"I also need access to any evidence regarding Ares and Li Wei from your group. Not hearsay. Evidence. As well as all the documentation your mob has about the Guardians. The Australian police will need it to build a water tight case against these pricks."

She paused to make her point clear. And her silent intensity of needing his assurance she was right to proceed caught the heaving energy force around him. She would use the negotiation to help the Guardians gain pertinent intel. Intelligence that could save more lives. The room heated up as she held his gaze.

"Everything Nicholas. I want to see and hear everything. This is not an overnight fix. Your organisation's co-operation on the Australian aspects will be needed for quite some time. We can hold them on the current charges but to really bind them up ... for that to happen, I'm going to need your full co-operation. If you can't do that, then I can't help you."

Francesca maintained her position. The air was sucked into a vortex between them and ignited like a powder keg.

"Mother of Mary, you're not afraid of the tough conversations Francesca!" Zanda said watching the silent exchange between the two and feeling the chemistry burn brightly between them.

"Trust Mario. I've built my career on trust, integrity and loyalty. And 'saying it like it is' is a brand new freedom for me, because I don't have time for sorting out your shit." She said all the while looking at Nicholas and trying to get a read if that kind of information was available. Her eyes narrowed.

"Those are my terms. What do you say Nicholas?" she said after a lengthy pause.

"I think that's a solid strategy." He said, still locked in her steely gaze.

"Right, well I need to make some calls." She said, blinking slowly, breaking the connection. "Excuse me gentlemen."

She left the room.

"Mother of God Nicholas, is it hot in here? I thought she was going to melt your face off with those eyes. I've said it once and I'll say it until the day I die, you two have the most insane chemistry. You have to try again with her."

"My life is complicated enough." He said, breathing again. "I'll wait for her if you want to go and get Lucia. I'll see you downstairs in thirty minutes."

"She hasn't emphatically agreed yet." He reminded the Capo.

"She will." Nicholas said. "I know her better than she does herself. She won't be able to resist the challenge of tying up loose ends."

92

....

"H e's gone." Nicholas walked into the bedroom, shutting the door. She nodded at him whilst talking quickly on her mobile phone. She indicated for him to stay and he sat on the end of the bed, waiting for her to finish talking.

Francesca leant forward in the armchair and rubbed her forehead. "I don't know yet." She said. "But when I do I'll let you know. You have the capacity to do this remotely? Good."

There was a pause.

"Yes, I'm sure. I'll be fine. I have support." There was another pause. She looked at Nicholas. "As a matter of fact he's just walked in and is standing right here beside me. Alright mate. Yep. See you."

Francesca handed the phone to Nic. "He wants to talk to you."

"Yes Johnno?"

"I'm asking Sinclair to come in with a small covert team and be on the ground for support. I'll not have my former officer at your mercy in this situation. Too much is at stake, including her life. If that's a problem let me know now."

"I don't have a problem with that." Nic replied, looking at Francesca.

"Good. Quite frankly, too bad if you do. It's now out of your hands. I'll be in touch in the coming days." Johnno said and hung up from the call.

Nic handed the phone back to her.

"He already knew this was going down." Francesca said looking at Nicholas. "He's been waiting for my call. Why would that be?"

"I'm not going to leave you exposed." Nicholas said. "What kind of person do you think I am?"

She shrugged.

"Do you actually know if there is something on triads in a magic Guardian document somewhere?" she asked quietly.

"To be honest I don't." He said. "But I do know if there was something, where it would be kept. Which is why I brought us all to Warsaw. Your father set up a safety deposit system in the event a Guardian was ever in this situation with an organised crime group."

"You mean having no real choice but to participate."

"Something like that." He said. "Alessandro told me of a certain protocol. The intent to access the system, triggers a series of procedures, including an alert to Interpol agents located within the bank."

"Does it work?" She asked anxiously.

"I don't know. To my knowledge this will be the first time it's ever been tested."

"Great. So the big plan is to entice two of the smartest operators we know into thinking I have this dossier on each other's operatives and others who have undermined their activities and lure them to a location. One of them is impatient and takes the bait. Instead of handing over this bogus document, Interpol agents arrest them on the spot because of their existing warrants. Then they're extradited to Australia to face charges and essentially turn on the other for some kind of deal."

"Yes, that's it in a nutshell." He said nodding slowly.

"Again, why do I feel like the bunny on this operation?"

He took her hands in his. "You won't be alone. I'm going to stay on the ground throughout the whole operation, as will my team. You'll be protected every step of the way. I have no fears about stepping in to protect you. I've done it before, and so help me I'll do it again."

93

Headquarters, The Nationalist Bank
Warsaw, Poland

"As soon as you arrive at the bank headquarters you'll feel intimidated. It's a U-shaped building with a small car park in the centre. All the external windows face the car park and directly into the office spaces opposite." Nicholas said.

"The main public entrance is via a small grassy parkland facing a busy street intersection and is framed out by a tall, glass hallway void. You will enter the building at the cross section of the U shape, accessed by a wide flight of stairs at the far end of the parking area. This is the investment and business banking entrance.

"Proceed up the steps and through the security doors into the foyer. You will need to pass through a security check so have your passport ready. There is a facial recognition scan as well as a bag check and full body scan like the international airports.

"When you go through security, the first thing you'll see is the wall glass overlooking a large concrete square piazza and gardens. A reception desk is centred in the middle of that space in the foyer area. Make yourself known to the staff. This is where you'll meet with a Director of the Bank, Mikel Thedeou.

"Armed security personnel patrol every floor and the perimeter. They'll escort you both to a suite on the top floor on the Eastern side of the banking complex. I have four team members installed as part of the security crew who'll be close to you the whole time, so I want you to relax and be as natural as possible. Remember your father set this up, so there's no need to pretend to be someone you're not. Any questions?"

"Not so far." She said. "Fairly standard operating procedure, even if I am a little out of practice."

"Do you remember the passwords for the security questions as well as the code to retrieve the item?"

"Yes."

"Good girl. Be aware but not alarmed Francesca. You're in safe hands. Okay I'll see you after." And he hung up the phone call.

Her vehicle pulled up to the bollards at the entrance of the bank and she confidently strode the last few metres to the steps. Francesca stopped to look around the intimidating building and get a feel first hand for the layout.

"I'm here." She whispered to herself. "I'm actually here going through with this." And she resisted the urge to cross herself in prayer.

I see you. Nicholas thought looking through the binoculars. He checked the surrounding landscape. "Alpha one, this is Nic. Eyes on package. How copy:" He said into the microphone attached to his earpiece.

"This is Alpha one. Good copy, thanks Nic." Detective Inspector Jonathan McCrae responded from the Tactical Operations Centre within the Australian Federal Police Headquarters based in Canberra.

Utilising the multiple angles available and in joint co-operation from his Polish counterparts, Johnno streamed real time footage from a security camera positioned within the foyer of the bank and watched his former partner advance through the verification process.

"This is Alpha one. Confirming eyes on package." He said, watching Francesca as she negotiated the bank protocol. After a short while she met her contact at reception as planned.

Next the Detective Inspector located the pair exiting the lift and walking along a long well-lit corridor. Here they met with a security officer stationed on that floor. Three entered the viewing suite on the top floor.

Johnno watched on, as the room's internal security camera system relayed the Director seemingly asking her a series of questions. She looked confident in her responses. He nodded and left her alone. Outside the room, a security officer stationed himself close by. The police inspector held his breath as she punched the code on a small electronic keypad and unlocked a small door.

She waited for a few moments and then activated another code to access the inner chamber of the safe. Francesca took the contents from the box, briefly looked at them and then up at the entry door to the room.

"This is Alpha one. Nic, confirm target." Johnno asked over the closed communication circuit.

On the other side of the world, the Capo's phone showed an image.

"Alpha one. Confirming vision of Giuliett Seta and her minder Loris Moretti."

"I don't like it." Johnno said. "Where is Robbie L?"

"Tango Delta this is Nic. How copy:" Nicholas asked his team leader who was stationed on Francesca's floor with two team members.

"This is Tango Delta. Good copy."

"Tango Delta proceed route to package. Standby further instruction."

"Copy that."

"I want them in there with my officer." Johnno said.

"Alpha one stand back." Nic said firmly. "That will throw the whole operation off line. Moretti has the nose of a bear. She's a smart girl and my team is very experienced. They'll get her out if needed."

"You'd better be right." Johnno responded watching between the tense interchange inside the small boardroom and on another screen, the shifting slides of the target floor and the small unit cautiously making its way closer to the banks small office suite.

"Frigging hell!" Johnno suddenly swore. He dialled in again using the passcode he'd been allocated by the bank's security team. It routed him to another room, went to a dark screen and then lit up as a small graphic of an egg timer flipped. "Geezuz!" he said exasperated by the technical glitch.

"This is Alpha one. Nic. How copy:" Johnno asked his unlikely counterpart. "My feed's dropped out. Can you patch me in?"

"Affirmative Alpha one. I'll access the room utilising mobile phone. You'll have vision and sound. Alpha one, prepare for live streaming. Connecting you now. Radio silence in three, two ..."

Johnno was presented with a clear vision of the inside of her handbag, but at least he could hear the conversation.

On the ground, Nic edged closer towards a second building entrance. *We need to be higher, he* thought. He messaged the commander of his small overwatch unit located in the western side of the complex. 'Stay on planned route. Unsecured target. Whiskey Delta scout to rooftop.'

'Copy that.' Came the written reply.

From his new location, Nic continued to watch the exterior's vulnerable zones for Robbie L. The biker wouldn't send Giuliett alone. Sure, as shit he was here somewhere.

94

· · · · · · · · · · · · · · · · ·

"I appreciate your need to feel a part of this negotiation Giuliett, but being Robbie L's new whore does not make you privy to his business dealings. The evidence I have secured is between Robbie L and me." Francesca said, holding the sealed capsule containing the usb close. "I will not discuss any part of it with you or anybody else. Besides which, I don't believe you. Such a man would not send you in his place for anything. The deal is a face to face transaction. Those were the terms."

Francesca looked at her watch. "Or ... maybe not. His time is running out. Your boyfriend has ten seconds to appear in this room as we arranged."

"Or what?"

"I walk." Francesca said looking at her plainly. "And the information on Li Wei's operations affecting Ares in Australia is off the table. I can't help him anymore."

"You're so smug. But then you always were." Giuliett sneered. "I should have finished you off on your fifteenth birthday like I wanted. But no, you had to run to Nicholas and cry your pathetic little eyes out. You've made my life hell ever since."

"Such a tragic little sob story. I'm not buying it Giuliett. You forget, I was present during those holidays too and I know the truth about you. You've manipulated everyone and everything for so long that you believe your own bullshit to be fact! But I

447

haven't forgotten a thing. We've all made choices." Francesca said. "I've chosen to make mine meaningful."

"By being the Capo's whore. Bravo!" Giuliett said sarcastically. "Well, unlike you, I don't care for approval. I do what the hell I want."

Francesca couldn't resist taunting her and unleashed on the girl who'd set the course for Francesca's adult life.

"Let's discuss that shall we? Nicholas. Carlo. *Zio* Enrico. We've all witnessed you lick it up for them. Poor Giuliett Seta. She never had the approval of her sick bastard of a father so she turned to whores and cocaine for comfort." Francesca said. "All these years later and you're still running with the same pathetic story. My life as a victim turned me into a narcissistic sexual predator."

"You have no idea what my life was like." Giuliett said coldly.

"Maybe not. Do I care? Not a stitch."

From across the desk Francesca leant in towards her childhood tormentor. Her eyes were just as icy. "All your life you've chosen the wrong side dear girl. I don't give a shit about you or your problems. And I was born with a most satisfying habit that I never bothered to rectify. Without regret or remorse I treat people as they treat me. That's not a good outcome for you dearest Giuliett. Goodbye Giuliett."

Francesca dismissed her, gathered her bag, the documents and stepped around the boardroom table between them.

"Take another step and you're a dead woman." Giuliett threatened. "You'll see who's on my side."

"Say another word and I'm arresting you on kidnapping, human trafficking and murder charges." Francesca said. "This meeting is over."

Francesca made it to the boardroom door and all hell broke loose.

"Incoming!" Nicholas yelled into the microphone on his headset as the connection was lost with her phone.

Someone pushed Francesca to the ground as the external window glass shattered. The room filled with smoke and Francesca grabbed at her jacket holding it up to her face. The gas stung her eyes.

A guard threw Francesca a breathing mask and eye goggles. Within seconds, the silence erupted with rapid machine gun fire and Francesca watched terrified as Interpol black ops soldiers entered the room from the window.

"Go! Go!" The same guard bundled her towards the doorway. He kicked it open. "Get out!" He pushed her into the hallway, following up with a spray of bullets towards Giuliett, Loris and her security detail who'd rushed into the room through a connecting door and were now caught between the two assaults. The guard rolled out after her and slammed the door shut.

The hallway was eerily quiet, not a sole to be seen.

"Where the fuck is Tango Delta?" she asked, searching for Nic's reconnaissance team stationed on that floor.

He frowned at the silent hallway. "This way." He said, leading her away from the elevator. He spoke into his headset microphone. "Victor Romeo, this is Romeo one. Package on boarding."

"Are you hurt?" The soldier asked her as they quickly moved forward. His face and head were covered in a black combat beanie.

"No. Are you?"

"No. Here, take this." He handed her a semi-automatic 9mm

pistol that had been clipped to his person. "We're heading to the roof extraction point. Rendezvous in five mikes to take you to safety."

Five mikes, five minutes. Francesca thought and looked at her weapon, recognising it at once. She checked the soldier, noting his combat kit, realising she'd seen it very recently.

She tapped the gentleman on the arm and smiled. "Nice to see you again. Tell Nicholas I'm safe." She said in his good ear.

He nodded and pointed upwards. *When we're in the air* she thought he meant and nodded in agreement. He held his hand briefly up to his lips to indicate silence as they approached the service stairwell doorway.

95

. . . .

n Canberra Johnno paced the operations room and swore. "Fuck! Fuck! Fuck!" He yelled. "This is Alpha one. Nic! Where are you? What the fuck is happening?"

"Already on it." He was breathing hard, running towards the building. He came to sliding standstill and dove behind a vehicle as bullets rained down from above.

"I'm under fire." He said into the mouthpiece.

"I see you. On it boss." Came the reply from a team member stationed at a western point.

"Where is she?" Johnno yelled. "Someone tell me where the fuck my officer is!"

"This is Whiskey Delta. Friendly bird incoming. Hold your fire. Hold your fire." Came the response from Delarno's rooftop commander, as the Interpol chopper, distinctive in blue and white markings headed towards the extraction point on the Eastern side. Three soldiers scrambled out and the aircraft immediately lifted and moved out.

"Thank fuck!" Johnno said as he patched them in. "This is Alpha one. Bravo Charlie: how copy:"

"Alpha one." Captain Sinclair McCrae answered. "This is Bravo Charlie." He glanced at Grant and Iceman who signalled to their commander. "All good copy and on board."

"Tango Delta: how copy?" McCrae asked.

"This is Tango Delta. Good Copy." Came the reply from Nicholas' reconnaisance team leader on the fortieth floor of the building. "Secure and commencing to checkpoint Echo Bravo."

"Copy that." McCrae answered, directing Iceman towards the eastern roof top checkpoint.

"Securing Extraction Zone." Iceman said.

"Copy." Came the reply.

"This is Whiskey Delta. Friendly overwatch in place. Sealed and secure. Bank lockdown procedures are go. I repeat emergency lockdown procedures are go. No one in and no one out."

"Where's my gunman?" Nicholas asked.

"He's down."

"I'm moving in." Nicholas said.

"This is Alpha one. Nic, stay mobile on the ground." Johnno intervened. "Satellite vision loading now. I should have external picture in four, three, two ..."

"I see the descent point from the roof to 4088." Iceman said. As he looked down, the camera attached to his kit streamed vision back to Johnno.

"This is Alpha one. Iceman, I have you." Johnno said splitting the computer screen to show the interior room and Iceman's vision.

"This is Alpha one. All in for situation report. 4088 internal camera back on line. No blonde and no package. Interpol agents have secured remaining offenders." Johnno said. "Package is mobile. Target is mobile."

In the Canberra situation room, Johnno spoke to his Polish counterpart. "All units, this is Alpha one. Interpol agents are checking every floor, security camera by camera to locate persons of interest. Stand by for instruction."

"Copy that Alpha one. Standing by on rooftop." Iceman said.

"Standing by on ground support." Nicholas said.

"Entering target area from designated roof portal." McCrae said. "Search and retrieve."

"This is Alpha one. Copy that McCrae. I see you. Proceed." Johnno said.

Giuliett stumbled onto the eastern rooftop, her eyes streaming with tears from the gas. Iceman watched her from his hideout behind a concrete air-conditioning unit.

"This is Iceman. Alpha one, I have eyes on Giuliett Seta. Eastern rooftop exit portal mark two. Permission to secure."

"This is Alpha one. Copy that Iceman. Secure threat."

"This is Whiskey Delta. Eyes on from the west. Your position is secure."

"Copy that Whiskey Delta."

Johnno watched as the Afghan national followed protocol, apprehended and secured her to a bollard at a designated checkpoint.

"All units. Threat secured." Iceman said after a few tense minutes. He looked towards the thud of rotor blades. "All units. Bird approaching Eastern rooftop. Stand by for confirmation."

Iceman sought cover as the chopper performed a reconnaissance flyover.

"All units. Hold your fire." Nicholas said, recognising the aircraft. "That's a friendly."

"That's Russian." Iceman said.

Some distance in front of him, the doorway of rooftop portal one opened slightly. Iceman witnessed the Russian combat soldier cautiously step forward and Francesca Salucci follow him out, protecting his back, as they moved towards the extraction point.

"This is Iceman. Eyes on package on route to extraction point. Has unknown support."

"All units. Let her go. This is a planned extraction." Nic said.

The Kamov ka226T circled back and dropped at the landing zone. Johnno watched as Francesca climbed in with the soldier and they lifted almost immediately.

"This is Alpha one. Confirming package is onboard and secure." Johnno said, watching them bank left. "Commence evacuation to designated location for debrief."

"This is Whiskey Delta. Bird approaching from the west at speed." Came the warning but it was already upon them. "All units. Hostile craft."

It flew low and fast, spraying both rooftops with bullets. Iceman pushed the girl hard and backwards into the concrete wall. "For your safety." He said at Giuliett's black look.

He watched as it quickly caught the Russian craft, peppering it with shots. The Russians retaliated.

"Who the fuck is that?" Johnno asked.

"Looks like an OH-58D." Iceman said.

McCrae and Grant pushed through the rooftop doorway Francesca had just vacated. "Nic." McCrae said and his voice was taut. "Talk to me."

"The Chinese have arrived." The Capo said and his worst fears were realised. "Standing by for instruction Alpha one." McCrae said, ducking behind a cement wall as the chopper returned with another barrage of gunfire. "We don't negotiate." The Federal police officer said. "Take it down."

"I'll cover you from the flank." McCrae said evenly to Iceman.

And the door behind him opened with a spray of gunfire, scattering the soldiers to shelter.

"Requesting aerial support." Grant said, ducking out from behind a large, squat concrete bollard to retaliate.

"Copy that. Aerial support engaged." Johnno said. "This is Alpha one. Where are you Nic?"

"Already on my way." He said, running up the stair well from the underground car park. He popped out on the third carpark level and snapped the window cleaner's trolley. It scaled up quickly to the fortieth level.

From there he levered up onto the roof using the black ops zip mechanism, popping up behind Li Wie's small outfit. Robbie L was crouching with them, intent on looking through the lens of a sniper's rifle towards McCrae's hideout. Nicholas crouched at the ledge. Staying there he was a sitting duck for aerial attack. Going over and he was dead before he could reach protection. He peered over the ledge again. It was a good fifty metre dash to the protection of a large concrete bollard.

"Alpha one, this is Nic. How copy:" Nic asked.

"Go ahead."

"Eyes on Robbie L. Eyes on three armed triad offenders facing Bravo Charlie. My position is in line with the initial black ops point of entry. I'm behind target."

"Copy that." Johnno said.

"Wei. Lark. Seta. They're working together." Nic said into the closed communication system. "I repeat. Three targets are working as one."

"Copy that." Johnno said.   "This is Whiskey Delta. Take shelter. Hostile bird coming on." The scout said looking northwards at the sound of the rapidly approaching craft.

"We'll cover you Nic." McCrae said from his hiding place. He motioned for Grant to track round to support the Capo.

Nic levered himself gently over the ledge and crawled silently towards the first small air conditioning vent. Luckily the small entourage remained intent on McCrae's assault ahead of them. The chopper drew in closer. Suddenly their attention moved towards Nicholas and Grant and there was no time.

Nic made the last five metres into a secure vent as the machine gun bullets hammered the concrete around him.

Amid the confusion death caught up with a triad operative who'd stepped out from behind the concrete wall as the enemy caught up with Delarno.

97

....

"Where the fuck is Delarno's detail? We can't leave them there. They'll get knocked off like flies." Francesca yelled above the rotor blades as she listened to the conversation through a borrowed headset.

"I agree." Sergei motioned to the pilot to turn around. "You ready?" He asked her.

She nodded, quickly familiarising herself with the Special Forces assault rifle. She positioned herself to have good leverage, sight and protection. The chopper picked up speed and Francesca felt the rush of engagement course through her.

"This is Alpha one. Reinforcements on their way." Johnno relayed to the ground team. "ETA fifteen mikes."

"Copy that." McCrae said.

Francesca smiled at the sound of Sinclair's voice coming through the headset, thinking *We'll be there in two.*

Li Wei's Kiowa Warrior hovered towards a second roof entrance located closest to the centre of the U-shaped building facing the oncoming assault from Nicholas and the Interpol officers.

Nic's eyes darted between the entrance and the last place he'd seen Robbie L. The Capo was caught in the middle. A sitting duck, but for Nic to move now was suicide. And he didn't have the fire power to take them on. So he waited for a split second opportunity.

"This is not good." Nic said as a flash of light headed in his direction. "On the east. Incoming! Look out!"

Nic ducked down for shelter as the grenade smashed into a concrete wall a short distance in front of him, blowing debris across the roof and over the buildings edge. He took the chance and ran back towards the air vents he'd first used as cover.

The wind picked up speed around the building. A violent rainstorm brewed closer. The air smelt of rain and concrete dust and burning metal. And still the helicopter waited.

It was a dangerous and gutsy manoeuvre. Updrafts rocked it from side to side. Nicholas sighted Robbie L and chanced a continuous volley of shots. The biker stumbled but kept running towards the Chinese owned chopper. A triad operative running beside him was not so lucky and fell to the ground.

"This is Nic. Two enemy down." He said into the microphone. He watched as Robbie L edged further away and out of range.

"Alpha One. Where's that back up?" Nic screamed above the noise filling his ears and frustration filling his lungs. "It's about to fucking piss down here and get very ugly. Where the fuck is Interpol?"

"ETA ten mikes." Johnno said. Ten minutes.

"This will be over by then." Captain McCrae said, thinking quickly to regain control of the rooftop standoff and retain the offenders. Delarno was isolated from the rest of them. Caught between the chopper and the extraction point. But he had the greatest opportunity for attack. Even though he was outgunned. McCrae signalled to Iceman.

"Whiskey Delta cover me." Nic said, stepping out briefly from his hideout, aiming at the chopper pilot. The retaliation from

Wei cut through the outside seam of his pants, grazing his thigh. He ducked back in, swore at the injury and then ignored it.

On the western side rooftop Whiskey Delta stepped into the clear. Nic again opened fire facing the chopper.

A flash of light and a terrible roar shook the building and the ground beneath the chopper collapsed inwards. The aircraft immediately started its upward ascent. He watched as Li Wei lost his balance and foothold in the sudden motion and was thrown onto the rooftop.

The building vibrated in the subsequent explosion. Nic regained his balance grabbing onto the air vent to steady his fall.

The chopper suddenly dropped. It's struts threatened to crush the Chinese crime boss trapped underneath. Caught in the destabilising drafts, it wobbled only metres from the ground.

Nic took advantage of the chaotic moments to make the final dash to safety. He caught a movement metres away and to his right side and ran harder towards it.In one quick motion Iceman dropped the machine gun he'd been using and from over the top of his chunky shoulder, he secured a grenade launcher attached to a rifle. He stepped out from behind a lift shaft, took aim and fired.

The chopper exploded in the air as metal shards and glass blew sky high and then rained down from the heavens. The remains peeled off to the car park in the centre of the building's office wings.

There was a moment's silence. A silent space that was immediately filled with the most horrendous crashing sounds as cars were crushed and blades dug into the glass and rock and concrete. It echoed in the U-shaped hollow of the building.

The Russians arrived at speed. They flew high over the carnage and circled back.

"All units. Wei and Robbie are active. Wei and Robbie are active." Nicholas said into the microphone.Above them the Russians swooped again.

It happened in slow motion. Through the settling dust Nicholas watched as Robbie L, now clearly positioned and exposed, took aim at the Russian pilot. Nicholas retaliated.

Through his scope, Nicholas saw Robbie L slump forward as the Capo's bullet hit its mark. In the same horrifying moment, the pilot took the fatal hit in the chest from the biker's rifle and the chopper dipped and spiralled.

Terror coursed through Nic's veins and came from his mouth in an anguished scream. "Francesca!" He watched helplessly as the chopper groaned. "Up! Up! Take it up! Take that fucking bird up!" He screamed running to the edge of the rooftop and pivoting between watching the scene unfold and protecting Iceman and McCrae as they stalked forward seeking out surviving triads.

Grant arrived beside him.

"There's nothing you can do there." She said indicating the drama below. "We need to move with them."

He remained close to the edge of the building.

"Delarno!" she said again. "This is our aim now. Protect our front men."

Nicholas didn't respond. Paralysed by fear and helplessness he watched the scene below.

"Move soldier." She yelled at him, physically pulling him away from the edge of the building. "You'll move with me. Focus."

In the commotion and left to her devices, Giuliett took a sweeping arc with her foot at a discarded pistol lying on the ground ahead of her. Secured to a metal pole, she used every small leverage to stretch out as far as she could. It was almost in reach.

She pulled on the pole and stretching to her body's limits, her toes caught the pistol's grip. She coiled back for a second's reprieve. Catching her breath she repositioned her body and stretched out again. Millimetre by millimetre she brought the handgun towards her. She almost had it. One more toe tap and it was hers.

Filling the background noise, the chopper was screaming. It was dropping heavily. Francesca scrambled to hold on and the gentleman jumped forward desperate to gain control. The ground was rushing up to meet them and Francesca prepared to bail at the first possible minute.

Then it almost stopped mid-air, poised barely metres from the ground in the green space beyond the eastern wall. They bucked and swayed. Then, they lifted. Ever so slightly. Ever so slowly. Bit by bit. Francesca held her breath and her body high, subconsciously urging them upwards.

The flying machine's engine groaned terribly as time stood still. Next they were suddenly airborne, rocketing towards the sky. Francesca's shoulders slammed against the interior supports. Sergei was the first to gain his senses and pulled the dead pilot towards the back seat. At the same time the gentleman clamoured to his new position in the pilot's seat.

She handed the Russian mob boss a sub machine gun, his only weapon of choice, retrieved her own assault rifle and took her position by the window.

The gentleman took a minute to steady the craft as they sat high in the clouds directly above the chaos below and said "Breathe Francesca."

98

· · · · · · · · · · · · · · · · ·

"This is McCrae. Confirming biker down." McCrae said.
Nicholas stalked forward. He and Grant spread out but remained in a steady formation.

"To the right! To the right!" he said catching sight of a quick movement close to McCrae. He was too late. Li Wei stepped out from a hole in the wall behind McCrae.

Neither could get a clear shot without injury to the soldier medic and they watched him turn to face the Chinese triad leader, raising his hands away from his body.

Grant and Nic held their pistols high, pointing at the back of Li Wei.

Behind them Giuliett singled out Nicholas. "I wouldn't if I was you." She threatened.

Grant and Nic paused.

"Drop your weapons." She ordered stepping closer, pushing her pistol into his skull. "Oh Nic. This is just too tempting." She said.

Giuliett moved her hostages forward towards Li Wei and placed the four captives in the centre of a circle. The three soldiers and Nic stood together, their backs to the centre, facing outwards.

"Now," Giuliett said. "Isn't this cosy?"

"What are your terms, Giuliett?" Nicholas asked immediately.

"Nicholas. Always the negotiator." She purred. "I should have guessed you'd be the first to talk. But that's okay. I have something I want to share with you. And now is as good as time as any."

She paused for effect. "Gatto told me a funny little story about you right before he died. Do you want to hear it?"

"Sure." Nic responded drily.

"He spent his last breath trying to convince me you were part of the Guardians." She said.

"Who knows how the mind and mouth of an old man works?" He said.

Giuliett laughed.

"Is it true Nicholas? Have you joined that whore and her team and betrayed all of us and everything we've worked for?" she asked.

"You want to know and I'd like to tell. In truth, my answer has bearing on the outcome today." He said calmly.

"Does it now?" she said. "Do tell Nicholas. Tell us all about it."

"I'd be very happy to discuss your concerns in private." The Capo said. "This is, after all, *our* organisation to manage. Discussions of this kind are between you and me. Seta and Delarno coming together. It has a nice ring to it, don't you think? There's no need for anyone else to get hurt. Those are my terms."

"You sound just like her!" she shouted in frustration.

"Come now Giuliett." Nic cooed. "Isn't this what you've always wanted? An exclusive arrangement just between you and me? This is your opportunity to lay everything down in our own, very private meeting." He stepped forward towards her slightly.

"Stop there. Ha, you may be right." She said. "Alas, my father taught me to never trust a Delarno. Besides, I already have a solid alliance with the Delarno clan in Robbie L. So, it is a pity for you. The time for talking is long past my friend."

She looked at Le Wei. "I know the truth Nicholas. You are a bigger traitor than even a Salucci could claim to be." She said.

"Now, here's my terms," she drew a deep breath. "My terms Capo are that you all die. And you can all rot in hell together. Isn't that what you've always wanted Capo? To be together forever with that bitch Salucci. Well then, today is your lucky day. I'm about to grant your wish." She took a deep breath of satisfaction.

"Now, I'm an old-fashioned kind of girl. I choose death by firing squad."

Wei nodded silently at her in agreement.

She moved to the side of the assembled group, motioning her pistol towards the closest roof entry point. "Go on then, off you go towards that wall or the famous soldier medic gets used as pistol practice." She shot him in the shoulder to prove her point.

"Move!" she yelled.

Four shuffled slowly towards the wall.

"I said move." She yelled again, pushing Grant in the back.

"When I say, we drop and roll." McCrae said quietly as they approached the wall. "Copy?"

"Copy." They whispered in unison.

"That's far enough." She said. "Now. Turn around and face me."

Giuliett looked at them in turn, a satisfactory smile spreading across her face.

"Any last words?" She asked. "No?"

She looked questioningly at them but there was no time for answers.

"I'll do the honours." She said to Wei. "This is my mess and I'm more than happy to clean it up." Li Wei looked at her for a moment and nodded.

99

....

"Where are they Johnno?" Francesca said in a direct line from the chopper to her colleague at the Canberra base.

"They're on the eastern side of that rooftop. Ten degrees north north east from the extraction point."

"We'll come at them from underneath." Sergei said.

"For fucks sake, hurry up man. McCrae's pistol-whipped and she's lining them up against the wall for execution. Wei is complicit. We have a hostage situation."

Francesca looked at Sergei and she knew immediately the direction of his thoughts.

The helicopter rose steadily up from behind the building like a nemesis rising from seabed. In the late afternoon light, the concrete dust and debris swirled around it like some ancient mist. To Johnno witnessing it from afar it was poetry in motion if it wasn't so terrifyingly real.

Undaunted, Giuliett turned away from the intimidating sounds and sight of the looming Russian chopper to face the four against the wall. She raised her pistol and pointed it directly at McCrae's chest.

In the blink of an eye, all four dropped and rolled in one movement. At that precise moment, Francesca and Sergei engaged on cue, unified in their response.

Li Wei momentarily distracted by the noise and threatening vision of the helicopter bearing down on them, caught Francesca in his sights. She gave him no second chance and watched as he and Giuliett fell almost as one onto the concrete rooftop.

Nicholas limped towards McCrae, assisting the soldier medic

to his feet. Four moved as one towards the designated landing zone.

The chopper met them there. From the Kamov doorway, Francesca faced outwards towards any further threats. Sergei pulled them into safety. The small team securely inside, the chopper lifted almost immediately.

"Do you have room for one more?" McCrae asked. "We have a friend on the western rooftop."

They bunny hopped to the landing zone, collected the Whiskey Delta leader and then rising steadily, pushed north towards St Petersburg.

Back up arrived and swung over the scene in a reconnaissance flyover, to return and land on the rooftop. Tactical response police officers piled out making their way towards the fallen.

A second wave of Interpol officers arrived on cue. Like ants, the soldiers crawled into the rooftop entry stairwells in well-practiced drills.

"Great work team." Johnno said. "Will be in touch for the briefing summary tomorrow. Over and out."

And with that, his phone rang. "Yes Minister, that is correct, a rapid incident is unfolding in Warsaw, Poland. I can confirm that one Australian citizen is deceased and three Australian citizens have been successfully extracted for medical treatment. Interpol agents are on the scene. Local police have secured a number of offenders."

100

·····················

Delarno Estate, Rapallo, Italy

"I have so much to tell you. So much has changed. We did it. You and I. She came to me, to us. At first she pledged to me, the Capo, but you and I both know I'd never invoke her into that organisation. I brought her into the Guardians. And secured her ongoing safety with the Commission. It has worked out as you and her father planned those many years ago. I wish you could be here to see it Zio. I wish you and Stefano could be here to enjoy this complicated moment."

Nicholas sat in the quiet space, high in the hilltop olive grove overlooking the sea and the small harbour, in the place he'd buried Alessandro. He offered his thoughts and prayers to his uncle.

The sun was rising and the sky was turning from cobalt to yellow. The waves crashed against the rocks of the sea wall below. It was peaceful. And Nic's emotions had settled at last after the volatile ending in Poland.

"I am ashamed Zio." He said solemnly. "The outcome could have been very different. I did everything I'd be trained not to do. I lost control of me and my fear took over. Somehow, this time, it worked out for us. I have learnt my lesson."

There would be hell to pay at next week's Commission meeting. But for now, the Capo found peace. Acceptance walked with him and so did relief. It had ended. Not how he would have preferred. But it was done.

Today Sebastino Nero would present his proposal. The long-awaited Immigration Strategy that both filled the Commission coffers and the Guardian's need for justice was to be ratified by the Italian Government.

At this moment, Nic was justified in the feelings of satisfaction that washed over him. Vindicated for all he and others had suffered. It was a complicated moment of the heart. But the head was sure and focused and helped the heart with promises of what could be in the future and somehow the two joined together settled and happy.

"You will see Zio. This is my duty, it is the place where I belong, but I know now, it is impossible for me to be here without you. I stand on yours and Stefano Salucci's shoulders. I will not let either of you down."

He watched Marionetta Castello begin the steady climb towards him. She held the small basket used for carrying refreshments.

"I do not know what the future holds, none of us do. But I thank you for giving me the support I need, when I need it most. And for giving me time and the understanding to use it wisely." The Capo said to his Uncle's spirit.

The young woman paused a little distance from him. Nic acknowledged her with a short wave.

"Good morning Signor. Excuse me, I do not wish to interrupt. I only brought caffe to nourish you."

"Good morning Marionetta. Thank you. You're welcome to stay. My uncle won't mind the extra company." He said teasing her. "Besides, it's a beautiful sunrise."

She nodded and sat cross legged on the grass beside him as the sun breached the horizon. "Make a wish Signor Delarno." She said huskily. "This is the precise moment that wishes are heard."

Nic turned to face her briefly. She was serious. Her eyes were closed, her face radiant from the exertion of the climb and her mouth moved silently in fervent wishes. Nic smiled at himself. He shook his head gently from side to side in disbelief for what he was about to do. Then for what is was worth, the Capo shut his eyes and made a wish too.

101

· · · · · · · · · · · · · · · · · · ·

Salerno, Italy

nd the water was calm and crystal clear, the colours of blue and green and the gentle waves lapped against the boat. Francesca reached down dragging her fingertips through the bubbly white caps.

She smiled. At the brilliant blue cloudless sky, at the white flapping sail, at the two little people sitting at the bow and the man who was watching her intently as he lay propped on one elbow beside her.

She linked her fingers with his. Turning his palm upwards she traced a love heart. She felt his smouldering eyes darken and as he pulled her into him, she weakened again, allowing herself to be wrapped in his love.

He kissed her passionately. Francesca sighed softly, bringing her fingers up to gently cup his handsome face.

"Could one person ever be as happy as I?" she asked

"Yes." He said. "That person would be me."

"I still can't believe ..."

"Shh!" Her soldier medic gently held his finger to her lips. She kissed it. "At this moment we live and make love for today. And that's all we have time to think about."

Francesca smiled and closed her eyes, resting in the warmth of the sun and the masculine scent of him, knowing she had everything she'd ever need on this little boat, sailing along the protected inlets of Italy's western coastline.

Can traitors be lovers?

When organised crime detective Francesca Salucci starts investigating the death of a biker, she unveils a trail of shady drug deals and internal power struggles tearing apart Australia's notorious crime gangs.

Her investigation leads her from Sydney to Rome all the way to a small town on the Italian riviera. There, reunited with a former lover, Francesca has no choice but to confront her past. She finds herself caught between her personal history and her desire for justice.

An action packed thriller that tells a story of love, greed, betrayal and moral conflict.

A secret, a revenge and the family caught in the middle.

Francesca Salucci is back. This time living in Fiji with a loving family and a promising new job. Yet her life is not as tranquil as it seems. Her former career as an organised crime detective may be over but her affair with the son of a dangerous mafioso is anything but forgotten.

The new life she has worked so hard to build is beginning to crumble and when her family is in danger she can't tell her allies from her enemies.

Serpent Sting takes us from war-torn Afghanistan to the stunning Fijian coastline; from the pomp of award ceremonies to secretive Venice, as one family's desire for revenge unravels against another's quest for peace.

THE TROUBLE WITH SERPENTS
TONI GRANT

		Qty
ISBN: 978 1 921596 84 1		
RRP	AU$24.99	.....
Postage within Australia	AU$5.00	.....
	TOTAL* $_____	

* All prices include GST

Name: ....

Address: ....

....

Phone: ....

Email: ....

Payment: [ ] Money Order   [ ] Cheque   [ ] MasterCard   [ ] Visa

Cardholder's Name:...

Credit Card Number: ....

Signature:...

Expiry Date: ....

Allow 7 days for delivery.

Payment to: Marzocco Consultancy (ABN 14 067 257 390)
PO Box 452

Torquay Victoria 3228

Australia

BE PUBLISHED

Publish through a successful publisher.

Brolga Publishing is represented through:

• National book trade distribution, including sales, marketing & distribution through Simon & Schuster.

• International book trade distribution to:
  - The United Kingdom
  - Sales representation in South East Asia

• Worldwide e-Book distribution

For details and enquiries, contact:

Brolga Publishing Pty Ltd

ABN 46 063 962 443

PO Box 452

Torquay Victoria 3228

Australia

markzocchi@brolgapublishing.com.au

(Email for a catalogue request)